WOLF HUNTS

Stoneridge Pack Series: Book One

CJ COOKE

Wolf Hunts

By

CJ Cooke

Version 1.0: January 2021

Published by CJ Cooke

Copyright © 2021 by CJ Cooke

Discover other titles by CJ Cooke at https://cjcookeauthor.wixsite.com/home

All rights reserved, including the right of production in whole or in part in any form without prior permission of the author, except in cases of a reviewer quoting brief passages in review.

This book is a work of fiction. Names, characters, places and incidents either are products of the author's imagination or are used fictitiously. Any resemblance to actual events or locales or persons, either living or dead, is entirely coincidental.

Cover design by: Mibli Art
Formatting by: Bookish Duet

❦ Created with Vellum

DISCLAIMER

This is a reverse harem romance novel. It covers sexually explicit scenes in a multiple partner relationship and is not meant for readers under the age of 18.

If you are offended by this type of material, maybe reconsider if this is the book for you.

1

CALLI

It was strange. I could remember some parts of that night so clearly, but looking back, it felt like just a dream. So impossible, that I wished it wasn't real. The red and blue flashing lights had lit up the street with eerie clarity, and then they just stopped. Almost like they didn't want to alert anyone else to the tragedy. There was no crowd of gawking neighbours listening in for the next round of neighbourhood gossip. No, it was just three knocks on the door: one to break my heart; one to destroy my dreams; and another to irrevocably change my life forever.

I could still remember clearly opening the door. It was nearly 11:00 pm, and there was no reason for anyone to be knocking at that time. Once it was open, I saw the two police officers' faces, and I just knew. It's strange, people talk about heartbreak, but it isn't until you feel it that you realise it's true. The crushing pressure on your chest as you try to pull in enough air, the noise around you drowned out by the pounding blood rushing through your head, and then you feel it in the middle of your chest. The tearing, the physical rip as your heart fragments inside of you and shatters.

My parents had gone out for a date night, leaving me to babysit my five-year-old brother. I was twenty and getting ready to head to university in a few months. I'd had some time off to travel and had only recently returned home. They hadn't expected another child so late in life, and they rarely got to do anything as a couple. When I came home from backpacking, they'd been so happy to see me, but I could see the strain on their faces. They needed a break, and I was only too happy to give them as much of a break as I could before I went off again. I adored my little brother, even if he could be annoying at times.

The officers said it was a drunk driver who had forced their car off the road, killing them both on impact. Apparently, my parents hadn't suffered. I don't know why they felt the need to tell me that. They were gone; that was all I could process at that moment. Someone would need to look at the accident scene when it was safe enough to look around. My father had quick reactions, whether he was driving or not. He was a shifter after all. I needed to make sure it was an accident and nothing else. Life wasn't safe for us.

My father was a wolf shifter, and my mother was a witch. I'm a hybrid—a never-before-seen born female wolf shifter, with a side sprinkling of magic. When I was born, my parents were shocked, to say the least. Never before had a female wolf been born. Female wolves had to be turned, and they resulted in some horror-movie version of a werewolf. They walked on two legs and took on some lupine features, but never truly became a wolf. You had to be born a shifter to be able to shift into your animal entirely. Shifters were born with a dual soul. You couldn't inherit one through the bite.

When I had started to show signs of magic, my parents were even more shocked. So far, my little brother appeared to be only a wolf, but time would tell on that. My father left his pack when he met my mother because they fell in love. They would never have accepted her in the pack. The Wolf Hunts had been going on for fifty years. When the witches discovered they could extract the magic from a shifter to increase their own, even if temporarily, they didn't even hesitate. And so, the Wolf Hunts began. But a shifter couldn't survive without their magic. To be drained was certain death.

My brother and I had lived our lives running from both sides. My parents were convinced that the wolves would never accept us; and the witches would just drain us. From what I'd seen of our world, I was inclined to believe they were right. If someone had found my parents together, obviously mated, they would have killed them on sight. I wore a talisman which suppressed my witch and wolf scent. I still had access to both sides, but anyone coming across me wouldn't know I was anything other than an ordinary human.

The Police Officers said what they needed to say and made the necessary sombre faces before leaving. It was back to work as normal for them, but for me, my entire world was starting to implode.

Quickly, I ran up to Jacob's room, wrapped him up in his blankets, and bundled him into my car. My parents had trained me on what to do if this sort of situation ever occurred and had made sure there was a plan. Leaving my cell phone in the kitchen, I grabbed our go-bags out of the hallway closet. I was to go to one of their closest friends, Sean Phillips, he would know what to do from there. I took one last look around the house; the living room where we had sat every year at Christmas opening our presents, the kitchen where we had eaten breakfast nearly every morning.

Slowly, I pulled my resolve around me as I pushed the

reality of the situation down into a place where I would have to deal with it later. Because now I had to be strong. I had to be strong for Jacob. I pulled the front door shut on the house closed on my old life, got into my car and drove away. It was time to run.

2

CALLI

SIX WEEKS LATER

I hitched Jacob up onto my hip so that his sleeping head lay on my shoulder, and walked toward the luggage carousel. Thankfully, he'd slept through most of the last flight, and I had been able to sit back and relax. It had been a long six weeks. My parents had made this plan for us long ago. As soon as Sean saw me at his front door, his face fell. There was only one reason why I would be there. He pulled me into his arms and held me while I fell apart. It was the only time I'd allowed myself to cry. After I pulled myself together, he patted me on the head and silently got to work, liquidating my parents' estate in England. They already had another home set up in Arbington, Maine. It was some kind of cabin they'd bought a few years ago under an offshore corporation they'd formed explicitly for that purpose. It was untraceable, and it was the escape plan if we were ever discovered.

At first, I didn't want to go. It didn't seem right to take Jacob away from everything that he had ever known. It had been an accident, after all. Sean had gone to check the accident site, and said he didn't see any signs of foul play, but he was getting a copy of the police report just in case. He was still convinced that this was the best idea though. Sean and my parents were involved in things that skirted on the edge of illegal in our society. In fact, screw it, they were totally illegal. When you helped people run from the Council—who were supposed to look after them—they tended to put laws in place to stop you from doing it. Shifter society was just as corrupt as human society though, and it was only people like Sean and my parents that made it survivable for some of our kind.

In the end, we'd gotten on the flight. I'd just have to worry later down the line if I was making the right decision. I was too exhausted to argue any more.

The flight had been pretty dead, thankfully. We had flown from Heathrow to Washington, D.C., and then on to Portland where we had just landed. We'd been travelling for nearly twelve hours, and Jacob had passed out as soon as we were seated for the second flight. He was taking everything pretty well, but I think that was just because he didn't realise what was going on. He was only five, after all.

Most of our things had been abandoned at the house. Apparently, there were supplies in our new home, but I would no doubt have to replace a lot of our belongings. I couldn't think about that right now, though. I was exhausted. I just needed to get our one checked bag, pick up the rental car and get us to the house so we could crash. I was running on fumes at the moment, but I needed to get Jacob somewhere safe before I could relax. My wolf was spinning out of control. She hated the enclosed space of the airplane and the upheaval of leaving our home, our den, behind. She was distressed enough at the loss of my parents; our pack. I'd need to go for a run soon, but I didn't have the luxury of doing that in the near future.

I gently laid Jacob down on a bench next to the luggage conveyor and slid my backpack under his head. He was so small. He was being so brave; I was so proud of him. He looked so much like my mother with his mousy brown hair and his big blue eyes. He was cute as a button, and he used that to get away with murder. 'I taught him well,' I thought, with a wry smile.

"Jacob, honey. I need you to wake up a bit for me, okay? We need to pick up our bag and get the car. You can have another sleep while we drive to the house." I gently shook his shoulder, and his eyes fluttered open as he grumbled beneath his breath. That, he got from our father. "Hey there, little guy. You have a good sleep?"

"I'm still tired," he said, sitting up and rubbing at his eyes.

"I know," I told him, running my hand through his unruly hair. He was going to need a haircut soon. "We're nearly there."

"Can I have some juice?" he asked. I rummaged in the backpack and pulled out a drink for him.

"Can you stay here while I look for our bag?" I asked him.

He nodded his little head and started to look around as he drank his fill. He'd been so quiet since it had all happened. He'd withdrawn into himself and barely spoke at all. I was out of my depth, but I hoped that we would find a way to deal with our loss together once we got settled.

When I looked back at the conveyor, I saw it had started to go around, and there were a few bags on there already. The plane had been pretty empty, so there shouldn't be that many to come out. We only had to wait for our one suitcase. I had gotten a few bits for Jacob and I while we were laying low at Sean's. There seemed little point in getting things we would then have to pay to ship here. Besides, it was bad enough having to lug this one case here. Thankfully, it quickly came into sight, and I grabbed it from the conveyor. Now we just had to find the car rental place. So close to being able to sleep!

The woman at the rental place was potentially some kind of an angel. She had set us up with a car seat for Jacob, whom she was completely smitten with, and arranged to have the car collected from our new home in two days. Because my parents had the house fully set up, there was already a vehicle there. I was only hiring the car because I didn't want to take a taxi. The rental was already equipped with a sat nav, and she had one of the employees set it up for us with our destination while she helped me get the car seat fitted. We only had a half an hour drive, and then we would be at the house—where there were beds and the sleep! I needed so much sleep!

Jacob fell asleep before I even had the engine of the car turned on. The sun was just starting to set when we pulled out of the rental's car park, and by the time we arrived at the house, it was pitch black. Thank god for sat nav! When we first pulled up, I was convinced we were in the wrong place. The "cabin" that I had thought we were going to was absolutely enormous. I had to give it to my parents, they had picked a beautiful home for us, even if they would never get to live here with us.

There was a beautiful two storey picture window on the front of the house. The front door was off to one side, and there was a matching window on the opposite side of the house, creating a symmetrical look to the front. There were two dormer windows in the roof, covered by a light layer of snow.

I drove up the driveway and circled to the two-car garage next to the house. There was some kind of blue truck already parked outside, so I pulled up next to it. Thankfully, Jacob was still fast asleep in the backseat. Leaving the engine running to keep the car warm, I got out to investigate. I still wasn't convinced I was in the right place and I didn't want to wake him up just yet. The house's front door opened as I got out of the car, and a man who looked to be in his early thirties stepped out.

"Calliope?" he asked, walking over and offering me his hand.

I took it with a sigh of relief. "Oh thank god, I was convinced I was in the wrong place. And please, call me Calli," I said.

He chuckled as he shook my hand. "Long journey?"

"Like you wouldn't believe."

"Let me help you get your bags into the house," he offered, as he stepped towards the car. "My wife came by earlier and opened up the house for you. She made up the bedrooms with fresh sheets and dropped a few things off in the kitchen to get you started."

"Thanks. I really appreciate it," I said, popping the trunk open. "Sleep is like the only thing I can think about at the minute."

"I'm James by the way," he said, grabbing the suitcase and looking into the back seat. "You want to take the bag, and I can grab the little one?" he asked, spying Jacob asleep in the backseat.

"No, it's okay. He's only twice as heavy as he looks," I laughed.

Leaning in, I turned the car engine off and then gently unclipped Jacob from his seat and lifted him out. He had gone full-on dead weight and snuggled into me with a sleepy grumble.

James led the way into the house carrying the suitcase. I realised that someone had salted the pathway for us and the thoughtfulness of these people nearly brought tears to my eyes. James and his wife had been the caretakers for the house, keeping it clean and making sure that it stayed in good condition. Good news for me because I was barely an adult, and there was no way I would know how to fix up a house if anything went wrong.

We stepped through the front door, straight into the open plan living room, dining room and kitchen. It was an enormous space. The living room portion was set in front of the giant picture window at the front of the house. As we walked to the back of the house where the kitchen was, James set the suitcase down and led me over to a small archway on the other side of the dining area. There were three doors, and he opened the one on the right, revealing a bedroom. My parents had obviously set this one up for Jacob. It was definitely a little boy's room. The room's walls were a deep blue, and there was a green metal-framed bed made up with blue polka dot sheets. A big cream rug covered the floor with large yellow circles on it, and there was a big colourful world map on the wall. Under the window was a little desk and a dresser sat at the end of the bed. There looked to be a built-in closet, as well. It was the perfect room for Jacob, and I felt a lump form in my throat when I realised that my parents had taken the time to make this into a home for us without us even knowing. James pulled the covers back on the bed for me, and I gently laid Jacob down, took off his shoes and tucked him in. He was only wearing joggers and a shirt; he could sleep in those.

We quietly retreated out of the room, and I released the breath that I didn't realise I was holding. James chuckled at me. "That's a cute boy you've got there."

I smiled at him in relief. "Jacob's my brother," I told him.

"Phew! I thought you were a bit young to have one that age," he said, looking a bit uncomfortable.

"Yeah, don't worry, I expect everyone will make the same mistake," I waved him off. "Can I get you a drink or something?" I asked him.

"Nah, I'll get out of here and let you get some sleep. Are your parents joining you soon?" he conversationally asked as he zipped his coat up, pulling some gloves out his pockets.

"No, it's just the two of us. My parents passed away a couple of months ago," I told him quietly. It was hard to say out loud, but I would have to get used to it. I had meant it before when I said that everyone would be making the same mistake. I had talked this through with Sean before we left. The most believable story was to stick to the truth; our parents had died in a car accident, and we had moved here to make things a bit easier for Jacob. He had offered to come out with us, to help get us settled, but I didn't want to impose on him any further. He had his own life back in England, and if I was going to stand any chance of doing this, I needed just to jump straight in and do it.

"I'm sorry to hear that," he said. He genuinely did look sorry. "My wife, Mary and I, run the local store. If you need anything, come by and ask for one of us. We're a fairly small town here in Arbington, but we look after our own. That includes you two now as well," he smiled.

It was a nice sentiment, and I hoped that Jacob and I could see this place as home in time. We would still need to be careful, but Jacob and I were used to small-town life. Kirkby Malzeard, where we had both grown up, was only a small village in Yorkshire. My parents were convinced that it was easier to hide in small towns. It was the big cities where everyone thought you would go to hide.

"Thank you. I'll probably see you tomorrow in that case, when we come by to stock up." I walked James to the door, and we said our goodbyes. He seemed nice enough, and I would have to thank his wife for opening up the house for us.

As soon as I closed the front door, I looked around myself, suddenly feeling a little lost. The house truly was beautiful. The living room had a massive TV which would make Jacob immensely happy. I would have to see about getting cable installed. That was American TV, right? I had no idea. I needed to make a list or something, but my brain felt like it was fast shutting down from lack of sleep. I wandered into the kitchen and checked the fridge. Mary, who was now my most favourite person in the world, had set us up with milk, cheese, bread, eggs, bacon and orange juice. A quick look in the cupboards and I discovered coffee but no tea bags. Definitely going to need tea bags, but at least we had something for breakfast in the morning.

Now all I needed to do was find a bedroom. I checked the other two doors where Jacob's bedroom was and found a bathroom and what looked like a guest bedroom.

There was another archway on the opposite side of the open plan living area, and I grabbed the suitcase and wandered through it. I was faced with another two door situation and what looked like a back door. I tried the door to the left and found it led to two dark staircases, one going up to the attic area and one going down to the basement. I quickly closed that door not feeling up to exploring that far just yet. Plus, it was a bit creepy! The other door opened to reveal the master bedroom. When I walked through the door, I felt the tears creep into my eyes. Obviously, this was the master suite because I could see a walk-in closet and an en-suite bathroom through an open door. But it had been set up nearly exactly like my room at home in soft greys. I had always thought that my parent's room was garish with its bright yellow walls, but my mother liked it, and my father didn't care what colour the walls were. The tears fell slowly down my cheeks when I realised they had never intended to come here with us. My parents had set this house up for us if anything ever happened to them. My wolf howled mournfully in the back of my mind, her own grief amplifying mine. I dropped the case next to the door, kicked off my shoes and fell onto the bed. Burrowing my face into the pillow, I cried softly until exhaustion finally settled over me and dragged me into sleep.

3
CALLI

I woke up the next day with a small foot jammed into the small of my back. Rolling over, I saw two little feet on the bed next to me. Lifting my head, I peered down the bed, and saw Jacob asleep sprawled out starfish-style, the wrong way round and snoring softly. I hadn't closed the curtains when I fell into bed last night, and sunlight was streaming through the window. When I checked my watch, I was pleased to see that it was nine in the morning. Hopefully, we would adapt to the time difference reasonably quickly.

I grabbed the foot that was slowly making its way up to my face and started to tickle it. Jacob squealed and giggled.

"Morning," I laughed. He really did have an infectious giggle even if he was a bed hog. "You want some breakfast?" I asked him, sitting up. Jacob just nodded and sat up. "How about you go get washed up, and I'll cook breakfast for us," I offered.

Jacob slid out of bed without a word and wandered out of the room. I sighed and got up myself. Realising that all our stuff was still in the case, I heaved it onto the bed and opened it. Grabbing Jacob's toiletries bag, I followed him out of the room and found him sitting on the sofa. I passed him the bag and ruffled his hair. He just got up and wandered back in the direction of his room and bathroom, and my heart broke as I watched him. I didn't know what to do to help him. Maybe it was the loss of pack feeling that was hurting him so much, but he was still young and hadn't come into his wolf yet. Sean suggested giving him time, but I didn't know how much time was too much before I needed to think about getting him someone to talk to. Would that even be possible? We had so much to hide. How could Jacob openly talk to someone about his problems when he couldn't even tell them the whole truth?

I wandered into the kitchen and quickly made us scrambled eggs with bacon. I sorted myself a cup of coffee and Jacob a glass of orange juice when he sat down. He ate quickly, and I was glad that he was at least hungry.

"I was thinking we could head into town after breakfast, pick up some more groceries and see what else there is." Jacob just nodded at me. "Little guy, I'm worried. I know you're hurting because I'm hurting as well. How can I help you?"

Jacob looked at me with his big blue eyes. "I miss them," he whispered.

"I know. I miss them too. You know they set up this house for us? I think Mum did a good job in your room, don't you?"

He just nodded sadly in reply.

"How about we see if we can find some toys in town for you to fill that new room with?" I suggested. That immediately brightened him up, just like I knew it would. I'd make this house as much of a home for him as I could, and hopefully, that would help him a bit. "I'll grab you some clothes and then let's get ready and go out, okay?" Jacob jumped off his chair and ran towards his room. "Brush your teeth!" I shouted after him.

I quickly put our dishes in the dishwasher, set out some clothes for Jacob and then jumped into the shower. There was something about a hot shower that always made me feel a bit better. I quickly got ready and found Jacob sitting on the sofa again, fully dressed and watching some kind of cartoons on TV. Apparently, we either had cable, or we didn't need it. While he was preoccupied, I rummaged through the kitchen. I had seen a folder on the kitchen counter earlier which had details of all of the utilities and house information in it, so I set it aside to deal with later. Next to it had been the keys for the house and the car and a note from Mary.

Calliope,

I hope everything is in order with the house. If you need anything, feel free to stop by the store anytime. James has filled the truck up with gas for you. He says it's running fine, but you might want to get it checked over at the garage as it's been parked for a while. We've also stocked you up with some salt for the driveway if you need it. It's in the garage with the snow shovel.

Hopefully we'll see you tomorrow, Mary.

I smiled when I read it. Mary and James were both very thoughtful. Grabbing the boarding card print out and pen out of my bag, I started to make a list on the back of it of what we would need at the store. I wasn't sure how big it was so I didn't go too crazy. I had looked up Arbington on google, and it seemed like a pretty small town. There was a bigger supermarket in the next town over if we needed it and Portland was the closest city. We were probably going to need to shop online for a lot of stuff to get Jacob set up and settled in though. Thank god for Amazon! With Jacob starting kindergarten in a couple of days he'd need school supplies too.

When my list was made, I grabbed the truck keys off the kitchen counter and joined Jacob in the living room where he was still watching some silly cartoon and laughing away. It was nice to see him laugh again. "I'm going to back the truck out of the garage and get it warmed up. Why don't you stay here where it's warm?"

Jacob smiled up at me happily and nodded. Even though he still didn't say anything, my heart nearly stopped at seeing him act a bit more like his old self.

I slipped on my coat and grabbed my bag before backing the monstrosity that was apparently a truck, out of the garage. Putting the heat on full blast, I jumped out and took another look at it. It was truly enormous. I'd never driven anything so big in my life! It was black, very shiny and looked pretty new. All I could tell you was that it was a Mercedes, had four doors and one of those flatbed bits at the back. I was used to driving a Renault Clio. I wasn't sure if I liked it, but it would have to do. I'd bet anything that my Dad had picked it out.

After managing to drag Jacob away from the TV, we drove into town and pulled up outside the store. Thankfully they had a small car park next to it because there was no way I was going to try to parallel park that thing.

I walked into the store with a sullen Jacob, who had realised that shopping was not as fun as cartoons. However, when he saw the rack of toys, he soon brightened up and skipped right over. The woman behind the checkout counter gave me a friendly smile and waved me over, after telling Jacob where I was going, I walked over to join her.

"You must be Calli," she said, coming around the checkout and pulling me into a hug. I awkwardly hugged her back doing one of those weird back pat things. "You are just like my James described, except far more beautiful," she said, holding me out at arm's length to inspect me. "I'm Mary by the way," she told me with a wink.

"Thanks, I showered and everything this morning," I laughed, and she giggled along with me. "We've just come to check out the town and get some shopping done. We didn't bring much of anything with us, so Jacob is having some pretty big toy withdrawals."

We both looked over at him as he was creating a stack of toys beside him that I would inevitably let him have. Thankfully it seemed to be limited to Lego, cars and jigsaw puzzles.

"James said you only had one bag. Are you having the rest of your things shipped?" she said, cocking her head to the side.

"No, it seemed easier to just sort it out at this end rather than ship everything. We came here for a fresh start after …" I trailed off and she laid her hand on my shoulder.

"James did fill me in. I'm sorry for your loss." She slipped her arm around my shoulders and gave me a side hug before letting me go.

"I just want to get Jacob settled. He's not doing so well," I said.

"Is he going to Pine Elementary? They have an incredible school counsellor. I'm sure he would be able to give you some advice."

"Yeah, he starts in a few days. I actually need to stop by there and finish up registering him and get the school supplies lists and stuff." I laughed as Jacob tried to carry his haul over to us by himself.

"You look like you've got yourself pretty much sorted out there, spud." I smiled at him, and it turned into a grin when he smiled back at me. "Is it okay if we leave these here while we go and grab some groceries?" I asked Mary.

"Of course, honey. I promise to keep them super safe for you," she said, smiling down at Jacob.

Jacob actually said "Thank you" to her and then we grabbed a cart and made pretty quick work of going around the store. It wasn't that big, but it had everything we needed. I planned on filling the fridge and freezer with enough to make a couple of meals for us that were big enough to create leftovers. The only thing that it was missing were my precious Yorkshire Tea teabags. I'd have to make do with the crappy Liptons that they had until I could find some way to get my hands on them. The worst news though, I wasn't old enough to buy alcohol here! That sucked more than I thought it would.

When we made it back to the checkout, James had joined Mary and was checking out the Lego that Jacob had picked out. Mary quickly rang up our groceries for us and got them bagged up. "This is some pretty sweet Lego you've got here, kid," James said to Jacob who grinned and nodded at him.

"If you want, you can leave Jacob here with us while you go and run your errands at the school and the like," Mary offered.

"That's very nice, but I couldn't put you out like that," I said awkwardly.

"It's no bother," James answered happily. Then he knelt and spoke with Jacob. "Mary never lets me play with Lego anymore," he said, rolling his eyes.

Jacob smiled shyly at him, whispering, "You can share mine if you like."

Tears came to my eyes, and Mary gave me a knowing smile as James took Jacob over to a small table set up next to the checkout, and they started opening the Lego boxes. "He hardly speaks at all anymore," I said quietly, and Mary rubbed my arm.

"Go on, get those errands run. He's fine here for a couple of hours."

I thanked Mary and James, who just waved me off, and Jacob happily waved back at me from where he was in full out Lego mode. I had the school to get to and also the garage. I figured that if I booked the truck into the garage, I could drop it off another day for them to check over while I hung out at the library or the coffee shop.

I decided to head to the school first. I had all of the school information I needed in my bag. Hopefully, I'd be able to make an appointment to speak with the school counsellor. The school was only a short walk from the store, but I decided to take the truck so that I could swing by the garage on the way back. Also, I needed the practice driving it if I was completely honest.

The woman in the school office, Holly, thankfully took pity on me and basically filled out all the forms for me and just showed me where to sign. She also mentioned that if I didn't mind waiting for ten minutes, I could see the school counsellor now. I was quite happy to, especially when she set me up with a coffee and a doughnut. It was a lovely little school. Arbington was the biggest of the towns in the area, so quite a few kids bused in to attend here. Holly was filling me in on the after school clubs when the smell hit me, and I froze in my seat. Wolf. There was another shifter here. I had been through this before, but it still terrified me every time. My hand automatically went to my necklace to check that my talisman was still there. Then I took a few calming breaths so that I could get my emotions under control. Some shifters could scent fear, and I couldn't draw suspicion to me.

"Ms. Fairchild?" I heard a male voice question.

I looked up and then glanced over at Holly in question to see her grinning at me and giving me a thumbs-up behind his back. I couldn't help the smile that hit my face at her antics, and thankfully I was able to suppress the laugh. He might be a wolf, the thing that I was terrified of being discovered by. But. My. God! He was gorgeous! Like, shockingly beautiful. He didn't seem much older than me, which I found a bit weird. He had brown wavy hair that was gelled back from his face and a short beard of stubble. His deep brown eyes were shining in amusement, and he had a cheeky grin on his face.

"She's doing something behind my back again, isn't she?" he laughed.

"Who would that be?" I questioned innocently.

"That's right, solidarity!" Holly laughed.

"You realise that you all but confessed you were, in fact, doing something behind my back," he laughed at her, turning around.

While I got my chance, I shamelessly checked him out. He might have been wearing a suit, but he filled it out more than enough. And his ass was amazing!

He was currently squabbling with Holly about being professional when I caught her eye, pointed at his ass and mouthed 'what!' at her. She burst out guffawing in laughter, but when he turned around, I just smiled sweetly at him.

"You two," he said, pointing between us. "Are not allowed to be friends!"

Holly pouted, but couldn't suppress her laughter for more than a few seconds before he shrugged in defeat and turned back to me. "I'm River Thornton. I'm the school counsellor. Why don't we go into my office, away from the children?" he said, glaring at Holly.

He led the way to a nearby office, and my nerves suddenly kicked in. I was going to be shut in a room with a wolf shifter. Be. Cool!

"Thank you for meeting with me at such short notice," I

told him as I sat down in one of the chairs in front of the desk. I was surprised when he sat next to me rather than on the other side of his desk.

The office was sparse, to say the least. There was just the desk with an office chair behind it and two guest chairs on the other sides. A stack of archive boxes in the corner rounded out the 'furnishings'.

"Homey," I nervously said as I looked around.

He did one of those amazing male laughs that makes your insides turn to liquid before hitting me with a glaring grin. "I only started this job this semester, so I'm still settling in," he said. "If you don't mind me saying, your accent?"

"Oh yes, Jacob and I have relocated here from England," I filled in. "I suppose it sticks out a bit doesn't it."

"Maybe a little," he smiled. He flicked open the folder in front of him, which held the forms I had just filled out. "I see that you are listed as Jacob's next of kin."

"Yes, I'm his sister," I confirmed. "Our parents passed away a few months ago."

He looked at me, and I saw a glimmer of pain in his eyes. "Do you have family in the area?" he asked.

"No, it's just the two of us."

He closed the folder and dropped it onto his desk. "Do you mind me asking what made you come to Arbington?"

"Not at all. My parents had a second home here. I didn't want to stay in my parent's home. A fresh start seemed like a good idea. I suppose it also seemed like a good idea to get Jacob settled somewhere that wouldn't remind him of our parents constantly. He isn't doing too well, but I suppose that's to be expected," I rambled.

"Ms Fairchild," he started.

"Please, just call me Calli," I cut in.

"Calli," he said with a smile. "How are you doing?" he stressed.

"Why?" I asked, cocking my head to the side in question.

"Jacob isn't the only one who lost his parents. But you also have the added pressure of having become your brother's guardian. It can be hard to deal with your own emotions when you're looking after everyone else, especially a young child," he said.

I bristled at the implication of his comment. "Jacob is very well cared for, Mr Thornton."

He held up his hands in surrender. "You misunderstand me," he said quickly. "I just wanted to make sure that you're okay," he said softly. "And if I am calling you Calli, it's only fair that you call me River."

"I'm fine," I said shortly, shutting the subject down. "My concern is Jacob. He's shutting himself down. He's all but stopped speaking. I don't know how he is going to cope with school. He went to a pre-school before we lost our parents, but my mother had started to home school him."

"You might find that school helps him. It will give him some more structure to his day. He'll start to socialise with other children, make some friends. Children can be very resilient, Calli. We will look after him while he's here," he smiled pleasantly at me, but my hackles were definitely raised now. My wolf didn't like the implication that we couldn't care for our brother, whether he had meant it or not.

"I hope so," I sighed, trying to calm my emotions.

"Well, he starts on Monday. If you want to bring him to the office first thing, I can introduce myself, and I'll take him to class and help him settle in. Did you get a supplies list?" he asked, standing up.

"Yes, Holly gave me one." I stood up and went to walk

past him. As I reached the door, he put his hand on my arm and turned me around.

"I don't want you to leave angry with me, Calli," he said softly.

I looked him in the eye, and I could tell that he was genuinely distressed. It was kind of ironic. If he knew what I was, he would no doubt be more concerned with putting me down rather than whether he had hurt my feelings. "No offence is taken, I assure you," I said tensely. Even I didn't think it sounded convincing.

He followed me out of the office, nervously rubbing the back of his neck. "So, erm, what have you got planned for the rest of the day," he said, trying to make conversation.

"Nothing much, I just need to go to the garage and see if I can get them to look at my truck sometime. It's been sitting in the garage at the house for a while, and James recommended getting it looked over."

"My brother owns the garage. I can give him a call and let him know that you're coming. I'm sure he'll be able to squeeze you in," he said with a shy smile.

If the garage owner were indeed his brother, then he would be a wolf too. If there were two wolves in the area, then it was likely there was a pack here. Why would my parents have sent us to a house where there was a pack nearby? Did they not know? Had they intended us to approach the pack? Fuck! There was no backing down now. We were here, and I needed some stability for Jacob. He hadn't shown any signs of magic, and my mother had recognised mine at an earlier age than he was now. If we were discovered, I could tell them that his mother was a wolf. Hopefully, they would only kill me and take him into their pack.

Fucking hell that sounded like a shit plan even to me! I'd

run before they could get hold of us, but we didn't have anywhere else to go, and I couldn't just drag Jacob around the world after me. He was traumatised enough as it was. I was pretty sure we could just lie low. I'd figure out who was part of the pack and make sure to limit my contact with them. It was the world's worst plan, but at the moment, it was the only one that I could think of.

"Thank you," I said, smiling at River and hoping my inner turmoil wasn't apparent. "That's very kind of you."

"It's the least I could do," he said before turning and going back to his office.

4

RIVER

Fuck! I was such an asshole. When I walked into the reception area and saw her, I'd nearly swallowed my tongue. She was so beautiful. And so not what I was expecting. I'd heard rumours, of course, about the single woman and a child moving into the cabin that had stood empty for so long. I'd expected her to be older. And definitely not as attractive as she was. She had long golden hair and beautiful, big emerald eyes. When she stood up to greet me, I couldn't help running my gaze up her long luscious legs, past her hourglass figure and then pull on every ounce of decency I had not to let my eyes linger on her breasts. Thankfully, she had been smiling at Holly and hadn't seen me thoroughly check her out. Holly noticed though, and there was no way I would hear the end of it from her. I could even feel my wolf huffing in amusement at me. It wasn't often that I found myself getting this worked up by a woman. The only problem was my clumsy attempt at conversation had clearly upset her, and I could understand why. I had basically insinuated she wasn't capable of caring for her brother. She was probably never going to forgive me.

Picking up the phone, I dialled my brother's number. He answered on the second ring. He always did. Grey was my biological brother, but he was also Alpha to the Stoneridge Pack; my pack. We were a relatively small pack and lived not far out of town. We had seven males, but no turned female wolves. Grey did well handling all of us, unmated males. Female wolves were rare because they had to be turned, and it was exceptionally hard to turn humans. None of us had ever found someone that we wanted to risk turning. Nash was currently dating Holly, but she had no interest in being turned. She knew what we were. A couple of people in town did. She didn't seem all that bothered about being turned though which spoke volumes on how long they both saw their relationship lasting. It was a painful process, but it either worked, or it didn't. Thankfully none of the women died if it failed. I don't know if anyone had ever tried twice though or what the consequences would be if they did. The problem was, our wolves would never accept a human as a mate. So whilst we could be with a human and form a relationship with them, it would never be what it could be if that woman were a wolf.

"What happened?" Grey growled at me.

"Why do you assume that something has happened?" I said, immediately annoyed. Grey was my older brother by four years. I was the kid brother that was always screwing up. But I went to college, got my degree, and now had a pretty good job. I'd grown up a lot over the last few years.

"It's the middle of the day, you're at work, and there's no other reason for you to call me."

I sighed part in frustration and part from lust. "There is the most beautiful girl in the world heading over to you."

Grey immediately started laughing, and I heard him call out into the garage. "Hey Tanner, you need to hear this,

River says the most beautiful girl in the world is on her way here."

I could hear all the guys laughing in the garage. Just wait until they saw her then they'd be sorry. "So, I may have accidentally upset her. Do you think you could help her out and maybe, I don't know, convince her I'm not an absolute asshole?" I muttered. I was never going to hear the end of this.

Now I could hear Grey and Tanner both laughing their asses off at me. "You need me to fix you up, baby brother?" Grey managed to get out between laughs.

Tanner, our pack Beta, and my brother's best friend came over the phone; apparently, I was on speaker. "Why didn't you just apologise to her?"

"I tried, but I majorly put my foot in it."

"Ah man, you sound pretty sad about this," Tanner sympathised. "I tell you what, when you get back to the packhouse tonight, we'll teach you how to talk to a girl." And then they were all just laughing at me again.

"Just leave it to us brother," Grey laughed.

"I already regret this, you know," I grumbled before we said our goodbyes and hung up. Maybe I should just send her some flowers.

I dropped my head into my hands and took a moment to feel sorry for myself. When I looked up, I was treated to the grinning face of Holly in front of me who had no doubt heard every word. "Would it make you feel better if I told you that she was totally checking out your ass earlier?" she asked.

That perked me up. "Actually yes, yes it would."

She sighed dramatically and passed me a post-it note. "Don't thank me too much. Remember, I accept gifts in the form of wine or chocolates."

I looked at the note and frowned in confusion. "I don't get it."

"It's the brand of her favourite tea, that she can't find and she really misses. It's the perfect apology gift that you could drop by her house with."

I grinned up at Holly. She could have chocolates *and* wine for this. "You really are the best, Hols," I shouted out my office door after her, as she turned and went back to her desk.

I logged into my computer quicker than I had ever before and set about trying to find the closest and quickest supply. Luckily for me, I found a shop two towns over called the British Corner Shop and a quick call to Nash, and the promise of letting him borrow my motorcycle, had him driving over to pick me some up.

5
GREY

My brother was such an idiot. I couldn't believe he had called me up to try and make nice with some woman for him. I was still laughing about it when the Mercedes truck pulled up outside the garage about ten minutes later. It was a welcome relief to what had been a tense few months. I was certain we had a vamp nest setting up somewhere in the area that we would need to deal with and, to make matters worse, we had scented witch magic near town nearly two months ago and were still on edge from it.

"Heads up," Tanner laughed. "This must be the most beautiful girl in the world." He leant against the side of the car I was working on and watched through the open garage door while I went back to my work.

"What a moron," I muttered. "You would have thought that after he went away to college …"

But then I was cut off by Tanner swearing. "Fuck me sideways."

"What?" I asked, following his gaze to the woman stepping out of the truck.

River wasn't wrong. She was a petite little thing, but the way that her jeans hugged her lean legs and the sweater stretched over her curves had poor Tanner drooling next to me, and I had to admit that I wasn't far off it myself. When she turned around and stretched back inside to grab her jacket, I thought Tanner was going to pass out with how heavily he was breathing. "God really does exist," he joked.

I slapped him in the stomach and laughed. "You stay here. You clearly can't be trusted. Breathe into a paper bag or something," I teased him, as I went to walk over to greet her. That was when I realised that River had failed to give us her name.

"Hi there," I said with a smile, stretching out a hand to her. She took it with a firm hold and smiled back at me with the most beautiful smile I'd ever seen.

"Hi, I was wondering if I could book my truck thing in for you to look at," she said, pointing back to the fancy Mercedes behind her. Good lord, her accent was just the icing on the cake.

"Well, truck things are my speciality." I grinned.

She laughed, and I decided there and then that River was out of luck. It was every man for himself in this game. "I'm not used to something this big. It's a bit of a monster." She flushed and then threw back her head and laughed. "God, I nearly said it was a bit much for me to handle, imagine all the jokes you could have cracked at my expense then."

"How dare you!" I said in mock outrage. "I'll have you know that I'm nothing but a gentleman."

Tanner rushed over to join us, clearly not content to sit on the sidelines any longer. "Hi, I'm Tanner," he said, sticking out his hand to her and giving me a devilish grin. "You must be the newcomer that everyone is so excited about."

"Calli. I suppose I'm the highlight of the town gossip, am I?"

"Well, if the town gossip is my brother, then yes," I laughed.

"I can't believe you just threw him under the bus like that. And here you were trying to convince me that you were a gentleman," she smiled.

"So, what's wrong with the truck thing?" I said, striding over to have a look at it. It was a really nice vehicle. Much fancier than we generally saw around here.

"Hopefully nothing," she shrugged. When I raised an eyebrow at her in question, she added, "It's been sitting in the garage up at the house for a while, and James said I should get you to check it out to make sure it's running okay."

"I can do that for you now if you like?" Tanner offered. "Should only take me an hour or so."

"Erm, would you mind if I just booked in for next week? I've got all the groceries in the back, and I need to pick Jacob up and take him home. James must be tired of playing with Lego by now."

"Aww, you should have brought him here, I never get to play with Lego," Tanner actually whined.

"I'll buy you some for Christmas," I said, slapping him on the back. "I tell you what, throw the groceries in the back of my truck, we can swing by and pick Jacob up, and I'll run you home. We'll look at the truck this afternoon and drop it back with you after we close," I offered, already formulating a plan on how to see her again after that.

"I couldn't possibly put you out like that," she said blushing.

"No problem at all. I need to grab something from the store anyway, and your house is on our way home," I argued. There was no way she could say no now.

"How do you know where I live?" she asked suspiciously, taking a step back, hopefully unconsciously.

"Yeah Grey, how do you know where she lives?" Tanner said, rubbing it in a bit more.

"Because the whole town knows where everyone lives," I laughed. "Stop trying to make trouble. I saw the beautiful lady first."

"Actually, River saw her first, I saw her second, and you were lowly third," Tanner argued.

Suddenly realising we were bickering over a woman standing in front of us, I turned back to her with a smile. "Maybe you could just forget that last little bit happened?" I said, smiling at the cute blush she had going on.

She just shook her head and smiled.

"I'll go and grab my keys then," I said, turning around and jogging back into the garage.

When I got to the office, I rummaged through my desk, trying to find my keys when Aidan stuck his head through the door. "Awww boss, that was just so goddamned adorable."

I grabbed the keys and walked past him, giving him a playful shove. "You're just jealous."

"I most definitely am," he laughed, as I jogged back to make sure that Tanner wasn't making any headway without me.

6

CALLI

What in the hell was going on with me? That garage had been swarming with wolves, and there I stood and flirted with two of them. And now! Now, I was sat in a truck with one while he drove me and my little brother, who I was supposed to be protecting, back to our home! I'd lost my damn mind. Or maybe my wolf had because she was just lazing in the back of my mind refusing to see what the problem was.

When we got back to the house, Grey unloaded the groceries and carried them in for me. Because that's apparently what I did now, I invited wolves I didn't know into my home. Wolves I should be hiding from because, you know, they would probably kill me when they found out what I was.

Why did they have to be so hot?! Grey had shaggy brown hair that he kept pushing back out of his brown eyes. His square jaw was covered with short stubble, and he had a typical mechanics body, you know the type, you usually see them on calendars, covered in oil and topless. Tanner was the same except he was blonde and clean-shaven. He had these dark brown eyes that seemed to be constantly filled with laughter. They were both sooo hot, shameless flirts, and did I mention fucking wolves!

Jacob happily ran into his room with his haul of new toys. It would at least keep him occupied for a while. Grey put the groceries down on the kitchen counter and then turned around to look at the house.

"I always wondered what this place was like inside. It's really nice," he said, wandering into the living area. "I may have to marry you, just so that I can share your TV."

I laughed and went to join him. "It is rather large," I said, looking at it. When I looked up at him, he had a massive grin on his face and was suppressing a laugh. "I was talking about the TV, get your mind out of the gutter," I laughed.

"What! I didn't say anything!" he said, raising his hands in surrender.

"I'd offer you a beer, but unfortunately I'm not old enough to buy beer anymore," I chuckled, walking back into the kitchen. "All I can offer you is instant coffee, water, milk or juice," I said, opening the fridge and checking inside. When I turned back around, I caught him staring at my ass and found that I actually quite liked it. Maybe it's a wolf thing? Maybe it's a 'my wolf likes wolves' thing? Why was my life getting so complicated?

"Why can't you buy beer anymore?" he asked, changing the subject.

"I'm only twenty," I said. "We have a lower age limit in Europe," I shrugged.

"You're only twenty," he said, cocking his head to the side. "But Jacob …"

"Is my brother," I laughed.

"But he lives here with you?"

"Yep."

"And your parents?" he asked, confused.

"No," I answered quietly, turning to the bags of groceries to unpack them. I needed a second to push the tears out my eyes before I could look at him again.

"I'm so sorry." I heard his voice from directly behind me. Then I felt his hands on my shoulders as he gently turned me around and pulled me against him.

I leaned against his chest and let myself feel the grief, just for a moment, as he held me in his arms. Then I pulled back and took a step away from him, taking a deep breath. "Sorry, that got weird fast," I said, trying to laugh off the awkwardness of having just hugged a practical stranger.

"Don't apologise for feeling pain, Calli," he said softly. As if he could sense my unease, he took a step away from me and picked his keys off the counter where he'd dropped them. "I should get back to the garage and have a look at your truck. I'll be back in a couple of hours though."

Thanking him again for his help, I walked him over to the door and watched as he climbed into his truck with a smile and a wave, then drove away.

"I thought we were hiding from wolves?" Jacob's little voice came from behind me. I turned around to see him standing outside his room, looking at me. It was possibly the most he had said to me for weeks.

I waved him over to the sofa, and we both sat down. "We were. I don't know why Mum and Dad would have sent us here, though. There's definitely a wolf pack in this area. We're going to need to be extra careful until I can figure this out okay. We won't be able to avoid them, so we just need to make sure that we keep our secret. Do you think you can do that?" I asked him.

"I can. I don't know about you," Jacob said with a giggle.

"Hey, what's that supposed to mean?" I said, tickling his sides just to hear more of his giggles.

"That man likes you," he said with a frown. "I'm the man of the family now. I'll have to make sure he's going to be nice to you."

"Oh! Who told you that?" I laughed.

"Uncle Sean did," he said. "He told me to look after you because I was the man of the house now."

"I tell you what," I said, pulling him closer to me for a hug. "How about you be a kid for a bit longer, and we just work this out together instead?"

"Okay," he mumbled into my sweater as he held me a little tighter.

Sensing the need to change the subject and keep him talking before he could slip back into his grief again, I suggested we start our Amazon shopping spree to get him some more toys and all his school supplies. Jacob ran to get the iPad, and I made us a couple of sandwiches. We sat on the sofa giggling and internet shopped for the next couple of hours. It was nice and almost felt like I had my little brother back.

By the time I heard the sound of the truck rumbling down the driveway, I was pretty proud of what I had accomplished for the afternoon. We had ordered all of Jacob's school supplies and a ridiculous amount of stuff for his room. I'd also ordered clothes for both of us. Most of it was going to be delivered tomorrow—gotta love next day delivery!

I'd even pulled up enough courage to explore the creepy stairs. We had a basement with a blessed wine cellar stocked to the brim, and a fully equipped gym down there. I was glad that I'd ordered work out clothes because I was dying to get in there. Upstairs was where the weirdness started. At first glance, it was a library. All of the walls were covered in bookshelves which were crammed full of books. There were a couple of armchairs up there and a coffee table. When I'd looked a bit closer though, all the books were on magic, shifters, witches and other supernatural stuff. Some of them also looked crazy old. It was something I just didn't have the heart to deal with right then, so I went downstairs and set about cooking a massive roast dinner. It had always been Jacob's favourite, and I figured we could use the leftovers for a few days.

Dinner was just about ready when I heard the truck outside. I went to the door and found Grey climbing out of my truck, with Tanner and River getting out another that had just pulled in. Three wolves in the house now! That had to be a record. I invited them in, and we all ended up standing in the kitchen.

Grey passed me the keys. "That is a really nice truck," he said.

"You marrying me for my truck as well now?" I laughed.

He just grinned as well. "Well if you're proposing," he shrugged.

"Was it all okay?" I asked.

"Mostly. We changed the oil and gave it a service for you. It's going to need a new oil filter, but I've had to order one in because we didn't have one in stock. If you drop by on Monday, I can fit it for you."

"Thanks, it's probably a good job I brought it in then." I picked up my bag off the dining table and started to rummage through it to find my purse. "How much do I owe you?" I asked while I searched.

"You can settle up with us at the garage on Monday," Grey shrugged.

"Oh, okay."

"Something smells incredible," Tanner said, peering in the oven.

"No close the door!" I shouted.

"Woah, sorry," Tanner said, slamming the oven door shut quickly.

"If my Yorkshire puddings don't rise now, I'm so telling Jacob that it's your fault," I said, trying to peer through the oven glass.

"What's a Yorkshire pudding?" Tanner said, looking into the glass beside me.

"It's a … Yorkshire pudding," I said lamely, not knowing how to describe it. "Don't you have those here? You have it with a roast dinner."

"A pudding?" Tanner said, looking even more confused.

"Well, here's something you can get here too, if you know where to look," River said, with a wink as he pulled a gift bag out from behind his back.

"You got me a present?" I asked, surprised, as I took the bag.

"Think of it as an 'I'm sorry I was accidentally an ass to you' gift," he grimaced.

I looked in the bag, and my heart nearly stopped. When I looked up, there were actual tears in my eyes. "Awww, did you fuck it up again, man?" Tanner asked, looking warily at me.

I just laughed and threw my arms around River in what was probably an inappropriate reaction to a kind gesture. I felt his arms come around me, and he gently sighed as he held me against him. "I'm sorry," he whispered to me.

When he let me go, I realised that it should be super awkward that I was hugging a virtual stranger in my kitchen, again, with his two friends here. "Is this weird? This feels a bit weird," I said self-consciously.

Grey just laughed and slung an arm around my shoulders. "It's only weird when you make it weird, English."

"I suppose I should ask you if you want to stay for dinner then?" I said. I usually wasn't as weird as this. Maybe it was me. Was it me? These guys made me feel like I was losing my mind.

"Do I get to try a Yorkshire pudding?" Tanner asked, with a grin.

"I can't believe you've never had a Yorkshire pudding." I shook my head.

"We would love to stay for dinner," Grey said. "Let me just call the house to let them know we'll be coming back late."

"Oh, I'm not keeping you from anything am I?" I said nervously. I hadn't even considered the fact that they could have someone waiting at home for them. But then again, they had been shamelessly flirting with me so I would hope that they didn't.

Grey just shook his head with a grin and stepped out of the kitchen to make his call, so I set about mashing the potatoes for dinner. River went to the sink and washed his hands before offering to help, and I set him out carving up the beef. Before long we had dinner ready to go, and Tanner was looking suspiciously at the Yorkshire puddings which were waiting to be dished up with everything else.

"I'll tell Jacob that dinner's ready," I said, excusing myself from the kitchen.

When I went into Jacob's room, I found him sitting on the floor building something with the Lego we had bought today. He gave me a stern look when I told him that dinner was ready and that the guys would be eating with us.

"We're supposed to be keeping the secret," he said with a frown on his face.

"We are, little guy, it's just …" and then the scent of wolf hit my nose. I turned around and saw Grey standing in the door with a sheepish look on his face.

"Tanner wanted me to ask if you want him to start setting the table?" he said slowly.

"Yeah, sure." I held my hand out to Jacob and helped him up off the floor. "Go wash your hands, little guy," I told him as we all left the room. Grey had obviously heard mention of a secret, and I just had to hope that he wouldn't think it was anything too serious.

Dinner was a bit quiet at first, and I was worried that Grey would ask me what Jacob had meant, but eventually we all flowed into easy conversation. It was pretty nice. Even Jacob was happy with the three of them which had surprised me. Tanner was officially obsessed with Yorkshire puddings and made me tell him three times how to make them. After we finished eating Jacob asked to be excused and skipped into the living area to watch cartoons. Tanner sprawled out on the floor with him, and they started a very in-depth conversation about Pokémon. Grey and River helped me wash the dishes, and I smiled as I watched Jacob chatting away with Tanner. "He's always been good with kids because he basically still is one," River joked.

"I heard that," Tanner shouted across to us.

Once Jacob was settled into bed at eight, Grey suggested that they head back to their house. I could tell that the other two were reluctant to go and it was nice to know that they had enjoyed the evening as much as I had. We all said our goodbyes and Tanner pulled me into a hug before they left, mumbling that everyone else had got one already apart from him. Once the door was closed, and I was alone again, I wandered into the kitchen, poured myself a glass of wine and decided to have a steaming hot bath before bed. Maybe I could use the time to figure out just when it was that I had lost my damned mind.

7

GREY

By the time we pulled up at the house, the guys practically skipped in the front door ahead of me, and I couldn't help but laugh at their antics. River grabbed us all a beer out of the kitchen, and we sat down in the living room. I could hear a few of the other pack members wandering around the house, but no one bothered us for now.

"Is this going to be a problem?" I asked them as I took a swig from my bottle.

"What, all of us falling for the same girl?" Tanner asked. "How could that possibly go wrong?" he laughed.

"She is pretty amazing," River sighed. Normally I would have laughed at him, but he wasn't wrong. She was pretty amazing.

"So, Jacob isn't her kid?" Tanner asked.

"No, he's her brother, parents died in a car accident a couple of months ago," River filled in.

Shit, I knew they had lost them, but I hadn't realised it had been so recently. When I'd held her for that brief moment in my arms this afternoon, and I felt her grief slam into me, I didn't want to let her go. I'd never liked anyone this much so quickly before.

"That's rough," Tanner said, gulping down his beer. "Jacob's a nice kid."

"Yeah, when I spoke with Calli this morning she was concerned about how he was going to do at school. Apparently, after their parents died, he pretty much shut down. He barely talks anymore. Tonight's probably the most he's said in weeks," River said thoughtfully.

It was strange that we had gelled so well with the kid as quickly as we had. Usually, human kids were a bit leery of us. My father had always told me it was because they could instinctually tell shifters were predators.

"We should try and help her out more," Tanner said, sitting up. He was clearly concocting his own plan on getting closer to Calli.

"I don't know," River said, frowning at him. "Jacob has been through some major trauma. You can't get involved in their lives if you don't intend to stick around. It wouldn't be fair to him or Calli," he warned.

"Who said I wasn't intending on sticking around?"

"Maybe I'm just hoping," River smiled.

"Okay, this is going to be a problem," I said, watching them both. "We can't all pursue her. I can't risk this disrupting the pack."

"Well, it's nice of you to back down, big brother," River said, slapping me on the back.

"Oh, no! I'm not backing down. I really like her. I'm all in," I laughed, slapping him back.

"So, we all date her," Tanner shrugged.

"I don't know, this is a small town, and humans don't do the multiple mates thing," I said, concerned. "They've both been through a lot, and this is a fresh start for them." I frowned, this was going to get complicated.

"Maybe, we're getting a bit ahead of ourselves here. We don't even know if Calli likes us. How about we just get to know her, be her friends and just see where things go," River suggested.

"Are you just trying to get us friend-zoned so that you win?" Tanner frowned. "And what was in the bag? That was some sneaky tactics there."

"It was just some tea," River smiled. "Her favourite kind that she couldn't find." He was definitely feeling smug about himself.

It was nice sitting around like this. We hadn't done it in so long. Tensions in the pack were always pretty high, but more than ever right now. We had two members who were married to humans. Wallace and his wife, Kelly, had a seven-year-old son, Coby. Blake and Jean were expecting their first baby in April and we already knew they were having a boy. We were reasonably confident that either we had a witch in the vicinity, or one had been passing through. Since we had caught the scent, we had been on high alert. Kelly was safe because she was human and didn't have anything that the witches would be interested in. Even though she was human, Jean had a shifter baby growing inside her and was potentially in danger. Little Coby and the rest of us could also be a target. We hadn't caught the same scent since or any other that caused us concern, but it would take a while for us to be able to settle when witches had breached our territory.

Tanner and River were goofing about, and it was nice to see them relax a bit. I'd have to check in with Blake. He'd been running a patrol today checking for any unusual scents around our lands. I might even take a run myself tonight. My wolf was too agitated to stay cooped up. Being an Alpha, we didn't take any threats against our pack lightly. Running into the beautiful Calli was not helping either. He wanted to be around her and he was sulking that we had to leave.

Tanner switched on the TV, and he and River settled back to watch some football highlights. Could we really share a mate? It wasn't unheard of in shifter society. She was human, though, would she even be willing to consider that? River was right; we were jumping ahead of ourselves. Getting to know her would be fun and I had made sure that she would be coming by the garage on Monday.

Jacob seemed like an adorable kid. Obviously, he and Calli were a package deal, and I was more than okay with that. Maybe pack life would help him. I could smell the grief on him. And fear, which I found surprising. It was what had drawn me to the bedroom doorway when I overheard him asking her about keeping the secret.

"What are you thinking so hard on?" Tanner asked me, nudging my leg with his foot.

"Something Jacob said tonight. When we were getting ready to eat, I followed Calli over to his room. I could smell the fear coming off him, and I was worried. I overheard him say something to her and ... I don't know," I frowned. Was he afraid of us?

"What did he say?" River asked, sitting up concerned.

"Something about them keeping a secret. I think it might have been us that he was afraid of." I looked at River, and I could see the same concern on his face that I was feeling.

"It would be understandable for him to be concerned about men coming into Calli's life. He's just lost both his parents, and she's all that he has left. The fear of losing her is going to be something that he will struggle with, especially at such a young age." He frowned as he thought about it more. "Keeping secrets isn't something that is going to be good for him at this age, considering their circumstances." I could tell that River was struggling with wanting to protect Jacob, which was essentially his job, and also not wanting to upset Calli again after their rocky start. He huffed out a sigh and slumped back in his chair. "I should speak to her about this," he muttered.

"Noooooo, that's a terrible idea," Tanner said. "Look, she'd obviously do anything for him. We don't know them, and we don't know their past. Challenging her about this is only going to push her away. Selfishly, I don't want that to happen. But putting my feelings aside, if they are running from something or are in some kind of trouble, I don't know about you two, but I want to be around to help protect them from it. You were right the first time. We should just get to know them. Once she knows that she can trust us, she will come to us if she needs help. If she doesn't, then we can think about speaking with her about it then. In the meantime, we keep an eye on them."

Tanner was my beta for a reason. He might be laid back and a bit of a goof at times, but when the situation called for it, he was my level head, and he also gave well-reasoned advice.

I nodded and stood up. "I'm going to check in with Blake and run the perimeter. I'll see you both in the morning."

8

CALLI

An obscene amount of packages arrived on Saturday morning. I'm pretty sure that the delivery guy was judging me as he was offloading them from his van. Hell, I was judging me when he brought in the fourth load. Now I was sat on the sofa, drinking some Yorkshire tea and just staring at the mountain of packages. Jacob was still asleep, the time difference was affecting him, and I figured that as he had school starting on Monday, I'd let him get the extra sleep as it was the weekend.

I was just about to start opening the first box when the doorbell rang. Heaving myself off the sofa, I opened the door. "Please, don't tell me you have something to deliver," I sighed.

Instead, I found a smiling Tanner on the doorstep. "Well, I do have a box of pastries, but I can just eat them all by myself if it's going to be a problem."

"Sorry, I thought you were the UPS guy again." I opened the door wider and invited him in. "Don't take this the wrong way, but why are you bringing me pastries?" I asked as I followed him into the house.

"Ah, don't be mad, but they're not for you. I promised my man, Jacob, that I'd drop some by. He was reluctant to believe me that the bakery here did the best ones in the world."

I laughed, that was definitely Jacob. He hated the expression, the best in the world. He was a tough kid to impress.

"Well, I'm afraid Jacob is still asleep."

We walked into the living area, and Tanner suddenly came to a stop in front of me. "Good lord woman, did you buy Amazon?"

Glancing at the mountain of boxes, I cringed. "Yeah, it does feel like it," I said, looking around. "We didn't really bring anything with us, so there was a lot to replace. I wanted to get Jacob settled into the house, and he needed school stuff and toys and clothes." I sighed and dropped onto the sofa. Leaving everything behind had been hard, but it was even harder on Jacob. He didn't understand why he had to leave all his things behind.

"I'll tell you what, I'll open and you can start organising what's inside," he suggested, surveying the stack.

"You don't have to give up your Saturday morning to help me out of my shopping hole," I said, desperately hoping that he wouldn't leave me to face it alone.

"It's fine," he said, dropping down onto the floor and pulling the first box into his lap. "This is the perfect excuse to get out of work. We don't have anything booked into the garage so I would have only ended up cleaning and Grey won't make me come back when I tell him that you need my help. You are the perfect escape plan," he grinned mischievously, and pulled a pocket knife out of his jeans and started to slice open the first of the boxes.

We made a pretty good team. The Amazon parcels were mainly stuff for Jacob, so I separated a pile for school supplies and stuff for his room. We quickly moved onto the stack of packages from other companies which consisted mainly of clothes for the both of us. "Do I have to check in my man card if I admit that these are adorable?" Tanner asked, holding up the pair of boots that I'd bought for Jacob.

"I won't tell anyone you said it if that makes you feel better," I laughed.

Tanner sucked in a breath and then made some kind of choking noise as he opened up the next parcel. He grinned over at me and then held up his next find. "These, on the other hand, are far better." Of course, he had found all of the lingerie I'd ordered, and was currently holding up a red lace thong.

"I'll just take that one," I said, leaning over and snatching the parcel away from him.

"Awww, but I wanted to see what else is in there." Tanner didn't let go as I reached for it and as I had dived forward so quickly, I suddenly found myself face down, ass up and draped across his lap. "Hmmm, now *this* I can get on board with too," he growled.

I floundered around like an octopus on dry land as I wriggled off his lap and reclaimed the parcel much to Tanner's amusement. I could feel the heat radiating off my cheeks from the furious blush that had taken up residence on my face. Suddenly, I found myself at a loss for words. What was it with these men? They were wolves! I was supposed to be running away from them, not falling all over them. Why would my parents even send us here if there was a pack in the area? From what I had found out from Sean, my parents had bought this house four years ago. So, maybe the pack was new?

"So, erm, how long have you lived in Arbington?" I spluttered.

Tanner grinned and settled back into opening up the remaining packages—no doubt hoping to find something else scandalous. "We all grew up not far from here, but we bought the house about six years ago, it needed some work doing to it, but with all of us pitching in it wasn't too bad," he shrugged.

So, they had already been here when Mum and Dad bought the cabin. Meaning they would've known there was a pack in the area. They weren't so careless to not have done their research. "You all seem close. Do you live together?"

"Yes, there's the three of us and a couple of our other friends." I caught him peering up at me while he kept opening the package he was on. "Five of us live in the house we first bought and then two of our other friends have built cabins on the land that they live in with their families."

I was surprised that he was talking about the pack with me. As far as Tanner would know I scented as human. "So, you all live together, like in a commune thing?" I said, hedging my bets. "You're not trying to induct me into some kind of cult are you?" I cracked a joke to try and make light of the conversation so I could keep pumping him for information.

"You've foiled my evil plan," he said dramatically. "Nah, we've all been friends for ages. It just seemed sensible when we saw the big house and the work needed, that we all went in on it together. Once it was done, I think we'd gotten so used to it that we just decided to keep living there together."

That must be the story that they tell everyone. It was pretty good and he was obviously used to saying it. I didn't know what other information to fish for without giving it away that I knew he was a wolf.

Before I could think of anything else to ask, a sleepy

Jacob stumbled out of his bedroom rubbing at his eyes. "Can I have some juice, please?" he mumbled.

"I got you, buddy," Tanner said, jumping up and heading into the kitchen. Jacob took the cup and wandered back to his room, closing the door behind him. I was pretty sure that even though he looked straight at Tanner and said thank you, that he had no idea he was actually here.

"He takes a while to get going in the morning," I explained as Tanner dropped back down on the ground with me. "I don't know how to put this without offending you," I said, biting my lip nervously.

"Go on. I always like it when a conversation starts out that way," he laughed.

"You don't have to keep coming round to check up on me. I'm more than capable of looking after Jacob. We don't need charity," I said, firmly.

Tanner cocked his head to the side as he thought before he responded. "I'm not here to check up on you. Well, maybe I am, but not for the reason that you think. Isn't it obvious that I like you, Calli?" he smiled softly at me.

Tanner wasn't like I'd envisioned a male wolf would be. He seemed considerate of my feelings and almost gentle. I had always assumed that they would be brash and overbearing. Not that my father was, but I'd always thought he was the exception to the rule. Perhaps I was naïve, because I liked him too. If I was honest with myself, I liked all three of them. But I couldn't allow myself to get that close to them. I didn't know if it was even wise to strike up a friendship with them. At least not until I could figure out what my parents had intended.

I felt inside to try and get a read from my wolf about the situation. She had always been who I turned to in the past when I was worried about something. Unfortunately, on this occasion, she was zero use. She was still just lazing in the back of mind, quite content to be around Tanner. Traitor!

"I can't," I said quietly. I felt the sadness swarm over me as I admitted it as much to myself as I was to him. I couldn't, even though I wanted to.

"Calli, it's okay, I know you're going through a tough time, and I'm not going to try and push anything," he said, reaching forward to try and lay his hand over mine.

I quickly whipped it back and stood up. "I'm sorry, Tanner. I … I just can't. I think you should leave," I said, taking a few steps away from him. I needed the distance. My wolf was already mourning the loss of him, and he was still in the room with us. I needed him to leave before he could sense what asking him to go was doing to me.

"Calli, I'm sorry," Tanner said, standing slowly and reaching out for me. His eyes were so sad, but I couldn't let myself get drawn in by them. I needed to be strong. I had to protect Jacob. I'd let it go too far already.

"No," I said, striding over to the front door and opening it for him. When I turned around, he was still standing in the same spot with his hands hanging down beside him. I had that distinct kicked puppy feeling, and it was beyond awful. "Please, Tanner, just leave."

Tanner walked slowly over to the door, pausing beside me, but I didn't look up. He didn't try to reach out and touch me this time, and I wasn't sure how I felt about that.

"I know I've fucked this up because I brought it up too soon. You haven't done anything wrong, Calli. And you haven't frightened me off. If you change your mind, or if you will accept just my friendship, you know where I am. And I will be waiting everyday for you to come and see me." At that, he walked out the door, not looking back.

Closing the front door, I sagged against it. Tanner

wouldn't have even made it to his truck by the time the first sob forced its way out of me. Why did this feel so bad? Why did I feel like I had lost everything all over again? I dropped to my knees and leant my forehead against the door and just let my tears come. After a few minutes, I rose to my feet and walked into my bedroom. I couldn't let Jacob find me like this. I set the alarm on my phone for half an hour and then I curled up under the covers, letting my misery take over. I could allow myself half an hour to fall apart. Then I'd pull myself together and walk out this room, wearing a smile as my mask, trying to convince myself more than anyone else that I could do this—I had to do this for Jacob.

9
GREY

Tanner's truck screeched up to the garage two hours late. Climbing out, he slammed the door shut behind him. Stalking across the garage to the storeroom, he slammed that door behind him too. Then he lost control. I heard his wolf rip from him. We listened to the snarls and the crashes as he ripped the room apart. Blake was the only other person working in the garage today. We always seemed to be slower at the weekend, and it didn't make sense to have more mechanics in. He looked over at me in question and I just shrugged in response, so he went back to work. I'd never seen Tanner like this. I could feel his anger and distress through the pack bond. There would be no containing him until his wolf wore himself out. Striding into the office, I made myself a cup of coffee, propped my feet up on the desk and waited for him to come to me when he was ready.

It was over an hour later before he emerged from the storeroom and came into the office. Tanner made a cup of coffee in silence before he slumped into the only other chair in the room. I let him stew for a moment. I could feel the tenuous grip he had on his wolf at the moment.

"I fucked up," he said between gritted teeth as he looked down into his coffee like it held all the answers to his problems.

"You went to see Calli this morning?"

"I fucked up really bad," he said hunching forwards on himself. I sat up immediately. I had known Tanner since we were kids, and I knew he would never hurt her, but I'd never seen him like this before. "We were having a good time getting to know each other. I know we said that we weren't going to push, that we were going to get to know her but … I don't know, at the time it just felt right. I told her that I liked her." He looked up at me, and I was shocked to see that tears swam in his eyes.

"What happened?" I asked quietly.

"She just said that she couldn't, and asked me to leave," he said, returning his stare to his coffee. Okay, that didn't seem too bad. "You should have felt the emotion that rolled off her. She was so … sad. And when I left …"

I didn't interrupt to ask him what. I didn't know if I wanted to know. "I could hear her … through the door ... crying. I heard her break apart. And I felt it, all her grief and her sadness and her pain." He paused before he added, "I did that to her."

Leaning forward, I braced my elbows on the desk as my heart broke for them both. I couldn't imagine what it must have felt like to feel Calli go through that and not be able to do anything to comfort her. "No, Tan, you didn't do that. Calli has lost two people that she loved, and she's had no choice but to hold it together to look after Jacob. You didn't cause that pain for her. It's part of her now, whether we like it or not. All we can do is just try and help her through it."

Tanner furiously wiped at his eyes before he lifted his gaze to look at me. "I don't think I can fix this."

"It's going to be okay, Tan. On Monday, she's going to drop Jacob off at school, and she'll talk with River for a bit. And she still needs to come back to change that filter on her truck. We'll make sure that she's okay. Just give her time. It's going to be okay, I promise. That is as long as you put the storeroom back together, because I sure as fuck am not going to do it."

Tanner laughed, and I felt some of the despair lift from his shoulders. "Why do I like her this much, so fast? We don't even know her," he said, shaking his head.

"I don't know. But whatever she hit you with, she got me too. And I'm pretty sure River as well."

Tanner just nodded before heading back into the storeroom. It took a hell of a lot longer for him to put it back together than it had to tear it apart. I really hoped that I wasn't going to break my promise to him. How this girl we didn't even know had become so important to us, I had no idea. I didn't know how to deal with upset women. Give me a pissed off shifter male, and I was in my prime. That was why I was the Alpha of my own pack. But we didn't have any women in our pack. Jean and Kelly may have married two of the guys, but they didn't want to go through the change. They weren't really part of the pack because they couldn't make that bond while they were human. I wasn't their Alpha; I was just their friend. Maybe I needed to get some advice from one of them.

10

CALLI

Monday rolled around so fast and Jacob was actually excited about going to school. I suspected it was more because he was bored of my company and wanted to make some friends his own age. I couldn't blame him. I'd been crap company since Tanner left on Saturday morning. Jacob practically threw himself in the car as we were leaving, and I couldn't help but laugh at him. They didn't have a uniform at the school, and he had spent a lot of time thoughtfully deciding what he was going to wear. He looked so cute with his backpack and lunch bag. Packing him a lunch this morning had really made me feel old. My life had taken such a massive detour, but I wouldn't change it. I'd do anything for him. In fact, I think I was going to miss him today.

I'd decided that I would pick myself up out of this slump I was in. I was going to drop Jacob off at school, quickly drop by the garage and get the filter sorted for the truck, and then I would drive into Portland, have some lunch and do some shopping.

I'd put a gentle wave through my hair and dressed in some of the new clothes I'd bought. I had on a burgundy skater dress with a leather biker jacket, some thick tights and over the knee flat boots. The dress was a bit shorter than I would typically wear, but the thick tights almost felt like wearing trousers, so I wasn't worried about feeling the cold—maybe just a strong wind and the potential of losing my dignity. Whatever happened, I actually felt a bit more like myself. My talisman hung down over the top of the dress, and I couldn't help playing with it. It was becoming a bit of a nervous habit of mine. It clashed a little bit, but I couldn't exactly take it off. The copper wiring that looped around the stone didn't look too bad, but the purple of the amethyst stone didn't quite go.

When I walked into the school office with Jacob, Holly looked up and whistled when she saw me. I did a little twirl for her, and she laughed. "Well, don't you look lovely. Hot date?" she asked.

"Nah, just decided to go and do a bit of shopping and treat myself," I said with a smile.

"Well River's caught up with some parents who just turned up, and I have no idea how long he's going to be. I can take Jacob and introduce him to his teacher if he wants," Holly said, smiling down at Jacob.

I could tell just by looking at him that he was smitten with her. It was pretty hard not to be. She did seem pretty awesome. "Yes, please," he said with a big grin.

"Okay, little guy," I said, kneeling in front of him. "You got this. I got this. We're a team remember."

Jacob threw his arms around me and gave me a big hug. "I think we're going to like it here," he whispered to me, and I gave him a big squeeze.

"I'll be right outside waiting for you at the end of the

day," I said, standing up. I felt like I could well up, and I coughed to dislodge the lump forming in my throat.

Holly patted me on the shoulder as she walked around her desk and came past me. "Let's go then, Jacob." She opened the door for him, and he just walked out without even looking back. It was good to see him comfortable and happy here. I just hoped that he was right and we were going to be okay. If that was going to happen, I needed to put space between the guys and me. I wouldn't avoid them, but I couldn't let myself form any kind of relationships with them. As much as I seemed to want them, I would not put Jacob at risk like that.

It was time to go and face the music at the garage. I could do this. As I walked out of the office, I saw River sitting at his desk. I didn't catch his eye as I went past. It looked like the two parents in there were reaming into him. It was probably for the best that he had been too busy to see me this morning.

The drive to the garage was far too short, and I was nervous when I got there. Grey had said to come by today, and I just hoped that it wasn't too early. If it was, I could always stop by after I had picked Jacob up from school. I suppose I just wanted to get this over and done with. I pulled up outside the door as I did the last time and took a deep breath to prepare myself. This was going to suck. By the time I was climbing out of the driver's door, Grey had already seen me and was walking out to greet me with a big smile on his face. Why did they have to be so goddamn beautiful? This would be so much easier if they weren't. I didn't miss how his eyes widened when he saw my outfit and deep down it did make me feel a little bit happier.

"Hi, I was wondering if you had the filter for the truck or if I need to come back later. I was going to head into Portland for a while, so I was kinda hoping to get it out the way and sort the bill before I went," I rushed out as I walked up to him. Part of me wanted to throw my arms around him—the crazy-ass, weird part. He was, after all, basically still a stranger. And, you know, part of an entire species that would probably kill me.

"It just came in. We can install it now. It only takes ten minutes. Why don't you come through to the office with me, and Tanner can sort it for you," he said, turning around and walking back to the garage. It felt like there was something off about him, but I wasn't sure what. "Tanner," he shouted into the garage. "Can you fit the filter on Calli's truck?"

I saw Tanner's head pop up from next to a car. When he caught sight of me, his mouth fell open, and I felt my cheeks blush. I raised my hand to say hi to him, and he gave me a big smile. Well, at least he wasn't upset about Saturday. I should definitely wear a dress more often if it were going to get this reaction.

Grey was standing by the office door, waiting for me, and I followed him through and took a seat next to the desk. It was actually pretty orderly, and I couldn't help but look around. A small pile of papers sat on the desk, a chair on either side and a filing cabinet in the corner. There were some pictures of various cars on the wall which I suppose was to be expected. There was also one of Grey and River grinning into the camera with their arms slung around each other's shoulders. It was nice. After running my eyes round the room, they fell on Grey, who was just sitting on the other side of the desk waiting for me to finish. "Do you like what you see?" he said with almost a growl, and I felt like my insides suddenly turned to liquid. My wolf preened at the noise, and it felt like he was asking about himself more so than anything else.

I chose the safest route. "It's not what I expected. There's not one naked woman stuck on the wall," I observed.

Grey's smile widened to a grin, and he rolled his eyes. Perhaps everyone said that. I grabbed my bag and started to rummage through it to find my purse. I needed to get this back into the realms of professional. "So, how much do I owe you?" I asked him as I located my purse and pulled it out. Why did it always seem like a small achievement whenever you could find something in your bag?

Grey picked up a piece of paper from the small pile on his desk and glanced at it. "Twelve dollars."

"That doesn't seem right," I said, dropping my purse into my lap.

"Too much?" he smiled.

"You know what I mean?"

"It is, it says right here," he said, showing me the paper.

"That's just a receipt for the filter. You haven't included any of the labour or any of the work you did on Friday," I huffed.

I pulled a hundred dollar bill out of my purse and shoved it at him. "Don't you have anything smaller? You can't expect me to break a hundred for a twelve dollar invoice," he grinned.

"Mr Thornton, I appreciate the sentiment, but I don't need your charity. I know my circumstances cause everyone to pity me, but I can assure you that my parents ensured that Jacob and I would be well provided for. I'm actually very well off." I didn't back down, and I kept the money held out to him.

Grey took the money with a sigh. "Calli, it's not charity, and no one is pitying you. It's just a friendly gesture. Perhaps, I'm just trying to ensure that you continue to give us your business."

I cocked my head as I looked at him. Could I have read this wrong? I stood from my chair. I couldn't waiver on this. This was the only way that it could be. "I'll wait outside for

Tanner to finish. If that isn't enough to cover the work, please let me know," I said as I reached for the door and let myself out of the office.

Tanner had pulled the truck into the bay that he was working in and made quick work of getting the new filter fitted. I didn't want to talk to him either. My wolf was nearly howling with grief inside me. She wanted us to laugh and joke and be the same as we were the other night at dinner with them. She liked having them around. I did, as well, even I could admit that to myself. But this wasn't about me. It was about Jacob. I was all that he had left, and it was my job to protect him. They may be friendly and nice to me now, but what would they do if they ever found out our secret?

I waited outside the garage and breathed in the fresh air. I loved being outdoors. I always found it centred me. It always calmed the wolf inside of me as well. Perhaps it was part of our nature to want to run free. I had never really had the chance to do that. I'd been on runs with my Dad but never for very long, and he would never stray far from my mother. I hadn't allowed myself to run in my wolf form since I'd lost them. I felt the desperate need from both myself and my wolf to just shift and run free, leaving all my troubles behind me. Clenching my fists hard, I felt my nails bite hard into my soft palms. The pain was enough to draw me back into myself and ride out the impulse to shift. A small part of me was worried that if I shifted, I would never come back, that I'd completely surrender to my wolf nature and leave my human life behind.

My truck rolled up beside me, and Tanner jumped out of the driver's seat. I caught him subtly scenting the air. He frowned when he looked at me. "You alright, Calli?" he asked.

"Yes, I'm fine, thanks," I said, giving him a bright smile that I forced on my face.

He reached out to pass me the keys, and when I went to take them, I saw the blood shining in the palm of my hand. I hadn't realised that my nails had cut so deep. That must have been what he was scenting. I turned my hand over to hide the blood from Tanner's view. "About Saturday," he started.

"It's okay," I said quietly. "I'll maybe see you around," I quickly added before my resolve broke and I told him that I hadn't meant it. The words were on the tip of my tongue, but I couldn't let myself say them. This was the best way. This was the safest way.

I jumped into the truck and started the engine. I didn't miss that Tanner hadn't moved from where he was stood, and he was watching me with a look of concern on his face. Pulling out of the garage, I headed out of town. I couldn't stop myself, and I glanced into the rearview mirror. He was still standing there, just watching me drive away.

11
TANNER

I walked into the office and slumped down into the vacant chair. Calli's scent faintly lingered in the air, and I sighed as I breathed it in. Grey just sat behind the desk with a grumpy look on his face.

"What happened?" I asked him.

"She was not happy that I was only going to charge her for the parts, and then she left," he grumbled.

"When I gave her keys back, her hand was bleeding," I said. I had caught the bloody nail marks in the palm of her hand. I knew she had tried to hide them from me. I wasn't going to push anything and ask her about them, not after Saturday. But I was starting to worry about her.

"Bleeding how?" Grey asked. "I didn't scent any blood on her when she was in here."

"Like she clenched her fists so hard she sliced open her palms with her own nails," I explained.

Grey sat back in his chair, thinking. I could see the concern on his face, no doubt mirroring my own. "Do you think they're in trouble?" he asked. "Maybe the dead parents story isn't true. Or even worse, maybe it is. Maybe they're running from something. It would explain the mystery secret."

"Or we could just be overreacting about a girl that we like, who doesn't feel the same way about us," I added. But I knew that wasn't right. When we had first met Calli, she had been so open and happy, and we had gelled when we crashed her dinner the same night. Something was happening that was causing her to shut down on us, but I had no idea what it would be. Maybe Grey was right.

"She called me Mr Thornton," he grumbled, crossing his arms over his chest.

That, at least, made me laugh. I wasn't the only one feeling the sting of Calli's rejection now.

"What do you think we should do?" I asked him. Grey was my Alpha, and if he told me that we were going to let her be, I would have to follow his wishes. No matter how much I didn't want to.

"Let's look into their story. It shouldn't be too hard to find a report of two loving parents dying and leaving behind two kids. Surely it would have been in the local papers. We know a rough time frame, and we know a rough area. Get Nash on it," he said, turning back to the work on his desk.

"Okay. How much of a priority is this? Nash is busy looking into the possibility of a vamp nest near here still. And we have the witch issue we need to decide on, as well."

"The witch scent hasn't returned in nearly two months. I think we should scale back on it. It seems more likely they were just moving through the area. It shouldn't take Nash long to look into this. I want a report as soon as possible. Once he's done, he needs to go back to the vamp situation. I want to know if we are going to have an issue. This is a small town. We can't afford any humans being taken and them drawing attention. Once we have the location of the nest, we need to tell them to move on," Grey said, leaning back in his chair.

"I'll let him know." I got out of the chair, pulling the phone out of my pocket and dialled Nash. After filling him in, I went back to the Ford that I had been working on, I was hoping to get it finished before the end of school. Then I just needed an excuse to drop in on River. I was hoping to get another chance to speak with Calli. I'm not sure when I turned into some love-struck highschooler making any excuse to see a girl, but I was past the point of caring. My wolf felt uneasy with the thought that she could be in trouble and was riding me pretty hard to protect her. I even really liked Jacob. I'd had fun playing with him the other night. I could tell that he was nervous about us when we had dinner. I had thought it was just because of what he was going through with the loss of his parents, but maybe it was something else. By the end of the night, he seemed to have relaxed around us though—the same as Calli had. I couldn't let her push us away. I didn't know what it would do to me, but I wasn't willing to risk losing her.

12

CALLI

I'd nearly driven back to the house after visiting the garage, but I made myself go, and I was glad I had. It was nice to relax and have some time to myself. I needed some kind of plan for what I was going to do. Yes, for now my life needed to be about looking after Jacob, but was I going to put my whole life on hold for the next thirteen years until he turned eighteen? I wasn't lying when I told Grey my parents had provided for us. We had more money than we could ever need. I didn't need to work, but that wasn't really the person I was. There was a University in Portland and the thought struck me that maybe I could do my degree here. Probably not straight away, but maybe in a couple of years.

I called the University when I parked the truck and spoke with a helpful woman in the admission department. When I explained my situation to her, she was optimistic about finding a way to fit my studies around Jacob's schedule. She warned me that it might take longer to get my degree, but to be honest, I didn't care about that.

Afterwards, I went around a couple of shops until I finally stumbled across a music shop. It had been years since I had played the guitar. I hadn't taken mine with me when I went travelling for those two years, and I had left it at the house when we ran. I hadn't felt the urge to pick it up again. But as I looked through the shop window at the guitars on display, I realised that maybe going back to old routines might be a good way to cope with everything that had happened. Music always helped me relax, and perhaps this would be a way to work through my emotions. I was still in two minds when I caught sight of the sales assistant smiling at me through the window. When she saw that she had caught my eye, she waved me in, and I couldn't resist.

"Hi," I said, walking through the shop door. I immediately spied the wall of acoustic guitars and started to head in that direction.

"Are you looking for anything in particular?" she asked me as she followed me over to the guitar wall.

"I'm not sure," I said, looking at the beautiful instruments in awe. "I left mine behind in England when we moved, and if I'm honest, I haven't played in a few years."

"Ah, it never leaves you, though," she sighed, running her hand over one of the guitars with a soft sigh.

My eye immediately caught a Gibson Hummingbird Studio guitar, and I couldn't help but walk over to it and run my fingers across the finish. It was so much nicer than the old guitar I used to have. It was a stunning instrument and obscenely expensive.

"You've got a good eye," she said as she picked it up off the rack and held it out to me. "Here, try it out."

My eyes blew wide in shock. "Are you sure?" I asked, my fingers already closing over the neck and taking it from her before she could reply. I wasn't going to turn down this opportunity.

She just laughed and pointed me over to a stool set up in

an area with amps and a music stand. I wasn't going to need any of those things, though. I sat down and quickly tuned the strings by ear. It was mostly in tune anyway and just needed a few tweaks. The sales assistant had moved over to the counter to give me some space. As soon as my fingers strummed over the strings, I closed my eyes and just gave myself to the music. It had been so long, but she was right, it never left me. I started playing Stay Alive by Jose Gonzales, quietly singing the words but leaving the guitar to do the talking. When I played the last cord and opened my eyes, I knew I would buy it. I didn't realise how much I had missed this.

"That was beautiful," the sales assistant said from in front of me. I had been so absorbed in the music I didn't even realise she had come over. Thankfully the rest of the shop was still empty. I never really played in front of anyone. It was just something I did to pass the time.

My cheeks flushed in embarrassment. "Thanks. I'll take it," I told her, passing the guitar back. Her eyes flashed in happiness, and I realised this was probably a pretty big sale for her. "Can you fit me out with a case, strap and some picks as well please?"

"Of course," she gushed, rushing back over to the counter.

We spent the next twenty minutes picking out the case and strap and grabbing a few other bits. I ended up getting a tuner as well. Whilst I could tune it by ear, I was never quite spot on with it. When she rang up the total, I passed her my card and just tried to not listen to how much it all cost. I hated spending this much money on one thing, but I knew my parents would've been glad I did.

After dropping the guitar off at the truck, I stopped by a small coffee shop for lunch and then dropped by the university's admissions office and picked up a prospectus and other information that the lady on the phone had put together for me. She made me promise to call as soon as I had looked it through, and it was a promise I intended to keep.

I got to the school a couple of minutes before the kids were due to leave feeling quite happy with myself. I had needed the break from reality for a bit, and I felt better now that I had the beginnings of a plan for the future forming. I didn't want to hang out with the school moms who seemed to be collected outside the school gossiping, so I hopped out of the truck and leaned against the door while I waited for the kids to start emerging. Flicking through the University prospectus, I began to look at the courses offered to pass the time. I was so engrossed in the catalogue that I didn't hear him approach.

"I'm sorry I missed you this morning," his voice rumbled from next to me.

I looked up and saw that River had come out to join me. "It's not a problem, Jacob was so excited this morning that I think he just wanted to get to class anyway."

"Thinking of getting your degree?" he asked, pointing at the catalogue in my hand.

"Well, it was the plan originally. After I finished school, I had two years out and went backpacking. I'd come back home to start getting ready to go to University when the accident happened. And, well, the rest you know," I said with a sad smile.

"Where did you go backpacking? I've always wanted to travel, but I've never really had the chance," he said, leaning against the truck beside me. I could see that I was getting the evil eye from a couple of moms. River was probably the school hottie they all came to school to see.

"I kind of bounced around Europe for a while, then through Turkey, Iran onto India, up through China to Mongolia, then I double backed down and went through Thailand and Vietnam. Eventually, I ran out of time and had to fly back home," I smiled. His mouth had dropped open as I went through the list. I had packed a lot in, but there were a lot of people and places that I needed to stop in on. It had been an incredible two years for me, and I would have loved to have done it again.

"That's a long way. I'd love to hear all about it sometime. You must have seen so much. Did you go with your friends or a, erm, boyfriend?" he finished awkwardly.

"Nope, I went on my own. Made a few friends along the way."

"That's a bit dangerous," he frowned.

"I can handle myself," I nearly laughed. Men always assumed that women were so weak and vulnerable. My father had taught me how to fight. It was all part of my parent's paranoia.

"Anyway, what are you thinking about doing for your degree?" he said, changing the subject.

"I'm not sure. I'm not even sure if I'm going to do it. I need to concentrate on Jacob at the minute and getting him settled in. Maybe next year, though. I just wanted to see what they had on offer." It sounded almost like I was trying to talk myself out of it.

"I think you should go for it. You can't live your whole life just for him. It's admirable, but you'll probably eventually go crazy."

"Ah, well, that's because you're assuming I'm not already crazy," I laughed.

He grinned and laughed with me, then the school bell rang. It was like it smacked me over the head to remind me that I wasn't supposed to be doing this. These wolves were just too easy to talk to, and it was easy to forget to keep my distance from them. It was almost like I could hear my wolf sniggering at me in the back of my mind.

I straightened up and watched the school doors as the kids started to flood out. Jacob came out of the doors and stood at the top of the steps hesitantly. I waved at him and when he saw me a huge grin blasted across his face and he ran at top speed to me. When he reached me, he threw his arms around me and held me tight.

"Hey, you okay little guy?" I asked, detaching myself and kneeling to be with him.

"Yeah, I had a great day!" he said, jumping up and down in excitement.

"That's amazing. I knew you'd have fun," I laughed. His happiness was just infectious.

"I got to use my crayons, and I drew you a picture," he said, brandishing a piece of paper at me. "It's you and me and our house."

"Well, that is cool. I think we should stick it on the fridge when we get home." It was actually pretty good.

"I'm glad you had a good day, squirt." River said, ruffling his hair. "I was just talking to your sister about all the travelling she's done."

"Yeah, she has a million photos of it," he sighed dramatically, and we all laughed.

I heard the scuffle behind the truck before I registered what was going on, then a large man came flying past with another man raging after him. Fists were flying, and from the smell of it, one of them was far too drunk for this time in the day. I pushed Jacob behind me, but I wasn't fast enough as one of them reared back and caught me in the shoulder before he punched the other man in the face. Jacob tucked himself against my body, shaking and crying, and I gritted my teeth against the pain. Somehow Tanner appeared out of nowhere and threw himself between the brawling men and Jacob and I. He wrapped himself around me, and River dragged one of the men back before Tanner turned and pulled the other back. Both men were screaming obscenities at each other. One of them, the drunk one by the smell of it, looked vaguely like the man who had been shouting at River this morning.

When it was apparent that the guys had them restrained, I quickly turned to Jacob and checked him over.

"You okay, little guy?" I asked him, running my hands over him.

Silent tears were running down his face, and he just nodded at me before burrowing into my chest. I picked him up and walked him around to the passenger side before putting him in the truck. Wrapping him up in my arms, he clung to me while he cried. I ran my fingers through his hair whispering reassurances to him until he calmed down and then I pulled back a little bit.

"You sure you didn't get hurt?" I asked him again, and he nodded.

The police showed up and were shoving the men into the back of a police car. Once the police had the situation under control, River rushed around to where Jacob and I stood. I could see him vibrating with anger but trying to keep it reigned in for the sake of everyone around us. The fight had drawn quite the crowd of gossiping onlookers.

"Jacob, are you okay?" he said, ducking his head down to speak with Jacob. They spoke quietly with each other for a minute, and I leant against the hood of the truck and tried to subtly feel out my throbbing shoulder. Tanner came up beside me while River was talking to Jacob.

"Let me see?" he said, pulling my jacket to one side and running his hands across the already forming bruising.

I hissed out a breath when he felt along the bones. "I think you're just going to get some bad bruising, but you should get it checked out," he said, concerned.

I couldn't risk going to a doctor, I could tell that I'd done some damage, but it would be fine by tomorrow with my shifter healing.

"I'll be okay. I'll go tomorrow if it feels like it's not going to heal up," I said, knowing that I had no intention of doing that.

He didn't seem convinced, but I could see River starting to look over at us in question and then with just a look they both traded places. It was nice to see how concerned they were about Jacob, and they were so good with him. Tanner immediately leant into the truck and held Jacob who looked like he was feeling a bit better, talking quietly with him. River did the same check over of my shoulder that Tanner had done.

"I know, I promise to go to the doctor tomorrow if it seems like it needs it," I told him, resisting the urge to roll my eyes. It was nice to have someone care, but they were getting a little overbearing with it.

River at least had the decency to smile when he realised what he was doing, but I noticed that he didn't let me go. He had his hand on my waist, and stayed close enough that I only needed to lean into him for it to be an embrace. I wanted to, so badly, and my wolf pushed me to make the move, but I had to think about Jacob. I had to think about us as a family and what was best for him. And as much as it pained me to say it, these three wolves couldn't fit into that.

"Ma'am," one of the police said coming over to us. "Would you like to file a complaint?" He looked at me in concern, and I'm sure the fact that River didn't seem to want to let me go made it seem a lot worse.

"No, it's fine, I was just stood in the wrong place," I told him.

"It isn't fine. You could have been really hurt," River said as anger flashed across his eyes. I could scent his wolf close to the surface, and I knew that he must be fighting the urge to shift right now.

I placed a hand on his chest to try and calm him down, to reassure his wolf that I was still here. "It's okay," I murmured to him. "I'm here. I'm not badly hurt."

River was starting to shake, and I knew we were reaching dangerous territory. I glanced over at Tanner, but he was busy talking to Jacob, who actually seemed a bit calmer and was talking back to him. I needed to learn how he was able to draw him out of his shell so easily. River was barely hanging on though, and was dangerously close to shifting in the parking lot at the school. The police officer left us with his card and walked away, and River watched him go. His wolf flashed through his eyes, tracking his movement. This was bad; this was really bad. Shifters who exposed what they were to humans were immediately sentenced to death. There was no trial and no opportunity to explain yourself. Most of them were killed before they were even taken into custody by the Council.

I reached up and took hold of his face in both hands, physically turning him away from the police car where the two brawlers were now handcuffed, so that he was looking at me. "Stay here with me," I told him, locking eyes with him. "Ground yourself here with me."

His wolf receded, and he blinked, looking down at me in confusion. Shit, shit, shit, shit.

I took a step away from him, uncertain of how to explain what had happened. He didn't say anything to me, and I was hoping that his confusion would prevent him from saying anything further. Tanner looked at us suspiciously, so I walked around to the driver's side of the truck and jumped in.

"Come on, kiddo, it's time to go home," I told Jacob, getting his seatbelt on him and making sure that he was okay. "Thank you for your help," I told Tanner who was still standing in the open passenger door looking at me with an expression I couldn't quite decipher. Quietly, he closed the passenger door and stepped back as I backed out of the spot and drove away with my heart pounding in my ears. What had I done?

13

TANNER

I stood on the pavement and watched Calli drive away.

"What just happened?" I asked, looking at River in confusion.

The crowd of gawking onlookers had filtered off, and we stood mostly alone. River strode past me back into the school building, and I followed him. Once we were inside his office, he closed the door and then started to pace the room. Given how small it was, he only made it about five steps before he had to turn back the other way. I grabbed hold of his shoulders and stopped him when I couldn't take it anymore.

"River, what the hell, man?" I tried to reign in the anger, but something wasn't right here.

"I nearly lost it. I nearly shifted out there," he said, running his fingers through his hair and then pulling it tight in his hands as he folded down on his knees. "But then Calli, she, I don't know man, she pulled me back."

I crouched down beside River on the ground and placed a hand on his back to try and calm him down. I hadn't seen him like this before, but I could feel the anxious energy radiating off him.

"I lost it. When I saw that man hit her, I couldn't hold my wolf back. He wanted to rip him apart for touching her and Calli … she … she talked me down," River said, looking up at me in confusion, before he stood up and started to pace again.

"What do you mean she talked you down?" This was confusing as hell, and I had never seen River freak out like this before. I quickly pulled out my phone and shot off a text to Grey to let him know that he was needed at the school.

"Okay, I think we need to calm down. Sit down, try and calm down and I'll see if I can get you a drink or something," I told River, pushing him down in the chair and then backing out of the room like he was a bomb I was waiting to go off.

"What's going on?" Came Holly's voice behind me which just made me shriek like a little girl as I literally jumped about a foot in the air.

The shit-eating grin she gave me as I turned around, told me that I was not going to live it down for a long time. Miming strangling her I growled. "Calli got hurt and River nearly shifted outside."

"What!" she whisper-shouted at me.

I just threw my hands up in the air in exasperation. "I'm going to grab him a drink and try and calm him down," I said as I still stood there in shock.

"Okay," Holly said, steering me to a chair and pushing me into it. "I'm going to sort out those drinks for maybe everyone. Wait! Is Calli okay?"

I assured her that she was fine and then she rushed out of the reception area and into the Principal's office, as I leaned to the side to see what she was doing I saw her grab a bottle of whiskey out of his bottom drawer and run back into the reception area with a grin. She grabbed a couple of mugs from the cabinet, we cautiously came back into River's office. Thankfully, he looked a little less like he was about to throw up from the shock. Holly poured out a drink for all of us, and then we sat in silence and drank until Grey showed.

"What happened?" he said as he burst through the office door. He was immediately by River's side, his hand grasping the back of his brother's neck as he looked him over. Grey was a good Alpha, and he was an even better brother to River. We may rib him from time to time, but there was nothing that Grey wouldn't do for River.

"Bud McFarley and Stan Jenkins got into it outside the school at pick up today. Calli got hurt," I filled him in briefly.

"WHAT!" Grey roared.

Holly shrunk down in her seat a bit. Even she, a human, could sense that the three wolves she was currently shut in a room with were far from happy. My own wolf was a snarling mess every time that we thought about it, and I kept seeing Bud rearing back for his punch and smashing his elbow into Calli while she tried to shelter Jacob behind her. Holly though, being the special kind of person that she was, went and fetched another mug and passed a mug full of whiskey across to Grey, who had now taken over the pacing where River had left off. I quickly looked River over, his brother's anxiousness had ramped his own back up, and he had a death grip on his mug. He didn't seem on the verge of losing it though, so at least it was a bit of an improvement. The tension in the room was making even me feel on edge. Sometimes being able to sense emotion had its downsides, and this right here was one of them.

Grey leant against the wall and swallowed down a mug full of whiskey before he sighed. "Why do I have the feeling that you haven't told me everything yet?"

River looked up. "I nearly lost it, I nearly shifted." His

eyes were wide, and I knew he was scared. River had been the unruly kid of the pack when we were first setting up. Grey had been far more patient with him than any other alpha would have been. But even back then, when he was reckless and wild, he had never come close to shifting in front of humans. The Shifter Council would have him put to death if he exposed us like that.

Grey's mouth opened like he was going to say something, then it closed again.

River was starting to look like he was going to throw up and Holly stood up and refilled his mug before looking around at us all and laughing. "I have never seen you guys so whipped over a girl before."

None of us answered. I got the feeling that this was a conversation that needed to be had between the three of us when Holly wasn't around. It wasn't that I didn't trust her. She knew all about the pack and had seen us all shifted before. She was, after all, dating Nash. But something was going on here, and if it involved Calli, I didn't want to share it further than the three of us. We couldn't expose Calli to others until we knew what it was that she was hiding from, and there was no doubt in my mind that she was hiding from *something*. When I found out what it was, my wolf and I were going to tear it apart, and we would prove to Calli that we were the wolf she needed to have beside her. I looked across the room at Grey and River. The only thing was, I wasn't sure if maybe she needed three wolves with her. I did feel territorial about her, but not when it came to them. Shaking my head, I downed the last of my whiskey.

"Come on, let's take this home," I suggested, standing up out of my chair and heading to the door.

Grey and River followed me out of the room, and Holly

gathered up the mugs to clean up the evidence of us stealing the Principal's liqueur. I dug my wallet out of my jeans pocket and passed Holly a fifty dollar bill. "Better replace that bottle." I smiled at her, and she just nodded and left us.

14
CALLI

Jacob had been quiet all through dinner and had then gone back to his room to play while I cleaned up the mess. Spaghetti Bolognese was another one of his favourites, but even that didn't seem to help. I had the dishwasher stacked and a glass of red wine in hand while I sat down on the sofa. I didn't know what I was going to do with myself. I'd really fucked up today. I didn't know what it was with these wolves that kept making me forget myself. I looked across at Jacob's closed door and felt like I was going to cry. I was all that he had left, but I felt like I was constantly letting him down. These three wolves could mean death for me. I wasn't sure what would happen to Jacob if we were ever discovered, but when death was even an option for him, we just couldn't risk it. If I couldn't trust myself around them, then there was only really one option—we had to leave.

I took a drink of my wine while I thought about it. If I couldn't trust myself around them, then we needed to go. There was no other option. Trying to avoid them had been a stupid idea. Just the thought of leaving had my wolf whimpering inside me, but I reminded her that we had to protect Jacob; we had to protect what was left of our pack.

I pulled my laptop across the sofa to me and opened it up. First things first, I sent an email to Sean to update him on what was happening. I didn't fill him in on the fact that I was lusting after the three guys and couldn't trust myself to keep away from them, just that there was a pack in the area that was deeply involved in this small-town community. I floated the idea that we needed to leave and asked for suggestions of where we should go. I was starting to think that we should return to the UK. Maybe hit Ireland instead of England. We could get something remote. I could homeschool Jacob for a couple of years. When we were sure it was safe, maybe we could return to England and get Jacob settled in a school. At least we would be closer to Europe, where I had made some contacts during my travels. I had met a few shifters and witches in my two years travelling that I trusted enough to take into my confidence. Some of them I met through Mum and Dad, but they made sure that I visited them so that, if I needed it, I had a network to turn to for support. Maybe it was time to call in one of them. I had met a Panther shifter in Portugal who could maybe steer us to somewhere free from packs.

I was just about to start looking at properties in Ireland when the doorbell rang, and I trudged over to answer it. The sight in front of me broke my heart and made me unbelievably happy all at the same time. The three of them standing there together was all I wanted right now, but I had to remember Jacob. I couldn't be this selfish anymore.

Grey held out a hand to me. "I brought your change," he said, passing me a receipt and some money. When I looked at the receipt, I was pleased to see that he had indeed included an hour of labour and the parts' cost.

I smiled up at them when I had read it. "Thank you." I was tempted to make some snarky comment about how it wasn't so hard to do it right, but I just didn't have it in me.

"Is Jacob okay after this afternoon?" River asked, and I nodded, not wanting to get drawn into a conversation about what had happened.

We fell into silence until Tanner lifted his nose and scented the air. "Aww, did we miss dinner this time?"

"You do realise that you don't live here, right? You're like stray dogs, I feed you once, and you keep coming back for more," I laughed.

Tanner laughed, but I saw Grey and River look at me quizzically. It was probably the dog comment hitting a bit too close to home. After today I was pretty sure that River was going to start suspecting me. I needed to be more careful around him.

Grey stuck out one hand to me. "It was a pleasure doing business with you," he said, waiting for me to take his hand.

I looked at Tanner, who was looking at Grey like he had gone crazy. When I reached out to shake his hand, he didn't let it go immediately and instead turned my hand over. He ran his fingers across the palm of my hand, and I couldn't suppress the shiver that ran down my spine. He saw it as well, and I saw his eyes flash with arousal, but then he suddenly took a step back. "We'll see you soon, Calli," he said, turning around and walking away.

Tanner and River looked confusedly between him and me. "I guess we're going then," Tanner said, almost like it was a question. He gave me an awkward wave and followed Grey, River following closely behind them.

I closed the door gently and then leaned against it. These wolves were going to be the death of me. Quite literally.

15

GREY

"Nash!" I roared, as I stalked into the house.

Tanner and River were hot on my heels. They knew something was wrong with me. I hadn't spoken the whole drive home. I was suspicious, and my suspicions were pissing me off. More so at myself for having them than anything else.

"What's up?" Nash asked as he appeared in the doorway of the home office. The office was Nash's domain. Some days it felt like he never left it. He was our guy when it came to needing any information on anything. The pack probably wouldn't survive without him. He was narrowing down the location of the vamp nest we suspected was nearby. He was also looking into recent real estate purchases to make sure we didn't have any witches moving in on the pack and, hopefully, he had finished looking into Calli's background.

"Did you finish the report I asked for?" I growled at him.

Nash raised his eyebrows. Everyone would be able to tell I was pissed. I was trying to hold back the waves of Alpha power that my wolf was throwing off, but it was proving hard. I was pissed at myself. My wolf was even more pissed at me. He did not like the fact that I was doubting Calli. Nash ducked back into the office and then reappeared again with a file folder that he passed to me. We all moved into the living room, and I dropped down into an armchair and opened the folder to see the newspaper print outs.

"On the surface, everything looks as you said, but when you scratch and look a bit deeper, it does get a bit suspicious," he said.

"Explain," I growled.

"I pulled up the newspaper stories of the car accident pretty easily. A drunk driver collided with their vehicle forcing it off the road, and both died on impact," he started.

"Wait, are you looking into Calli?" River asked, shocked.

I pinned him with a glare and turned back to Nash. "Go on."

"So, I had my guy contact the local police up there. Apparently, they turn up at the house to inform the next of kin of the accident and speak with the daughter. They give the bad news. It's late at night, they leave. Next day they go back to the house with a family liaison officer and it's empty. No one gets in contact with the liaison, and no one hears from the daughter again. This comes up to the officer in charge who thinks that's a bit weird. She was young, she's lost her parents, and he's concerned about her and her younger brother. So, he looks into it further. The bodies of her parents were claimed by a Sean Phillips who is the family lawyer. Both cremated. No service. No sign of the kids. So, I looked into the house. It was bought four years ago by a Pine Harbour Corporation. It's just a shell. It doesn't do anything. It's registered in the Cayman Islands and the money filters through there from an account in Switzerland," he finished.

"When was the accident?" I asked him.

"Seven weeks ago," Nash filled in after checking his notes.

"Do you have any confirmation on when they arrived in the States?"

"Yep, came via Washington, D.C., last Thursday," he gave me a questioning look waiting for me to give him further information.

"She can't be our witch from two months ago then," I sighed in relief.

"What? Of course, she isn't a witch," Tanner scoffed. "All we can prove is her parents died exactly how she said they did. She left their family home when she found out. Which we also sort of already knew and her parents bought this house through some shady company."

"This morning, you said her hands were bleeding. There were absolutely no marks on them now," I argued. "She's defensive. And … I don't know … I feel strange around her," I said, throwing my hands up in the air. I didn't want to talk about this in front of Nash.

"What do you mean strange?" River questioned, who had just remained silent up to now. I knew my brother. He wasn't happy that I'd questioned Calli's honesty.

"Have you ever felt this way about a woman before?" I asked him flatly.

"No. That doesn't mean that something nefarious is going on though." River waved me off, but his eyes were flicking around suspiciously. He was hiding something.

"I can't stop thinking about her. My wolf obsesses over her. Fuck, I obsess over her. When she's near me, it makes me feel happy. I just want to wrap my arms around her and hold her and never let her go. When I'm not with her, she's all that I can think about."

"Yeah, I know the feeling," Tanner grumbled.

"We need to keep an eye on this. Something isn't right." I felt frustrated. Every ounce of my being just wanted to go back to her house and refuse to leave until she told me she felt the same way too. I knew that she did, but I also knew that something was scaring her as well.

"What if she knows about shifters?" River asked cautiously.

"What did you do?" I sighed. I didn't have the energy for this right now.

River shifted guiltily in his seat. "Nothing more than you already know," he muttered. "It's just something that Calli said to me when I was struggling to hold back the shift." He looked down at the floor frowning.

I was just about to reach across the room and slap him across the head in frustration when he continued. "She told me to stay there with her. To ground myself with her. It just … fuck, I don't know! It came across like she was trying to help me hold back the shift. It worked too," he huffed, crossing his arms and slumping back into his seat.

I needed to remember to speak with River about this. He had always been the screw up when he was a kid, and I knew it had broken his confidence. He tended to beat himself up when he felt like he'd let anyone down.

"She can't know," Tanner said, frowning, almost like he was trying to convince himself more than anyone else. "Maybe she thought you were having a panic attack or something."

I dug my fingers into my temples. I could feel the stress headache already forming. We had too much shit going on right now, and it was stretching us too thin.

"I can look into her parents a bit more," Nash suggested. "See if there is anything in their background that would suggest they've come in contact with shifters in the past."

I gave him a nod, grateful again that we had Nash to do shit like this for us. "Have you found anything on the vamp nest?" I asked him feeling the need to change the subject.

"Nothing solid, but I think I might have narrowed it down. Just running some last checks. I should have something for you by tomorrow night."

"Good," I grumbled.

We sat in silence, all consumed by our thoughts. The relief that washed over me when Nash confirmed that Calli couldn't be the witch we had scented had been nearly overwhelming. But something wasn't right, and as much as I wished we could go on like nothing was wrong, we needed to get to the bottom of it.

16

CALLI

I'd spent the last hour in the gym and had a good sweat starting up. I sometimes found that running on the treadmill could help when I was feeling the need to shift. I still hadn't dared shift here yet. It was going to be difficult to tell when it would be a good time. Ideally, I needed it to be when Jacob was somewhere else, where he was safe. At the moment that was only when he was at school and shifting in the daytime seemed dangerous. Especially for me because my white coat would show up like a bitch if I were seen. The thin layer of snow we had when we arrived still lingered in places but nowhere near enough to provide me with camouflage. The problem was if I waited until night, I was still going to stand out, but it would also mean leaving Jacob alone in the house. It was one of many on my very long list of problems at the moment.

When my phone started ringing, I glanced down and saw that it was Sean finally calling me back.

"Hey."

"Tell me about this pack," he said. I could hear the worry in his voice.

I climbed off the treadmill and grabbed my towel before heading up the stairs to the kitchen.

"It seems to be fairly small. I think they mentioned that there were about seven of them."

"Mentioned? What the fuck Calli?" he swore.

"Yeah, one of them works at Jacob's school as his school counsellor, and then I ran into the other two at the garage. It's impossible to avoid them. They just keep showing up everywhere," I scoffed.

I grabbed a bottle of water out of the fridge and then sat down on one of the dining chairs. Thankfully Jacob was asleep because I needed to have a frank conversation with Sean, and I didn't want him to hear.

"What do you mean they keep showing up? Do they know what you and Jacob are?" he asked quietly, almost like he was afraid to hear the answer.

"No, well, it seems like it's more because they sort of, well, you know, like me," I stuttered. Talking about this with Sean was just plain weird.

"Only you could get a pack of wolves to fall in love with you," he chuckled. "How long have they been there? I remember your Dad researching the sale, he went to look around the house and the area, and he said there was nothing to worry about there."

"It's not a whole pack, it's only three," I mumbled. "What do you mean he came here? If he came here? There's no way he wouldn't have known there was a pack here."

I tried to think, but it just felt like my mind was spinning out of control.

"I don't know what to do, Sean. This whole situation is just confusing. If it were just me, I'd wait it out. Dad had to have had a reason to send us here where there was a pack close by. But it's Jacob. I can't risk him. I can't lose him as well," I told him quietly.

"Are you sure there is nothing in the house that your parents could have left you to explain this?" Sean asked me.

"I haven't seen anything, unless it's up in the creepy attic library," I mumbled more to myself than him.

"Creepy attic library?" he laughed.

"I mean, it is what it is, I can't make it any clearer. It's a creepy, witch library, in the creepy attic."

Sean laughed, and the sound made me smile. It reminded me of every Christmas we had ever had. He always spent Christmas with us. He truly was Uncle Sean to Jacob and me as well, I suppose.

"Well strap on your big girl pants and go and have a look at the creepy witch library in the creepy attic. I'll see what I can find out about this pack from this end. I'm going to start looking at another safe house for you guys as well. Any preferences?"

"I was thinking Ireland, but I have a contact in Portugal who can probably assist location wise if you think that the UK is too dangerous."

"If you went remote enough in Ireland you would probably be okay. The only pack over there is around the Belfast area so if we go as far South as we can you should be fine. I'd like to speak with this contact though in case they have a better option over there, can you send me their details?" I could hear him tapping away at his laptop already.

"Yeah, I'll send them across for you now."

This was all getting pretty real, too quickly.

"It's probably sensible to have a few safe house locations set up even if you decide to stay and, Calli, don't take this the wrong way or anything, but I think we need to make some kind of arrangements for Jacob, just in case. He needs an escape route," he ended quietly.

"That would actually make me feel a lot better," I admitted.

"Okay, so you go and check out the library for anything that your parents could have left and I'll look into safe house locations. Be safe, Calli. I'll call you in a couple of days." I could still hear the worry in his voice.

I was starting to regret not taking him up on his offer to come over and help us get settled in. I had been so adamant about getting here and doing it on my own and then the first sign of trouble I went running back to him. I completely sucked at this adulting crap.

"I will. We miss you, Uncle Sean."

"Miss you too, kid," he said before hanging up the phone.

I looked at my phone and saw that it was coming up to ten at night. Jacob had been asleep for a couple of hours now. I glanced over at the door to the attic staircase, grabbed my bottle of water and strode over there. At the last second, I swerved into my room, deciding to take a shower first. It definitely wasn't because I was scared of the attic. Probably.

Unfortunately, there was only so long you could stay in the shower, and once I was clean and in a fresh pair of pjs, I once again found myself standing at the door to the attic. This was ridiculous. *"I am a grown-ass woman. I am responsible for another life. I might be doing a terrible job at keeping him safe because my hormones have apparently found a way to override my brain, but I was doing the best I could. I can, therefore, go into a creepy attic and not even be scared. I can totally do this."* I thought as I walked back into the kitchen, and grabbed a bottle of wine, poured myself a glass and took a large mouthful whilst staring at the door.

Grabbing the glass and the bottle as well, because you

know, I headed to the door, flung it open with far too much purpose and stormed up the stairs. Thankfully the light switch was at the bottom, and I flicked it on as I stormed past. When I reached the top, I took another look around me. It was just a whole load of bookshelves and a few armchairs with a coffee table. I didn't know what I was making such a fuss about. No, that's a lie, I did know what I was making such a fuss about. It was Sean's implication that there would be a message up here from my parents. I didn't know what would be worse. If there was a letter, or if there wasn't.

All of the emotion drained out of me. It was just all too much, everything that had happened and was happening now. I wasn't ready for this. I set the wine glass and bottle on the coffee table and curled up in one of the armchairs. Pulling the throw blanket off the back, I wrapped it around myself.

I could feel them breaking against the wall I had built in my mind. The emotions that were rolling through me that I had tried my best to hold as far away from me as I possibly could. It was time. It was time to let myself feel again. Jacob was fast asleep in bed, there was no one else here to see, and there was nothing here that I needed to hide from. A couple of weeks after we had turned up at his house, Sean had warned me that I would need to let myself feel the pain, that I couldn't let it fester inside of me. I knew it would break me if I did, and I couldn't do that to Jacob. I was all that he had left now, and I had to be strong during the day time for him. But now, here in the darkness, where no one could see me, this was the time when I needed just to let go. If I didn't let myself finally fall apart, I wouldn't be able to find a way to heal.

I felt the wall start to crumble, and my emotions began to slip through. Grief has a funny way of completely overtaking your mind. It fills every part of you. It somehow physically hurts. My eyes ached from the need to cry, and I finally let it go. The tears came slowly at first, I panted through the confusion, through the pain and the despair. But the tears soon started to come quicker, and the pants turned into sobs.

I curled into myself, and I rode the pain of the heartbreak. The loneliness and confusion overtook my mind. How could this happen? I didn't want to be alone. Why would they leave me? Common sense slipped away from me as self-doubt took over. I couldn't do this without them. They didn't prepare me for this, and I was already failing Jacob. Finally, the hate and the anger set in. Why did this have to happen to me? I was terrible at caring for Jacob. He deserved so much better than me.

Then, like a ray of light in my mind, I felt my wolf. She was tearing apart with grief as well, but she was there. She was with me. She would always be with me. I would never be alone when I had her with me. I sent her soothing thoughts, and she sent some back to me. I could almost feel her curling around me, trying to offer me comfort. My tears slowed, and I built the wall again in my mind. It wasn't as strong this time, there wasn't as much to hold back anymore, but it's mere presence almost felt comforting to me. It was what helped me get through the day. It was what would make the world believe I was okay. It was completely and utterly unhealthy for me, but for now, it was what I needed to function. I couldn't afford to just give up and curl up in a ball for weeks on end, letting myself float away on my grief. I had Jacob. He needed me, and selfishly I needed him as well. He gave me a purpose.

I swiped the tears from my cheeks and cleared my throat. Taking a deep drink from the glass of wine in front of me, I stood up and turned my attention to the bookcases. If there were going to be a message here for me, it would be in there.

Three walls of the attic were lined entirely with bookcases. Some of them had cupboards built into the bottom; some were just floor to ceiling shelves of books. The books were piled and stacked. A few, which looked like the oldest of them, sat on stands with the front cover facing the room, almost like they were on display.

My mother had loved books, and I knew that she would have been the one to set up this room out of the two of them. I looked across the shelves, not knowing where to start. There were hundreds of books up here. But then it caught my eye, in one of the corners there sat an old weathered book on a stand, it's front cover would have been facing the room had it not been obscured by the photograph. It was a picture of us all. I walked over and picked it up. I couldn't remember when we had taken this. It must have been a while ago because Jacob looked to be about three in the picture. We were all laughing and smiling at the camera. My father had one arm around me and one arm around my mother. She had Jacob sat on her hip while she wrapped her arms around him. She was smiling down at him with a look of such love on her face. My father and I were laughing at each other. It was a nice picture. It was a perfect example of our family. We had been happy.

I gently picked up the old book behind the photograph and took it to the armchair. When I opened the front cover, there laid against the first page was an envelope with my name on it and one with Jacob's Setting aside the book for later, I stared down at the envelope with my father's familiar writing on the front and tried to draw enough courage to open it up. When that failed, I opened it anyway, resigning myself to another breakdown in a few moments.

My beautiful Calli,
There is only one reason why you would ever be reading

this, and all I can say is how sorry your mother and I are that we aren't with you anymore. I know this is hard, and this is more than a parent should ever have to ask of a child, but we need you to protect Jacob.

If you are reading this letter, then you are already at the house. Your mother spent so much time putting it together for you both, so if you hate it, it's all her fault. I had no input. You know what your mother is like. Seriously though, we have done as much as we can to provide for you both. Don't doubt yourself. You are a beautiful, strong, and capable woman. So much like your mother. You have everything that you need. Just look inside yourself. Trust your wolf. She won't steer you wrong.

Hopefully, you find this letter before you find out that there is a wolf pack in the area. If you don't, then I'm sorry. I suppose we should have prepared you for this. Maybe it was selfish of us not to. We only wanted you to have as normal of a life as possible.

I've spent time in the area, I've watched this pack, and I've spoken to them. They are good men, Calli. Your mother tells me that this is where you need to be, but she won't tell me why. She says that you need to find out for yourself. I know that we have always taught you to hide, to be cautious. But you are going to need help if you are going to have any kind of a life. I truly believe that these men are the ones that you can trust to help you.

Your mother and I sent you to Europe to make contacts. While I'm writing this you're somewhere in Portugal I think. Those people will be able to provide you with a lifetime of advice and information. But you need to live your own life Calli. We don't want you to spend it always on the run and looking over your shoulder. Give this place a chance. Give this pack a chance.

I've written something for Jacob as well. Please give it to him when he's older, when he's old enough to understand.

I love you, baby girl. I wish that I could be there with you now. I know that you're sad, and that's okay. It's okay to cry. We will always be with you. We love you and Jacob more than anything else that we had in our lives. You were both the best thing that we ever did in life.

Dad

The tears were falling fast by the time I reached the end of the letter. I didn't have it in me to think over what the message had said tonight. I dried my eyes and left the attic. I didn't want to look through the books or anything up there. Taking the photograph and both letters with me, I checked on Jacob to make sure that he was still asleep and then crawled into bed. Pulling the covers around me, I fell back into the grief that filled me. I didn't need to make any decisions tonight. I could afford to give tonight to myself. And with that, I let the tears take me before exhaustion finally pulled me into sleep.

17

CALLI

The next morning, I woke up with a fuzzy head and a mood that seemed to match the grey, dreary day starting outside. My alarm was nice enough to wake me up at 7:00 am, and I dragged myself out of bed and into the shower. Jacob was still asleep, so I started making his packed lunch and getting breakfast ready. I definitely needed pancakes this morning.

Jacob sleepily came out of his room, and I passed him a cup of juice before he turned around and shuffled back into his room. He was always so funny in the morning. It was impossible to be in a funk when Jacob was around. I heard him shuffling around the bathroom, and I got to work on the pancakes and chopping up some fruit.

"Jacob, do you need help picking out your clothes?" I shouted into his room when I heard him emerge from the bathroom.

He stuck his little head out of the doorway and gave me one of his massive smiles. "Nope," he said before he disappeared back into his room.

Just as I was plating everything up, Jacob emerged

wearing a pair of jeans, a dinosaur t-shirt, and a hoodie over the top. He hadn't combed his hair, but he still looked pretty good. He was a cute looking kid.

Jacob managed to put away three pancakes and a whole bowl full of fruit. That kid was like a black hole.

"You all ready for school today?" I asked him.

"Yep," he smiled. "What did you pack me for lunch?"

"Ham sandwich, apple slices, and crisps. I've also put you some popcorn in to have as a snack at break."

Jacob gave me a smile of approval, and I almost sighed in relief. I'd been worried that yesterday was going to put him off going back to school, but if anything, it didn't seem to be on his mind at all—me on the other hand, I was shitting myself. This was worse than the first day of school. How do parents do this every day?

However, we were in the car on time and at the school five minutes early, so I was going to chalk that up as a life win. Was I completely avoiding the issue of my father's letter? Yes. Was I going to stop? Absolutely not.

I was just about to get back into the car when I heard someone shouting my name. Holly came jogging across the car park with a big smile on her face.

"Calli, I'm glad I caught you. River told me about yesterday, are you okay?"

"Yeah, I'm fine. It was nothing, right as rain by the morning. Just a little bit stiff," I said, completely forgetting that I was supposed to be injured and trying to subtly slip my bag off my supposedly injured shoulder.

"So, I don't get much of a break, but I'm hoping that I can convince you to have lunch with me today, if you're free that is," she said, giving me a blinding smile, which I was pretty sure was the one she used to get whatever she wanted.

I was about to turn her down, but then I thought about my

father's letter and what he said about living my life. "Actually, that sounds good. I'd love to," I told her.

"Well, don't sound so surprised!" she laughed swiping for me as I dodged out of the way. "I usually grab lunch at 12:30, do you want to meet back here then?"

"Awesome. I'll see you then."

I made my way back to the house, and after walking through the front door, I just stood in the middle of the living room, realising that I was alone for the first time in a long time. I had no idea what I was going to do. I felt my wolf brushing against the edge of my senses. I suppose I could shift and let her out finally. I had no idea how she wasn't raging out of control at how long it had been. I'd never shifted alone before. I'd never had to with my father around. Just thinking about it now though, I couldn't. It was too soon after finding the letter. I was still too broken. I just needed some time to try and glue the cracks together inside of me before I risked taking another hammer to my heart. I needed a way to start to work through all of this. That was when I realised that I did have a way. Striding into my bedroom, I found the guitar sat in the corner where I had left it.

Walking into the living room, I pulled the case onto the sofa beside me. Flipping open the lid, I ran my fingers over the instrument. It was stunning. Probably the most expensive thing that I had ever bought for myself. I spent the next ten minutes getting it perfectly tuned and then fitting the strap to it I had bought. It didn't need one, but the battered old guitar my father had taught me to play had one, and it just didn't feel right not to have the strap any more.

Once it was ready, I sat with it in my lap, cradled in my arms and closed my eyes. I could still remember how my father had patiently taught me all of the cords. At first, I didn't want to learn, but it was something my father had wanted to share with me, and I had humoured him at first. Then, I started to enjoy it. Once I became an angst-ridden teenager, I hadn't appreciated how my father had provided me with a way to express and process my emotions, even if I had frequently made use of it. Right now, though, I could appreciate what he had done for me and I'd never felt closer to him. I could feel the tears prickling behind my eyes, and I just moved my fingers over the strings, a haunting melody taking shape. As beautiful as it sounded, I just couldn't. My fingers came to an abrupt stop, and I gently placed the guitar back in its case and closed the lid. Why was this so hard?

I couldn't just sit there anymore, so the obvious answer was to make a cup of tea, which I drank leaning against the kitchen counter as I glared at the guitar case on the sofa. Right, I needed a plan. I wasn't going to live my life moping around like this. I needed to make a list. A 'getting shit done' list. I pulled out my phone and opened up the list app because I realised I had literally no stationary in the house now that the pad in my bag had run out, unless I wanted to use some of Jacob's crayons and drawing paper.

Okay. I could do this. First, I stared at the empty screen as it seemed to speak to me in my inner bitch voice, accusing me of wasting my life. With an internal slap and a mental shake, I started to type. *1. Get a life.* Then I dropped my phone on the counter and decided another cup of tea was a better idea as I ignored my inability to know what to do in any given moment.

It felt like it took about a year until lunchtime rolled around. By the time I was pulling into the school's car park, I was halfway to hating myself and failing to find any reason why I shouldn't. However, I did have a loose plan for the afternoon that was sort of making me feel like I was getting myself together.

Holly was waiting in the car park for me when I arrived, and she hopped up into the passenger seat of my truck.

"You fancy going to the coffee shop for lunch?" she asked.

"Yeah, that sounds good." I backed out, feeling a sense of pride at not hitting any other vehicles. Holly directed me to the best place to park, which was basically anywhere in the vicinity of the coffee shop.

It smelt like fresh coffee and cinnamon rolls when we went inside, and my mouth was instantly watering, not for that gross, hot, bean sludge but for the cinnamon, sugary goodness. Even better yet, when I ordered, they told me they were just out of the oven and would bring one over when they'd cooled a bit. Holly thought my little happy shimmy at the counter was hilarious, but I was having a bad day, and I deserved this in my life.

We found a small table near the window and the waitress brought over our order. I'd gone with a diet coke, and a panini and Holly had the most enormous coffee I had ever seen and a chicken salad baguette. It was nice sitting and having just a normal conversation with Holly. She was impossibly optimistic about everything.

"So, what have you been up to today?" she asked, cradling her coffee between her hands.

"Well, I dropped Jacob off at school this morning, and then I got home and realised I had nothing in my life and I didn't know what to do with myself," I told her, plastering a fake smile across my face.

"So, an average Tuesday morning then?" she laughed.

"Yep. So, after I had a brief quarter-life crisis, I decided to make a list."

"I love a list, pass it here," she said, holding out her hand to me. I obligingly pulled out my phone and got up my list before passing it to her. She stared at the screen with the most serious look on her face I think I had ever seen on her. "Number one, get a life. I like the way that you've managed to really group everything together into just one point here. It makes your list very compact. Almost like it's not a list."

I took the phone back off her, and she finally cracked out a smile. "Have you ever considered that you might be being just a little hard on yourself?" she laughed. "How long have you been in town?"

"Nearly a week," I realised. It seemed like so much longer than that.

"And, would it be reasonable to suggest that maybe, in less than a week, it might be a bit much to expect to have your life completely together then?" she pointed out, taking a deep drink from her coffee. Her serious point being drowned out by the whipped cream moustache she was currently sporting.

"You may have a point there. Perhaps, I need to break down that list a bit more."

"Or, and I'm just floating ideas here, maybe take it easy for a bit, give yourself a break and start making a list in say, six months or so." Holly reached across the table and took my hand. "No one expects you to have it all together. You're doing an amazing job with Jacob. You don't need to do everything all at the same time. Just take some time to settle in and find your feet. I think you'll be surprised how things tend to come together on their own."

I slumped back in my chair with a sigh. I knew what she was saying to me was right, but I couldn't help but feel like I wasn't doing enough.

"I'm sorry, this is depressing, and you only have an hour for lunch," I started, I was never going to get invited to lunch again at this rate.

"You're right; this is depressing. So, tell me how River's gift went over. How did it go? Did you instantly forgive him and then fall in love? Have you kissed him yet? And what's going on with Grey and Tanner?" She eagerly leaned forward and laughed at what I can only assume was a shocked look on my face.

"Very well, yes and I'm not sure, no and again I'm not sure," I said, holding up a finger with the answer to each corresponding point.

"Okay, two more questions. Do you hate me? And why are you making me dig so hard for this information?" she said, holding up her own fingers.

"No, I think it would be impossible to ever hate you. And I don't know where I stand and I'm really confused, and I don't know what to do," I answered on a sigh. Everything seemed quite hopeless, but then I realised that Holly could maybe help me work through some of this and I was suddenly grateful that I had someone to talk to. Perhaps I do need therapy?

"Okay, so I met River first, you know because you were there." I nodded across at her. "And then I went to the garage and met Grey and Tanner. Then, I'm not so sure. They're all great guys, and Jacob seems to like them. They had dinner with us when they dropped the truck back at my house, and we had a really good time. But, it's weird right, because there's three of them. I do like them. Maybe a bit too much. It kind of feels a bit too soon to be jumping into something though." I frowned as I spoke because I realised that this actually was how I felt. I did like them, but I wasn't so sure if it did feel like it was too soon. In all honesty, the only thing holding me back was the whole wolf/witch issue. Now that I had the letter from my father though, I was wondering if maybe I needed to take the leap and see what happened. If I could do it in a controlled fashion, maybe make arrangements for Jacob to be away for a few days and then if it did go horribly wrong, he would be safely away from the danger.

"Well, have they asked you to choose?" Holly asked with a wicked smile on her face.

I spluttered in embarrassment until I realised that I wasn't forming any words. Holly's smile just increased in intensity, and there was a distinct eyebrow waggle going on.

"Oh please, like you haven't thought about all three of them together getting hot, sweaty and rolling around in that empty, lonely bed that you have," she said fanning herself with one hand.

"Yeah, that's exactly what I was thinking of doing, a foursome while my little brother sleeps in the other room," I said seriously which just made Holly bust out laughing even more. "Enough about my imaginary love life. Tell me about yours. Is there someone out there that is the victim of all of your devilish sex plots?" I asked.

"Nash," she swooned. "He's amazing. Total geek but with a body to die for."

She looked so happy, and part of me was jealous. My wolf was happily prancing around in my head at the thought of all three guys, and I was fairly certain the lack of attention had finally driven her insane.

"He's actually friends with your three guys," she added, almost like an afterthought.

"I don't think you can really call them my guys," I pointed out. "We had dinner together once and a handful of conversations."

Wow, I'd never thought about it that way. We hardly knew each other and never spent any time together, and I was thinking about telling them my darkest secret and putting my life in their hands. It was official, I had gone insane, or perhaps my wolf had, and she had dragged me along with her.

"So, what you're saying is that you want to go out with them," she said grinning at me. I could already tell that she was up to something, but all I could manage was a huff of amusement, not quite sure what I was seemingly about to agree to.

"That's not quite what I was saying. It's not that easy for me anyway, I have Jacob, and at the moment—I'm sure you're going to enjoy this bit—you're right, I need to take time to settle us in here."

"While it's always nice to have confirmation of my supremacy, maybe a few coffee dates here and there, nothing serious, just something casual between friends. I hate to think of you rattling around in that house all day on your own." There was something in her eye that looked awfully like sympathy, and I needed it not to be there right now.

"Supremacy might be more your word than mine. Anyway, what if they're just being friendly and aren't interested like that. I can't just start dating them all anyway. It wouldn't be right."

"I didn't say date. I said coffee with friends, and they totally like you. You should have seen them yesterday. When River told Grey that you got hurt outside the school he was all like, 'whhhaaaattttt, I am man hear me roar' on your behalf." She smirked as she beat against her chest, doing her manly roar in the middle of the coffee shop. No one paid her any attention which I thought spoke volumes about Holly.

"Okay, I don't even know what to do with that," I laughed. Thankfully at that point, my cinnamon roll was dropped off, and it smelt heavenly.

"Maybe you could pick up a couple more of those and drop by the garage. Maybe have a chat with some gentlemen and express a bit of interest. Perhaps try and gauge from any subsequent conversation their potential interest."

It wasn't the worst idea, and when I looked over at the counter, the waitress was already watching to see what I was going to do. It seemed like they were maybe paying a bit more attention than I had initially thought.

"I guess I'll take half a dozen more," I shrugged at her, and she beamed a smile back at me before putting them in a box.

"We should do this again," Holly said, standing up. "I feel like your relationship is going to be the best entertainment we've had around here for a long time. How is your shoulder anyway? River said that you were hit when the fight broke out."

"Oh it's fine, it was a bit sore last night, but a soak in the bath and some ibuprofen straightened it right out," I said shrugging. This was the best way to start a new friendship, with half-truths and lies. I was going to make a fantastic friend.

As we passed the counter on the way out, the waitress gave me a box of cinnamon rolls, and I added my own on the top before settling the bill. Holly kept fake swooning and laughing at my expense. As annoying as it was, it was still fun, and I was glad that we had done it. Unfortunately, this was a ridiculously small town and while that had seemed like a good idea to start with it took far too short a time for me to drop Holly back off at the school and then pull up outside the garage. Now I was sat in my truck, holding onto the steering wheel with both hands and desperately not turning my head for fear of catching someone's eye. That was why I let out the most embarrassing girly shriek when Tanner knocked on the window five minutes later.

"Calli, you in need of something?" he asked, frowning in

confusion. It would seem that my time sitting in the truck hadn't gone unnoticed.

"No. I mean ... well ... I was with Holly ... I brought cinnamon rolls!" I suddenly blurted out.

Tanner chuckled and then opened the truck door. Holding out a hand for me, he waited for me to unbuckle my seat belt, and then taking his hand, I slid out of the truck. I suddenly found myself standing very close to him, as he had failed to step back to give me room to stand. I could feel my wolf practically spinning in circles in my head in response to his close proximity, and I couldn't help myself. My other hand just seemed to come up of its own volition, and before I realised what I was even doing, I could see it laying against his chest. I felt the rumble of pleasure come from his wolf before he coughed to try and cover it up and subtly stepped back to make room for me.

"Grey is a couple of towns over meeting with one of our suppliers, so that means you've got me all to yourself," Tanner grinned. He dropped his arm around my shoulders and walked me into the garage.

I caught sight of another of the pack working in the far corner under a car, but he didn't pay us any attention. Tanner led me over to the office where I had spoken with Grey a few days ago and pulled the door shut behind us, enclosing us in silence.

"So, I know this is a bit weird with how we left everything but I ... I don't know. Ten minutes ago, when I was talking to Holly, this seemed like a good idea." I was suddenly cursing Holly out in my head for the impromptu confidence she had managed to instill in me.

My father's letter blazed to the front of my mind, and I could almost hear his voice repeat the words, 'trust your wolf'. My wolf was spinning in circles in joy at the forefront of my mind. She wanted out. She hadn't pushed this hard against me since, in fact, I think ever. She wanted to be with Tanner. She wanted to show off to him, to meet him and his wolf.

Will you just calm the fuck down. We will in time, but we need to lay the foundation first. We can't tell them the truth until we have Jacob somewhere safe, just in case.

I immediately felt her start sulking, and I could almost see her hunching down with her ears pulled flat against her head. The bond between my wolf and Jacob was solid, she would never put him at risk, even if these three wolves seemed to have her forget herself every so often.

"This is an excellent idea," Tanner smiled, snapping me out of my thoughts. "Do you want a coffee?"

I scrunched my face up in disgust. I could stomach coffee if it were the only thing around, but I had to be desperate enough for caffeine before I was willing to gulp it down.

"Water would be fine for me," I sighed. I really needed a cup of tea, but I knew they wouldn't have any.

"Not a coffee fan then I take it," he laughed as he grabbed a bottle of water out of a small mini-fridge sat next to the filing cabinet and then filled a mug from the coffee pot that sat on the top.

"Not hugely. I can stomach it if I'm desperate. What can I say, I like to embrace my stereotype and tea is the only way to my heart," I smiled as he passed me my drink.

"I'll have to try and remember that."

"Tanner, about the other day. I'm sorry. I shouldn't have just thrown you out of the house like that. I … I don't know, things are just still hard, but I don't want you to think that I don't … well … that I don't like you," I mumbled. Why was this so hard? I had the distinct feeling that I was making a fool of myself right now.

"You don't owe me any kind of apology," he said, pulling the chair from around the other side of the desk so he could sit next to me. "I get it Calli, and I probably jumped the gun a little bit. It's just, when I'm around you it's hard not to want everything all at once."

As if he wasn't sweet enough, I practically melted on the spot at his words.

"The others …" I started, but then I had no idea where I was going to go with that. You can't tell a guy who just admitted to liking you, that you also liked his friends.

Tanner just laughed. "Definitely feel the same way too." He didn't seem upset about that idea. It was almost like he was waiting to see what I would do, which was difficult because I was a human as far as he was aware.

I opened up the box of cinnamon rolls and offered him one before taking one for myself. They were still slightly warm, and I couldn't help shoving it into my mouth to take a massive bite.

Tanner just laughed at me as I unashamedly got icing smeared all over my face. I wasn't even embarrassed. This was amazing. I took another huge bite and groaned in delight as I slumped back in my seat. Instant regret at handing over the box of the rest of them hit me. Jacob didn't even like cinnamon rolls, but I definitely should have just kept them all and eaten until I thought I was going to throw up.

I realised that Tanner wasn't laughing any more and when I looked back up at him I saw the heat banked in his eyes. The realisation of the sex noises I had made while eating hit me at the same time as I felt my cheeks heat to the temperature of what I can only assume was the same as the surface of the sun.

"You're adorable when you blush," Tanner smiled as he

took a bite of his cinnamon roll. "Oh, fuck me, that is good," he mumbled, making me laugh.

There was something about Tanner that could instantly make you feel at ease. Even with my stumbling attempts at conversation. He felt so ... familiar almost. It was disarming. Being in his presence made me forget all of the reasons why I shouldn't be with him.

"So, not that this isn't the best thing that's happened to me all week, but what brings you to our door?" Tanner asked me again.

"Well actually, if you remember correctly, I was sitting outside like a weirdo stalker, and it was you that brought me to the door," I corrected him.

"That is a good point," he conceded, taking another bite.

"Would you like to go for lunch with me sometime?" I rushed out and then because I was a massive weirdo, shoved another enormous piece of cinnamon roll into my mouth because it would prevent me from saying something stupid in the next few minutes when I started to die of embarrassment.

Tanner's mouth had dropped open in shock at my question, no doubt because I was giving him emotional whiplash from how I constantly pushed him away and then pulled him close again. But then, just as I was starting to wish that the ground would open up to swallow me, he broke into the most beautiful smile.

"I would love to," he grinned, and my heart did a little flip flop like a fish out of water. For some reason, that analogy seemed incredibly appropriate for me.

As soon as I had swallowed my mouthful of food, a sigh of relief gushed out of me. I don't know what I had expected his response to be. Actually, that was a lie, I was pretty sure he was just going to laugh at me, but I couldn't be happier with the one that I had gotten.

"So, when do you want to take me out?" he smiled.

"I'm taking you out?" The cheeky fucker.

"Well, you did ask me," he frowned in faux confusion.

"You do have a point there. Well, when are you free? I just spend my days sitting around with nothing to do, so we should probably just work around your schedule," I suggested.

"Hey, you're doing an amazing job with Jacob, Calli. Don't be too hard on yourself. You don't need to get it all done at once you know," he scolded me.

"You're the second person to say that to me today. And I know. I suppose I'm not used to just not having something to do. Even when I was travelling, I always seemed to be busy. I don't know what to do with myself at the minute." I think that was my main problem. Not being busy was just making me feel so lost at the moment.

"Well, how about you start by taking me out for lunch on Thursday. It's my day off. We could drop Jacob off at school and make a morning of it. Grab some lunch and be back in plenty of time to pick the little guy up," he suggested.

"Sounds perfect," I said, standing up and dusting off my sticky fingers against my jeans.

Tanner stood at the same time and gently put one hand on my waist. He waited a moment before pulling me towards him, almost like he was giving me a chance to make a run for it or push him away if that was what I wanted. I didn't, though. I went willingly and leant against his chest. Tanner's eyes widened in surprise as I reached up on my tiptoes and laid a gentle kiss on his cheek. He nuzzled his head against my neck, and I felt his sigh of happiness as he did. I took a step back before anything had the chance to get out of control.

"If you can get to mine by 8:00 I'll even make you breakfast," I smiled at him.

"Breakfast and lunch, now you're just spoiling me," he joked as he opened the office door for me.

We walked back out to my truck, and he opened the door for me, even if I did catch him checking out my ass after I climbed in.

"Say hi to Grey for me when he gets back."

"Oh, he will hear all about this, every hour of the day for at least a week," he grinned, and I knew that he was being serious.

"Don't be mean to him," I scolded him playfully.

"It's not like he won't do the same thing when he gets to go out with you," he laughed as he closed the door.

I drove away with a smile on my face even if I was slightly confused about what we were doing. Tanner had basically given me permission to date Grey as well. Or was he just trying to make it clear to me that we wouldn't be entering into anything serious together? I huffed in annoyance at myself. Why did this have to be so complicated?

18

CALLI

I pulled up outside my next destination and shook my head to clear my thoughts of men and upcoming dates. Now was time for me to take a few baby steps in getting my life together.

First stop, the library. As soon as I entered the building, I inhaled that book smell all libraries had and sighed as it gave me an instant calm. A woman was standing behind a desk looking through a stack of books and working away at a computer. She was so engrossed in her work that she didn't notice I had walked in. Although I suppose early Tuesday afternoons were not going to be the busiest time in a small town library like this. While she was distracted, I took a moment to look around myself and take in the building. It was clearly one of the older buildings in town; in fact, it had an old schoolhouse look about it. It looked to be one big room, there wasn't really a ceiling as such, and the building just opened up into the rafters. It was impressive being able to see all the old wooden struts crisscrossing around, although I bet it was pretty terrifying when the weather turned and probably freezing in the winter. The library itself was just row after row of books. It looked like the end of each aisle was labelled, and that was about it. I couldn't see any seating or desks, although they could have been further into the stacks where I couldn't see. It was an impressive collection for such a small town, but it wasn't exactly warm and friendly.

"Can I help you?" I heard a feminine voice ask.

When I looked up, I saw that the librarian had finally noticed I'd walked in, and I approached the desk.

"Yes, I'm new to town, and I'd like to sign up for a membership for myself and my little brother, if you have a children's section," I told her.

"Of course." Her face broke into a smile, almost as if she hadn't been sure if I would be friendly initially but was now willing to help even if she had offered before. "The children's section is in the far corner. I'll show you once we have you all signed up."

We went through the process of registering. It was far easier than I had first thought because small-town gossip meant she already knew who I was and where I lived. Even in the small village back in England where I grew up, the gossip wasn't quite as efficient as this. Once I had mine and Jacob's cards in hand, she gave me a brief tour of the library. The children's section was pretty nice. There was a collection of soft rugs down over the hard wooden floor, and the shorter stacks were painted bright colours. There were even several beanbags scattered about together with some child-sized chairs and desks.

"We do a toddlers session on Mondays and Wednesdays where we have storytime. For those who are a bit older, we have a few creative writing workshops after school. I can grab you a pamphlet on the way out if it's something that Jacob would be interested in? There is one which caters to his age group," she told me. I hadn't expected them to have something like that arranged and I had to admit that I was impressed. "We also hold an art session at the weekend for his age group if he wants to attend that."

"Wow, this is far more impressive than I had expected," I admitted, hoping that I wouldn't insult her. Thankfully she just laughed like she was used to hearing it.

"We have a few families with children of a similar age, and it sort of came together when there was a gap in after-school activities for them. The PTA at the school got involved in setting it up with us, and they even help with the funding," she explained.

"The PTA. I suppose that's something I'm going to have to brave at some point." I shuddered at the thought. That was something I hadn't considered.

"Don't worry. They're a friendly bunch. I'm Diane by the way," she said, holding out her hand for me to shake.

"Calli," I said and then cringed. "Sorry, you already know that. I suppose it's just a reflex to say my name back."

"Don't worry about it. Is there anything else that you'd like me to show you?" She seemed like a nice woman, but I was nervous to admit to her the section that I wanted to find. "Don't worry, I'm like a doctor, whatever you tell me stays between us, it's the librarian's promise," she said quietly almost like she could sense my reluctance.

I laughed, but it was more due to nervousness than anything else. "I was wondering if you have a self-help section," I admitted.

Her eyes softened, and I knew that the gossip mill had included the details of why we had moved here as well. "Of course. It's just over here," she told me, leading me a couple of stacks back. It was quite well stocked. "This is the section on grief, and I believe we had a couple that dealt with grief in children as well," she said, running her fingers along the spines of the books as she looked for something. "Ah, here it is. My friend said that this one was particularly helpful when she lost her husband," she said, pulling out a book and passing it to me.

I held the book in my hand and stared at the front cover *Children and Grief: When a Parent Dies*. It was almost like the world stood still as I looked at it. I was still a child too. This was so overwhelming, not to mention panic-inducing. Sometimes it felt like I couldn't breathe, and I felt like the walls were closing in around me. I didn't hear Diane talking to me until she laid a hand gently on my shoulder.

"Are you okay, Calli?" Diane asked me gently.

"Yes, sorry, I just zoned out there for a second," I said, shaking my head.

"Calli, I hope you don't think I'm overstepping here, but my friend also attended a grief counselling group which I know she found helpful. Would you like me to get the details for you?"

My first instinct was to tell her no and that I was okay, but then I looked down at the book in my hand, and I realised that I did need help. Anyway, just because she gave me the details, didn't mean I had to do anything with them just yet.

"Yes, please," I whispered.

Diane spent ten minutes with me going through the books until I had settled on two that I wanted to take home with me. She checked them out as an extended loan for me, and she promised to text me the details of the grief support group. When I left the library, I felt emotionally drained, and I was tempted to not go to my last stop, but I gave myself a shake to pull myself out of my funk. I knew this wasn't going to be easy when I sat myself down on the plane with Jacob sleeping at my side. But this was what we needed to do. I didn't only need to make a home here for Jacob. I wanted to make one for myself as well. But before I could do that, I needed to find myself first. That was why I stepped into the hardware store next. This was my crazy idea about how I was going to go about taking the first step.

The hardware store smelt like cut wood and was like a completely different world to what I was used to. I grabbed a basket from beside the door and started to wander my way through the aisles. My mission was to put myself together a home maintenance toolbox thing—I was still working on the name—but I intended to have the things I would need to do anything around the house that needed doing. It was my first step in being an adult and a homeowner. I might have to borrow a book on how to do DIY, but I was still counting it as a step forward.

So far, I'd grabbed a set of screwdrivers, and now I was browsing the hammers. I had no idea that there were so many different types, and I had no idea what type I needed or even why there were so many different types in the first place.

"Something wrong at the house, Calli?" Someone asked from behind me.

I turned around and found James standing behind me.

"No, not yet," I told him, holding up the hammer I had in my hand. "I'm making a toolbox." I might have said it proudly because I weirdly was.

"Okay, you know if anything happens up at the house, I'm more than happy to come over and help you out," James said leaning away from the hammer which I appeared to be swinging around with no concern of the consequences.

"I know, and I will probably have to take you up on that at some point. I just kind of want to be prepared and learn how to do the very, very, very small things myself."

James reached forward cautiously and gently took the

hammer off me that I was starting to use to punctuate my words with now.

"Well to start with, that's a pin hammer, and you don't want one of those." He looked down into the basket. "And you don't need that many screwdrivers for what you want to do," he said, removing the pack from my basket and shoving it back onto the shelf in entirely the wrong place.

James guided me back to the start of the aisle and then went around the store with me and started to pick out what I needed and explained what they were used for.

"I'm sorry that I've kind of hijacked your free time," I said suddenly as James finished explaining why it would be more beneficial for me to have a power screwdriver as well.

"Nah, it's nothing. I'm like a romance novel, small-town guy. The hardware store is like shoe shopping for me. This is the most fun I've had in ages, not counting my afternoon playing Lego with Jacob. I'm still waiting for a repeat invite by the way," he grinned, and I could tell that he genuinely meant that. My parents had done an excellent job of picking us a good community to settle in should the worst happen.

"Did you ever meet my parents?" I asked him, not finding the courage to meet his eye as I did for some reason.

"Mary and I spent some time with your mother when she came over to start furnishing the house, and we took the caretaker position. Even though we didn't spend much time together, Mary and I still considered her a friend. She was a good person, Calli, and I imagine your father must have been as well if she chose him. It shows with what an excellent job they did bringing you up. They'd be proud of how good you're doing with Jacob." His voice grew gruff as he spoke, and I could tell that he was struggling with the same emotions that I was. My parents had been like that. Even when they only spent a brief amount of time with anyone, they seemed to be able to touch their lives.

We finished up in the hardware store by getting a toolbox to keep all of my new tools and supplies in. It came in handy when I checked out because James put everything inside it as it was rung through and I had something to carry it all home. I even got to leave all the packaging in the store, so I didn't have to deal with it at the house. James really must enjoy the hardware store because he seemed to know the man at the checkout well. However, that could have just been part of the small-town dynamic. In any event, they both had great fun organising my new tools, so much so, that I wandered off at one point and bought a plastic storage bin and some small containers for the other things I had purchased. I was now fully stocked with things like light bulbs and batteries. I was prepared for all eventualities, including a blackout which apparently could happen if the storms were bad and we didn't have a generator up at the house.

James helped me carry everything to my truck and load it into the flatbed. I was starting to see the convenience of having one now. It really did make shopping a lot easier.

"So, any plans for breaking in your tools?" James laughed as I proudly looked at my shiny red toolbox.

"Yes actually, I'm going to use my brand new tape measure to measure out space in Jacob's room so that I can order something to store his ever-growing Lego collection and some other things," I said proudly and then realised that I might be going a little more stir crazy than I had first thought.

"Well, if you need help putting it together you know who to call. Let Jacob know that we've restocked the toy section with some pretty sweet Lego sets. I'll see you around, Calli," he said, waving goodbye.

"Thanks again," I shouted after him, and he just waved one hand over his shoulder at me.

Checking my watch, it was nearly time to collect Jacob from school, so I decided to head that way and read some of my book in the car while waiting for him to finish up.

19

GREY

Tanner had been insufferable all day. I had no idea what it was that made him act like such a dick, but he was getting on my last nerve by the time we were locking up the garage. At first, I'd assumed it was because Calli had dropped by with the cinnamon rolls, but it was definitely something more than that. He was playing it close to his chest, though. I was gutted I'd missed her just for some boring meeting with a supplier. That was probably why Tanner was grating on me a bit more than usual. I was just being a grumpy bastard.

We pulled up at the house, and I was hoping that River had thought to put something on for dinner because I was starving. I bet Calli had made something amazing. I was going to need to find a reason to check in with her at some point around dinner time again because she was an excellent cook, or maybe it was just because I got to spend time with her that made it seem so good. Either way, I definitely wanted to drop by again, and I wanted to do it soon. Maybe I could stop by tonight and pretend I was checking up on her after yesterday.

"River! You home?" Tanner shouted as soon as we walked in through the front door. He was practically vibrating on the spot, and I had no idea what had got into him.

"In the kitchen," River shouted from deeper inside the house. Thank fuck. Hopefully, that meant he was cooking.

Tanner practically sprinted ahead of me, and I shook my head and followed him. Sometimes it was like I lived with a bunch of kids. By the time I arrived in the kitchen, which had to be less than a minute later, Tanner had a beer out of the fridge and was passing one to River before handing one back to me. River looked to be cooking some steaks, and I was beyond grateful for the fact that he got home before us right then.

"I think we need to make a toast," Tanner said, trying to sound casual but the fact that he was practically bouncing on the spot was ruining it for him.

"What's got into him?" River asked me, ignoring Tanner.

"I have no idea, but he's been like this all afternoon," I said, taking a deep drink from my beer. What was it with cold beer that just seemed to set everything right in the world? "Go on then. I know you're dying to get it out," I finally said to Tanner, who just grinned at me before clearing his throat and holding his beer in front of him with a serious look on his face.

"To me and wishing me luck on my date on Thursday," he grinned.

"Ha!" River burst out joyfully. "And then there were two. Just me and you to fight it out for the lovely Calli then brother," he said, jokingly shoving my shoulder.

"You're lying," I accused Tanner, refusing to chink my bottle against his.

Tanner was grinning and shaking his head when River realised that he was missing something. "What?"

"You do not have a date with Calli!" I accused.

River gasped in shock and accusation, and I found it amusing even though I was reeling from the thought that Calli had agreed to go out with Tanner.

"I definitely do. She ... Asked .... Me!" he bragged. "It started out as a lunch date and ended up with me joining them for breakfast then we're going to spend the whole morning together and end with lunch," he grinned. It was nice to see Tanner so happy, but I won't lie and pretend I wasn't gutted.

"It's over then, she made her choice," River said sadly, turning back to the stove.

It crushed me to see my little brother hurting, nearly as much as it crushed me to feel the same way myself.

"Ah, stop moping, you're ruining my good vibes. You haven't lost out. As much as I'd love to lie to you, she hasn't chosen me. She didn't come right out and say it, but she made sure that I knew she liked you guys too and I assured her that the feelings were mutual. In fact, she even told me that I wasn't allowed to be mean to you when I bragged about it." I could see that he was trying to be serious, but the grin that had been on his face all day was trying to force itself back there. "You're lucky that I'm such a good guy and I didn't just steal her away from you."

Feeling the need to change the subject, I turned back to River, who was still fussing over the stove and not turning back to us. Tanner looked across at me, worried before he stepped up beside River and slapped him on the back.

"So, what's for dinner?" he asked.

"Steak." River said quietly, pointing at the pan.

I knew this was going to be a problem when we first discussed it. I just let them assure me that it wasn't because I wanted Calli so much for myself. I probably would have agreed to anything. But seeing my brother hurting now was hard. It agitated my wolf, not only because he was our brother but because we were his Alpha.

"You do realise you are the only one out of all of us that has a legitimate excuse to talk to her," I reassured him. "And there are over twenty-four hours between now and this idiot's date with her. Over twenty-four hours when you get to see her at least twice."

River cocked his head to the side in thought, and I could almost see the cogs turning in his head. By the time he turned around from the stovetop to announce that the steaks were done, which was literally minutes considering we all liked them cooked rare, he had a sly smile on his face. I immediately felt my wolf settle, and couldn't help the sigh of relief that gently left me. River was oblivious to me as he bustled around laying the food out on the table and no doubt fine-tuning the details of whatever plan was forming in his head. Tanner, however, always seemed to be able to read me like a book and patted me on the shoulder as he moved past me to take a seat at the table.

Nash came to join us at the table, and Aidan was close behind him. The others always ate with their families unless it was a special occasion. We really should get the pack together again soon though, it helped with our bond, and it wouldn't be long before we would be welcoming a new pup into the pack. As we ate, the others made quiet conversation, but I was lost in my thoughts of Calli and Jacob. I think pack life could help Jacob with the grief he was feeling. I wanted them both to be part of the pack but to do that officially I would have to turn Calli. I'd never tried it myself, but I had been present when my father had tried to turn a female for one of his pack members, and it had been horrific.

I didn't know whether I could put Calli through that. The woman had writhed on the ground in agony for hours. I could still hear the sound of all of her bones breaking, setting and rebreaking as we watched them moving around underneath her skin. When she finally fell, limp and unconscious she remained in her human form, the turning had failed. I was only about eleven at the time, but I was convinced she was dead. I didn't see how a person could go through what she had just done and survive. She did survive, though. It took a week before she was strong enough to get out of bed, and then we never saw her again. The love that had apparently been so strong she was willing to be turned, had broken along with her body during the turning attempt. She became a cautionary tale through the pack, and there were very few attempts after hers.

My wolf grumbled in my head. He was adamant that Calli would be pack, but he was also adamant we would never allow her to feel any pain. I didn't understand him at times, but the bond he was forming with Calli was strong. It felt like he wanted her more than I did, and I wouldn't have thought that was possible.

The other problem was going to be that none of us were going to be willing to give her up. I could see sharing a mate with River and Tanner. My wolf and I had no problem with that. They would be able to keep her safe when I was distracted with Alpha duties. Between the three of us, she would never have to be alone, and Jacob would always have someone to care for him. But how would Calli react to such an idea? Tanner seemed to think that she was okay with dating the three of us at the moment, but she was human. This wasn't something that humans did. Would she really be okay with it if we wanted something more than just a few casual dates? I shouldn't forget that not only was Calli still hurting, but so was Jacob. Was he even ready to let us into her life? What he thought was always going to be the final deciding factor, and it should be. Jacob was such a good kid. Her parents must have been really good people to have raised two kids like them.

"Grey!" Tanner shouted at me.

"Sorry, did you say something? I was miles away." I shook my head in surprise but also to try and clear my thoughts.

"Nash thinks he's found something," he told me, his eyes filling with concern. "Do we need to talk?"

"No, it's fine, I was just … I'll tell you about it later," I sighed. "Sorry, Nash. What were you saying?"

"No problem, Alpha." Nash smiled. "I think I've found a property where the nest could be located. It's in the next town over. There haven't been any problems with locals going missing, but there have been reports of two missing hikers and a break-in at the local clinic. They were cleaned out of a lot of the drugs but also their whole blood supply. I think they took the drugs to stop any suspicions being raised, but they'll also probably sell them for funds. It's actually a good idea, the human cops have already floated the idea of it being gang-related. They think someone is setting up their own hatchet clinic." Nash drifted off as he started going over the facts in his mind. He did that sometimes.

"What led you to the property?" I prompted to bring him back to the conversation.

"Right! Sorry. Yes, the property. I didn't see it at first because it was bought over a year ago. Looking into Calli gave me the idea. I wasn't getting anything on the recent purchases, so I hacked into the water and electric companies and started looking at properties which had been vacant and just had the utilities turned on. That gave me a much shorter list, and then I was able to look at the purchase transactions. The one I think we should look at was purchased under a shell company that I can't see much activity for, apart from the purchase of several domestic dwellings and one warehouse property in Portland. Most of the properties still seem to be vacant. I think we might have a bigger nest than we realised moving into the area. These seem to be the first but judging by the scale of the property purchases, not to mention the funds needed to acquire so many properties; we may have a bigger problem on our hands than we first realised. We might need to take this to the Council."

"Ah, fuck! I hate dealing with the Council," Tanner grumbled.

"That's because you hate speaking with your father," Aidan laughed.

My wolf, who had only just calmed down about the whole Calli situation, was now pacing angrily in my head again. This was the first major breach of our pack lands. Our pack was only starting out and far too small to deal with a full-scale vampire nest moving in. The closest pack we had for support was my father's. He was on the other side of Portland. This was going to be an issue for him, as well.

"Where are the other domestic properties located?" I asked Nash.

"None in Arbington, four in the towns surrounding us and then five in the towns surrounding your father's pack lands. They've been careful not to buy anything on pack lands," Nash said, shuffling through a file of papers which I hadn't noticed sat by him on the table until now.

"Any activity at the warehouse yet?"

"No, but there have been applications filed for a change of use. I'm trying to get copies to see what it is."

"Okay, keep an eye on the properties. Let me know as soon as there is any kind of activity at any of them. I want a copy of the change of use application as soon as you have it.

Also, we need to try and identify which nest is moving in here and why. I'll contact my father to let him know the situation. Once we have the rest of the details, we're going to have to decide if we need to take this to Council."

I looked at Tanner out of the corner of my eye, and I could see him shifting uneasily. He hated getting involved with the Council because he hated his father. It went far beyond him not liking to talk with him. Tanner's father was disappointed that he wasn't Alpha of his own pack. He tried to push him to challenge me for the Alpha position the last time he saw him. Tanner had no interest in being an Alpha, and if his father had taken any time to get to know his son during his childhood or adult life, he would know that Tanner was an amazing beta.

My wolf was finally starting to settle now that we had a plan in place when I felt a rush of emotion through the pack bond: sudden and overwhelming panic and fear. One of our pack was in trouble. I bolted to my feet and rushed to the front door with Tanner, River and Nash on my heels.

"Who is it?" Tanner asked. "Who is it coming from?"

I couldn't filter the feelings with my own, and I threw back my head and let loose a howl. The sorrowful howl that answered it was un-mistakenly Wallace. All four of us shifted and ran towards the cabin he shared with his family. His fear was slamming through the pack bond, and it had my wolf racing, ready to fight.

When we reached the cabin, the front door was open, and Kelly was curled in a ball on the floor just inside, weeping hysterically. Wallace had shifted, and he was scenting the ground around the cabin. He was running back and forth, trying to catch a scent. His grief and panic were nearly overwhelming. Sensing no threat in the area, we all shifted. Nash went straight to Kelly and pulled her into his arms, and she just clung to him crying. Wallace bared his teeth at the sight of Nash with his wife and lunged for him. I caught him by the scruff of his neck and shook him harshly.

"Shift!" I yelled at him. He struggled against my hold, and I forced a wave of my Alpha power toward him, forcing him to comply. It was a painful process, and he landed on his knees beside me panting.

"I'm sorry, I … my wolf is losing control," he panted. "Coby …" He was looking around the cabin, his eyes wide with fear.

"What's happened?" I asked crouching beside him.

"He's gone, Coby is gone," he shouted. I could see Wallace struggling to contain his wolf and the urge to shift becoming overwhelming. "They've taken him."

I put my hands on Wallace's shoulders and fed a wave of my power down into him. Not as harsh as the last, but gentle and calming. I needed him to be calmer. "You need to control your wolf, Wallace. I don't want to have to cage you. We need to know what's happened so we can find Coby. Who has taken him?" I asked, even as the dread started to form in my stomach.

"We put him to bed about half an hour ago. He wasn't feeling well. When I went in to check on him, he was gone. His room, there's the scent of a witch in there," he finished on a sob, and he hung his head as tears rolled down his face. I pulled him to me and held him. Coby was the first pup born to our pack, and it was the happiest day in our pack history. We all doted on him.

"Tanner, I need you to shift and run the perimeter as quickly as you can. I want to know anything you can pick up, any foreign scent at all, no matter what. River, go back to the house and gather the pack, we need to spread out and search the area. Nash, will you stay here with Kelly?" I asked.

He nodded grimly. Kelly was curled in his lap rocking. Silent tears fell down her face, but she had stopped making any noise.

"Wallace, I'm assuming you want to search with us?" I asked him.

Wallace determinedly got to his feet, and nodded once at me. He went over to his wife and pulled her from Nash's lap, holding her close. He whispered in her ear, no doubt telling her he was going to find their boy. I only hoped we wouldn't make a liar out of him. Witches could hide their scent for short periods. If they could cover enough ground while doing so, we could lose their trail.

Everyone scattered to do their jobs. I shifted back into my wolf and took off to run the perimeter in the opposite direction than Tanner had taken. We needed to be quick. Once they had him in a secure place, it wouldn't take them long to start draining the natural magic out of Coby. He was only seven, and I didn't know how long he would last once the drain began.

20

CALLI

Jacob was getting ready for bed, and I was pacing the house, my mind racing with thoughts of the guys and the letter my father had left. I didn't understand what my father had meant about trusting my wolf. My wolf was pushing me towards the guys, but that wasn't safe for Jacob. I didn't know what to do. My wolf was just as confused and distressed as I was. The urge to shift was overwhelming. It had been so long. I was stupid to keep putting it off. If I didn't shift soon, any emotional overload could cause a spontaneous shift, and I couldn't afford to do that in front of anyone else. I had enough troubles without alerting the Shifter Council to my presence as well. I shuddered, and it was almost like I could feel the fur just under my skin, aching to push through. Fuck! How had I let it get this bad? Why was I continually fucking this up?

My wolf was worrying about Jacob just as much as I was and I realised that if I could maybe reassure her on one of our problems, she might be a bit less volatile. I could hear Jacob climbing into his bed, and with a sigh of relief, I let the change take over me. I had never had any trouble with changing. It didn't hurt at all; it felt more like a sense of calm that took over. Some times I wondered if the wolf was my true form, and I was actually a wolf that could turn into a human rather than the other way around. As soon as I had all four paws on the ground, I shook out my white coat and padded across the house into Jacob's room. We used to do this all the time before I went away travelling and I don't know why I hadn't thought of it before.

Jacob was already snuggled down under his covers, but his little face lit up when he saw me, and he sat up again.

"Calli!" he cheered.

I jumped up onto the bed and nudged his chest with my head to make him lay back down again. I couldn't communicate with him when I was a wolf because Jacob hadn't shifted yet. I had been able to speak with my father when we were both in wolf form, and it was another reason why I was a freak. It shouldn't have been possible, but the pack link which my father and I had formed, allowed us to speak with each other. He had explained to me that he had never heard of any other packs being able to do so and we chalked it up to something else screwy that my magic let me do. Once Jacob went through his first change, and we formed a pack bond, I was hoping we would have the same kind of link. Thankfully headbutting was also an effective form of communication though because Jacob laid back down in his bed. I laid down next to him, and he curled his little body around me, holding onto my fur tightly in his little hands. My wolf sighed in happiness. We may not have a formal pack bond, but Jacob was pack to us, he was our pup. I should have realised that being with her pack would help my wolf through this.

"I've missed you," Jacob whispered, burying his face into my fur. I felt his tears against my fur, and I felt like the worst sister in the world. I should have realised that Jacob would need this pack bond as well. I felt like I was constantly failing at everything at the moment.

I shifted slightly on the bed so I could lay my head on his chest and look up at him.

"I miss them," he whispered to me. "I know you miss them too."

I whimpered in agreement. It was the only way I could speak with him in this form.

"I think I can feel my wolf," Jacob admitted, and my ears pricked up in interest. Jacob was only five. He shouldn't be able to shift until he hit puberty unless he had an Alpha that was able to help him through the shift. I had first shifted when I was four, but that was because of my magic. We had always assumed that Jacob hadn't inherited any magic when he didn't shift last year, but if he felt his wolf now, he must have something. This was the downside of Jacob having a permanent protection spell. Mine was in my amulet so I could take it off, whereas Jacob's was a tattoo. His was a next-generation spell that Mum's friend had thankfully continued working on after she'd made mine. But because Jacob couldn't take it off, there was no way to tell if his scent had changed.

"He's sad too," Jacob told me, and I felt my heart break for him. "But he helps me to feel better. He looks after me, and I will look after him. You haven't been looking after your wolf Calli." He had such a serious little look on his face, and it was adorable. Annoyingly though, he was also right. "You need to let her run."

I whimpered again and laid my head on his chest. My ears flattened back on my head. My baby brother was telling me off.

"I'm not a baby. You can go outside and run when I'm

asleep, you know." He was completely serious, but I wasn't sure if I agreed with him.

What if something happened? What if someone broke into the house? Or if there was a fire? Or if Jacob got hurt and I wasn't here to help him?

"Stop hogging the bed and go for a run. I'm trying to sleep," Jacob sighed, rolling over.

I rolled my eyes and jumped off the bed. Sometimes it felt like he was just a really small forty-year-old man. It was hard to be annoyed with him though, because this was the most he had spoken since we had lost our parents. It was like he was his old self again. I should have realised he would have found talking to my wolf easier than talking to anyone else. He had always told her all of his secrets.

The cabin we lived in was set back in the woods and isolated. We had a lot of land, all of it forest. There wasn't another house around for miles. The problem was that my land backed up to the pack lands. I couldn't afford to run into one of them if I was out for a run. But, the chain on my talisman was long enough that I could keep it on even in my wolf form, so I didn't have to worry about leaving a scent trail.

Deciding that Jacob was right, I slipped out of the back door. I didn't want to leave him alone in the house. He was far too young and my wolf and I were both anxious about leaving him. I consoled her that we would have a short run, but we couldn't move out of hearing of the house. She was more than happy with the compromise. As soon as I had the lay of the land, I would be able to risk shifting in the daytime when Jacob was safe at school.

My white coat wasn't exactly conducive to camouflaging me in the night, but with the thin layering of snow on the ground, it worked quite well in this weather. I stretched out, enjoying the feeling of finally being able to be shifted outside. I lifted my nose and scented the air. There was nothing nearby apart from a few critters, and I took off at a slow run into the forest. If I stayed near the treeline, the house would always remain in sight, and my wolf could easily hear if anyone were approaching it.

My wolf was ecstatic to be free to run. We quickly scented a rabbit and chased it joyfully. We had no intention of catching it. We weren't hungry, and we couldn't afford to get too distracted and wander too far from the house.

About fifteen minutes in I heard a noise that didn't belong. I flattened myself down into a snowdrift and listened. It was definitely the sound of running, but it sounded more like people rather than wolves. It was coming from the North, in the direction of the pack lands but it was heading towards me. When they stopped, I could hear a low murmured conversation. I stayed low to the ground and crept forward on my belly. I needed to know if these people were a danger and if they were heading towards the house so that I could quickly return to Jacob. My wolf did not like that we had these people on our territory. Especially not so close to our den and our brother. No one should be in this part of the forest because it was part of the land that belonged to our property.

Before I reached them, I heard two people take off running in separate directions. Neither was heading towards the house, so I decided to creep closer to those who had stayed. Once I was close enough, I hunkered down behind a large tree and peered into a small clearing to see what they were doing. There were three people, two men and one woman, standing in the clearing talking. It seemed like they were arguing, but they were speaking low, and the wind was blowing in the wrong direction for me to make out much of what they were saying. There was something off about them.

The woman was clearly agitated, and she threw her hands up in the air in defeat before turning her back on the men. That was when I caught the scent of a witch. They must have been masking their scent until now. They could only do it for short periods. My talisman was the only reason why I could hide my scent permanently, but it was an age-old secret that one of my mother's friends had discovered and the process was not common knowledge. Thankfully she disagreed with how the covens were being run, and it was a secret which she would never make known. It could have devastating consequences if it were.

They continued to bicker, clearly not paying attention to their surroundings. If they were, they would have surely heard it coming. An enormous black wolf burst out of the trees and took the woman down, tearing its teeth into her throat. She was dead before she even hit the floor. The two men separated and started to try and circle the wolf. He was incensed, snapping and slathering at the two male witches. I caught his scent on the wind, and I realised that this wolf was Grey. He was magnificent. Bigger than any wolf I'd ever seen. I had heard that Alpha wolves were larger, but I had never seen one. The only male wolf I had ever seen was my father, and he wasn't an Alpha. One of the witches feinted towards him, causing Grey to dart forward, snapping his teeth.

I was frozen to the spot. I didn't know what to do. These witches were obviously used to fighting wolves. They had separated so that one of them could stay in Grey's blind spot. It may sacrifice one of them, but between the two of them, it seemed unlikely that Grey would make it out of this fight unharmed. He no longer had the element of surprise on his side. I wanted to help him, but I didn't know what he would do if he realised who I was. I couldn't risk Jacob. My mind was racing, and I was torn between two terrible outcomes.

In the end, the decision was made for me. One of the witches darted into Grey, and he leapt to engage him. The witch he had taken his eyes off pulled a vicious looking hunting knife and leapt for Grey's back. Instinct took over. I couldn't stand by and watch them kill him. I darted out of my hiding place and lunged for the witch with the knife. I latched my jaws around his wrist and shook with all that I had. He screamed and dropped the knife. I lost my grip, and the witch fell to the ground and started to crawl away from me. I could hear Grey snarling and snapping behind me, but I didn't dare take my eyes off the threat in front of me. He couldn't be allowed to live. He had seen me, and I couldn't risk him telling someone about me. I lowered myself closer to the ground and stalked towards him. He was terrified, so I felt fairly confident that he had no other weapons. Once I was close enough, I lunged killing him as quickly as possible. I wasn't the type of person that would want him to suffer, but I wouldn't put his life above that of Jacob's, and I would do anything to keep my brother safe. As usual, I had fucked this situation up enough already.

As I turned to see what was happening in the fight behind me, I saw Grey locked down on the arm of the last remaining witch. The witch screamed in pain, but I saw him pull his hunting knife from his back. There was no way that Grey could know he had done so, I barked out a warning as I saw the witch swing the knife across Grey's belly. The sound of his yelp tore into my soul, and my wolf flew at the witch who dared harm him. He was so distracted with trying to dislodge the wolf on his arm that he didn't even see me coming. I leapt at his back and locked my jaws around the side of his neck. I felt his jugular pulse once before I closed my jaws and ripped it open. Grey released his grip from the witch's arm and dropped to the ground. He crawled a short distance away before his great head dropped with a huff. The witch had already fallen to the ground dead.

I ran over to Grey and snuffled my nose into his neck. I could scent blood all over him. The knife must have cut him deeply. He took a deep pained breath, and then he shifted back to his human form in front of me. His eyes locked with mine and I saw pain and confusion moving across them. I looked around us. There was no one else here, and I couldn't hear anyone else coming to his aid. I couldn't leave him here to die, not when I had the power to help him. I whined and lowered my head to him again. He raised his hand with a look of wonder on his face. I thought that he was going to stroke my head, but he stopped short at my neck. I realised then that he had the talisman in his hand having recognised it.

"Calli?" he whispered and then his eyes rolled back in his head and he passed out.

I shifted back to my human form and rolled him onto his back. Moving his shirt aside, I could see a deep gash running straight across his abdomen. He was bleeding out heavily. I was already on my knees next to him, and I clutched my hands in my hair. A terrible, terrible part of me realised that I could just let him die here and no one would ever know. My secret would die with him, and Jacob would be safe. But I couldn't do that. I couldn't do that to him. I shook out my hands at my side and gently placed them over his wound. I felt deep down inside me for the magic I kept suppressed, and pulled it up to the surface. My hands started to feel pleasantly warm, and I knew it was working. It was the only magic my mother had ever risked to teach me—the magic to heal. The wound was deep, and Grey had already lost a lot of blood. I could feel that he was teetering on the edge of death. The more magic I flooded into him, the more I felt him moving away from that ledge and tears came to my eyes, falling fast down my cheeks.

I pushed as much as I could into him, but it still wasn't enough. Any one witch could only hold a certain amount of power. Once that well of power was drained, continuing meant drawing on your own power, your own lifeforce. I could hear my heartbeat slowing in my ears. My vision was becoming cloudy. It wouldn't be long before I would use more than I could sustain, and I would lose consciousness. I needed to bring Grey back enough that he would be able to protect himself once I passed out. I could only hope that if I begged, he would understand. "Come on, Grey, come back, don't do this," I pleaded with him.

The last thought that I had before I slipped into unconsciousness was of Jacob. What had I done?

21

CALLI

I came to slowly. It was like I was waking up from my feet up. I knew I was sitting up. As I tried to shift my weight, I also realised that I was bound to a chair. I guess Grey hadn't been as understanding as I had hoped. *You've really fucked up here Calli!*

I tried not to move too much. I needed to come back to myself before I gave away that I was awake. Breathing in through my nose, I didn't recognise any of the scents around me. I was definitely inside, but I could feel the sun on my skin. It must be the next morning, which would mean I had been out of it for several hours. I could smell the scent of wolves thick in the air, so I had to be at the packhouse. Well, at least I wasn't with the witches. That was one small positive out of this whole shit show.

"I know you're awake," a male voice growled from in front of me.

I hesitantly opened my eyes, and I saw a tall man in front of me with buzzed dark hair and a days worth of stubble on his face. I didn't recognise him. He was over six foot tall and well-built, both of his arms had full tattoo sleeves, but the most noticeable thing about him was that he was definitely a wolf. When I locked eyes with him, he angrily strode forward. Grabbing my shoulders, he tipped the chair backwards, screaming in my face. "Where is my son?"

Panic flooded me. I was locked in a room with an angry shifter, and I had no idea what he was talking about. "I don't know. I don't know anything about your son," I whimpered.

"Don't lie to me," he seethed through gritted teeth.

I barely even saw him move, but pain exploded in my face as he backhanded me. The chair tipped precariously to the side, but he caught it and pulled it back towards him before backhanding me again. The pain was nearly unbearable. Tears poured down my face, and I begged him to stop. I cried out that I didn't know what he was talking about but the more that I begged, the angrier he became. He punched me hard in the stomach, the bindings preventing me from bending forward in response to the blow. I'd been in fights before, and I had sparred in class, but I had never faced the full wrath of a shifter. He backhanded me again on the other side of my head, and I felt blood starting to pour from my eyebrow with the explosion of pain. He followed it with another brutal punch to my stomach. I knew that blood poured from the corner of my mouth, and I was pretty confident that he split one of my eyebrows open as I could feel something warm running down the side of my face. Then it was like my brain just let go of reality to try and save me. The blows kept raining down on me, and I felt my ribs breaking with blow after blow. The pain was unbearable, and I could feel the blackness starting to creep in around my vision again.

There was a scuffle at the door, and it was ripped open with people running inside. Two men tackled the shifter who was beating me and dragged him away. I sagged forward as much as my bindings would allow. Blood was pouring out of my mouth. I think I'd bitten my tongue at some point. Unconsciousness was pulling at me, begging me to just let go and feel the bliss of nothing for a while. They dragged the angry shifter out of the room, and then I heard the door lock behind them. Gritting my teeth, I panted through the pain. I couldn't pass out now; I needed to get out of here. When I had sucked in enough air to calm my tears, I hesitantly looked around me. I was in a small room that was unfurnished apart from the chair that I was sat in. There was a small window behind me that I could just make out over my shoulder. I needed to get out of here. I needed to get Jacob, and we needed to run. From what I could see out the window, the sun was only just rising so I hadn't been out of it for as long as I had initially thought. Hopefully, Jacob hadn't woken in the night. He would be so scared if he woke up and found me gone. I had been so stupid. I should never have gone on that run. I should have just shifted in the house to tide me over for a while.

I struggled against my bindings, but they didn't budge. When I looked down, I saw that they were some kind of nylon rope, similar to a climbing rope. It would be strong, and there would be no breaking it. I might be able to cut through it though. I shifted one of my fingernails to form a deadly claw. My father had been so proud of me the first time I had managed it. Only the strongest of shifters can partially shift a part of their body. It was a rare talent. It took me several painstaking minutes, but I was able to saw through the ropes at my wrists.

When I did so, I felt the rope around my chest slacken and then drop. I pulled my arms back to my front. My shoulders screamed out in agony at the movement, but I couldn't afford to stop. I had no way of knowing when someone could be coming back. I made quick work of the ropes at my ankles, and I staggered to my feet and over to the small window. I knew that some of my ribs were broken and it was difficult to breathe. Every movement I made was pure agony, but I could feel the adrenaline starting to pump through my body. I just needed to make it out of here and get Jacob to safety; then I could crash. But right now, I couldn't afford to let myself give in to the pain that wanted to flood through my body.

I was careful to stay off to the side as I peered out the window, just in case anyone was standing guard. I couldn't see anyone, and I knew that my time was running out. I quietly unlatched the window and pulled it up. No one shouted out, and I heard no movement, so I pulled myself up and climbed out. I fell more than jumped out of the window and landed heavily on my knees. The pain flared through me, and white light flashed across my vision. It took everything in me to suppress, not just the scream of pain that I wanted to make, but also the surge of vomit trying to force its way out. The tree line was only twenty metres or so in front of me. If I ran and I could get enough of a head start I might make it. I pressed myself against the wall while I took one last look around. I couldn't see anyone, and it was now, or never, so I took a deep breath and then pushed off from the wall running for all that I was worth.

"Not so fast witch," came the voice of the buzzcut shifter from behind me. Normally I would have kept running, but Jacob's scent filled my head, and I stopped and slowly turned around.

I saw him holding onto a squirming Jacob, who was trying to get to me. There were two other men with him that I didn't know—the ones who had pulled him from the room. I wrapped one arm around my stomach and winced as the pain from the beating pounded through me. Where was Grey? I was sure I'd healed him enough before I passed out. Surely, he wouldn't have just left me to these men.

The front door of the house burst open, and Tanner appeared in the doorway. I had never seen him so angry, and I'm pretty sure that a large amount of that anger was directed at me.

"Wallace, what are you thinking?" he shouted, storming down the steps towards him.

"You should stay inside Beta. We decided you would stay away from the witch because we don't know what she has done to your wolves," he snarled.

Tanner clearly didn't like the challenge in Wallace's voice, and he snarled at him. While the two stood off with each other, Jacob took the opportunity to sink his teeth into Wallace's arm, who swore loudly and thankfully loosened his grip on him. Jacob tore towards me, and I had never felt as relieved as I did when I had him in my arms. I pushed him behind me. "Did they hurt you?" I asked him through gritted teeth. My wolf was angry. This man had dared to touch Jacob, and she was ready for blood.

I felt Jacob cling to me and his head shake. He was shaking, and I would never forgive myself for putting him through this.

Tanner seemed to have gotten control of the situation. "We would never hurt him Calli," he growled.

Wallace just snarled. "He may not, but I will rip him apart in front of you if you don't tell me where my son is."

Everything happened in slow motion then. I pulled Jacob's arms from around me, and my wolf burst out of me a snarling, angry beast. No one was allowed to threaten our brother. I stood in front of Jacob, shielding him with my body as I snarled and snapped in the direction of the male shifters. They all staggered back in shock.

"How is this possible?" Tanner murmured.

"It's just a witch trick," Wallace barked.

"No," said one of the men clearly and calmly from behind him. The two of them had remained silent until now, but he stepped forward and laid his hand on Wallace's shoulder. "Only those with a dual soul can shift form like this. She would have to be a born shifter to be able to become a full wolf."

Tanner and the other wolf stared at me in wonder, and I continued to bare my teeth at them. I felt Jacob's little hand clutch at the fur at my back, and I curved my body so that I could lean against him but keep my face, and more importantly my teeth, in the direction of those that would harm us.

The front door burst open for the second time, and Grey staggered through, his arm around River who was helping him walk. "Stand the fuck down," he bellowed, and a wave of Alpha power flooded the area.

Wallace and the two other shifters dropped down to one knee under the pressure of the wave. Tanner wavered, but he didn't fall. Jacob whimpered and clutched me tighter, making me snarl and snap at the shifters even more.

River's eyes were wide in shock as he helped Grey walk down the steps and in front of the other shifters. When he stood still between them and me, Grey pushed River away. "Calli, look at me," he sighed.

I looked him dead in the eye, but my upper lip was pulled up and my teeth fully on display. "I will never hurt you or Jacob. I could never. I didn't understand before. You're an impossibility; how was I supposed to know what I was feeling." Then he added quietly, "Mate."

Grey dropped to his knees in front of me, making sure that he held my gaze. I felt it then, what I had always felt and didn't understand, what I felt for all three of them. My wolf calmed, and I took a hesitant step forward towards Grey. The other shifters behind him had fallen silent. Jacob let go of my fur, and I took a few more steps to Grey. He sat back on his haunches, and then he did the only thing that he could to gain my trust in him completely. He leant his head to the side and exposed his neck to me. I walked cautiously to him. I kept casting my gaze from him to the pack of shifters behind him. They didn't move. Once I had reached Grey, I tentatively reached out with my nose and sniffed his neck. I saw Wallace flinch and I pulled back from Grey and immediately snarled.

"It's okay, Calli," Grey said. "No one will hurt you. I will protect you with my life. Both of you." He smiled gently at me, and I moved forward, bumping my head against his chest.

The relief that flowed through me was immense. He was mine. He had named me mate, and my wolf assured me that he was right. Though, she didn't need to. I could feel it.

Grey brought his arms slowly up to hold me, but as soon as he touched my left side, I whimpered loudly, and he pulled his arms back quickly with a confused look on his face. I felt the pain come rushing back as my adrenaline started to fade. I took a steadying breath and shifted back to my human form. The pain was excruciating, and I cried out before slumping forwards. Grey was there to catch me, and he held me gently. His right arm wrapped protectively around me, and his left hand hovered over my face. It was probably starting to bruise now. I must look terrible.

"Who harmed my mate?" Grey roared.

Wallace immediately dropped to his knees and bared his neck to Grey. "I didn't know. I didn't know," he muttered over and over again.

Grey was beyond pissed, and if he didn't have me cradled in his arms, I think he would've killed Wallace. I couldn't concentrate on him now, though. There was only one person that mattered. I pushed Grey's arms off me and struggled to my knees. I had to get to Jacob. I crawled one step toward him before falling forwards on my hands. My head and my torso hurt more than I could have ever imagined. I shuffled forward another step. Even though he was terrified of every other shifter who stood in front of him, Jacob ran to me. He was the bravest kid that I knew. I held out my arms to him, and he fell against me. The pain flared again so much that I thought I would be sick, but I didn't make a noise as I held him tightly against me.

"I'm so sorry, little guy. I'm so sorry. I said that I would protect you, and I failed." The tears fell from my eyes, and I wept just from the pure relief of holding him.

I heard Grey muttering to the people behind us and some of them moving inside and away from us. Grey staggered back to my side and dropped to his knees beside me. He gently ran a hand soothingly over my back, and I sighed at the touch. I lifted my head and looked at him over the top of Jacob's head. Tanner and River were both stood behind him looking anxiously at me.

When I finally had my tears under control, I felt like I was able to speak. "What happened to his son?" I asked.

"Coby was taken from his bedroom last night by a witch," Grey said sadly. "He's only seven."

The shock hit me hard. That could easily have been Jacob if his scent wasn't so well hidden. I would never forgive Wallace for what he had done, but I could understand why.

Grey gently placed his hand against my face. "I'm so sorry. I was still unconscious when they found us. I didn't have a chance to tell them that you saved me," he smiled.

It was then that I remembered his wound and I quickly pulled up his shirt and ran my fingers over his now flawless stomach before sighing in relief. "I wasn't sure I would be able to heal you enough before I passed out."

"You are one ferocious little wolf," he smiled. "I am honoured to call you mate."

Tanner and River watched us anxiously, and my eyes flicked back and forth from them to Grey. "It's okay, Calli. I know they feel it too, and my wolf has no problem recognising them."

Tanner and River moved forward, so the four of us were surrounding Jacob, who was now curled up against me. They dropped to their knees simultaneously and bared their necks to me. I leant toward Tanner, who had dropped down next me, and I ran my nose up the side of his neck. He shuddered and sighed. Then I placed a small kiss on his neck, and he whispered, "Mate."

Then I leaned forwards to reach River and did the same to him. It was awkward with Jacob curled between us, but I would not let go of him for all the world at the moment. River sighed, "Mate," when he felt my touch, and then they all moved as one and carefully embraced me. It felt right to be surrounded by my mates, and my wolf sighed happily deep inside me.

I sat back and untangled myself from their arms. "There were two others, I think," I told Grey. "I was out running when I heard people moving through the woods then stop. I could hear them talking. I went to see what was happening, but before I got there, I heard some run off. I think there were two that left. When I reached the clearing, I saw the remaining three arguing and then you burst out of the trees and you know what happened next," I panted in pain. Talking was not easy when you had several broken ribs.

"Yes, you saved me … twice." He smiled, and Tanner and River smiled at me, clearly proud of their mate.

"Do you have a map?" I asked them. "I think I can point you in the direction they went."

Tanner and River quickly got to their feet, and River rushed to the house no doubt searching for a map. Grey leant down and ran a hand down Jacob's back. "Can you forgive us for misunderstanding little man?" he asked Jacob.

Jacob looked up, his face streaked with the silent tears none of us had known he was crying, and my heart broke for him. A look of complete anguish bled across Grey's face as he realised what they had truly done. He held out his arms to Jacob, and he fell into them. Grey held him gently to him, rocking him and stroking his hand up and down his back. "I'm so sorry, Jacob. I can never make up for what has happened here today." Jacob's little arms wrapped around Grey and he snuggled into him.

Even though it must have hurt him, Grey stood with Jacob cradled in his arms. Tanner was immediately at my side. I tried to stand, but he swept me up into his arms. He nuzzled his face into my neck, and I felt his tears. When I looked back, two had fallen onto his cheeks. "We failed you," he said simply, and I stroked my hand down his cheek.

"It doesn't matter now. We need to find the missing boy," I told him.

Tanner gave me a sad nod and started to walk back to the house. We followed Grey into a living room where he had put Jacob onto a sofa and wrapped him up with a soft blanket. He sat by his side and lifted one arm so that he could snuggle up against him. River brought the map into the room and laid it out on the coffee table, but before he did anything else, he turned to Jacob and asked him, "Do you need anything, little man?"

River nodded as Jacob whispered something to him, and then he got up and left the room. He returned a minute or so later with a glass of milk and cookies, which he passed to Jacob with a smile. Jacob sipped on his milk and looked a little better for it. I hoped that this had not traumatised him so much that he was set back to how he was when he barely spoke to anyone.

Kneeling at the coffee table, I peered down at the map. "Can you point out where you found us?" I asked.

Tanner looked over the map. "This is your house, our house and where we found you," he said, pointing at the various places on the map.

I followed my finger from my house to the route I thought I had taken when I was running and stopped at the clearing. "They came this way." I said, moving my hand over the map, "and then two of them split off from the clearing, one heading this way and the other this way. I'm sorry, I can't tell you more. I didn't see them, so I don't know if they had the boy with them."

Grey shuffled to the edge of the seat and looked at the map. Two of the men from earlier came into the room as I explained what I heard. One of them was on a laptop, and the other stared at the map with us. I hadn't missed Wallace come and stand in the doorway, but I couldn't look at him, not yet. Not while I was still hurting so much.

I noticed something on the map and went to point at it. The sudden movement caused a flash of pain through my side, and I grunted at the sudden pain. "What's this?" I breathed out.

Tanner was immediately at my side. "Come on," he said, lifting me onto the sofa and settling me back. "Blake, can you get me the first aid kit, please?" he asked the other man who had come to look at the map too.

"I'm fine Tanner. You don't need to fuss over me," I said, trying to swat his hands away.

"You are not fine. You're in pain, and your eyebrow has started bleeding again," he said, pointing at my face. I reached my hand up to my face, and sure enough, it came away with blood on it.

Blake rushed back in with the first aid kit and opened it up beside me. He passed Tanner a gauze pad who pressed it against my eyebrow. "Hold this here for a minute," Tanner instructed me, and I reached up to press my hand against it. "Calli, I need to lift your shirt and check your abdomen, is that okay?" he asked me gently.

"Erm, okay," I said, suddenly nervous.

Tanner gently pushed my shoulders so that I was leaning back against the sofa, and then he took the bottom of my shirt in his hands and slowly pushed it up. If it weren't for the pain that I was trying to pretend that I wasn't in, it would have been quite erotic. I could feel myself growing wet despite how much I was hurting. I knew Tanner caught the scent of my arousal because he looked up and grinned as his need flashed through his own eyes. That fell away, however, when he looked down and saw the state of my stomach. There were angry red marks across most of my abdomen and two spots, one over the bottom of my left ribs and one over my right kidney, were darkening to purple. A growl started low in Tanner's throat, and I ran my hand through his hair to try and calm him.

Grey was obviously watching, and I was glad that he was taking Jacob into account and not completely losing it. "River, fetch some ice and call Aidan to join us. I need to address the pack."

River got up silently, but I didn't miss the way that he shoved Wallace out of his way as he left the room.

I turned my attention back to Tanner, who had tucked my shirt into the bottom of my bra to hold it up out of the way. "We're going to get some ice on that, to help with the bruising," he said gently. Then he reached up and pulled the gauze away from my eyebrow. He leaned in closer to look at the wound. "It shouldn't need stitching. We should be okay with just a butterfly bandage. Do you heal the same as we do?" he asked, sitting back and rummaging through the first aid kit.

"Yes, I think so."

"Wait, can't you heal yourself like you did me?" Grey asked.

"Unfortunately, no. Even if I could, I'm going to be tapped out for quite a while. You completely drained me," I answered quietly.

"So, you are a witch," Wallace snarled from the doorway just as River returned with his ice and a man that I didn't know followed behind him, who must have been Aidan.

All of the men watched quietly as Tanner wrapped the ice in a towel that River had brought with him and laid it on the bruising over my right kidney area. I hissed as he pressed it against me, but then I held it against my side so that he could apply the butterfly bandage to the cut above my eye. When he was done, he gently nuzzled into my neck, and I rubbed my head over his as he did it.

No one said anything for a while. Aidan was the first to break. "What happened to her?" he stuttered.

"Wallace," Grey growled.

Wallace didn't even look ashamed of himself, as far as he was concerned, I had deserved a beating just because of what I was. I might be currently sat in the home of my mates, but it wasn't safe here. Aidan had turned to Wallace with a look of horror on his face. "What the fuck, man?"

"She's just a witch," he scoffed.

A vicious growl ripped from Grey and Jacob tensed at his side. As soon as he did Grey's growl dropped, I felt the calming Alpha waves coming off him as he tried to settle Jacob again. Grey looked over at Tanner, nothing was said, but Tanner just nodded and then stalked out of the room. As he passed Wallace, he grabbed him by the scruff of the neck and hauled him out of the room.

Grey turned to the rest of the men in his pack. "This should not need to be said. Stoneridge is a small pack, but I believe we are a pack with honour. We do not beat women. I don't care what anyone thinks they are or what they have done. Calli is my mate. She is mate to Tanner, River and I. You will treat her with respect. Wallace is going to have a lesson in where his place is. I will not afford anyone else the luxury of the same lesson. If anyone steps out of line on this, I will consider it a direct challenge, and you will face me personally. Do we have an understanding?"

The men in the room all sounded off with a, "Yes, Alpha," and then we drifted into an uneasy silence.

Aidan looked at me, and I could see he wanted to say something. I gave him a smile and a nod hoping that he would realise I wouldn't be upset by the question he clearly wanted to ask. His eyes flicked to Grey and then back to me. "You can ask," I told him. "I know that you have questions and you won't insult me by asking them. Perhaps it will help clear some air."

Aidan again looked at Grey who I saw out of the corner of my eye give him a small nod. "Are you a witch?" he asked quietly.

"I'm a hybrid," I clarified. "My mother was a witch, and my father was a shifter."

"That shouldn't be possible," said the man with the laptop who I believed was called Nash.

"Why?" I asked him.

"I have heard of other mixed species couples," he shifted nervously looking around. Perhaps this wasn't information that the rest of the pack had. "None of them were able to conceive a child."

"Well, I am living proof that it is possible. And so is Jacob." I smiled across at my brother, who was peeking out from behind Grey, and he gave me a small smile back.

"So, you can shift?" Aidan asked.

"Yeah, and she shifts into a beautiful white wolf," River smiled.

"And you have witch magic too?" Aidan asked again.

"Yes, but I don't know the extent of it. My mother only taught me how to heal. We lived under the radar, constantly looking over our shoulders. She didn't think it was safe to actively teach me magic," I said quietly.

"You're a healer?" Blake asked, perking up.

"Yes, I can heal most wounds and some illnesses, but illness is a bit more tricky than a physical injury." This didn't seem to be going too badly so far, with the exception of Wallace. But his son was missing, and if that had been Jacob, I'm not sure that I would be acting any differently than him.

Blake leaned forwards in his seat. "Would you look at my wife? She isn't feeling well, and she's due to have our baby in the next few months."

"What's wrong with Jean?" Grey asked, suddenly looking concerned.

"I'm not sure. It's been coming on for a week. She's tired all the time. At first, we put it down to the pregnancy, but it's getting really bad. She couldn't get out of bed this morning, and she can't stomach any food without being sick. She's barely keeping water down." He looked near frantic by the time that he had finished explaining.

"You should have said something earlier," Grey told him.

"If you take me to her, I can look at her now. I don't know

how much I can do straight away, though. It took all of my magic and more to heal Grey's wounds." This wasn't good if she felt this way, and she still had two months of the pregnancy to go.

Blake got out of his chair. "I can take you to her now. We live in a cabin just a short walk from here." He had a look of relief on his face, and I hoped that I could live up to the hope that he now seemed to have.

"Wait, what are you going to do about the child?" I asked, turning to Grey.

"We'll scout in the directions that you heard the others go in and see if we can pick up Coby's scent," Grey answered. He got up and started to organise the pack into two teams.

"What did you see earlier, Calli? When you were looking at the map," Nash asked me.

"Oh," I looked back at the map and scanned it again to try and find what had caught my eye. "Here, there's an access road that comes off the main road and runs through the forest for a few miles but then ends in nothing. Seems strange to build a road to nowhere." I ran my finger along the road I had seen.

Nash looked at the map. "I think there's an abandoned wood mill there," he said. He went back to his computer and started furiously typing. "You might be on to something. I haven't been able to find any trace of witches coming into the area through property sales or rentals. They could have set up shop in an abandoned building."

He turned the computer around and showed Grey something on the screen. He nodded and turned back to me with a look of pride on his face. It was nice to see him looking at me like that, and I felt the blush coming to my cheeks. "Calli, I'm going to run with the pack to scout. Will you be okay here? Wallace is locked in the cage. He won't be bothering you."

"Of course, go, I can look after myself and Jacob."

"I will protect her with my life, Alpha," Blake said, lowering his head.

"Nash, go with them to Blake's house, you can hook the laptop to the wifi from there if you need to. Make sure you keep your phone with you in case we need you." Grey ordered leaving the room with the pack following closely behind him.

I walked over to Jacob, who was still snuggled in the corner of the sofa and looking fairly sleepy. "Hey, little man. How are you doing?" I asked him, pulling him into my lap. It hurt like hell to do it, but I didn't want to show any sign of it and scare him any more than he already was.

Jacob didn't say anything, and he just nuzzled into me. Tears sprang to my eyes, this was my fault. I felt Blake's hand on my shoulder, and when I looked up at him, he had an understanding look on his face. "Bring him with us. He can sleep at my house for a while. It's a lot smaller than here and a lot less intimidating."

"Thank you," I whispered. I don't think I could have spoken any louder without the tears starting to fall in earnest. I gathered Jacob up against me and followed Blake out of the room. It hurt so much, though, and my ribs were protesting the extra weight in my arms. Blake gently took Jacob from me, and I walked by his side, holding Jacob's hand. Nash followed closely behind with his laptop and a bag.

Blake was right, and his home only took a few minutes to get to. It was a cute wooden cabin, similar to what I had thought our own home would be like before we arrived. When we entered, it was lovely and warm, and there was an open fire burning in the living room. He put Jacob onto the sofa, and he snuggled down. I could see his eyelids drifting already.

"I'll sit with him," Nash offered, taking up the armchair

across from the fire and setting up his laptop. I gave him my thanks, but I could see that Blake was hovering anxiously by a door across the way from us.

When I followed Blake into his room, I was immediately hit by powerful energy engulfing the room. "What's wrong?" Blake asked.

I shook my head at him, not wanting to worry him too much at the moment and also because a very frightened looking sick woman was watching us from the bed. I walked over and knelt beside the bed so that she wouldn't have to crane her neck to look at me. She was lying on her side, curled up. She had kicked the covers off her, and her simple white nightgown was drenched in sweat. "Hi, I'm Calli," I said, reaching out and taking her hand. "Blake said that you're not feeling too well. Do you mind if I have a look at you?" I asked her gently.

She shook her head, and I gently placed my hand against her head. She was burning hot with a high fever which even I knew was very dangerous for the baby. "Can you get some towels and cold water?" I asked Blake, and he hurried out of the room.

"Jean, has your baby been moving around very much?"

She shook her head and tears sprang to her eyes. "I haven't felt him moving for a few hours." She whispered her voice hoarse.

Blake rushed back into the room with the towels and the water, and I immediately soaked them and wrung them out. I ran them along her face and her arms cleaning away some of the sweat and cooling her burning skin. She sighed in relief. "I'm going to need her to lie flat so that I can have a look at her, but being on her back will be difficult for her. Can you help me get her propped up on some pillows?" I asked, turning to Blake.

He nodded grimly and set about helping me get Jean in position. When she was sitting comfortably, reclining back on the pillows, I wet the towels again and laid a small one over her forehead and one on the back of her neck. I passed the other to Blake and instructed him to keep running it over her arms and chest to try and help her cool down.

"Jean, is it okay if I put my hands on your belly?" I asked her, and she nodded. Her eyes were drooping, and I could see that she was fighting to stay awake.

I sat on the side of the bed and placed a hand on either side of her belly. Closing my eyes, I called forth my magic into my hands. I had very little left, and it wasn't easy to get it to cooperate at first, but once it was where I needed it to be, it seemed keen to help. It was a strange way to describe it. My magic had always felt like a warm presence. Almost like it had a personality of its own. I could feel Jean's essence, and it was not shining as bright as it should be. Worse was that the baby's essence was barely shining at all. It was flickering like a candle. I pulled my magic out of my hands and pushed some of it out into the room. There was something here. Something dark and heavy. It seemed to be somehow tied to Jean and the baby. I sat back and frowned. Jean wasn't ill. There was some kind of magic at work. I nodded to Blake to let him know that I was done and then I stood up. "I'll give you both some time. I'll be out in the living room," I told Blake, leaving the room.

Jacob was sound asleep when I went back into the living room, and Nash was quietly working away on his laptop. He glanced up at me as I approached. "He was out like a light before you'd even left the room." I smiled at him and went over to the small window to look outside. I always found that it helped me think when I could see outside at least if I couldn't be running free in it.

I pushed a little of my magic into this room, but the energy that was flooding the bedroom wasn't in here as well. It was either tied to the room or Jean herself.

Blake came out of the bedroom a few moments later and rushed over to me. "Can you tell what's wrong with her? Can you heal her?"

I didn't want to be the one to have to do this. I guided him over to another armchair in the living room and sat him down. Nash had set his laptop aside and reached over to clasp Blake's shoulder. He must have been able to tell from the look on my face that it wasn't going to be good news. "Jean isn't sick," I told him.

"She is, you saw her," Blake said, shaking his head.

"Someone has placed some kind of spell on her. It was what I could feel when I went into the room. It's drawing energy from the baby, and Jean's body is trying to replace that energy with her own. It's draining them both," I told him.

The look of shock on Blake's face near broke my heart. He started to shake his head in denial as silent tears streamed down his face. "No, no, she's just sick."

"I'm sorry, Blake," I said, taking his hand. "Your baby is very weak. He doesn't have much left to give."

"Can you stop it? Can you break the spell?" he asked me urgently, squeezing my hand.

"I don't know any magic apart from how to heal," I said sadly. Then I started to think about it. There were all the books in the library back at the house. Maybe there would be something there that could help us. The problem was going to be time. I didn't know how much time we had before the baby would die, and I suspected that Jean would closely follow.

"You thought of something," Nash said. "What is it? Anything could help."

"There is a whole library of books back at my house. Maybe we can find something?" I said hesitantly.

"Let's go now," Blake said, standing up.

I cast a look at Nash, and he gave me a sad smile. I took Blake's hand and pulled him back down to the chair. "Blake, the problem that we have is time." He frowned at me, not entirely understanding what I was trying to say. I didn't want to have to be the person that said it. "I think that the solution that we are going to need to look for is to try and do something to save Jean."

Blake just nodded blankly. "I know that," he said trying to stand up, and Nash pushed him back down to the chair again.

"Blake, what I'm trying to say is that I think it's already too late to save your child," I told him.

He just nodded slowly, his eyes going vacant. "You will try, though, won't you?" he asked me quietly.

"I have no experience in this, but I will do whatever I can," I promised him. We all stood up as one. "We need to take Jean with us to my house. The spell in your bedroom is powerful. It may slow down the progress if we remove her from where the energy is collected. Plus, if she is with us and we do find something we can hopefully treat her immediately."

Blake rushed to the bedroom door. "Nash, pull my truck around," he instructed him.

Nash sprinted out of the door, and Blake ran into the bedroom. I could hear him whispering to Jean, and he quickly appeared in the doorway, holding her cradled in his arms. I scooped Jacob up off the sofa and quickly pushed down the sudden urge to vomit. I don't know if it was the pain of picking him up or the realisation that Blake was pinning every hope he had on me saving his family, and I had absolutely no idea what I was doing.

22

GREY

We found the abandoned wood mill. Tanner and River had headed in the opposite direction, tracing the other trail while Aidan and I headed towards the abandoned wood mill. This part of the forest was well outside of our lands. There was something about it that felt abandoned and void of life. The wood mill was beside the river which ran through here. Its old water wheel had collapsed and been washed away a long time ago. The building was old stone and had clearly been abandoned centuries ago. It looked like it should have been condemned and knocked down years ago. Half of the building had collapsed, and the roof was long gone. It had been abandoned for long enough that a relatively large oak tree now grew through the insides of the mill and had sprouted out the part where the roof would once have been. It was kind of ironic if you thought about it.

We ducked down into the undergrowth to watch the building. There was a faint stench of magic floating in the air. It wasn't the light, pleasant fragrance I had smelt when Calli had healed me. It was dark, heavy, and it had a lingering smell of death. I had no doubt we were in the right place.

We knew there could be two witches inside, but we didn't know if there would be more than that. We needed to get a look inside without alerting them to our presence, but I was worried that they'd know we were there as soon as we got close.

To make it easier to talk to Aidan, I shifted back into my human form. I could send him some images and feelings through the pack bond, but it was quicker and more efficient just to speak this way.

"We need to get a look inside to see if they have Coby without them realising we're here," I said.

Aidan nodded and looked grimly at the building. It stood in a clearing, and we had no covered route inside. "I could draw them away while you check inside," he finally said.

"No. I can't put you at risk like that." The best way inside looked to be through the collapsed portion of the building. If we went through the door, there would be no cover, but if we scaled the fallen stones, we should be able to get to the top floor to look inside. The problem was if we dislodged any of the stones in the climb, it would be evident to anyone inside we were there. "I think it would be better for you to return the way we came and meet up with Tanner and River. Bring them back here. I will try and get a look inside while you're gone. If you get back and I'm not here then Tanner will know what to do."

I could see that Aidan wanted to argue with me, but we were in an impossible position. We didn't know how much time Coby had. We couldn't afford to delay. Aidan nodded and said, "Yes, Alpha." Then he shifted back to his wolf and took off at a run, back in the direction we had come from.

We had run for just over an hour to get here. Assuming

that the others were still searching in their direction, it would be several hours before anyone got back here. Sunset was a long time off, and I didn't think Coby had long to wait.

I crept to the edge of the trees and then laid low on my belly, watching the building closely. I couldn't see anyone or any movement inside. There was no way to tell when was going to be a good time so, I guess, now was as good a time as any. I burst from the trees as fast as I could, sprinting across the clearing until I was flush against the wall. The wall must have collapsed some time ago because I could see that the fallen stones were held together with plants and grass growing between the stones. Hopefully, that would help hold them together when I did the climb. I listened carefully and could faintly hear some movement inside. Creeping along the outside wall, I crouched down underneath one of the ground floor windows, listening as hard as I could. There was definitely someone in there. I could hear somebody moving around, but I needed to be able to see what was happening. I crept back along the way I came and looked up at the fallen stones skeptically. This wasn't going to be like climbing some stairs. I could see a clear route but the stability of the stones was a real concern. I was fairly sure that the plant life I had seen earlier should hold the stones stably, but I wasn't sure that I was willing to bet Coby's life on it. I nervously took a few steps up the stack, making sure to keep listening for sounds of anyone approaching. I felt like my heart was beating in my throat. It was hard enough to tolerate a threat to my pack, but for that threat to be against our only pup was nearly unbearable.

I made good time scaling the stones. They were solid as I had thought, but I still made sure to make my way cautiously. The hole in the outer wall on the second floor let me enter the building onto a walkway. Or rather it was a walkway now. On this level, the middle of the floor had collapsed entirely, leaving just a walkway around the outside walls. I crept over to the corner of the building where it was darker and watched the room below.

I could see a young man; he looked in his twenties. He was pacing in the middle of the room. Interestingly there was no rubble inside on the ground floor. It looked like someone had cleared the area out. There were a few boxes stacked on one side. Bags and supplies were stacked up next to them. It looked like they had been holding out here for some time, probably since we had first scented them in the area.

"Where are they?" he huffed, continuing his pacing.

"Just shut up and sit down. They're probably keeping an eye on the first specimen. Once that one is drained, we can drain this one and get the hell out of here. I don't like being so close to this pack," a second voice complained.

The two of them shut up, and I could hear more shuffling down below me. I couldn't see the second person that had spoken, and I couldn't see if there was anyone else in the room below me either. The smell of magic was much more pungent than it had been outside. I couldn't help but wonder why Calli's magic smelled so different.

I crept to the edge of the walkway. As I approached the edge, it whined under my weight. It clearly wasn't as steady as I had thought it had been. Freezing, I hoped it wouldn't collapse from under me.

"What was that?" came the second voice again.

"What?" the pacing man asked, freezing.

"That noise, I heard something."

"Please, this place makes noises constantly. It's only a strong wind away from collapsing. You're being paranoid, like usual," he scoffed.

No one else made any comments. I could hear a soft sniffling sound below me, and it made my ears prick in hope. It could be Coby. I hurried back away from the edge. I needed to get a better view of the part of the room that was below me. One side of the walkway was blocked with some rubble but there looked to be a way around on the other side, even though the floor had degraded nearly all the way to the wall. I shuffled around as quietly as I could. I couldn't afford to make a noise. They would be listening even more closely now.

It was hard going, but I pressed myself to the wall and crept along. My fur ruffled against the rough stones as I nervously made my way across the narrow ledge. I couldn't afford to lose my footing and fall. The fall wouldn't kill me—it might hurt a bit—but I couldn't afford to lose the element of surprise I currently had working in my favour.

Once I managed to creep around to the other side, I could see him. Coby was curled up in the bottom of a cage. It made my blood boil. They had caged him like he was nothing but an animal. I could see the person that the second voice belonged to now. It was another man, but this one even younger. He looked like he could still be a teenager. No wonder he was so nervous. I was pretty sure they wouldn't cause me any problems. I crept closer to the edge, keeping close to the ground. The older witch was still pacing. I would wait until he had his back turned before taking him out first.

"Have we got the crystal ready to store the next essence?" the older witch asked.

"Yes, Aurelia set it up before we went to take the second subject," the younger witch explained.

"Aurelia was right about taking the young ones. The essence we have taken from the first one is far stronger than any we have taken before. She will be pleased with us when we return with these. It's going to make the rising much easier," the older witch smiled.

Finally, he turned around to pace back towards the other side of the room, and I leapt. I landed right on top of him, and as my jaws closed around his neck, and I felt his blood start to run, my wolf growled in appreciation. This man was a threat to our pack, and now he would die as a consequence. The younger witch started to scream. He didn't even have the sense to run. He just stood there as I slowly advanced on him, snarling with my teeth bared. There was a distinct smell of urine just before I leapt. He didn't even try to put up a fight. I tore out his throat, and he was dead before he even had a chance to hit the floor.

I shifted and ran to the cage, flipping the latch and swinging the door open. As soon as the door opened, Coby flew into my arms. I held him tightly then pulled him away from me, running my eyes over him. "Did they hurt you?" I asked him urgently.

He shook his head and then gripped me tightly again. I stood with him still in my arms. We needed to get out of here as quickly as we could. There was no way to know when others would get here, but it could be hours, and I had no idea if there were any more witches in the area.

I looked around, but there were no crystals like they had talked about. It was just a couple of boxes and the cage. I frisked through the pockets of the young witch who was lying dead at my feet and found a mobile phone but nothing else. Luckily, I knew the numbers of all of the pack by heart. Something that came in handy when you shifted. Clothes came with us, anything in your pockets was smoke though. I called Nash quickly. If any of the others had problems or needed to check-in, it would be with him.

"Yep," he answered. He was always suspicious of numbers he didn't know.

"Nash, it's Grey. I've got Coby," I said tensely, scanning the trees outside. I didn't like being stuck here without any of the pack as a backup.

"Thank fuck. We're at Calli's house. Something really bad is happening with Jean. We need you here," he rushed out.

"Okay, Tanner, River and Aidan are still running. They should be heading in my direction, but it could take hours for them to get to me. I'll leave a signal for them here to head back to the packhouse. Can you bring the truck to pick Coby and me up? We're at the abandoned wood mill," I instructed him.

"I can be with you in fifteen minutes. I'll call Kelly on the way and tell her we have Coby. How's he doing?" he asked nervously.

"He's okay," I said, squeezing him tightly to me. "We'll head up the road and meet you on the way in. The further away we get from this place, the better."

I took a moment to lay out a ring of stones at the spot where I told Aidan to look for me. Tanner would know that it meant to return home. Then I shifted into my wolf, Coby clambered up onto my back, and he wrapped his arms around my neck in an almost stranglehold as I headed up the road to meet up with Nash.

We were about five minutes down the road before I saw Nash in the truck, and I felt Coby's relief once I got him inside. Just before we left, I threw back my head and howled. Hopefully, the rest of them would be close enough to hear it and know that they should return to the packhouse. It would have us all reunited quicker, and I was reluctant to have the pack separated when we didn't know if there were any other witches in the area.

"Can you drop me at Calli's house and then take Coby back to his Mum and Dad?" I asked Nash. He just nodded and floored his foot on the accelerator. I could feel his distress through the pack bond. When I went to ask him to update me, he just caught my eye and subtly shook his head, his eyes flicked to Coby who was curled up in my lap. I knew that I should go back to the packhouse with Coby to reunite him with his parents, but something was clearly going on with Jean, and it had seriously rattled Nash. Our pack had never faced any challenges like this before, and I just prayed we could make it through.

23

CALLI

Jean was resting in the guest room, and I had tucked Jacob up in his bed when we got to the house. I quickly called the school and left a message on the machine to tell them that Jacob wasn't feeling well and he wouldn't be at school for the next few days. He had only managed two days at school, and now everything was falling apart. I was the worst. Nash got a call from Grey to say that he had found the missing boy and I could see the relief on both his and Blake's face. While Nash got in the truck to go and pick them up, Blake and I went up to the library.

We stood in front of the bookcases, unmoving, just staring at the sheer volume of books in front of us. There had to be hundreds.

"I guess we start with the ones on magic and witches," I shrugged. This task seemed impossible. We had no idea what we were looking for. I had no experience with this sort of magic.

Blake strode determinedly over to the bookcase and finding the right section pulled half a shelf of books into his arms and carried them over to the coffee table and chairs. I followed him and collected the rest off the shelf.

Ten minutes later, I heard a knock at the front door. I looked over at Blake who was still engrossed in the book he was looking through and then got up to see who it was. I didn't think he could deal with anything else right now. I ran down the stairs and threw open the door. When I saw that Grey was standing on the other side, I all but fell into his waiting arms. He held me gently, not wanting to aggravate my injuries, and then I led him inside. Thankfully, the painkillers were still going strong, and I probably had another hour or two before the pain came back to bite me in the ass.

"Tanner, Blake and Aidan are still in the forest. I'm hoping they're on their way back, but it could be hours before they reach us," he told me as I closed the door behind him. "Where's everyone else?" he asked, looking around.

"Jacob is asleep. Jean is resting in the guest room, and Blake is up in the library." I told him.

"You've got a library?" he said, looking around like he was trying to find it. When his eyes came back to me, I just pointed up, and he smiled. "How's Jean?" he asked.

Any smile I had immediately fell from my face as I explained the situation to him.

"Do you think that you can save the baby?" he asked me quietly.

I shook my head. "I don't even know what's wrong with them. I don't know how to stop it. I might not even be able to save Jean. The only thing we could think was to come here and look through the library to see if there was anything in the books."

Grey pulled me into his arms and held me for a moment. "We will get through this together," he told me.

I nodded and then grabbed some drinks from the kitchen

and showed Grey up to the library. I caught him looking around in amazement before he walked over to Blake and crouched down beside him. He spoke softly to him for a moment, and I saw Blake's shoulders fall, and his head drop. He nodded sadly and then he got up and left the room.

"He's going to check in with Jean and make sure she's comfortable," Grey told me. He looked around again and then asked me. "What do you need me to do?"

"I don't know, I'm just making this up as I go along," I said, feeling the tears coming to my eyes. I already felt like if we lost the baby or Jean, it would be my fault. I was only twenty. I shouldn't be responsible for trying to save two people's lives.

Grey rubbed my shoulder and then held me close again. "We all are," he told me softly. "But we have to try."

I nodded and then turned back to the chairs and the coffee table. "We're going through the magic books first to see if we can find anything. "

Grey nodded and sat in the chair Blake had vacated and pulled a book from the table and started to look through it. I picked up the book I was looking through before and kept looking. Blake came back about ten minutes later telling us that Jean was sleeping and we all sat in silence going through book after book.

A few hours in, Jacob came up the stairs in his pyjamas dragging his bunny with him. He came over to me and crawled into my lap without saying a word. I brushed the hair back from his face and cuddled him while I looked through the book a bit more. It hurt to have him cuddled up against my ribs, but I wasn't ready to let him go. He started to shuffle about a little bit after a while. This had to be boring for him.

"Are you ready for something to eat?" I asked him.

He looked up at me and just nodded, and my heart broke

by his silence. I had failed him, and I had failed my parents, who had expected me to be able to look after him. Checking my watch, I found it was already ten o'clock in the morning.

"Come on, how about you go watch some cartoons, and I'll make some bacon and eggs for everyone," I told him.

Jacob climbed off my lap and just silently walked back to the stairs. Once he disappeared down them, I couldn't keep hold of my tears, and some slipped silently down my face. I looked down at the ground to try and hide them, but Grey had seen them anyway. I saw him kneel in front of me before he slipped a finger under my chin and raised my head, so I was looking at him. I was surprised to see that he had tears in his own eyes.

"I am so sorry, Calli," he said, looking over at the stairs where Jacob had gone.

I just shook my head and got up. I couldn't deal with this right now.

When I got downstairs, Jacob was silently sat in front of the tv watching something, and I started pulling things out of the fridge to feed as many as I could. We had bacon, sausage and eggs. I filled the kettle and got to work whisking the eggs while it boiled. If there was ever a time when I desperately needed a cup of tea, it was definitely now. I got the sausages started and gave Jacob a glass of milk. When I checked on Jean, she was sat up in the bed, but she wasn't asleep.

"Can I get you anything?" I asked her, sitting on the edge of the bed and taking her hand. She gave it a weak squeeze.

"I need you to promise me something," she said. She swallowed hard, and I picked up the glass of water next to the bed and helped her take a sip. "If it comes to it, you need to cut the baby out of me and save my son."

I reared back like she had slapped me. "I can't … I don't know how," I told her, shaking my head.

Jean gripped hold of my hand tighter. "I want you to promise that you will save my son's life before you save mine," she told me sternly.

"Jean," I had no idea what to say to her. "I think you should talk to Blake about this, not me," I told her.

"I tried. He won't listen," she said, shaking her head.

I couldn't tell her that the baby wasn't going to survive. I knew it was selfish, but I just couldn't. I gave her hand one last squeeze, and then I stood up. "I'll get Grey and Blake to come down. This is something that you should talk to them about. Grey will be able to reason with Blake for you if that is what you want." She nodded sadly at me, and I quickly left the room.

Jacob was still sitting on the sofa, and Grey stood at the stove cooking breakfast. For a moment, I felt a strange sense of warmth when I saw him that had a smile flicker across my face. It quickly faded. This was not a day when anyone should smile.

I joined Grey in the kitchen, and he gave me a sad smile. I felt like this should have been a happy day, but it couldn't be anything further from it. But that wasn't what I should be concentrating on now. Right now, the only things that I needed to focus on were Jacob and trying to help Jean as much as I could.

"I need to talk to you," I told Grey quietly. I saw his shoulders slump and he turned to me with the saddest look on his face, that it broke my heart. He gently slipped his hands around my waist and drew me close to him. He dropped his head down and placed his forehead against mine.

"Please Calli. Don't make this decision now. I know that everything has spiralled out of control but please, please just give us a chance," he whispered.

I ran one hand down his cheek. "Oh, no, Grey. That's not what I meant. It's about Jean."

He cleared his throat and looked down for a second, and I saw the tears glistening in his eyes. "Come on," I told him, taking his hand and drawing him into my bedroom. "We need to talk about this, but we don't have the time right now. I know all of this is crazy and we have so much to talk about, but we have to deal with this first."

Grey smiled and pulled me closer to him. "I think I was supposed to be the one to say that," he told me.

"Why, because you're the man?" I scoffed.

Grey just chuckled again. "No, because I'm the Alpha and because all of what is wrong at the moment is because my pack fucked up," he sighed sadly.

"And I need to make this terrible situation a million time worse," I told him.

"Oh god, what now?" he sighed, his head falling back as he looked at the ceiling.

"I just spoke with Jean. She asked …" I looked at him and just didn't know how to finish it.

"What, sweetheart?" he asked, gently running the backs of his fingers down one of my cheeks.

"She asked me to promise that we would save the baby before her. She wants us to cut him out of her," I finished on a whisper. It was too terrible even to say.

"I don't even know what to say to that," he said, looking panicked. "How long do you think we have?" he asked.

I just shook my head. "I think we're already out of time. I don't think the baby can survive this. We just don't have enough time to find a solution."

And then it hit me. Time. We were looking for the wrong thing. We weren't going to find a way to solve the problem with the drain on the baby and Jean. We needed to find a way to get more time.

"What? You just thought of something," Grey said, sounding hopeful.

"We need more time," I muttered. "Can you finish breakfast? I need to call someone," I said, suddenly looking up.

"Sure," Grey said with a leery smile. He opened the door, and just before he was about to walk through, he put one arm around my waist and pulled me tight against him. "But the next time you bring me into your bedroom, you don't get to leave until you've screamed my name."

"I could just do that now if you want me to," I joked, taking a deep breath but before I could shout anything there was a knock at the front door, and Grey went to go and answer it with a laugh.

I found my phone in my bag on the dining table and scrolled through my contacts. When I had been travelling, I had made several contacts. It was the purpose of my going if I was completely honest. I managed to find a few people who would be able to help if it ever came to that. I had no idea that it would become necessary so soon. I found the contact for Marie, a witch I had met up with in the South of France, who was a friend of my mother. It was Marie who had made my talisman and worked with another witch on the masking spell. She had been able to give me the names of some other people who may have helped us if we needed it. When she answered her phone on the fourth ring, I sighed in relief.

24

TANNER

Getting back to Calli's house was the most relief I'd ever felt. I hadn't had a chance to speak with her properly since this morning. I couldn't believe that she was my mate! She was so beautiful. I hoped she was as happy about this as I was. It was so confusing, though. Shifters didn't sense a mate like this, but I suppose that's because we always thought that female shifters were an impossibility until Calli charged into our lives, blowing all of our beliefs out of the water. Is that why she didn't smell like a shifter to us? Could there be more out there like her that we just had no idea about?

Grey filled us in on what was happening when we arrived. He and River were currently talking quietly with Nash about what we were going to need to do if it got to the point where we were fulfilling Jean's wishes. I couldn't believe they were even considering it!

Calli was at the dining table searching through her bag for something. My eye caught Jacob, who was just sitting quietly on the sofa staring at the TV. Fucking Wallace! Jacob was such a nice kid, and he'd been having a hard time with the loss of his parents. I couldn't help but feel responsible for him being traumatised even further. When we found Grey in the forest, River and I were so caught up trying to get him back to the packhouse and find out what was wrong with him, that we didn't consider what the others were doing. I knew that they were going to put Calli in the basement until one of them came to and we could find out what had happened. I thought that she would be safe there. I had no idea that Wallace was going to abduct Jacob from his bed. And what he did to Calli. My wolf had relished the beating we laid on him when I threw him in the cage. He was lucky we didn't kill him. Deep down, I understood that he was out of control because of his worry for Coby, but I didn't think I could excuse his actions even with that in mind.

I went and sat down with Jacob, but he showed no sign of acknowledging I was there. He didn't even look at me.

"Hey little man, you doing okay?" I asked him.

Jacob just nodded. He didn't move. He didn't look at me. He just sat and stared at the tv. I'm not even sure he was seeing what was on it. My heart broke. We had done this to him.

"Have you had your breakfast yet?" I asked him quietly.

He just shook his head.

"I'll go sort it out for you," I said, standing up. I could feel the lump lodged in my throat. We needed to fix this, but I didn't know how.

When I went into the kitchen and saw that someone had started putting some breakfast stuff together, I just carried on where they had left off. Calli had found her phone and was scrolling through it with a serious look on her face, not paying any attention to anyone else. I hoped she had an idea that was going to work. I didn't know how the pack would weather losing Jean and the baby. Grey and River came into the kitchen to help with breakfast, while Calli paced in front of us with the phone to her ear.

"Marie, j'ai besoin de ton aide. C'est une urgence," she said with a flawless French accent.

Grey and River both froze on the spot at the same time as I did.

"The English accent was hot, but this just takes it to another level," I murmured, and they both agreed with me.

Calli continued talking away in French to someone on the phone, and we turned back to the food, there wasn't much, but we could run out in a bit for more supplies. The important thing was getting Jacob fed.

Calli started getting agitated, and her French was coming out thick and fast. By the time we had finished cooking, she had hung up the phone, and she looked devastated. River took some food over to Jacob and went to sit with him, while Grey and I went to see what Calli had found out. She had sat down at the dining table with her head in her hands. Grey knelt beside her, rubbing her back, and I took one of her hands in mine, rubbing my thumb across her knuckles.

"It's okay, Calli. We know that what we are asking you to do is probably impossible," Grey told her.

She looked up at him with the saddest eyes. "I think I have an idea," she whispered. I didn't know why she was so sad about it, though.

Calli looked between Grey and me before she said. "I need you to make me a promise."

"Anything," Grey and I said at the same time. And I knew we both meant it. We would give her the world if we could.

Calli looked over at Jacob. "If anything ever happened to me, make sure that Jacob is okay. Look after him for me," she said quietly.

"Calli, nothing is going to happen. We will protect you both with our lives," I told her fiercely.

"What are you planning?" Grey asked. "You can't risk yourself," he added quietly.

Calli ran one hand down Grey's cheek, and she smiled at him. It didn't quite reach her eyes, and I could tell she was trying to reassure him. Something wasn't right.

She suddenly stood up. "I need to do this upstairs," she said, and we all moved over to a staircase behind a door that I hadn't seen before. I followed her and Grey upstairs but paused at the top of the stairs looking around us in wonder. It was incredible. Calli had an entire library in the eaves of the house.

"Where did you get all of these?" I asked, looking along the shelves.

This amount of information on magic and the supernatural world, in one place, was unheard of. This would be like a dream come true for Nash, and I couldn't wait to see his face when he saw it. But then I saw Blake, sitting in one of the chairs frantically scanning through a book and my heart dropped. His sadness permeated the air, and my wolf whimpered as the feeling rolled over us.

Grey went over to him and put a hand on his shoulder. I could feel the calming Alpha waves coming off him as he tried to soothe Blake's wolf. The last thing we needed was another one of the pack to lose control. Blake's head dropped down, and the book he was scanning dropped into his lap as he relaxed under Grey's touch. "Thank you," he whispered quietly.

I went over to help Calli who was on her knees rummaging through a cupboard which took up the bottom half of one of the bookcases. She seemed to be gathering supplies for some sort of spell. When Blake realised what she was doing, he shot up out of his chair and ran over to her.

"Did you find it? Did you find out how to stop it?" he asked her.

Calli looked up at him and winced. "No. But I have an idea. In fact, it needs to be your decision if we try this," she said, turning to him. Blake dropped to the ground next to her waiting to hear what she was going to say. "I don't know how to stop the drain," she told him, and I saw his hope shatter. "What I think I can do is put Jean and the baby in a sort of … stasis. It would just be like they were both asleep. It would pause the spell that is on them causing the drain. While they are sleeping, I might be able to restore some of their energy with my healing magic." Blake looked up at her and tears shone in his eyes.

"Yes, anything," he said, throwing his arms around Calli and hugging her tightly.

"You need to understand the risk here," she said, drawing slowly back from him. "If we take the stasis off them before we find out how to stop the drain, it will just start all over again."

Blake just nodded. I realised what she was trying to say, but I didn't know if Blake did. Calli laid her hand on his shoulder. "I need to make sure that you fully understand what I'm saying to you. If we can't find how to stop the drain, you won't be able to wake them up," she told him.

Blake's face went blank, and then he just said. "We will. We will find a way."

"You shouldn't make this decision without considering that we may not be able to," Grey sighed, kneeling beside them both.

Blake just started to shake his head. "We will find a way. We have to."

Calli nodded and gave him a small smile. "This will buy us the time to look for an answer. But it could take a long time for us to be able to find it. I also can't guarantee that I will be able to restore the energy that has already been taken. Although my friend who I spoke with is certain that at least that much is possible," she told him.

Blake looked at the ground for a few moments, and I could see that he was thinking it through. Then he came to the same conclusion I already had. "We don't have any other choice. If we don't do this then they both die anyway," he said quietly.

"Yes, they will," Calli told him. "But that is your other choice, to let them go now," she told him gently.

Blake reared back like she had slapped him. "No, that is never a choice for me," he told her fiercely.

She just smiled and patted his shoulder. "We need to hurry then." And she turned back to the cupboard and started pulling things out again.

I couldn't help but feel like we were missing something here and that there was something she wasn't telling us. Calli looked over at me and asked, "Can you get my laptop from my room. My friend is going to email across the instructions." I nodded and quickly took off down the stairs.

It was easy to find Calli's room because her gorgeous scent was flooding out of it. I saw her laptop sat by the side of the bed. I had the stupidest thought of picking up her pillow so that I could breathe in the scent of her. Instead, I shook that thought out of my head and ran back up to the attic where the others were waiting. Calli had set up a massive bowl on the coffee table and was organising the supplies she had around her. She had a look of complete dread on her face.

Grey picked up one of her hands and pulled her over to the corner, and I followed them under the pretence of passing her the laptop, but really, I wanted to know what the hell was going on as well.

"There's something you aren't telling us," Grey said, getting straight to the point.

She looked him straight in the eye, and I could see the indecision flicker across her face. I realised she didn't want to tell us because she thought we would stop her from doing whatever she was about to do. She frowned before she slowly said. "I need to use a talisman to imbue it with the spell and attach it to Jean. The only talisman I have that I can use is mine," She said, holding on to the pendant which hung around her neck. As far as I knew, she always wore it.

"Okay," Grey said with a frown. "I'm going to be blunt because I don't understand all of this. Why is that bad?"

"Once the spell is placed on the talisman, it will be changed. I won't be able to change it back to what it is," she said, then she sighed, and her shoulders drooped. "The talisman masks me from everyone. It's why you aren't able to scent me as a wolf or a witch. If I take it off, everyone will be able to tell what my heritage is."

Grey and I looked between ourselves for a moment. She couldn't do this. "Can you get another talisman?" Grey asked her.

"No," she slowly shook her head. "The spell won't be effective on me through a different talisman. It's a one-shot deal."

"And you can't use anything else?" I asked.

Calli just shook her head. "We don't have the time to get another one. They have to be specially made through ritual to have the necessary properties to permanently hold a spell."

"I don't think you should do this," I told her seriously. "We don't know how much of a risk this is going to place you in. I know that's selfish, but I'm not prepared to risk your safety to save anyone." I pulled Calli into my arms. My wolf was agitated, and he was not happy with the idea that our mate could be placing herself in danger. This whole situation was beyond fucked up. Calli willingly came into my arms, and she tucked herself in against my chest. The fact that she was welcoming my touch made my chest swell. It was easy to forget that this whole mate situation was brand new and that it hadn't got off to the best of starts. At least she wasn't holding it against us even if she would be entirely reasonable to do so.

Grey was looking between Calli and Blake. "Does Jacob wear a talisman?" he asked, and I felt Calli stiffen in my arms.

"Yes, even if we could, I would not allow you to use Jacob's talisman," she said sternly.

"I wasn't suggesting that," Grey said holding his hands up. "Calli you have to believe that I would never do anything to put Jacob at risk. What Wallace did was reprehensible, and he will be dealt with accordingly even if you hadn't been my mate. We do not treat women and children that way. I was just wondering what it was because I hadn't noticed anything on him," he ended quietly. Poor Grey. He hadn't worded that well.

Calli snuggled back in against me, and I smiled over the top of her head at Grey. I didn't miss the slight squint of his eyes. After this was over, we needed to sit down and discuss our new relationship and what it meant for us.

"Jacob's talisman is a tattoo," she explained. "When I was born, my parents didn't know that I would have a mixed scent. They had assumed I would be one or the other. No one had ever spoken of any hybrids before. They had no way to know any different. They were able to have a friend help make my talisman when I was about six years old. Until then, they kept me away from everyone. I rarely left our house. When my mother found out that she was pregnant with Jacob, they already knew what to expect. Her friend, who had helped before had continued researching the subject for years after she made my talisman. She was there when Jacob was born, and she tattooed the sigil on him straight away. The spell is in the ink," she said comfortably. I was surprised that she would be happy to give us this much information, but then she must be feeling the mating link as strongly as we were. I would tell her anything if she asked me.

"We can't use the tattoo technique with Jean?"

"Not if you ever want her to wake up, the spell would be permanent," Calli sighed.

"And they can't give you the same tattoo?" Grey asked, even though we already knew the answer.

"No," she said sadly. "The spell only works once on someone. Once the talisman is destroyed, there is no way that the spell could work for me again."

"What about something different?" Grey said, looking thoughtful for a moment. "What if your mother's friend was to change the spell so that it had a different effect. Rather than masking your smell entirely what if it only covered your witch scent?"

"I don't think that would work, but I've never asked her. There was no need to. I suppose it could be a possibility. I don't know enough about magic to be able to give you a definite answer," she said, looking around at the books surrounding us. I knew what she was thinking. We were probably all thinking it. We had the perfect opportunity right here to learn what we needed. We just didn't have the time to do it right now.

Grey sighed and started to pace. You always knew he was struggling with something when he began to pace. "I still don't like it," he said. I could sense that there was a but coming and I wasn't so sure I was happy about it. "But ultimately it's your decision. I think that you should at least talk to Jacob about it before you do it though."

Calli pulled away from me, and I immediately felt lost without her. "You're right," she said.

Blake had sat back down on the same chair he had initially sat in, with his head between his hands. I couldn't even begin to understand what he was feeling right now. Grey walked over to him and suggested they both go and check in on Jean so that Calli could prepare for the spell. He would have been able to hear what we were saying, and he hadn't intervened. He was a better man than I was.

We all filed back into the living room. Jacob and River were sitting on the sofa. Jacob was still rigidly sat watching the TV. There was an empty plate on the coffee table in front of him, so at least he had eaten something. River was giving him some space for now, but I could see how downcast he was. I was torn. Jean and the baby were our priority at the moment because of the urgency of their situation, but my wolf and I were firmly in agreement that we wanted to do something to help Jacob.

Calli knelt in front of Jacob and clasped both of her hands over his knees. He didn't move to touch her, and his eyes stayed fixed on the TV. The poor kid had just shut down, and the guilt of our failing slammed through me.

"Jacob honey, I need to talk to you about something," Calli started. "You know that Jean and her baby are poorly? That someone is hurting them?" she asked him.

Jacob's eyes flicked to where the guest room was, and he gave a small nod of his head.

Calli seemed relieved by just that little movement. "Well, I think I can help her. I spoke with Marie, and she thinks we can put a spell on them so they go to sleep and the other person can't hurt them anymore. A bit like sleeping beauty." She paused for a second, but he made no move to show that he was listening or understanding. "I would need to use my talisman to do it, though," she added quietly.

Jacob's eyes snapped to her, and he stiffened. Calli started to rub his knees soothingly, but it didn't help.

"I would have to take it off and give it to Jean," she told him.

"No," Jacob whispered.

"Jean and the baby will both die if I don't do this," Calli explained.

Jacob launched himself off the sofa and wrapped himself around Calli. She held him tightly against her, and I could feel the tears stinging at the back of my eyes. Grey came out of the guest room, giving Blake and Jean some privacy and stood watching. He looked as torn as I was. The need to go and comfort Jacob was riding me strong. My wolf accepted that he was not only pack but that he was our pup now. I was uncertain that he would welcome any of us right now. How could he? He must blame us for what happened. I was usually so sure about myself in these situations. I was the Beta of our pack. I always knew what to do to make my pack feel safe and secure. But now? Now, I just felt like I had utterly failed Jacob and I didn't know how to put that right.

River dropped down off the sofa to kneel beside Calli and Jacob and started to rub his back, whispering soft words to him gently. That was when I realised that the poor little guy was crying.

I looked across at Grey. He was holding back the same as me. He seemed just as unsure as I did. Then he did something I would never have expected. Grey transformed into the massive black wolf of his other half, and he softly padded over to Jacob. I could feel his waves of Alpha power softly filling the room. Jacob's eyes flicked to him, and he looked unsure, but Grey lowered his head and moved slowly towards him. Jacob pulled back a little from Calli to see what the massive wolf was about to do. He didn't seem to be frightened at least. Grey lowered himself to the ground next to them, and he gently placed his massive head onto Jacob's tiny lap. I saw his hands grip onto Grey's fur like it was a lifeline.

"They will protect you?" Jacob whispered, looking back at Calli.

She nodded, not saying anything. The tears were already streaming down her face in response to her brother's distress.

I slowly walked over and dropped to my knees next to them. When Jacob looked up at me, he didn't seem scared, and I took that as a good sign. The fact that he had even said anything was a massive step.

"We will protect you both with our lives," I told him seriously.

He gave us a little nod and then climbed back up onto the sofa. Grey jumped up beside him and curled protectively around him. Jacob snuggled down into his soft fur and continued watching television with a massive black wolf protectively keeping watch over him. If we could get through this, I would do everything in my power to make that little boy smile again.

25

CALLI

I read through the instructions on the email one last time and then checked the bowl before me to make sure I had followed every step correctly. There was only one thing left to do, and it would be the hardest thing that I had ever done.

Tanner, River and Blake were all in the corner watching quietly. I couldn't decipher the emotions running across Tanner and River's faces. I barely knew them.

My eyes flicked across to Blake. He had one fist pressed hard against his mouth, but I could see the hope blazing in his eyes.

A deep, deep, dark place inside me wondered if this was all a trick. If they were just using me to save Jean and the baby. The despair and the hope in Blake's eyes was real. But the caring and love in the other guys' eyes seemed real as well. Did it matter though? Jean and especially her baby were innocents, and if it was in my power to do so, I should help them. That is one thing I knew my mother would have said. She was the kindest soul anyone would have ever had the privilege to meet. But doing this could place Jacob at risk. In fact, I was kidding myself; there was no might, he would definitely be at risk if we did this. And that was one thing I knew she would not be okay with. I wish she were here to give me some kind of advice. She would know what to do right now.

The indecision must have been apparent on my face because Blake came and dropped to his knees beside me. "I know what you are sacrificing by doing this. I know that he is your biggest concern right now. So I will make you a promise, more than a promise, I will pledge my life to Jacob. I will do whatever it takes to keep him safe. When Jeanie recovers, I'm going to send them far away. I know somewhere where they will be safe, even if that means I can't go with them. I will stay by Jacob's side, and I will protect him from anything and everything even if that means I can't be with my family. But please, please, I just need them to live," he said, looking deep in my eyes while he begged for the life of the woman that he loved and their child.

"No," I whispered. It felt like I had to force the words out of my mouth; my throat was so dry. Blake stiffened, and I saw the tears swimming in his eyes. "I would never keep you from them. You have to be with them. You need to hold them both every day and give them all the love you have. Otherwise, what are we even doing this for?"

I quickly pulled the talisman from my neck and dropped it into the bowl before I could change my mind. The tears I had so desperately been trying to hold back, flowed unchecked down my face, and I felt my heart break for a second time. I prayed that my parents would forgive me; I prayed that my brother would be safe; I prayed that I hadn't just made the worst mistake of my life.

The magic tensed in the air, and then I felt it snap in place. Hooking the talisman back out of the bowl I passed it to Blake. "Tell her whatever you need to, then put this around her neck. Once it's on, she will sleep," I told him.

Blake rushed out of the room with the talisman clutched in his hand. No one went with him. He was going to say goodbye to his wife. He shouldn't have to do that with people watching him. My hands were shaking as I reached out for the bowl to start clearing away what I had used. Tanner's hands came over mine, and he held them tightly before drawing me up off the floor and pulling me into his chest. Dropping his face down into my neck, he inhaled deeply, taking in my real scent for the very first time.

26

GREY

The scent of lilacs and twilight jasmine hit my nose, and I knew that it was done. I knew that my mate had just sacrificed the only thing that was keeping her safe, for the sake of the lives of two of my pack members.

My wolf whimpered, and Jacob curled himself around us even tighter. His small hands clutched desperately in my fur, and I heard him whisper. "It's going to be okay. We will protect her together."

I tucked my head around him tighter and pulled him into me. I had meant it when I said to Calli that I would make sure that Jacob would always be protected. She may have been my mate, but Jacob felt like more than a pup in our pack. He felt like he was my pup. And I was so proud of this scared little boy, who was taking the time to try and comfort me when he was so terrified himself.

Blake rushed down the stairs, and the others followed behind a few minutes later. He had rushed into the guest room, and everything fell quiet. I could feel the terror and the hope lashing through the pack bond. By the time the others made it down the stairs, I felt the relief and sorrow rush through in its place. It was done. Or rather it was just starting. Tanner locked eyes with me and gave me a nod. I had a terrible feeling we had made a massive mistake here, but we had at least bought some more time for Jean. I knew I should be relieved, but I couldn't help but dread what would happen next. I could only hope it was all worth it, that I hadn't just let my mate risk herself and her little brother for nothing.

Everyone drifted over to the living room and slumped down into the seats. Jacob gave me one last squeeze, and then he crawled over me and snuggled against Calli. I transformed back into my human form, and Calli reached across and took my hand. She looked at me over the top of Jacob's hand and just mouthed the words 'thank you' to me.

"What do we do now?" River asked quietly.

"I don't know. How long will the spell last on Jean?" I asked Calli.

"Indefinitely, as long as the talisman stays on her," she said with a yawn.

Tanner jumped up off the sofa and strode into the kitchen, putting together a plate of food, he slapped it in the microwave and then brought it over to Calli. "It might not reheat well, but you need to eat something. Then I think you should take a bath to soak those ribs and get a bit of sleep. You're exhausted."

Calli nodded her thanks and tucked into her food. I watched her eat for a minute. It satisfied my wolf to know that she was here, and she was safe. Then I climbed up and went to grab some food for myself. While I was in the kitchen, River joined me and filled the electric kettle, turning it on. He was reading the packet of tea he had bought for Calli when I interrupted him.

"What can we do for Jacob?" I asked him, looking out

into the living room where he was still cuddled up against Calli.

River put down the tea packet with a sigh. "I don't know. This is trauma on top of trauma. I think the best thing to do is give him time and reassure him as much as we can and see how he gets on. He might need to go into therapy," he said sadly.

"We did this," I told him quietly.

"No," River said firmly. "Wallace did this," he nearly snarled.

"I know, brother, judging by the smell of his blood on Tanner earlier, I would say that he has been told the error of his behaviour, but I will be paying him a visit this afternoon as well."

"He's a threat to Calli. You saw what he was like at the house. He hates her because all he sees is a witch." River said, frowning. I knew what he was suggesting, and I had already thought about it myself.

"I know. I will give him time, in case the way he feels changes now that Coby has been returned. But if he continues the way he is, he won't be able to remain in the pack." I would not turn away a wolf easily, but I would not allow a threat to our mate to remain in the pack either.

River finished making Calli her tea, and we both went back into the living room. Blake had come out of the guest room while we were talking and was sat in one of the chairs looking completely drained.

"We need a plan going forward," Tanner said with a frown. "Is it safe to move Jean back to her house?" he asked Calli.

"I don't know. I think you should leave her where she is for now, though. The bedroom at their house was thick with magic, I don't think it would be a good idea to put her back in there, at least for now," Calli said. Her head had flopped back on the sofa, and she was staring up at the ceiling. She looked exhausted.

"Okay, so we need to find a way to break the drain on them. The best place to do that is going to be in Calli's library," I pointed out. "You mind having a few guests for a bit?" I asked her quietly, realising that we had all just basically crashed into her life and her home and she had very little say in it.

"Wallace is not to come near this house or Jacob," she growled.

"Wallace is going back in the cage after he has had some time with Coby. He won't be allowed anywhere near here," I told her adamantly.

"Good. I know he'd lost his son, but I can't put aside what he did. Not yet. The rest of you are more than welcome as long as it doesn't upset Jacob." She clung to her brother who was snuggled against her watching the cartoons which were on tv.

"We're going to need supplies," Tanner yawned. "I can make a run to the store."

"Before we do anything I think we should all get some rest," I said, looking around at everyone slumped on the sofas. "We've had a mad twelve hours, and I think we all need to sleep even if it's not for long. We can decide what we are going to do next later on tonight."

Blake just sat, staring at the guest room door.

"You can stay with her," Calli said quietly to him.

He looked over at her. I don't think he had the capacity to process any more emotions today. "Thank you for this and everything. I know that our pack has not treated you properly and you could have just turned us away if you wanted to. The fact that you have done this for us, after everything that

Wallace did ... you're a better person than anyone I know," Blake said, shaking his head.

He was right. Calli was selfless, and she had a pure soul. Even when she was sitting on the ground outside the packhouse, beaten and only just reunited with Jacob, she wanted to know what had happened to Coby. Not only that, but she didn't even need to think about whether she should help, she just did.

There was a quiet knock on the door, and everyone looked at it for a moment before Tanner laughed and stood up to answer it. No one else clearly had it in them to get up right now. Nash followed Tanner back through to the living room and dropped down onto a seat beside him.

"Coby is back with his parents, and I've moved them into the packhouse where it's a bit more secure. Aidan is going to stay and watch over things." Nash told us. "How's Jean?" he asked quietly.

"She's okay for now," I told him and everyone had a weary smile on their face at the idea. We needed to chalk up today as a win. Jean was out of imminent danger, and we had brought Coby back to us.

"Okay, I think, for now, we all need to rest and get some sleep. Let's get together for dinner tonight and decide what we're going to do from there. Calli has offered for Blake and Jean to stay here. Nash, I know you just got here, but do you mind staying at the packhouse and working with Aidan to keep Coby secure?"

"Sure," Nash said, getting to his feet with far more energy than the rest of us had. "I brought Blake's truck back so I'll shift and go through the woods so I can leave it here for you."

"Actually, I'm going to go back to the cabin and grab a bag. You can ride with me," Blake offered.

"There's a spare key in the kitchen drawer," Calli told

him. "Might as well take it then you can come and go as you need."

"Thanks, Calli," Blake said, striding into the kitchen.

"You're better than we deserve," I told her.

"Come on, spud, let's set you up with a movie on the iPad in your room," Calli said, lifting Jacob in her arms as she stood from the sofa. I didn't miss the pinch around her eyes as she did so. Her pain killers must be starting to wear off.

"I'm going to run Calli a bath." River said, getting up and striding out of the room. I could feel his tension through the pack bond. Seeing Calli hurt was hard on all of us, but River seemed to be taking it especially bad. I hadn't seen him struggle to contain his wolf so much before.

I turned to Tanner and saw that he was frowning in concern as he watched Calli leave the room. "We need to decide on what we are going to do about Wallace," I told him.

Tanner nodded thoughtfully. "Give him tonight with his family, and then we can speak with him tomorrow. If there is any animosity towards Calli, and I mean even just the slightest amount, I want him back in the cage," Tanner said, a growl rolling through his chest.

I nodded in agreement with him even though I wasn't sure it was the best way to go about it. Caging Wallace could prove to just deepen his animosity against Calli, not improve it.

27

CALLI

As I slid into the bubbles, I felt the sting of the hot water slowly climbing up my body. There was something about taking a bath which was just on the side of too hot, that truly soothed the soul. I had taken some more painkillers before I got in and I was glad that I had. I should be mostly healed by tomorrow, but the pain around my ribs felt like it might take a bit longer. I can't believe that I even thought I had the skills to stand before a shifter in a fight. I'd been kidding myself; Wallace more than proved that. My father had been taking it easy on me all those years, and I was arrogant enough not to see it. This past week had highlighted too many of my character flaws, and I was starting to feel a bit like a fuck up.

But mates … three mates! I didn't even know where to go with this. It explained my weird trusting behaviour over the last week, I suppose. But I'd never heard of this. I'd never heard of this kind of instant connection. My wolf was adamant, though, and I felt it as well. Those three men were mine, they were meant to be with me, and I was meant to be with them.

Grey was right that we needed a plan for how we were going to go from here. He'd been talking about the whole witch situation at the time, but we needed one for us as well. What were we supposed to do? I still didn't even really know them, and before we were going to take any drastic steps, we needed to remedy that. Plus, even though they were my mates, I still had Jacob to take into account. Despite my recent reckless behaviour, he had to be my top priority. And it was reckless. I could see that now. Going out on that run was the single most stupid thing I had ever done in my life. But Grey would be dead now if I hadn't done it. I shook my head, almost like I thought it was going to clear my thoughts. I couldn't think about all that right now. It was done, in the past and there was nothing I could do to change it. There was too much going on now to worry about things I couldn't change.

I quickly shaved my legs and washed my hair, rinsing it out under the showerhead and then washing down my body as well. Stepping out of the bath, I wrapped myself up in one of the bath sheets and started to towel dry my hair. My hairbrush was in the bedroom, so I stepped through the door intending just to grab it and brush out my hair but froze on the spot while I took in the sight before me. All three of my mates were waiting for me on my bed. River and Grey sat on the edge, elbows resting on their knees, quietly talking to each other. Tanner had taken the liberty of stretching out and was laid back, hands behind his head, with his eyes closed. They all looked just as tired as I was. As a pack, they'd been through a lot today as well.

Grey's and River's heads snapped up as I walked through the door. Tanner didn't move. I suspected that he'd fallen asleep. I was suddenly very aware of the fact that I was only wearing a towel and feeling very nervous about it.

River cleared his throat and then stood up. "Have you had

any more painkillers?" he asked me, rubbing the back of his neck like he was suddenly nervous as well.

"Yes," I told him quietly. I wasn't sure why they were here or what they were wanting or even expecting. I wasn't even sure what I wanted. My body felt flushed, and I could feel the heat gathering between my thighs. Scratch that, I knew exactly what my body wanted, but my mind was the one having trouble catching on to the idea.

The corner of Grey's mouth twitched up, and I knew that he would be able to scent my arousal. "We just wanted to make sure you were okay, Calli, and maybe talk about what we were going to do. I can't believe I'm about to suggest this, but why don't you put some clothes on and then we can talk."

Tanner suddenly sleepily sat up. "Clothes on?" he asked, confused, looking around like he wasn't quite sure where he was.

It at least broke the tense mood, and I laughed, shaking my head and went over to the dresser to grab some pyjama shorts and a tank top. They had been right earlier when they said I needed to get some sleep, and there was no way I would get changed again before that happened. I slipped back into the bathroom and got dressed and then came out and slid under the covers so that I at least didn't feel quite as undressed as I was. Tanner was still lounging on the other side of the bed, but he had turned on his side and was propped up on one elbow. Grey was pacing the room, making me nervous, and River was just leaning back on the closed door, almost like he was waiting for me to try and bolt from the room. Before finding out they were my mates, this would have terrified me. But now, it was kind of funny.

"Okay," Grey said, suddenly stopping his pacing. "We're mates," he said definitively.

I couldn't help but smile. He was obviously nervous about something, and it was pretty cute.

"You're a wolf. Like a proper wolf," Tanner said, shuffling a bit closer. "I like it better now that I can smell your scent. It's beautiful, Calli. Just like you."

Okay, maybe Tanner was the cute one. I couldn't help but reach out and stroke one hand across his cheek. He closed his hands and leant into my hand. It was strange how right it felt being with them. My wolf was just lazing in the back of my mind, content to be surrounded by them. I had never felt her so at peace before.

"Tanner!" Grey said sharply, and Tanner's head snapped up to meet his eye. "Let's try and get through this first," he smiled.

"You're not getting lucky," I said, looking at them all. "I really am going to go to sleep."

"We know," River laughed. "Grey just means before he rolls over and gives you his belly to rub."

Tanner whipped one of the pillows off the bed and threw it at River's head, who dodged out of the way still laughing at him. Grey rolled his eyes and just sat on the bed next to me, leaving them to it.

"Are you happy about this?" he asked quietly.

I cocked my head to the side and thought. Was I happy about this? "Yes, and it's nice to finally understand why I've been having all of these conflicting feelings. But I still have to make Jacob my top priority. I don't know what, if anything, I can promise you right now," I told him honestly.

"No one is asking you to make any promises. Let's just get to know each other and see where it takes us. And as far as Jacob is concerned … shit, I don't even know how to say this without sounding weird," Grey frowned. "I will always see Jacob as my pup and part of my pack. I hope, I hope that's okay," he said, trailing off at the end in uncertainty.

"He's right, Calli," River said, dropping down to his knees in front of me. "Jacob will always be ours. We will always protect him and be there for him, no matter what."

"Your pup?" I asked in confusion.

"Yeah," Tanner said, sliding back onto the bed behind me and wrapping his arms around me. "He's ours.

I don't know if they realised just how much it meant to me for them to say that, but it was everything. If anything were to happen to me, Jacob would still have a family and nothing would get past these three strong wolves. For the first time since I opened the front door to those Police Officers, I realised that Jacob was safe. Maybe I hadn't epically fucked up just as much as I thought I had. Jacob had a pack now, and I knew they would do anything they had to so they could protect him.

"Will you stay here with me while I sleep?" I asked them, flushing in embarrassment for even asking.

"Of course we will," Tanner said, pulling me down into the bed with him as he snuggled in closer behind me.

Grey stood up, pulling off his shirt and then his hands dropped to his jeans. "Do you mind?" he asked.

I shook my head, biting my lip. I very much did not mind. He gave me an evil smirk as he unbuttoned his jeans, almost like he knew what I would be thinking. Pushing them down, he stood before me in just his boxer briefs. The ability to speak wholly left me. He had the perfect body that I knew he would have and his clothes had hinted and teased me with. His boxer briefs clung to him tightly, and part of me wished he would turn around just so I could check out his ass. What he was concealing in the front wasn't exactly disappointing though. In fact, good god, I'm not even sure that monster was going to fit.

My eyes tripped across his skin trying to take it all in at once. Grey had a huge tattoo that started on the right side of his chest and wrapped around the top of his arm. It was an intricate forest scene, not unlike the woods that surrounded the packhouse and I couldn't help but wonder if it was maybe a real place.

Tanner reached around from behind me. "I'm just going to get that for you," he laughed, sliding one finger under my chin and closing my mouth for me.

Grey laughed and slipped into the bed in front of me, pulling me close against him. Tanner didn't let go of me and slide along the bed so that he could stay flush against my back.

"We're not hurting you, are we?" Grey asked softly, as he held me in his arms.

I sighed and snuggled in deeper. "No," I could feel my eyes starting to flutter closed. This content feeling of being held by my mates calmed my spiralling mind, and I finally found peace for the first time in months.

"I'm going to go and check on Jacob," I heard River murmur just before I slipped into sleep.

28

CALLI

Everyone apart from me was still sleeping. I'd never been good at napping in the day. There was something about the daylight that just made my body unable to rest.

When I managed to slide out from between Tanner and Grey, I found River asleep on the living room sofa. He had one of the massive books from the library open on his chest. I wasn't too sure why he hadn't joined us, although it could have been a lack of space problem. Also, Grey was his brother, so maybe that was a bit weird. That might be something that we need to talk about.

Jacob had fallen asleep on his bed. The Minions Movie menu was playing on a loop, so I don't know how far he'd made it into the film. Judging by the enormous Lego fort that had been constructed on his bedroom floor, he couldn't have been asleep long. There was no sign of Blake, and I assumed he was sleeping in Jean's room because his truck was parked outside the house.

I was pottering around the kitchen, making food. I went with something easy and filling and basically what I had enough ingredients to feed all of the people currently napping in the house. It was also one of Jacob's favourites, which couldn't hurt. I had a feeling that kid was going to be getting his favourite everything for a while. I'd been blown away by the guys' declaration of seeing Jacob as like their own pup. How was that even going to work? How was any of this going to work? There was no way I was going to move us into the packhouse. Especially not with Wallace about. I may have been able to stomach him if it was just me, but there was no way he was ever getting anywhere near Jacob again.

A growl rumbled through my chest as I whisked up some batter for Yorkshire Puddings. I was going to make a triple batch, so hopefully, there would be some left to put in the freezer, but I had a feeling they wouldn't last that long.

I was going to need to hit the supermarket if things were going to continue like this. A weird part of me felt like I needed to make sure that Blake was looking after himself and eating. Perhaps I did have some kind of maternal instinct going on. Or, I just didn't want Jean to wake up one day and see that I had let her husband waste away.

I pulled two enormous cottage pies out of the oven and put the muffin trays in to heat up for the Yorkshires. They were the only things I had that I could make a large batch of them in and they would do for now. Almost like the smell of food had drawn them out of their sleep, Grey and Tanner stumbled sleepily into the kitchen.

"Coffee," Tanner grunted rummaging through one of the cupboards beside me before he pulled out the French press and some mugs.

Grey just shook his head at the ridiculousness of Tanner and his sleepy antics. Clearly, this guy was not one who could function without his sleep.

"You didn't have to cook for us," Grey said, sliding up

behind me and gently placing a kiss on the back of my shoulder. I shivered against him realising this was the first time he had ever laid his lips against my skin. How weird was it that we had all just snuggled up for a nap together and I hadn't even kissed them yet?

"Well, Jacob and I needed to eat, and it's not that difficult to just make it basically ten times bigger," I laughed. I was going to pass it off saying that I had doubled the recipe, but with four full-grown shifter males to feed it was a lot more than that. I was hoping there would be enough if anyone else happened to drop by as well. It had definitely cleared out the fridge and most of the freezer of all the minced beef that was for sure.

"Oooo Shepherd's Pie," I heard Tanner say as he inhaled deeply and sidled towards the food. He looked down at the batter in the bowl and bounced up and down on his feet. "Are you making Yorkshire Puddings?"

"Yes," I laughed. "And it's Cottage Pie," I said pointing at the two big dishes.

Tanner ducked down and peered into the side of the glass dishes. "It definitely looks like Shepherd's Pie," he said, squinting suspiciously.

"Well, I cooked it so, I can tell you for definite that it's cottage pie," I said, taking the hot muffin tins out of the oven and filling them with the batter before quickly putting them back in. That was the trick, straight into hot oil in the bottom of the tin and then quickly back in the oven before they cool down.

"I'll set the table," Grey offered.

"Do you want to see if Blake is in with Jean and if he wants something to eat?" I asked Tanner. "I didn't want to disturb him earlier."

Tanner nodded and went to see how Blake was doing

while I slipped into Jacob's room. He had woken up again and was back at work on his Lego fort. "We're going to need to get you some more Lego if you want to make this bigger," I told him.

He looked up at me with a soft smile, and it nearly broke my heart. This was how he had come back last time. Small steps. Seeing him smile was a massive relief though and a welcome change from the near-catatonic state he had earlier.

"Go wash your hands, spud. It's almost time for dinner. I made you Cottage Pie and Yorkshire puddings," I told him and was rewarded with another smile before he jumped up to do as he was told.

I couldn't help the sigh of relief as I walked back into the kitchen and started to get everything into serving dishes. I had green beans and roasted baby carrots to go with everything and of course gravy. I don't think Jacob could survive more than two days without gravy featuring in his diet. I dished Jacob's food up straight away so that it would have time to cool down. He hated it if it was too hot.

Tanner came out of the spare room with Blake in tow. He didn't look like he had got any sleep, and he had dark circles under his eyes. Tomorrow I would work on the energy transfer with Jean and see if I could at least help with some of the burdens of what he was carrying.

Once the food was on the table and everyone had helped themselves, we all kind of fell into a heavy silence as we ate. It was a bit awkward. Thankfully, we had Tanner to break us out of it.

"No, this is Shepherd's Pie," he told me seriously.

"It's not," I laughed. "It's made with beef; therefore, it is Cottage Pie. Shepherd's pie has lamb in it, hence why it has Shepherd in the name," I informed him. Jacob was just looking at him like he was crazy.

Tanner cocked his head to the side in thought. I knew that he didn't believe me and when he pulled out his phone to google it, I almost threw a carrot at him.

"She's actually right," he said in shock. "All this time," he shook his head looking down at his cottage pie like it had somehow betrayed him.

"What do you mean 'actually right'!" I gasped. "Rude!" I muttered but then laughed.

"I'm almost afraid to ask what this is in case she launches something at me," Blake added poking his Yorkshire pudding with his fork.

"Oh man, you've got to try it, it's amazing," Tanner gushed. He had four Yorkshire puddings on his plate, and he and Jacob had actually each stuck one on a fork and cheers'ed them earlier. I could see that the two of them were going to be trouble.

"You have to put gravy on it," Jacob quietly told Blake, and we all smiled and tried not to make a big deal out of it.

Blake managed to get Jacob to give him instructions on the best way to get gravy on his Yorkshire pudding, and I was grateful at the gentle way that these massive shifter men were slowly trying to coax Jacob out of his shell and gain his trust. When Blake had his first taste of gravy-soaked Yorkshire pudding his eyes widened in surprise, and he looked down at the serving dishes looking for more.

"Right?" Tanner said, happily munching on his own.

I rolled my eyes at their antics, and Jacob giggled. I could see it now that I was going to spend the rest of my life making Yorkshire puddings. There were none left over for the freezer. Maybe I could spend tomorrow making a tonne to save myself some grief in the future.

We were just at the stage where I was finishing up, and the guys were helping themselves to seconds when someone knocked on the door. River jumped up and went to the door to answer it and let Nash in, who immediately homed in on the food. Tanner grabbed him a plate and then we went around on the whole cottage pie and Yorkshire pudding thing again. Jacob thought it was hilarious, and his beautiful giggles set us all off.

"I kind of wish I'd made dessert," I admitted as we all sat around the table after we had finished eating. Even I could admit I was stuffed, but weirdly I was craving some lemon meringue pie.

"If I eat anything else, I'm going to puke," Tanner sighed, rubbing his belly.

Even Jacob looked like he was going to explode and had a little pot belly food baby going on.

"We need to decide what we are doing going forward," Grey said, breaking the mood. "The other issue we were dealing with can be put on the back burner for now. Nash, keep an eye on those properties, and I will send word to my father, other than that, I want us focusing on Jean and the witch problem." His gaze shifted to Jacob and then back to me, and I understood what he was subtly trying to say. This other problem wasn't something he wanted to talk about in front of Jacob. But fuck my life, another problem! Do you ever get that feeling that the universe hates you? Maybe not hate, I think it just thinks my life is a massive joke.

"I need a few days to recover before I can start trying to restore any of Jean's energy, so I'm going to concentrate on research in the library," I told everyone.

Nash raised his eyebrows in surprise and then quickly furrowed them in confusion.

"Dude, you are going to squeal like a little girl when you see upstairs," Tanner laughed. All of the guys seemed to find this funny, but I didn't get what the joke was.

Nash just started looking around him, no doubt scoping the place out for the stairs. The thought of stairs gave me a brilliant idea, and I excused myself from the table and went down to the basement. I grabbed a couple of bottles of wine out of the cellar when I heard a masculine gasp behind me and figured that one of the guys must have found the gym. When I made my way in there, I found River looking around with a massive smile on his face.

"This place is amazing," he smiled when he saw me walk into the room. "This is a really nice house, Calli."

"Yeah, my parents thought of everything," I said, sitting down on a weight bench and putting the wine bottles on the floor next to him. "Can I ask you for some advice?"

River came and sat down next to me and held my hand. "You can ask me for anything, my beautiful mate," he smiled. I really wanted to kiss him right now, but I needed to try and be a grown-up for a minute.

"I'm just thinking about Jacob and what will be best for him going forward," I told him, frowning as I tried to put my thoughts into some kind of order. "I don't know if I should encourage him back to school or give him some time."

River thought for a moment before he said anything. "He seems to be gradually making some progress tonight, but it will be a while before he comes back into himself again." He looked so guilty and sad as he said it and I squeezed his hand in support. "On the one hand, it could do him good to get back to a routine and see some friendly faces. Spend time with kids his own age. On the other hand, if you push him into an unfamiliar environment alone, it could make matters worse."

"Thanks for speaking out loud what I was worried about and somehow making me feel worse," I joked.

"Sorry. That wasn't very helpful, was it?" he said, giving

me a reluctant smile and I suddenly felt terrible. Maybe now wasn't the time to try and deal with my emotions through my inappropriate humour.

"No, but don't feel bad about it." I nudged him with my shoulder to try and show I wasn't holding a grudge. Something seemed to be bothering him, and I just didn't know him well enough to know what to say to him.

"Maybe give him tomorrow and see how he goes and make a decision from there. Take it on a day-by-day basis," River suggested.

"That's a good idea. Thanks. You were right before, when I was worried about him going back. I'm glad I've got you to talk to River."

He looked up at me, and I could see a question brimming in his eyes, but he also seemed to be reluctant to say it.

"It's hard because we haven't had a chance to get to know each other very well yet," I told him, hoping it would help.

River sighed, and I shuffled closer to him on the bench, so I was pressed up against his side. His head tilted towards me, and he ran his cheek over the top of my head before keeping it there. It was nice sitting here with him. It was a shame I was possibly about to ruin it.

"Maybe if you just say it while I'm not looking at you, it won't feel so hard," I suggested.

He let out another puff of breath before he spoke. "How can you ever forgive us, Calli? I'm worried I've lost you before I even had a chance to have you," he told me quietly.

"Do I look like I'm going anywhere?" I said, gently laying a hand on his thigh. "What Wallace did was wrong. In fact, wrong doesn't even feel like the right word. But his mistakes and his actions are not yours, River. This is still new to all of us, I don't know about you, but I'm looking forward to seeing where it's going to take us."

He gently wrapped one arm around my shoulders, almost like he was expecting me to run away despite what I had told him. It felt right, being here with him, in the quiet.

"I suppose we should go back upstairs. Unless you know how to get this cork out, then I'm totally down for hanging out down here for a bit," I said, grabbing the bottle of wine off the floor.

River looked at it like it had betrayed him. "Maybe we could find a screw top," he said, giving me a squeeze.

River reluctantly got to his feet, and I followed him back upstairs. He didn't let go of my hand, and there was something about holding hands with River that made me smile. It was such an innocent action, but it was making me deliriously happy.

When we got to the top of the stairs, we found Nash loitering about at the doorway. "Can I go upstairs?" he blurted out as soon as he heard us.

"Erm, sure. You could have gone up without asking you know," I told him, watching him shuffle back and forth on the spot like he was getting ready to run.

"Thanks, Calli," he shouted as he ran up the stairs, Tanner quickly followed after him with a massive grin on his face.

"Come on," River laughed, dragging me up the stairs after him. "This is going to be hilarious."

We all seemed to reach the top of the stairs at the same time, so we were fortunately in time to see Nash's reaction when he got to the library. He squealed like a little girl and then rushed from bookcase to bookcase gasping as he went. It was like he was having his own Beauty and the Beast moment but in a very small library rather than the impressive one that they had. Tanner was just pissing himself laughing at Nash. Admittedly, watching the big burly, red-headed wolf run around while he squealed in excitement was pretty funny.

"Wait ... Nash," I said as realisation struck me. "Are you Holly's boyfriend?" I asked, and he finally stopped his squealing and turned to me with a devastating smile on his face.

"Yeah, how did you know?" he asked.

"She told me when we had lunch ... yesterday? What day is it?" Too much had happened in the last few days.

"Really, what did she say about me?" he grinned, dropping himself down into the armchair where Blake had sat earlier and shuffling through the books which were still on the coffee table.

"Nothing much, but she said your name like this ... *Nash*," I breathed, bringing my hand to my chest and fake swooning for him. "So I think that pretty much speaks volumes."

The guys all laughed, and River held up the bottle of wine, which I had completely forgotten he was still holding. "I'm going to go and open this and get you a glass. Anyone else?" he offered.

"Sure, I'll drink Calli's wine," Tanner said, dropping himself down in the other armchair.

River disappeared downstairs, and Nash was immediately back on the subject of the library. "Calli, do you know how amazing this all is?" he said, clutching one of the books to his chest.

"I think she got that from your squealing. Dude, if you just want to leave your man card on the table before you leave, I can get that shredded for you," Tanner laughed.

"Don't be mean," I chastised, slapping him upside the head, but gently.

I wandered over to the bookshelf, where I had found my father's letter and pulled the old book off its stand. Running my fingers over the cover, I could feel the magic that was soaked into its pages as it warmed my hand. It was almost like it was saying hello to me. It reminded me of the soft feel of my mother's magic.

"I think my mother put this here for me. To help me," I said softly. It was obvious really that she had. I had no idea how she had managed it, but there wasn't anyone else other than my father that could have installed the library here.

River appeared back up the stairs carrying a couple of wine glasses, and Grey was behind him carrying more.

"Jacob's fallen asleep on the sofa," Grey told me, dropping a kiss on the top of my head and passing me a glass of wine. "Do you want me to put him into bed?"

I smiled up at Grey, wondering how we were suddenly in this weird place. It was nice, don't get me wrong, but it felt a little like we had missed several hundred steps in the middle. "He'll be okay there for a little bit."

"I don't think a collection like this exists anywhere else in the world, Calli. Apart from maybe at the Council's building. Your parents must have had some pretty good connections to get people to part with all of this information. Usually, each supernatural faction guards their secrets tightly. Your parents shouldn't have been able to access some of this information," Nash said, giving me a strange look.

I pulled my father's letter out of the book and passed it to Grey. I was interested in what he remembered, if anything, about my father. Nash was still watching me carefully as I took a seat on the arm of the chair Tanner was sitting in. I knew he suspected something and his suspicions made me wonder how much he already knew from personal experience.

"There are two very different worlds," I told them carefully. "The one that you grew up in: where you belonged to a pack; where you did as you were told and abided by the rules of your Council. And then there is where I grew up. On the outside."

Grey finished reading the letter and then looked at me. "I think I remember him," he said, passing the letter across to Tanner who read it, giving my leg a reassuring squeeze.

"Do you think they knew we were your mates?" Tanner asked when he had finished and then passed the letter on to River.

I just shrugged, it wouldn't surprise me if they did. I didn't know the true extent of my mother's magic. She had always been too afraid to use it around us, just in case it drew the attention of anyone to her children. What she did when she wasn't around us? I had no idea. Well, that's not entirely true. I had some ideas. I had learnt a lot while we stayed with Sean. They had run an underground network of sorts that helped anyone who needed to disappear. People like me.

"What are you trying to say?" Nash said.

Nash was naturally inquisitive, and he was intelligent. I wouldn't be able to hide anything from him. But as I looked around the room at my mates, I realised that I didn't want to. I wanted to share everything with them.

"I need to speak with someone before I can tell you everything. Is that okay?" I said, looking around at them all.

Nash just looked excited at the prospect, but Grey looked concerned. I couldn't blame him. This was his pack. He wasn't just responsible for these wolves; he cared about them all as well. He gave me a tight nod, and I felt like I had just lost a little bit of respect from him at that moment. The underground was bigger than all of us, though. Tanner gave my leg another squeeze. He must have felt the slight wilt of my body against him.

Clearing my throat, I stood up from the arm of the chair.

The sudden movement jostled my sore ribs, and I sucked in a pained breath which I am sure was noticed by all of them.

"I'm going to get Jacob into bed," I said, walking out of the room.

I couldn't take the look on Grey's face. It was a cross between confusion and disappointment, and I just didn't have it in me to suffer through it right now. Slipping down the stairs, I saw Jacob curled up snoring on the sofa. He does these cute little soft snores that get me every time. I scooped him up gently and huffed out a breath when the pain caught around my ribs again. I really needed to find myself some more painkillers, but I didn't feel like I had time to do anything to look after myself. As soon as I laid Jacob down in his bed, he immediately snuggled down into his covers with a snort. I couldn't help the smile that pulled across my face. I allowed myself a moment to watch him sleep like a weirdo, and then I slipped out of the room and gently closed the door behind me.

The guys must have still been up in the library because there was no one else in the open plan living area. Finding my phone on the dining table where I left, I opened up my contacts and called Sean before I could chicken out. He answered immediately like he always did.

"Has the situation changed?" he asked instead of a greeting.

Slipping out of the sliding door at the back of the house, I curled up on the outdoor sofa to speak with him privately. Thank god for patio heaters. The snow may have melted, but it was still cold outside.

"Yes, but not how you would expect." I took a deep breath because this was going to be the weirdest conversation we had ever had. "They're my mates," I blurted out.

"I'm going to need you to expand on that a bit more," he said stiffly.

"There was an incident, which I will tell you about later, I was exposed in my wolf form to the Alpha. He, his beta and his brother are all my mates. The pack is here now. I guess I'm joining it." I ended almost in a question because I'm not really sure how that works.

"I've never heard of wolves recognising someone as a mate like that before, but I suppose you are pretty different from any other female shifter. But that's good news, Calli," he said slowly. "Why do I feel like you're softening me up with the good news first though?"

"Because I totally am," I sighed. Then I launched into as detailed an explanation as I could manage of what had happened. Including the now sleeping beauty in my guest room and the fact that the way she got to be like that was by me sacrificing the only protection I had.

"Fuck," he breathed out as soon as I finished. I mean really there wasn't much more than that to say.

"Yeah, one of them floated an interesting idea, though. I know I can't reapply the same spell to myself, but what if it was a different spell. One that was just used to mask my witch scent?"

"I don't know enough about magic to be able to give you the answer to that, Cali, but I can look into it. See if I can get back into contact with Sera, if you like?"

"Yeah, I'd be grateful if you could. There's one other thing?" I said with a wince when he just sighed in defeat. "With the library here and the contacts I have, I'm going to need to tell them about the underground. They're already asking questions, and I don't feel like I can keep stuff from them."

Sean went quiet, and I could understand why he did. A lot of people's safety relied on the integrity of the underground. I only knew about the tip of the iceberg, and I had absolutely no desire to know any more than that. Not because what they are doing was wrong, but because knowing is what made it all so dangerous. Sean, I'd gathered from the six weeks that we spent with him, knew a hell of a lot more. He might be one of the people at the very top, but I'd never asked him, and he'd never told me.

"I understand what you're saying. How close are they to the Council?"

"I have no idea," I answered honestly.

The Council should be the thing that the underground had become. They should be the body that protected their people. They weren't. They're the thing that people needed to hide from. Those of us who were impure. Those of us who loved someone they deemed wrong. Those of us who wouldn't stand idly by and let their greedy and corrupt ways rule over their lives. Some never got to see the darker side of the Council, and their activities. Those who did usually died or became part of the underground.

"I trust your judgment Calli, and I trust that your parents would never have set up that house for you if they didn't think they could be trusted as well. Just make sure that you ask them about any Council ties they have before you tell them. Make sure nothing has changed in their circumstances since your parents looked into them four years ago." He didn't even sound nervous as he said it, he was always that confident in my parents. Everyone was. They had been the best of us.

"Okay. I think it would be sensible to set up those two safe houses still, just in case. It's always good to have options." It's not like I couldn't afford it and we would have just painted a target on our backs as soon as we went against the witches that came after the pack. It was only a matter of time before someone came back to find out what had happened, and I didn't have my amulet anymore to protect me. I couldn't afford for this to affect Jacob. I needed to make sure I had a safe place for him and a plan to get him there.

"I will. Be safe, Calli. I'll call you when I've spoken with Sera," he said before hanging up the phone.

After the call disconnected, I stayed sitting on the sofa, looking out into the darkness of the woods that surrounded the house. It was peaceful out here. I felt like I should be thinking of our next steps, considering how I would speak to the guys or putting together an emergency escape plan for Jacob. I just didn't have the energy to do it though. My mind felt numb. I just needed to go to bed and sleep, sleep away this terrible day and then wake up tomorrow in a different world, a world where I could have my mates beside me and not have to worry about what was waiting in the dark to try and take everything I loved away from me. We were going to need some kind of defences against the witches. They would be coming for us, and we needed to be ready.

29

GREY

Calli had gone outside to speak with someone on the phone. I could hear her voice quietly drifting towards me through the closed doors. I could have listened in if I wanted to, but I didn't want us to start our life together that way. I had seen her face when she left us in the library, and I knew she was upset. More so, my wolf was very aware I was the one that had upset her, and he was pissed at me. I'd never been able to school my emotions well. I wore them loud and clear for everyone to see. It was part of why I needed to leave my father's pack and start my own. I loved my father. I didn't want anyone ever to think I didn't. He was a good man. I knew he was. But sometimes I doubted him. I doubted his motivations, and I didn't like being that person. He had always been very much to the letter, the path of the law. A man who lived by the old ways and I kept finding myself not understanding some of the rules and decisions laid down by our Council. Decisions that he was happy to follow without question.

I had to leave in the end. It was not in my nature to just stand idly by. It would have only ended with me having to challenge my father, and that wasn't something I would ever have been able to live with.

It turned out to be the best decision I'd ever made and not just because it ultimately led us to Calli. We were a small pack, and our pack lands were small enough that the Council ignored us. It meant that we got to live our lives in relative peace.

River and I still saw our father. His was the closest pack to us and a valuable ally because we didn't have the numbers to defend our lands if we came up against a large force.

The library had fallen quiet since she left. Nash was back to looking through the bookshelves and every so often making little squeals of excitement. Tanner, however, was glaring at me across the top of his wine glass.

"You need to go and talk to her," he said, finally breaking the silence.

I knew he was right, but the fact that I also knew she was keeping something from us wasn't sitting well with me.

"If you don't go and talk to her, then you're never going to find out," River added.

"Plus, you should probably go and check on Blake," Nash said from the corner of the room. I hadn't realised he was even aware any of us were still in the room.

I left the library grumbling about how I was the Alpha and people shouldn't be telling me what to do, and the sounds of the laughter of the others followed me out. Knocking gently on the guest room door, I heard Blake call from inside. When I went in, my heart broke when I saw him lying next to Jean on the bed, watching her sleep. I could feel his sorrow flooding out of him into the room.

"This is my fault," he said, not taking his eyes off her sleeping form. "They only came after her because she was involved with me."

"This is not your fault Blake. You didn't ask for this; you didn't invite this. The blame for this lies solely on the shoulders of those who tried to hurt her and Coby," I told him, sitting on the edge of the bed.

I gently laid my hand on his shoulder in reassurance, and I felt him relax a little under the comfort of my waves of Alpha power.

"I should have said something earlier when she first started to feel sick. I should have known that something was wrong," he said quietly. "We had already scented the witch around the property, I should have known they were doing this to her," he sniffled quietly.

"I know that it hurts. I know watching the woman you love go through this is the worst kind of torture. But even if you had realised earlier what would it have achieved? We didn't know about Calli then to be able to ask for her help. All it would have done would be to cause you, and most of all, Jean, a lot more heartbreak. She would have had to live through days of knowing they were draining the life out of the baby inside her, and there would have been nothing she could have done about it. I know you wouldn't have wished that on her."

Blake rolled over to meet my eyes, and I could see his tears swimming there. I knew that no matter what I said, he was going to feel guilty about this. I couldn't blame him. I would do exactly the same in his position. I honestly did believe what I had said, though. There was no way they could have known what this was any earlier, and even if they did, there would have been absolutely nothing we could have done about it.

"Stay with her tonight, talk to her. You don't know, she might still be able to hear you. Then tomorrow we start making a plan. We will beat this, Blake. I promise you I'm going to do everything in my power to try and help Jean."

Blake nodded and then rolled over, snuggling back up against Jean's side. I quietly left the room to give him some peace. We were going to need to keep an eye on him to make sure that he didn't just give in to his grief. Jean would never forgive us if we let him wallow in that room by her side for however long it took to get her back to him.

I looked over to the sliding doors and could see Calli sat outside on the outdoor sofa. She seemed to have finished talking on the phone and was just soaking up the moonlight. She was so fucking beautiful. My wolf huffed in agreement in the back of my mind. He was straining to stake a claim on her, but we barely knew each other. The way that our relationship had been revealed had made us all feel awkward and unsure of ourselves. We suddenly went from trying to sneak a glance of her, to sleeping at her house while she tried to save a member of our pack. I couldn't even think about the beating Wallace gave her in between all of that happening. I would have to go back to the packhouse tomorrow to deal with that situation, and I fucking hated that idea. How had I gotten to the point where one of my own pack was a threat to my mate?

I shook my head and went into the kitchen to make Calli a cup of tea. She was British, and I was pretty sure that this was a thing they did. Drink tea when they were stressed out. Even if that wasn't the case, she was so happy when River found it for her. It was pretty obvious it was one of her favourite things. My wolf relaxed, knowing we were doing something that was going to make her happy. All he wanted was for her to come and live with the pack so we could watch over her and protect our new pup. How was that ever going to happen now, though? I was pretty sure Calli wasn't going to go back to the packhouse ever again. Were we going to live here? This house was amazing, but it was no way big enough for all of us.

When I was pretty sure that I had the tea made right—it was my first go so I hoped she would let me down gently if it was crap—I stepped outside and went to sit down next to her.

"Oh, thank you, you are truly a god among men," she smiled as she took the tea from my hands. My wolf was practically spinning in happy circles in my mind, and even I felt a little proud of myself that she was so happy from such a small thing.

The problem was now I had sat down, I didn't know what to do next. I didn't know what to say. Fuck, why am I failing at something as simple as spending time with my mate? I wasn't even entirely sure that she was happy about being my mate.

"This had been the craziest twenty-four hours of my life," Calli said, breaking the silence as she sat back into the cushions cradling the mug in her hands.

"Tell me about it. I have a terrible feeling this is just the beginning as well."

"I've been thinking about that. I know I said I would start looking for an answer for Jean straight away, but I wondered if maybe we should look into some kind of wards for the houses first. It would make me feel like Jacob was a bit safer at the very least."

"Is that something you can do?" I asked, immediately interested. I was aware of the concept of warding but seeing as witches and wolves were basically enemies, it wasn't anything we had ever had access to. Anyway, what would be the point in asking the person you needed protection from to put up the wards for you.

"Who knows?" Calli shrugged. "I've done more magic in the last twenty-four hours than I have in my entire life.

But what's the worst that can happen right? Might as well try."

"Let's try not to think about it," I said, awkwardly sliding my arm along the back of the sofa, and putting my arm around her. "Let's just have tonight and then start thinking about it all again tomorrow."

Calli ignored my awkwardness and snuggled up against me. "You don't even want to talk about earlier," she asked quietly. It didn't take a genius to know what she was talking about.

"I'm not going to make you talk about something you don't want to," I told her. Even I could admit that it came out a little sullenly.

"Grey," she said, sitting up. I immediately felt the loss of her touch and curled my fingers into the sofa cushions to stop myself from pulling her back into me. "It's not that I don't want to tell you. It's bigger than you and me. People's lives are at stake."

I frowned in confusion and then the worry set in. What the fuck was my mate involved in?

"Are you in danger?" I asked, a little more heated than I probably should have. If anyone asked, I was blaming it on my Alpha nature.

"When am I not in danger?" she chuckled. "I was in danger the second I was born, and I will be until the moment I die."

That one comment brought it all home. Because she was right, the world that we lived in didn't accept people like Calli. Even worse, the two sides of her heritage hated each other. She would probably have a better chance with the wolves than the witches. The witches would drain her dry the second they laid eyes on her. The wolves might give her a fighting chance. But even as I thought that I realised it wasn't true. Wallace had wanted to kill her, and she had called a witch to help her when we needed it the most. What did it say about us that someone I would have considered my enemy had proved more help today than one of my pack?

I was snapped out of my thoughts by River, who opened the sliding door and came to join us. "Tanner's gone to the diner to get pie," he said, sitting down on the sofa next to us.

Silence came over us all again, and I almost wanted to cringe at how awkward it all was.

Calli once again came to the rescue. "What kind of pie?"

"At this time of night, probably whatever they have left," River answered honestly.

I looked down at my watch and realised that it was almost ten at night already. Judging by the amount of food Calli had ready by the time we all woke up from our nap, she couldn't have gotten much sleep. She must be exhausted.

"Are your parents still around?" Calli asked suddenly.

"Our father lives about three hours away from here. His packlands border our own. Our mother died when I was fifteen though," River told her.

We still felt her absence deeply, but over time it had got easier.

"I'm sorry, that must have been terrible," Calli said quietly.

"When she passed, I read something that helped me. It said that grief is like a suitcase you inherit when someone dies. It's filled with all of the memories and feelings we have of that person. When you first pick it up, it almost feels like it's filled with rocks and the weight is unbearable. It feels impossible to know you are going to have to carry it with you every day. But over time, you gradually get used to the weight of that suitcase, until there comes a day when you don't even realise you're carrying it. There will still be days when you remember that it's there and you feel the weight of it again, but it doesn't feel as bad any more because it's those days that you remember all of the memories contained within it. It's through those memories that the people we love get to live on. It's an honour to carry that suitcase and guard the memories of the ones that we love inside it," River told her quietly. He'd never told me that before.

"That's beautiful," Calli told him, squeezing his knee. "Do you still see your Dad much?"

"Not as much as we probably should. Life gets in the way sometimes, you know. We should probably make more of an effort, though." I admitted.

"He must be proud of you, setting out and forming your own pack."

"I'm not sure proud is the right word. My father is very old fashioned. He expected me to stay in the pack, learn the ropes and take over the position of Alpha when he was ready to retire," I told her. "That just didn't feel like the right path for me, though. The pack we grew up in was big. My father, and therefore the whole pack, are very rigid and set in their ways. I wanted to start something new. Something different. A pack where everyone was valued for their contribution. I may as well have set out and started a hippy commune, which is actually what he told me once," I laughed.

River laughed along with me. "Oh man, when he finds out that Calli is mate to all three of us, he's going to start believing that."

I hadn't thought of that. It wasn't uncommon for wolves to share mates that had been turned, especially because it was so difficult to turn a human woman. Calli's very existence and her status as our mate could change everything for wolves. What if she could be the start of female wolves being born? Would our daughters be true wolves too?

"Tell me something about your childhood." Calli requested, coming back against my side to lean against me.

River leant down and scooped her feet up off the floor and pulled them over his lap as he started to tell her the story of how I nearly drowned in the lake because I was convinced that there was treasure in the bottom of it. Halfway through, Calli pulled my arm off the back of the sofa and wrapped it around her chest, twining her fingers with mine. It was nice, sitting here like this, telling her our stories, even if they were all going to be about me doing something stupid when I was a pup.

Tanner came back soon after and slipped out of the house to take a seat with the rest of us. He had three pie boxes and some plates and forks with him. Calli immediately zoned in on the boxes and Tanner's chest puffed up in pride. It seemed like our little mate had another weakness as well as tea.

Tanner laid the three boxes out on the table and opened them with a flourish. "Rhubarb apple, blueberry and chocolate cream for my main man Jacob when he wakes up in the morning."

"Oooo, I want to try rhubarb apple, and you are not giving Jacob chocolate cream pie for his breakfast," Calli said, clapping her hands together.

Tanner cut her a slice and passed it across with a frown on his face. "But he's going to love it."

"Of that, I have no doubt, but it's not really breakfast food." She groaned in delight as she had her first bite and we all became immediately focused on her and the fork that she was slowly sliding out from between her lips.

"Oh my god," she snorted. "You are such horn dogs if that was enough to turn you on," she laughed.

Tanner, who had started eating the chocolate cream pie

then made a similar noise, and she shuffled uneasily in her seat. "Okay, point made," she admitted.

We spent the next hour eating far too much pie and telling stories about the stupid things we had done when we were kids. It was nice. It was like we were getting round to one of the steps we had missed —actually getting to know each other.

When Calli finally couldn't hide her yawns any more and admitted that she needed to go to bed, she shyly asked us. "You are going to stay, aren't you?"

"Of course," Tanner said, pulling her up off the sofa and then scooping her up in his arms. "We'll take turns to sleep beside you and keep watch," he told her as he carried her to her bedroom.

"I feel like I should offer to take a shift, but I think I need to sleep for a few days," she admitted.

To be honest, I didn't know how she was even still awake. Not only had she drained herself to heal me, then been beaten to near unconsciousness, but she'd also then spent hours finding a solution to Jean's magical drain. I was pretty sure she had barely slept for the last forty-eight hours. Even if she had been fully alert I wouldn't have let her take a shift on watch. There was no way that any of us were going to be able to sleep while she was outside, alone, looking for danger. It went against my very nature. I had a feeling Calli wasn't going to be wholly impressed when we started in on that though. The poor woman was going to have to cope with three of us as well.

"I'll take first watch," River said, hovering in the doorway of Calli's bedroom. "Calli, I'll sort out with the school about Jacob not going in tomorrow, and one of us will be around in the morning when he wakes up. Sleep for as long as you need."

Calli rose up on her tiptoes and softly kissed River's cheek. "Thank you. I'll see you in the morning. And don't let Tanner give Jacob chocolate for breakfast," she ended with a smile.

"Hey, I don't need watching over," Tanner scoffed in fake outrage.

"Hmmm. We'll just have to see about that," she said, giving him a cheeky smile while she pulled some pyjamas out of her closet and slipped into her bathroom.

"We should probably get some things from the house tomorrow if we're going to be staying here," Tanner said, stripping down to his boxers and climbing into bed.

"Are we going to be staying here?" I asked. This situation was beyond weird.

"Of course you are," Calli said as she came out of the bathroom. "If you want to, that is. I'm not holding you hostage or anything."

She was wearing a pair of soft pyjama shorts and a tank top that stretched tight across her breasts. Even as she yawned widely and crawled into the bed, I had never seen anything as sexy in my life. There was nothing I wouldn't do for her. Climbing into bed beside her was the happiest I had ever been and feeling her snuggle up against me meant I wasn't going to go to sleep for hours. I felt Tanner slide closer, cuddling against her back. It should be weird sleeping like this with another man, but we were wolves, and we found comfort in being close to each other. Plus, he was Calli's other mate, and it just felt right that he was here. The only thing that would make this moment complete would be if River were with us too. It was like we were a pack within a pack. My wolf wanted them all close by where we could see them. The fact that River was outside making sure that Calli was safe while she slept was the only thing that was appeasing him at the moment. She had quickly become the centre of our world, and it felt right in a way I couldn't even put into words.

I laid back and enjoyed being close with my mate, even if she was shuffling around like she was uncomfortable. My wolf huffed in amusement because we knew the reason why she was uncomfortable. The sweet scent of her arousal was slowly drifting into the air. It would seem that our sweet little mate was just as affected laying between us as we were.

"How are you not asleep yet?" I heard Tanner mumble in exasperation against her back. It must be the sweetest kind of torture for him to have her ass rubbing against him every time she moved—which was currently a lot.

"I'm suddenly not tired," she mumbled quietly, and I nearly laughed at her avoidance of the real reason.

Tanner lifted his head and caught my eye as he gave me a wicked smirk. I already knew exactly where he was about to go with this, and I for one thought it was a fantastic idea.

Dipping his head back down, Tanner laid his lips against Calli's neck as he softly kissed his way to behind her ear. She froze as he moved his lips across her neck, but judging from the way that her chest heaved from her panting, it wasn't because she was scared.

"Does that feel good, mate," I murmured as I picked up her hand and kissed the pulse point at her wrist.

I could feel her heartbeat pounding against my lips and the soft moan she gave in response, set my cock hard.

"I think our beautiful mate needs something to help her sleep," I smirked at Tanner.

I saw his lips flicker in a smile against the skin of her neck before he gently bit down at the juncture of her shoulder.

Calli's eyes rolled back in her head as she moaned low and deep from the sensation. Her body bowed against Tanner, pressing her breasts forward towards me. I ran my thumb over the peak of her hard nipple that was pushing through her thin tank top and her eyes suddenly locked to mine.

"We can stop, now or whenever you want," I told her seriously. "But let us make you feel good Calli. Let us wipe away every thought in your mind."

Calli pinched her lower lip between her teeth and nodded in agreement. I knew she needed this. She needed something to help her mind just let go so that she could fall into a deep blissful sleep, and I was more than happy to do it for her.

Tanner's hands gathered the hem of her tank top and slowly started to work it up her body, exposing all her beautiful skin to me. Her creamy soft stomach was the first thing to be revealed to me and I shuffled down the bed to lay my lips against her. The bruising that had marred her skin was already fading; her shifter healing had started to remove the marks that offended my wolf and I so much.

My wolf growled in appreciation at our Beta unveiling our mate to us; it pleased him to feel like the Alpha in this situation.

As Tanner kept moving the material up, it almost felt like I was chasing it with my lips. When the curve of the bottom of her breast slowly came into view, I ran my tongue along the edge until I reached her cleavage. Calli leant up to meet me, and with a flourish, Tanner quickly whipped her top away, leaving Calli topless before me. She was pure perfection. Her dusky pink nipples sat atop her creamy white breasts, and I licked my lips in appreciation.

Tanner's hand moved to Calli's chin, and he tilted her head back so that his lips could reach hers. I watched as they slowly kissed, Calli's tongue slowly slipped out as she ran it across his lips and Tanner groaned, opening his mouth wider to give her access.

His other hand started to slip up towards her breast, but I took hold of his wrist to stop him. I wanted to watch this, I wasn't ready for him to move it forward into something else yet. Tanner's eyes locked with mine as he felt me stop his movement and the heat in them banked higher before he fell into that kiss with renewed passion.

His tongue slid into her mouth, and Calli whimpered in need, her hips writhing, seeking out any kind of contact.

My wolf was basking in the sense of controlling their enjoyment; their pleasure was ours to give. There was so much that we wanted to do in this moment, but tonight had to just be about Calli. It was too soon to take this too far, and I knew she wasn't ready. I didn't want her to regret anything in the morning.

Moving slowly, keeping my eyes on the show in front of me, I took Calli's hard nub into my mouth, gently biting down on the hardened peaks of her nipple. Calli's hands came up to cradle my head as she pulled me tighter against her. I couldn't stop the smirk of satisfaction as I cradled her breast in my hand and set about licking and biting the other.

One of Calli's legs slowly moved up, her thigh slipping across my hip as she tried to pull me in against her body.

There was nothing that I wanted more than to sink my cock into the heat of her body. To let her feel just how much I wanted her, while I watched Tanner feast on her breasts. But I held back, I didn't want to start something that was going to be too painful to stop, and I was determined to make tonight about Calli and Calli alone, no matter how much enjoyment I was getting out of being in charge of this show.

I ran one hand up her thigh, towards the heat of her pussy. I could smell her arousal on the air, and it was intoxicating. Slipping my fingers inside her shorts, I trailed up her thigh until I found her core. I lingered there, giving her a chance to pull away if that was what she wanted but all she did was whimper in frustration, grinding down trying to seek contact.

I grinned against her breast but ultimately pulled myself away. I wanted to watch her face. I wanted to see her expression when I finally gave her what she wanted.

I waited for the moment that Tanner drew back slightly from their kiss before I pushed two fingers inside her wet core. Calli's whole body bowed as she groaned at the sensation. Her breasts pushed forward as her head fell back to Tanner's shoulder, her hips grinding as she chased the sensation of finally having something inside her.

Tanner looked at me in question. It turned me on more than I ever thought it would to see him waiting for permission. I pumped my fingers twice into Calli's core before I withdrew them.

She lifted her head, looking like she was about to protest until she watched in fascination as I raised my hand, pushing my fingers into Tanner's waiting mouth.

His eyes rolled back in his head as the taste of his mate filled his mouth, and my cock grew impossibly harder as he sucked her sweet nectar from my fingers.

"I need you to tell me that you want more, Calli," I spoke low, the echo of my wolf's growl vibrating with my mate. "I know you wanted to take things slowly and this doesn't have to go any further if you don't want it to."

I needed her to say something, everything about our relationship had started out wrong, and I needed this not to be the same.

"Please, don't stop," Calli whispered.

And that was all I needed to hear.

My hands tore at the waistband of her shorts as I pushed them down her legs, removing the last piece of clothing that hid her away from me. Hooking her leg over my shoulder, I saw Tanner watching me with the lust burning in his eyes. I nodded permission to him, and his hands finally came up to cradle her breasts as he rolled her nipples between his fingers.

Calli's eyes were locked with mine as her mouth fell open on a sigh of sensation. I slowly lowered my face to the apex of her thighs, holding her gaze as I moved. She was the most beautiful creature I had ever seen, and I wanted to watch every sensation and every ounce of pleasure blaze across her face.

When my lips finally met her core, the sweet wetness of her pussy meeting my mouth, I growled in approval. She tasted like heaven, and I would die a lucky man with the taste of her on my lips.

Sinking two fingers back inside again, Calli's hips started to move to match the rhythm of my movements. I circled my tongue around her clit before sucking it into my mouth and rolling my tongue across it.

I could tell that she was close as her pussy quivered, tightening around my digits as I pulsed them inside her.

Tanner groaned in delight as he rolled both her nipples between his fingers and dropped his mouth back down to her neck to softly bite down. Just watching his teeth meet her skin had my wolf quivering in satisfaction and I filed that weirdness away to think about later.

Calli's soft moans filled the room as her body bowed between us. I felt Tanner grind against her ass, his hard cock brushing against my hand that cradled her ass, pulling her closer to me. I'd never shared a woman with anyone, let alone with Tanner, but everything about this felt right.

Her pants increased as she rushed to meet her orgasm, and I pulsed my fingers quicker inside her. My tongue lashed against her clit, and no matter how much I wanted to close my eyes and savour the taste of her, I kept them open and fixed on her face. My need to watch her come overriding everything else.

She shattered in the most delicious way as her pussy clamped down around my fingers and her head was thrown back as she moaned. I could tell that she was holding back, that she was trying to be quiet and I would let it go for now. We had others in the house, and as much as I wanted to hear her screaming in ecstasy, I also didn't want others listening in on her pleasure.

Calli panted softly as she came down from the high of her orgasm and looked down at me with a soft smile just as I pushed my fingers into my mouth, humming in satisfaction as I licked the taste of her from them.

I could see the heat starting to build again in her eyes, and my wolf growled in appreciation at how responsive she was. I couldn't wait to have her in here for a whole night when I could do all the things I wanted to her.

Tanner dropped soft kisses against Calli's neck as I moved up her body, trailing my lips across her skin as I went. Tanner moved back when I reached her lips, and I gently pulled her into my arms, careful not to jostle her ribs.

"Now, sleep," I mumbled against her lips as I kissed her softly again and then brought her to lie against my chest.

Tanner scooted closer to her and Calli hitched one of her legs over my hip as she settled in.

"I feel bad that neither of you …"

"Tonight wasn't about us, and you have nothing to feel bad about," I told her. I could already feel her breathing starting to ease out, and my wolf settled in my mind that she was finally going to get some sleep.

Seconds later, she was fast asleep. She hadn't even been awake long enough to put her clothes back on, and I found that I liked the fact that all of her skin was pressed against mine as she slept. I could get used to sleeping this way.

Even though my mind was trying to sort through all the problems we seemed to be accumulating, it didn't take long for me to follow her into sleep.

30

CALLI

I woke up the next day from the best sleep I think I had ever had. Unfortunately, I was now alone in bed because I was very much looking forward to a repeat of last night.

The sun was shining brightly outside, and I rolled over to grab my phone and check the time. When I saw that it was nearly 10:00 am I was surprised. It wasn't like me to sleep in this late. I suppose I had been pretty exhausted, though. That was the first time I'd experienced a drain on my magic to that level, and it's not something I wanted to rush into experiencing again. I could still only feel a faint glow of it inside, and it felt all kinds of weird.

I could hear movement out in the house, and I knew that the guys must be out there with Jacob. I needed to make sure I made time to speak with him today to see how he felt about them all being around. This was his house too, and it seemed like they were going to be a permanent fixture. I needed to make sure that Jacob was ready for this step with everything that had happened recently. If he wasn't, then the guys and I would have to take a step back and wait for him to be ready. It would hurt, but I would do anything for my little brother.

I dragged myself out of bed, took a shower and dressed before going out into the house to see what the plan was for today.

Tanner and Jacob were lazing on the sofa watching cartoons, and I could see River and Grey outside talking on the outdoor sofa. I flicked the kettle on and made myself a cup of tea before throwing a couple of slices of bread into the toaster. When I grabbed the things I needed out of the fridge, I noted a distinct lack of pie.

"Jacob, honey, what did you have for breakfast?" I asked in what I hoped was my sweetest voice as I leant against the kitchen counter as casually as I could.

Jacob is the worst at keeping secrets, and when he looked across at me with a massive grin on his face, complete with chocolate smeared around his mouth, it was fairly obvious what he had.

"Quick run for it!" Tanner shouted, lifting Jacob off the sofa and throwing him over his shoulder. Jacob squealed and giggled as Tanner sprinted them into Jacob's room and then slammed the door behind them. I couldn't even be upset that they let him have chocolate for breakfast when I got to hear those giggles.

"Like I said, Tanner's good with kids because he basically still is one," came River's voice from behind me.

I turned around to see him by the sliding door just as I heard Tanner shout out, "I heard that."

River just rolled his eyes with a laugh. "Do you want to join us outside Calli?"

He almost seemed shy as he asked. I needed to spend more time with River. The two times I had fallen asleep with them in my bed, River hadn't been there. I needed to make sure there wasn't a reason behind that.

"Sure," I said, smiling brightly. I quickly finished up my toast, then grabbed my cup of tea and another slice before heading outside to sit with them.

Just as I was sitting down, Tanner came out to join us, diverting my hand of toast so that he could steal a bite.

"What kind of man-imal are you?" I said in shock, looking at my toast which his big mouth had taken at least a third of. I pulled it into my chest to guard my food as I glared at him over my cup of tea.

River and Grey just laughed at us, and part of me wanted to accuse them of not protecting their mate's food, but even I didn't want to get Tanner into that much trouble. Instead, I shuffled a bit closer to River, who sat on my other side and hoarded my food closer. Now if he reached out to take my tea, he'd be pulling back a nub instead of a hand, that stuff was sacred.

Grey awkwardly cleared his throat and then shuffled in his spot, glancing uneasily at River. It seemed like they were talking about me earlier. I supposed it was inevitable that this was going to have to be a conversation we had.

"So, Calli, we were talking earlier, and we were, erm, wondering ..." he awkwardly started off.

"You want to finish the conversation from yesterday," I said, feeling sorry for him and getting him to the point quicker.

"Yeah," he sighed, rubbing the back of his neck. It was a strange move for this Alpha wolf to be undertaking and I couldn't help but wonder if maybe my mate was a bit of a softy on the inside, at least when it came to me. Outside of the bedroom at least as images of last night flashed through my head.

"Okay," I sighed, trying to figure out where to start. "You said last night that your father is very stuck in his old ways. How close is he to the Council?"

Grey frowned in confusion. I could see that this was maybe a strange place to start off. It didn't take a genius to figure out why I was asking them this, but I was hoping that it seemed more like I was some kind of fugitive, which I suppose I was, rather than anything else.

"He lives by their rule, but that's it, if that's what you're asking," Grey said confused.

I looked at Tanner to make it clear that I was asking him the same question.

"My father and I don't talk. I'm his biggest disappointment in life, and I think he's an absolute asshole," Tanner said calmly.

I was taken aback by how calmly he said the words. Whilst it was something that I might need to speak with him about in the future, if that was something he wanted to do, it wasn't something I could do anything about now.

"Erm, okay. And you, how much do you have to do with the Council?" I asked. I felt almost ashamed to do it. It's like I'm questioning whether or not they were good men. I knew they were, but once I told them why I was asking, I couldn't help but worry they were going to wonder about the motives behind my questioning.

"We're too small for them to care all that much about and just common wolves," Grey filled in. I think I heard a bit of resentment in his voice, but I'm not sure. I didn't know him well enough to be able to gauge it. Whilst that was something I planned to correct, it was only going to come with time. We frankly just hadn't had enough time together yet.

"Okay. I need you to understand first that the reason why I didn't tell you everything last night, the reason why I asked you these questions now, isn't because I don't trust you. This is bigger than you and me. The people we protect deserve to have a peaceful life. That is what it's all about," I explained uneasily. The three of them just looked confused. "I said before that there are two worlds. You grew up in a pack under Council rule. I grew up on the outside of that. No one would have claimed us. My father would never have been allowed membership to a pack because he loved my mother, and she was a witch. She could never return to her coven because they would have drained my father and her children on sight."

Shadows of memories flickered through my mind of harsh whispered arguments in the night, running and hiding with one of my parents.

"My parents were not the first to fall in love with what your Council or the covens would have called 'undesirables'. There are others. Others who have suffered because of the people they love. Who had suffered because they saw the corruption in your system first hand and couldn't abide by it. The stories that I have heard," I trailed off with a shudder. "They needed someone to save them, but there was no one. The very people who were supposed to protect them were the people they were running from, so they did the only thing they could, they saved themselves. Then they started helping others and soon a whole network, an underground, a resistance began."

I looked between the three of them. The three of them were born and raised in a pack. They know nothing of this. They still believed that the world was perfect, and the Council was there to help them.

"Makes sense," Grey said, suddenly nodding.

Fucking, what!

I tilted my head to the side in confusion and Tanner thankfully took pity on me and explained.

"There's always been something a bit off about some of the stuff that comes down from the Council. It's one of the main reasons why we separated off to form our own pack. Our Alpha was very old school, a 'what the council says goes', kind of guy. Even when it didn't fully make sense, he didn't believe in asking questions. It didn't sit right with us, and eventually, we decided that we didn't want to just stand by and participate in it any more," he explained.

I nodded in understanding. When I took those two years to go travelling, I met many people who formed part of the underground and did some work with them along the way. A lot of them had similar stories. They didn't realise what was going on at first, or something had felt off and then suddenly they were under a microscope and saw what was really happening, it wasn't 100% a shock to them. I didn't know how an entire society could function suspecting that their leaders were corrupt without ever doing anything about it. But I suppose some of them did, that's why a lot of them ended up having to turn to the underground.

"You realise that once they find out about me, they will come for me," I said quietly.

This was something that we needed to discuss, even if I didn't want to. Grey was an Alpha. He was responsible for his entire pack even if it was small. Being with me could mean he lost everything, that he lost them, his pack.

Grey got up and came and knelt in front of me. "I'm pretty sure I speak for all of us when I say that we would do anything for you, Calli. We meant it when we said we would protect both you and Jacob with our lives. And if that means we have to leave all of this behind and start over somewhere else with you, we'll do it. Even if it might be painful to do at first."

The guilt of what he was suggesting was crushing. They

would give up everything for me. They would leave their home and their pack behind.

"I don't know if I can let you do that," I whispered, tears building in my eyes.

Grey pulled me off the sofa and into his arms. I ended up straddling his knees on the ground.

"I've lost so much, and I know what that is like. I can't ask you to give up your pack for me," I said, burrowing my face into his neck.

Why did it have to be like this? Why did it have to be such an impossible choice? I didn't know if I would survive walking away from them.

Tanner laughed and slipped off the sofa, squeezing down behind me and wrapping his arms around me. "We wouldn't be giving them up. They'd come with us," he said like it's a forgone conclusion as he squeezed both me and Grey in his arms.

This was a difficult position for me because we were pretty much wedged in here between the sofa and the table. Grey and Tanner took up all the space, and I was pretty much perched on Grey's thighs. What I wanted to do was turn around and look at Tanner with a "what the fuck?" look on my face, but I couldn't shift my body that way and ended up just huffing in annoyance.

"You can't expect everyone just to leave their homes and follow us to god knows where!" I said, throwing my hands up in the air in exasperation.

"I don't think you understand sweetheart. It's not the packlands. It is the pack. We stay together. We always stay together. If we need to move on, then we move on. The house, the garage, they don't matter. We can have that wherever we end up. What matters is what is in the best interest of the pack and if people are coming for you, if people are coming for us, then the best thing for the pack is to move on," Grey explained to me.

"But what if it's not in the best interest of all of the pack members?" I asked.

This didn't make sense to me; these people had a life here. Why would they give all of that up for me?

"They can stay behind if they want to, but once you are a part of a pack, it becomes a part of you. They will want to stay together." I felt Tanner shrug behind me as he spoke.

I realised just how much my father had sacrificed to be with my mother, but also just how much we had missed out on by not having a pack around us as we were growing up. If we'd been part of a pack when my parents died, the pack would have come together and cared for us. We would have had not only a support system, but a family, even if they weren't blood relations, they would have still been pack. The Council was responsible for taking that from us. They were responsible for taking it from a lot of our people.

"We don't have to make any decisions now. We know that it is a possibility and we can make plans accordingly, but for right now we have other situations to deal with here," River said, placing a hand on my shoulder.

That made me feel a bit better. I couldn't add this to the pile of things we already had to deal with.

"Okay, moving forward we need to prioritise what we are going to tackle first and then go from there," Grey said, taking charge. It was weird to have this conversation straddling his thighs while we were all huddled together like this.

"Whilst this is lovely, can we move back to the sofa? I feel weird trying to talk this out with you guys sitting like this," I admitted, I felt my cheeks flush with heat and even I wasn't sure what it was exactly that I felt embarrassed about.

Grey chuckled, and I felt Tanner move from behind me.

Standing suddenly he scooped me up with him and then dropped us back down on the sofa, me still sitting in Grey's lap. His arms banded tightly around me, and I knew that for right now, I wasn't going anywhere. Not that it was any hardship for me, sitting here, so I snuggled into his chest and took what I could while we had the time.

"Calli, you mentioned something about warding. Can you look into that today?" Grey asked.

"Warding?" River said, frowning.

"Yes, Calli raised the point that now we've pissed off the witches it would help if we had some kind of system to tell us when they are breaching our lands. I think it's a good idea if we can pull it off. It would definitely make me feel better about us being spread across the two properties," Grey said nodding.

"In principle, it's something that I should be able to do, but I've never done it before, I don't know anything about it, and I don't know if I'm even at a point where it is something that I can do alone," I reasoned. "So at the moment it's more of a pie in the sky idea than anything else," I shrugged.

"Your mother didn't place wards around your home in England?" Tanner asked.

"No. We were completely under the radar. If we had wards placed at the house, any passing witches would have known someone inside could perform magic. It would be a glaring beacon confirming that we wanted to protect something. We couldn't afford that kind of attention. I figure that's not an issue here. The witches already know about you, and we need any help we can get if they decide to come back and investigate."

"It could draw attention to you and Jacob," Tanner warned.

"I don't have my amulet anymore; they'll be able to sense

my magic if they come into the area now anyway." I swallowed the lump forming in my throat.

Maybe I should think about sending Jacob away for a while, to one of the other families in the underground. Just for a little while. Him being around me drew attention to him. He would be safer if he weren't with me.

"We will protect him," Grey murmured, holding me tightly against him, almost as if he knew exactly where my thoughts had taken me.

I nodded in agreement, and we fell quiet for a while as we all got lost in our thoughts.

"Okay, about that, I have to ask, and I'm sorry if it comes out as insulting or something, but I just can't wrap my head around it," Tanner rambled away before taking a deep breath. "Why don't you stink?"

Laughter burst out of me. That wasn't really what I had expected him to ask.

"Well, I'm glad you don't think I stink," I laughed, but it quickly merged into a soft moan as Tanner shoved his face against my neck, inhaling deeply and running his nose up the length of my neck.

"You smell like lilac and jasmine and summer rain," he groaned. "It's almost as beautiful as you."

"He means," River said, clearing his throat. "Witch magic can smell kind of offensive to us. Maybe it's because your part wolf or because you are our mate," he reasoned.

"No, it's because I'm not corrupted," I explained.

They frowned in confusion at me, and I realised I would need to explain more to them.

"This is something that all of the packs should know, but your Council keeps it from you. There is more than one type of witch, just as there is more than one type of wolf. The only witches which you have ever come across are those that are there to drain your energy. I imagine it would be the same for all of the packs. Not all witches agree with the practice. Those that don't have the same type of scent as me. My mother always told me that it was because what those witches were doing was unnatural. It corrupts them and their magic. She always said that it was the smell of the rot that was taking hold of them," I said, reliving the memories of my mother and the way she would always be in the kitchen baking as she tried to explain the world to me when I was little.

"So, we could find allies in the witch community," Grey said, sounding interested.

"No," I answered honestly. "The rot goes deep, all the way to the coven heads. Those people who disagree with the practice are mostly part of the underground now. It is unlikely that they would come out of hiding to help us. They have just as much to lose as we do."

I could see that Grey was disappointed.

"They just want to live their lives in peace with the people they love. They take risks helping where they can in the underground but exposing themselves would mean death. It would mean running for their lives again," I said, and he nodded sadly in understanding. "I have someone looking into the adjustment to the original spell like you suggested," I told them quietly, trying to change the subject.

Thankfully they either could see what I was doing or just moved on, but the mood between us had grown heavy and sombre.

"I'm going to head to the store and grab some supplies for here, as it seems we have eaten Calli out of house and home," Tanner grinned, trying to break the mood. "I'll take Jacob with me. I promised he could look at the new Lego sets they'd got in."

I couldn't help but roll my eyes, that kid was obsessed with Lego. I suppose it could be worse, though.

"I need to head back to the packhouse and deal with Wallace. Can you come with me?" Grey asked River.

"I'd love to," he grinned back.

Okay, not going anywhere near that. I get it. They were male wolves feeling the mating call, and Wallace was a risk to their mate. They needed to get this out of their system. And maybe I'd like the idea of him getting his ass kicked a bit.

"Then it's settled. I'll get Blake to stay here with Calli. I think he needs to stay by Jean for the next few days anyway. Nash is up at the house so we can speak with him when we get there, and Aidan is finishing up at the garage and freeing us up for the next week," Grey nodded.

I climbed up out of his lap and went to head into the house. If I had a day of reading and researching ahead of me, I wanted another cup of tea to get me through it. If I couldn't find anything out on my own, I could always try and contact Marie again, but we tried to limit contact between the underground unless it was an emergency. I needed to learn how to do this myself. I flicked on the kettle and grabbed a tray out of the cupboard, deciding that an entire pot of tea was the way to go and started to load up on snacks as well.

31

GREY

River and I pulled up outside of the packhouse and just sat in the cab of the truck. It felt like we hadn't been here in ages. So much had happened over the last twenty-four hours. I clenched the wheel of the truck in my fists. I had never felt so betrayed by one of my pack brothers as I did right now.

"I don't know how to deal with this," I admitted quietly to River.

He was sat staring out of the passenger side window into the trees surrounding the house. I could feel the same conflicting emotions raging from him that I was feeling myself.

"I don't know either," he admitted.

We stayed like that, sitting in the truck, lost in our thoughts until Nash headed out of the packhouse. With a sigh, I climbed out of the truck, leaning back against the door as I waited for Nash to approach. He looked nervous, and I knew that whatever it was, he wanted to say to us out here instead of inside. There was no way that this was going to be good. When he reached the truck, he stood in front of me, casting his eyes to the ground in respect, before shuffling on his feet.

"Get to it," I sighed. I just didn't have the energy for this. We were fighting on too many fronts right now, and the fact that one of those was our own pack was unforgivable. Unforgivable that one of our pack brothers would move against us, and inexcusable that I had given him the impression as his Alpha that was even a choice.

"Wallace has been in the cage all night like you requested. He says that he wants to apologise, that he understands he was wrong," Nash said, but there was something shifty about him.

"What else?" I growled at him.

"I … erm … I'm not sure that I 100% believe him," he said quietly, looking down at his feet. I could feel the shame radiating from him.

Fuck. This could tear apart the pack. It needed to be dealt with quickly and properly. We were too small to be able to weather something like this.

I put one hand on Nash's shoulder, and I felt some of the tension leave him. "Thank you for telling me. I know this is a difficult situation."

Nash nodded and moved away from us to head back into the house. River had silently stood by my side throughout. He would never insert himself in something like this usually. Even though he was my brother, he never tried to step on Tanner's toes as Beta. This must be hard for him, though. Calli was just as much his mate as she was mine.

"Let's get this over with," I told him, striding towards the house. I didn't wait for him. I knew he would follow.

The cage that we had set up at the packhouse was in the basement. It was actually in the room next door to where they had held Calli when they brought us both back to the packhouse. That seemed like so long ago, but in reality, it was less than 48 hours.

The basement of the house was split into four rooms: the storage room where they had held Calli, the cage, and then we had fitted out a gym and a rec room down there. The gym saw a lot of use, the rec room not so much, and this was the first time we had to use the cage. Wallace was the only wolf in the pack who had ever needed to be caged.

I strode straight into the cage room and came to a stop just outside of arms reach. Wallace was sitting on the floor with his back in the far corner. He had his elbows braced on his knees and his head hanging down. He was the picture of shame and guilt, but Nash was right, it wasn't entirely believable. He waited for me to speak first like a good little wolf. He didn't even raise his head to look at me.

"Not even going to plead for forgiveness?" I snarled.

My wolf was slamming against the walls of my mind. To him, there was only one solution, and that was for us to go in there and kill the wolf that had dared to touch our mate. It wasn't that simple, though. There was the life of a child to be considered, a child that needed a father.

"What's the point?" he sniffled. "What I did was unforgivable, even if she hadn't been your mate. You should leave me here to rot."

River stepped closer to the cage, and I could see his resolve breaking. He always did have a kind heart. It wasn't because he loved Calli any less than me. It was because he loved his pack brother too.

"You're correct it was," I said stiffly.

Curious about how Wallace was going to play this I added nothing else and stood silently waiting by the bars, waiting to see what he would do next. He shuffled uneasily on the spot and didn't even last a minute before he looked up and finally met my eye.

"I'm sorry, Alpha. I shouldn't have acted the way I did, even if she is a witch." I caught his gritted teeth as he spoke and like Nash, I couldn't tell if he was entirely honest with us or if he just hated having to apologise to me.

"Does Kelly know the reason why you are sitting in this cage?" I asked him.

"She knows," was all he would say to me.

"Good." I turned around and strode out of the room.

I didn't particularly want to look at him anymore, and I wasn't entirely sure if he would be honest with me. I could sense deep-seated anger rolling through him, but that was all. I had no way of knowing who that anger was directed at, me or Calli. I had absolutely no doubt that it wasn't directed at himself as he would have me believe. I could understand why he would be pissed at me. I did have him sitting in a cage rather than with his wife and child. I just couldn't afford to let him loose if that hatred and animosity were going to be directed at Calli. Wallace had turned into a loose cannon, and it was my first time having this type of problem in my pack. It was funny, really. I wasn't keeping him in the cage because I didn't know what to do with him, I was keeping him in the cage because I knew exactly what I wanted to do with him. The cage was the only thing keeping him safe because the only thing that would satisfy me right now would be if Wallace were dead.

I found Kelly upstairs in one of the guest rooms, Coby was sitting on the bed beside her playing with his phone. He looked like he always did, like a typical kid without a care in the world. Kelly, however, had dark circles under her eyes which blazed with anger and sorrow.

"Kelly, let's talk down in the kitchen," I suggested, as she looked up and took me in.

Kelly wasn't technically part of our pack because she was still human. The Council would only ever allow her the status of friend of the pack. Coby was a pack member because he was male and would come into his wolf around the age of eleven when he started to go into puberty. In the bigger packs, it usually meant that these women had no rights and definitely no protections. It wasn't uncommon for packs to keep the male children and cast out the women. I had even heard some rumours of packs holding female humans captive if they were proven to produce male wolf heirs. No one has ever been able to corroborate those stories though. Until Calli, I had assumed they were nothing but rumours. But having her confirm the underground's existence, I couldn't help but wonder if there was some truth to them.

Kelly followed me down the stairs and into the large kitchen. We had renovated the kitchen with the intention of the pack expanding one day. It was big enough to cater to the pack we one day wanted to be. It was easy enough to set up the cabins on the grounds and even extend the packhouse if we needed. But we wanted this to be a place that could cater to the whole pack if needs be. Perhaps it was a stupid dream. Right now, it was nothing but a dream. I would miss this house when we inevitably had to leave it behind. But that didn't mean I wouldn't do it. Calli was my mate, and I would do anything for her.

When we reached the kitchen, I pointed Kelly over to one of the stools at the breakfast bar before setting out to make us both a cup of coffee.

"How is Coby doing?" I asked her.

"He seems fine, but I can't seem to take my eyes off him.

I keep expecting him to be snatched away from me again at any given second," she whispered.

I could understand how she felt. She had been through something no mother should ever have to go through.

"Thank you, Grey. Thank you for bringing him back to me." She stared into the coffee as she spoke. "The witches who took him …" She trailed off, but I knew what she was trying to ask me.

"As far as we know, they're all dead," I told her. "There is the potential that there could be one left out there, but we have no way of ever finding out."

I knew it wasn't what she wanted to hear, but I would never lie to her. Not about something like this.

"The pack will remain vigilant. If you want to stay here at the packhouse rather than go back to the cabin that would be completely fine."

She nodded numbly. I knew that what she and Coby really needed was to go back to their normal lives and try and put all of this behind them. I just didn't know if it was going to be safe for her to do that.

"And Wallace?" she asked quietly.

"I haven't decided yet," I told her honestly. "I can't tell if he is going to be a threat to my mate."

"So you would put your mate above him?" she snapped.

"Yes."

"You have known him since you were a child. You call him pack brother," she accused.

"I have, and I do. But the Wallace that I grew up with, the Wallace that I call pack brother would never have tied a woman to a chair and beat her until he broke her ribs and she suffered internal bleeding. He kidnapped a fucking child for christ's sake," I snapped back at her.

Kelly's breath caught, and her face snapped towards me.

"I didn't know," she told me. Her eyes told me that she was telling the truth, as well.

"What did he tell you?"

"That they found you and a witch unconscious in a clearing in the woods. He said that he hit her to try and get information. He never told me that he did that to her. He never told me about the kid." Her eyes filled with tears. Perhaps she was only now understanding how dangerous a situation Wallace was currently in.

"If I believe he is a threat to my mate, I will kill him," I told her, making sure to drive the point home to her.

She nodded numbly. "I understand. Few men would do any different. Before this happened, I would have denied he would ever do those things. I still don't understand. The man I love, the man I married would never do that to a woman."

"He believed he was within his right to do it because he believed her to be a witch," I explained.

"She is still a woman, and he is a wolf. He is stronger than any human man," she frowned as she was no doubt running through the facts in her mind. "I know you don't need to listen to me, Grey, that I'm not a member of your pack. But I would beg for Wallace's life if you would allow me to. I need him. I don't feel safe, and I don't think Coby is safe. Wallace needs to protect his son. I need him with us."

When she looked back up at me, the tears were running freely down her cheeks. I understood her position. She loved him. She always had. They were always that couple that made you want to puke. They never fought; they were nearly inseparable. She knew him better than any of us.

"Is he a threat to my mate?" I asked her, looking into her eyes. I needed to see her honesty.

"If you tell him you will only let him out to protect Coby and that he isn't to stray from his side, tell him there could be another witch out there and you don't know if Coby is in danger, then no I do not think he would risk being parted from his son," she told me.

I could see her point. The only thing that Wallace loved more in this world than her was his son. It was why his wolf was halfway to rabid when we had found him after Coby had been taken. I just didn't know if that was the reason for his behaviour with Calli. I hated myself for not knowing for sure because this was the one thing I couldn't afford to be wrong on.

"If he sets one foot out of place, I won't throw him in the cage next time," I warned her. "If you don't think he's ready then you need to tell me now."

"He will do this for his son," she said confidently.

I could only pray she was right.

32

CALLI

I woke with a snort, snapping my head up from the table where it had been laid. I quickly swiped a hand across my face, feeling the trail of drool there and inwardly cringing, hoping no one was looking at me. As I glanced up and saw the cup of tea which had been put on the table in front of me, waking me, that cringe turned into a happy smile, and I gratefully wrapped my hands around it. Blake was silently laughing at me from where he stood next to me.

"I thought you could do with that if I were going to wake you up," he smiled.

It was the happiest I had seen him since I had met him and almost as if he had the same thought his smile quickly flickered away and he slid back into his chair on the other side of the table.

We moved down to the dining table when it got to lunchtime so we could get something to eat but also so we just generally had a bit more space. I would need to get some sort of desk up there if this was to become a regular occurrence, which I was pretty sure it was.

"Can we just not tell anyone about that?" I asked sheepishly, trying to subtly check that I didn't have any more drool running down my face.

"Your secret is safe with me," he said, then he sighed. "I feel like I should be curled up in a ball crying somewhere."

Blake and I would be spending a lot of time together over the coming months, and we had been alone all morning. Tanner had taken Jacob to the store to check out the new Lego sets, and then he had called to say that they were going to hang out with James for a bit, then grab some burgers from the diner for lunch. They had offered to bring us something back, but we had decided against it. I had gotten to know Blake a bit better during the time we had been alone, and he seemed like a really good guy. He was obviously smitten with Jean, but every time one of his stories steered in her direction, he got this crushed look on his face. I had tried to steer him off the topic of her as much as I could. This whole situation couldn't be easy for him, even if he were convinced we would be able to find a solution to her problem. Every so often, he would go into the guest room to check on her. When he wasn't, his eyes would constantly flick in that direction. I had told him I could work through the warding issue alone if he wanted to spend time with her, but he was adamant he would help. I was pretty sure that he would be sticking by my side until we had a solution. He seemed to think that he owed me something for helping her. It said something about our world that not everyone would have done the same thing as I had done if they had the means to. After all, it was witches that had done this to her in the first place.

We had found the information on warding in the books reasonably easily. It looked like it was one of the spells that everyone learnt as they were starting out. It seemed relatively simple, in fact. The problem was the warding would be connected to whoever cast it and what I needed was a way to connect it to Grey and maybe some of the other wolves, ideally to the whole pack. That was where we were currently running into difficulties. The rest I was pretty sure I had understood. I was going to try a combination of wards to see if it would prevent not only witches crossing it but also casting spells across it. It was just going to take the right combination of stones. Once we had what we wanted and we had mapped out the area where we wanted the warding cast, I would need to bury whatever we were casting the warding on in the four corners, imbue them with my magic and then there was an incantation for when the final stones were set. It was surprisingly easy. In fact, it felt a little too easy. I was starting to worry that I was going to accidentally blow something up instead.

"I've found an online store we can order the majority of the supplies from, and they do next day delivery as well," Blake said, tapping away at my laptop.

"How very modern of them?" For some reason, I hadn't thought we would be able to have everything we needed delivered, let alone get a next day delivery service.

"Helps that the humans have taken up Wicca I suppose," Blake shrugged.

He had a point. Everything seemed to be available online nowadays.

It was an hour later when Grey and River turned up with Nash. I could tell as soon as they walked in that they weren't in the best of moods. I knew they had been up to the packhouse to deal with Wallace and I wasn't sure how I felt about it. No, that wasn't true; I was still pissed. But I had also gotten to a point where I kind of understood. If I had been in his position and Jacob had been missing, there was nothing I wouldn't have done to get him back.

They all sank onto the sofas with grim looks on their faces. Blake and I just looked between each other, not knowing what to do. My stomach sank, and at that moment, I realised I didn't want Wallace dead.

Blake broke first, and I was glad he did, I didn't dare ask.

"What happened?" he asked softly.

"Wallace is back with his family for now. He's keeping guard over Coby at their cabin and Aidan is going to keep up patrols. We'll swap up a rotation," Grey said. I caught him glancing nervously at me.

"That's good," I said. "Someone will need to keep a close eye on his son, at least until we can get the wards set up."

Grey smiled sadly at me. We would need to talk about this later together. I didn't want him to think he was failing me in any way.

"You can put up the wards then?" River asked, getting up from the sofa and moving over to the table where we had the books spread out. He actually looked interested in what we were going to try and do.

"Yeah, putting the wards up seems pretty easy. Blake was just about to order what we need on the internet. We should be able to get something in place by tomorrow. The bit we're struggling with is tying the wards to you guys rather than just to me," I sighed.

My eyes were starting to get that grainy, itchy feeling from reading for too long, plus I was beginning to feel hungry.

"I'm thinking blood," Blake mumbled reading the page he was currently on.

"No. We find something else." My head snapped toward him, but he was oblivious to the annoyed expression on my face because he was so engrossed in whatever he was reading.

River sat down beside me and took hold of one of my hands. I was still squinting in annoyance at Blake as the others got up and joined us at the table as well. After they had sat down, Blake finally looked up and then frowned in confusion.

"What?" he asked.

"Blood magic is dangerous, and I have cast a total of one spell in my entire life. Now is not the time to experiment with it," I told them all, mainly because I could see the others would be just as happy to follow along with his suggestion.

"It takes a part of you to warp something to your will. My mother had always warned me that it was addictive, and the more you used it, the more it takes until you are just a shell of what you once were," I warned. "I think we should try and join the ward to an amulet," I suggested instead.

"That looks to be a lot more complicated. I saw something about that in one of these books," Blake said shuffling through the stack of books before pulling one out and slowly starting to flick through it.

"Why does Blake get to be the researcher?" Nash huffed, slumping back into his chair. "I wanted to look at the books." He was definitely pouting, and it was kind of funny because I thought he was actually being serious.

Just as Grey rolled his eyes and was about to speak, there was a loud knock on the door, and before I could even move, River jumped up out of his seat to answer it. Was this weird? It felt normal, but I think other people might think it was strange.

As River opened the door, I could hear Jacob's giggles, and Tanner walked in with Jacob slung over one shoulder and a handful of shopping bags. Following him was Holly with a couple more bags. Nash was immediately on his feet to take the bags from her and wrap an arm around her shoulders. I already knew from talking to her that she was head over heels for him but seeing them together was pretty cute as well. He clearly felt the same way.

"Where is he?" Holly suddenly raged, and everyone in the room froze.

"Who?" Nash said, looking confused, frozen to the spot.

I'd bet anything these wolves had seen the temper fly out of this little woman before and they all seemed hilariously terrified of it.

"Wallace. Where is he?" she shrugged out from under Nash's arm and was on me in seconds, patting me up and down.

"You searching me for a blade or something?" I laughed.

"Don't you joke about this with me, missy," she said, standing back, hands on her hips, staring me down. "Some wolf beats the bejeezus out of you, and you don't even have the decency to let me come and look after you! I thought we were fated friends, me and you against these animals! And you!" she screeched, whipping back around to Nash. "You tell me in a text that my best friend got beaten up without immediately bringing me to her."

I'm not sure if she's joking now, but I'm pretty terrified. Nash, who either knows her better or is a man with a death wish, just grinned and pulled her back into his arms.

"She's fine, buttercup, and I hadn't realised you had claimed her already. Plus, in answer to your question, he isn't here." He snuggled against her neck, and Holly seemed to deflate on the spot.

"Good, I'd have a thing or two to say to him if he was," she sulked as she sunk against Nash.

When she turned to look at me, I could see the worry and the sadness in her eyes.

"I don't think I'd put even you in front of an angry wolf, buttercup," Nash told her, no doubt trying to calm her but it had the opposite effect completely.

"Let him try something. I'll wax every hair off his massive wolf body."

All of the men winced, I had to admit it was an inventive punishment, and it sounded like it would be excruciatingly painful. I liked it. If he ever apologised and asked how to make it up to me, I was totally going to get Holly to wax him.

"I'm sorry Holly, at the time, I didn't know how much you knew and I had thought that Jacob and I were going to be kept a secret." I scowled at Nash who had the decency to look embarrassed.

I wasn't quite sure what to do with this situation. Is this how it was going to be now? We were effectively outed and everyone was going to find out. Jacob was happily stood at the kitchen counter where the bags had been left, extracted what looked like another box of Lego. My wolf was pacing in my mind. She wasn't happy. Holly wasn't pack, and she knew Jacob's true identity. She was eyeing Holly as a potential threat. The last few days had been so tiring that I was having trouble holding her back. The force of her fury bent me double with a wince.

I felt strong hands gathering me up and leading me to the sliding door. As soon as the door closed behind me, a growl bubbled up through my throat, and I clenched my hands into fists. The pain of my nails digging into my palms drew me back to myself. All I could think of was danger. We had spent so long hiding what we were, that for it to be told to someone so easily, played against my nerves. My wolf didn't understand, and I felt the almost vibration against my skin as she tried to push against me to start the change. I crouched down on to the ground, wrapping my arms around myself, almost as if I was trying to physically hold back the shift.

I could hear Grey talking softly beside me, but his words just weren't registering to me. I was too lost in my wolf to listen. Too lost in the need to change, the need to protect. Grey was pushing calming waves of Alpha power across my skin, but it just infuriated my wolf more than anything else. She didn't want to be calm, she wanted to rage, and she wanted to protect.

I heard the door slide open and closed again before small hands came and braced either side of my face. Looking up, I saw Jacob's little face smiling down at me.

"It's okay, Calli. They're our friends," he simply told me before he wrapped his arms around me and crushed himself against me.

My wolf was happier with him closer to me, but she needed out. She needed to be with Jacob, but the thought of changing now, with all of these people, terrified me. I'd never shifted in front of anyone, apart from my father and Jacob, and I wasn't counting the time at the packhouse because I wanted to shred them all apart at the time. I didn't know how my wolf was going to react around the others. If I would lose control of her. But I needed this more than I needed to breathe right now.

Looking up, I caught Grey's eye, who was still crouched by the side of me. He had a soft smile on his face, and he was gently rubbing my back.

"I need to shift," I told him. If anyone were going to understand it would be him. "I can't hold it back, I … I haven't shifted around people before. You might need to protect them from me," I said shamefully.

"Calli, you can do this. They don't need any protection

from you, but I will be here if you need me." He grinned. "Plus, I think it might actually do you good to let your wolf meet the others. It will help you form the pack bond."

"Can I shift too?" Jacob asked.

Grey cocked his head to the side in confusion. I could understand why. Most wolves didn't shift until they hit puberty, and Jacob was a long way off. I had first shifted at four, and Jacob was already feeling his wolf at only the age of five. It wouldn't be long until he shifted naturally on his own. Technically with the help of an Alpha, he could probably shift now, but I wasn't sure how it worked.

"I shifted when I was four," I told Grey in explanation. It was almost comical the way that his mouth dropped open. "Jacob feels his wolf. It won't be long before he can shift alone."

"That's incredible. I can help him through the change if you want me to." He almost looked excited as he said it.

I looked down at Jacob, cringing as I tried to hold back the shift. It was painful to try and push it back down, and my wolf was forcing it forward now.

"I have to shift now, Jacob. I can't hold it back. Do you want Grey to try and help you shift? You can wait for it to happen naturally if you want, there is no pressure for you to do it now." I wasn't sure if this was a good idea, but it was Jacob's decision. He may only be young, but only he could tell how close his wolf was.

I was happy to see his nose crinkle up, which was his tell that he was thinking something through. He was too smart for his own good, and I could already see the problems he would cause me in the future.

I bent down and smacked a kiss on his forehead before letting the change sweep through me. Once I was down on all four paws, I jumped onto the outdoor sofa and gave Jacob a big lick across the face. He squealed and pushed me away, wiping his face in disgust. I knew he was only playing though, Jacob loved my wolf nearly as much as I did.

"Doing okay, Calli?" Grey asked.

I noticed that he didn't approach Jacob, and I appreciated that, even though my wolf and I agreed that Grey would never be a threat to either of us. I walked across the sofa cushions and nuzzled against his side so that he would know we were happy with him being here. He was our mate. My wolf wanted him by our side always.

"You are such a beautiful wolf, Calli," he sighed, sitting down so that he could nuzzle his face against my neck.

My wolf wanted to roll over and let Grey rub her belly, but I managed to hold her back. Now really wasn't an appropriate time for us to start rubbing all over each other.

I heard the door slide open again, and my head immediately snapped at the sound. Everyone else came cautiously outside to join us. Tanner and River smiled and immediately came and dropped down on the sofa. I crawled over their laps before flopping down on top of them. Tanner just laughed at me and started to run his fingers through my fur which almost had my eyes rolling back in bliss.

There was a feminine cough from behind us, and I reluctantly lifted my head to look at Holly. My wolf was a lot happier, but perhaps still a little annoyed, and I was fairly sure that as long as she kept her distance from Jacob, I wouldn't launch myself at her. That wouldn't exactly be a good way to start a friendship, and while I did consider Holly my friend, sometimes it was hard to separate my emotions away from my wolf's.

"I'm sorry, Calli." I heard Nash say. He did actually sound sorry as well, which weirdly made me feel better. "I shouldn't have spoken to Holly about you. It's just that she has known about the pack for so long and helped us out so much; it didn't even occur to me that I should be keeping it from her," he explained.

I sort of got it. He obviously loved her, and with that came trust. The problem was that all of these people were so new to me and, with the exception of my mates, I hadn't had time to form that trust yet. With my background and how I was brought up, trust was not something that I readily gave.

I gave Nash a nod, it was the most I could do in this form, and I was kind of grateful for it because it would give me some time to work through my thoughts.

"Can we do it?" Jacob suddenly asked, and we all turned to look at him. "I'm ready."

He was looking at Grey and standing tall, he could be such a little man at times. Our parents would have been so proud of him. I couldn't believe how much he had suddenly come out of his shell just by spending time around Tanner. Part of me was a little sad that I hadn't been able to do that for him, but I was grateful as well that Tanner could. That one of my mates already had a bond with him.

I looked up at Tanner and gave him an extra drooly lick on the chin. He just looked down at me and smiled. He wasn't even bothered that I'd slobbered on him.

"What are we doing?" River asked, looking at Jacob.

It showed a lot that they were asking him directly and not just talking over him.

"Grey is going to help me shift," Jacob said, bouncing on the spot.

I could see the excitement shining in his eyes. It was something I hadn't seen in him since we had lost our parents. I realised he needed this. I couldn't remember life before I found my wolf; I was too young. But now, she was a part of me, a big part of me. And she had been a great comfort to me since I lost my parents. I wanted Jacob to have that for himself.

"What? How?" River asked, sounding confused. I couldn't blame him, Jacob and I were changing the rules on everything they once thought was impossible.

"Jacob can feel his wolf already. Calli's first change was when she was four," Grey explained.

"Always the overachiever, hey Cal?" Tanner laughed, and I rolled my eyes at him.

Grey grabbed the table in front of the sofa and moved it out of the way to make more room. I could feel Nash and the others gathering closer to the back of the sofa, and I was okay with where they were for now. When he was done, Grey sat down on the ground in front of Jacob, who knelt eagerly in front of him. The little guy was practically vibrating on the spot, he was so excited.

"Okay, this is what happens. I want you to put your hands on my chest, and I will change. Feel the energy inside of me, Jacob, and how it changes. If I can feel your wolf close when I start to change, I can feed a part of my energy to him and push him along. It will feel a little like a tugging sensation in your chest," Grey explained to him. "I promise you that it doesn't hurt. It should almost feel like a relief. Like when you have a big stretch in the morning when you wake up."

Jacob just nodded in excitement. He was always like this. Once he made his mind up, there was no persuading him any different.

I clambered off Tanner and River and jumped off the sofa. I made sure to keep some distance between us because I didn't want to interrupt the process, but I needed to be nearby in case Jacob needed me. He looked over his shoulder at me with a big grin and then turned all of his attention back to Grey. The fact that I was happy for him to do this in front of the others, Holly included, just went to show how much I was starting to trust the pack.

Grey started his shift, and I could almost see the change come over him. He must have been slowing the process down so that he could get a feel for Jacob's wolf before he surrendered to it. I hoped that it didn't hurt him. Trying to hold a change back could grow painful. I had no idea how it must feel to slow an actual shift down.

My eyes locked on to Jacob. I had shifted myself the first time, and I had never seen what happened if an Alpha triggered the shift. My father wasn't an Alpha, so we didn't have that choice when I was young.

Jacob shuffled uncomfortably on the spot which I took as a good sign. Grey was holding his shift at a midpoint. I could see him gritting his teeth from what I hoped was the strain rather than any pain he was feeling.

All of a sudden it seemed to happen all at once, Grey huffed out a sigh and let his change take him over, and Jacob fell forwards onto his hands which turned into little fluffy paws and before us sat a little pot-bellied wolf pup.

I was immediately at his side, snuffling my nose against his neck to make sure that he was alright. He rolled to his side, unsteady on his feet, and Grey was beside him immediately pushing him back to his paws with his nose. I could remember how disorientating it was when you first shifted and having to get used to suddenly having four legs instead of two.

Jacob yipped happily and clambered up to his feet, with the assistance of a gentle push from Grey, and started to shakily move around as he got used to his new form.

"That is the cutest thing I've ever seen!" I heard Holly gush.

"Incredible. This is something no one else has ever witnessed before," Nash said from beside her.

"What do you mean?" she asked, I could hear the confusion in her voice.

"Wolf shifters don't ordinarily have their first shift until they hit puberty. By that time, they are adolescents. I've never seen a shifter pup before because we aren't supposed to be able to shift this early," Nash told her.

"Calli and Jacob are special." Tanner smiled down at the little pup who was now tugging on the leg of his jeans doing an adorable little growl. It would seem that Jacob had decided that now he was more confident moving around, he wanted to play.

"Is that why Calli looks like you guys? Like a real wolf?" Holly asked.

"Yep," Tanner said, scooping Jacob up and blowing a raspberry on his little tummy which just made him yip and growl.

"I'm not gonna lie, babe, if I could look like Calli's sexy wolf, I'd be more down to trying the shift," Holly laughed. "Do you mind if I sit down here, Calli?" she asked me, and I appreciated the fact that she did.

I nodded my head to let her know that I was okay then I bounded a few steps away and yipped to Jacob to encourage him to come and play with me. He tottered over to me, unsteadily on his feet before he pounced at me. I rolled onto my back, letting Jacob clamber over me and huffed my wolf laugh as he wiggled his little butt and tried to jump on top of me. Grey came over to join us and, not to be left out of the fun, Tanner and River shifted and bounded over to join us.

We spent the next hour playing on the lawn and then taking Jacob for a very short run into the forest. It didn't take long for his little legs to get tired, and we headed back to the house to lie on the grass and relax. Nash and Blake stayed outside at the seating area with Holly keeping watch over us as we played.

It was a nice way to finish up the afternoon and just forget about our troubles for a while, of which it felt like we had many.

33
CALLI

The warding supplies arrived at my house around mid-morning. Blake and I had spent most of the night going through the books in the library trying to find a way to link the warding to the pack members. We'd had quite a few disagreements over whether to use blood magic or not. I was adamantly putting my foot down that I wouldn't even consider it and Blake kept bringing it up as the easier option. We had given up at 2:00 am and gone to bed after River couldn't take listening to our bickering any more and actually sent both of us to bed.

I spent the morning looking into linking the wards to the guys, and I thought I might have cracked it. Blake, much to the annoyance of Nash, had become my study buddy and was starting to have the same basic foundation knowledge of magic.

"I'm still not sure that it will work. Maybe ..." Blake started

"I swear to god if you mention blood in the next words that come out of your mouth, I will start looking for a spell to turn you into a toad or something," I huffed.

A cup of tea suddenly appeared on the table in front of me, and I looked up to see a smiling Tanner next to me.

"You're the best," I sighed, as I gratefully wrapped my hands around the cup. I might be addicted to tea, but considering my life at the moment, it was the least of my problems.

Looking around me as I sipped, I couldn't help but feel shocked at just how much my life had changed in such a short amount of time. Jacob went back to school this morning along with River going back to work. I knew he was only doing it so he could be close to Jacob, and I was grateful that he was thoughtful enough to do it. The rest of the pack was taking some time off work whilst we tried to handle the witch situation. I had thought about keeping Jacob out of school, maybe even homeschool him for the year, but I wanted him to have as normal a life as possible. He still had his talisman tattoo working, so his scent was still masked. My parents would have wanted this for him. They always tried so hard to let us have a normal life. How would they feel if they could see what I was doing now? How disappointed would they be in me? I was under no illusions that they wouldn't be. I had given up the only thing I had that kept me safe, and in doing so, I had shone a spotlight on Jacob. I missed them so much. I wished I could just speak with them to ask my Mum for her advice one last time. I needed to feel my Dad wrap his arms around me and tell me that it was all going to be okay.

My chest physically ached from the grief, and my eyes burned with the tears I was holding at bay. I almost felt like if I wanted to, I could just stop. That everything about me would stop, and I could drift away to be with them again. That all I needed to do was decide, as easy as placing one foot in front of the other. But then Jacob's little face flashed in the front of my mind, and I knew I would never leave him.

Fingers gently brushed against my chin, and when my

eyes focused, I saw a worried Tanner knelt beside me, his eyes flicking between both of mine.

"Hey, where did you go then?" he asked me softly.

"Nowhere. It's fine. I think I have an idea about linking the wards to you guys, how many and who do you want linked?" I asked him, trying to change the subject.

Tanner stared at me, his brow furrowed and I knew that he wanted to question me more. I was ready to beg him not to. I didn't want to have to talk through my grief. I wasn't ready to go there, to share the pain and the thoughts, not yet at least.

"Ideally the whole pack but I suppose if you are limited on the number, you'll want to link Grey first, me, then River, and we work our way through the others," he replied, but I could tell by the tone of his voice that he wasn't going to just let it go.

"What are you thinking?" Blake asked, looking warily between the two of us.

"Okay, at the moment it's just a theory, and I might need to call someone to see if they think it's possible or if someone of my level would even be able to do it." I huffed out a breath realising that I was rambling. "At first, I thought about linking the warding to an amulet to alert the wearer, but then I realised that alerting one person wasn't going to be enough. Then I got thinking about my talisman, and then I started to wonder if instead of linking it to an amulet, we could link it to something else physical that someone could wear. Something like ink."

As I explained it, I realised that it just sounded stupid and probably impossible, but I couldn't stop thinking of the way that my mother's friend had got the protection spell to link with the ink of Jacob's tattoo.

"So, then we could tattoo whoever in the pack we wanted with that ink," Tanner finished off.

"I think so," I mumbled.

"It worked on Jacob," Blake pointed out.

"Aidan could do the tattoo, he has the equipment, and I bet he even has ink that we could use." Tanner shrugged. "I mean the theory sounds solid to me, but then again, I don't know anything about magic. Who would you need to call?"

"My Mum's friend who did the tattoo on Jacob. Sean is already trying to get into contact with her about changing my own masking spell. I could ask him to get her to call me or ask her for the information himself. I don't know how long it will take though. She's not exactly easy to get hold of. My Mum said she's basically a bit of a hermit. If he's already put out a message for her and is still waiting for her to get back in contact with him, then it should be a bit quicker," I shrugged.

Sera had never been easy to get hold of. I had heard the rumour while I was travelling that several coven heads were trying to find her because they knew she was helping the underground. I didn't know exactly how true that was though. Whatever the cause, she had gone to ground and locating her was always tricky. It was frustrating as hell in an emergency, but when we needed someone to disappear completely—and I mean like, they must be dead, kind of disappear—she was always the person we called. No one could hide a person on the run like Sera could, but it came with a sacrifice. No contact with the outside world. Whoever was running had to be desperate enough to drop off the map and leave everything about this world behind them. When it came down to it, very few were willing to take that step. I hadn't been. If it had just been me, I might have, but I couldn't do that to Jacob. He was too young, and he deserved a chance at a normal life.

"Okay, so we have a plan, we have all of the supplies we

know we need at the moment, all we can do now is wait," Tanner pointed out.

Well, when you put it that way, I suppose he was right. I looked across the table at Blake, who had a similar expression on his face that I expected I did. What were we supposed to do now? Tanner laughed at the both of us looking lost and rolled his eyes.

"Why don't we put some lunch together, Grey will be back from the garage any minute with Aidan and then we can float the plan past him?" Tanner suggested.

This was weird. I wasn't used to Tanner being the sensible one. Blake just nodded and stood up, moving over to the kitchen, but I seemed cemented to my seat in shock.

"You get used to it," Blake called over his shoulder at me.

Tanner looked confused until Blake called out again.

"It's like he's got a split personality or something. One minute he's the fun-going, easy one and then suddenly he's in charge."

We must have had the fun going Tanner back at that point because he just laughed and agreed.

Grey and Aidan turned up a short while later just as we were loading sandwiches onto a platter. I hadn't really had the opportunity to speak with Aidan much, apart from the morning he saw me battered and bruised by one of his pack brothers.

"Hey, Calli," he said, looking a bit sheepish and rubbing the back of his neck with one hand.

"Hey, Aidan. Come and help yourself to something to eat," I told him brightly.

Hopefully, we could just move past that morning and not speak about it. I didn't want it to rule over my life, and I was hoping that blindly ignoring it would make it go away. That was the best way to deal with problems, right?

"Thanks, Calli," Aidan said, giving me a bright smile and going to help himself.

These boys could eat! I was going to need to reassess how much food I was buying. Maybe wholesale was the way to go, and I would definitely need to grab at least one big freezer to put in the garage.

"What you thinking so hard on?" Grey asked, dropping a kiss on my cheek and taking a seat next to me.

"The logistics of keeping you all fed," I said as I took a massive bite out of my sandwich. It was absolutely amazing. Why are sandwiches always better if someone else made them for you?

"Yeah, sorry about that," Grey mumbled, and he even looked embarrassed as he said it. "We should probably come up with some kind of permanent plan for all that."

"Well, you know you're all welcome here, of course, I want to sit down with Jacob at some point and make sure he is okay with it all too. Otherwise, we will need to reassess. Jacob and I will need to stay here. This is his home, and he's had too much upheaval in the last few months." I didn't realise I was nervous about that until I said it. I had just assumed that Grey, Tanner and River would stay here with us, but they would want to be near the pack as well.

It was only on the other side of the woods, so it's not like it was miles away, but what if they wanted to go back to the packhouse. I didn't want to move there, and I didn't want Jacob to have to move again as well.

Grey put a reassuring arm around me, and I relaxed into him.

"We'll work it out sweetheart, but I think we need to have that conversation when River is here as well, and once you've had a chance to talk with Jacob. We don't need to make any decisions straight away." He was right, of course. But a part of me just needed for something in my life to have some stability.

We settled into an eerily, peaceful lunch together. The guys discussed what was going on at the garage and the plan for when they reopened in a couple of weeks. I just sat and listened, enjoying the normality of the moment. It was almost like a glimpse into what the future could be like for us until Tanner went and ruined it.

"We should stop by the house this afternoon and get Nash to catch us up on the vampire situation," Tanner suggested.

I tried not to look like I was taking too much interest in their conversation. I hadn't heard any of them talk about a potential nest nearby before. I had met some vampires when I was travelling. They had a very different type of community than shifters did. Whilst they did have a central Council, each clan had far more autonomy than the packs did. Some of the clan leaders were part of the underground and had helped some witches and shifters escape when they needed help. I hadn't heard of a clan in this area though, and I didn't know who the clan leader was. This was information that Sean would want to know when I spoke with him next, but I wasn't sure what to tell Grey. I knew that they already knew about the underground, but I hadn't gone into any great length. They talked about moving the clan on and seemed to have the same view of vampires as most shifters or the belief that the Council told them to have. But I didn't want to keep anything from them, and I didn't want there to be secrets between us.

Getting up, I moved into the kitchen and put on the kettle to make a cup of tea. I grabbed my phone off the side and sent a message to Sean, asking him to get Sera to call me when she called because I needed her help with something else. For now, we had far more pressing issues than which clan had decided to make Maine their home. I'd see if Sean knew anything about it and just put it on the back burner for now. Once the witches were dealt with, and the pack turned their attention to this properly, I'd talk with Grey. Was that just putting off my problems for the future? It absolutely was! But that was future Calli's problem, and I didn't have it in me to care right now.

"We're going to head back to the house to speak with Nash, sweetheart," Grey said, walking up to me in the kitchen. "Tanner and I will be back in a couple of hours, and Blake is going to stay with you. We were thinking of grabbing pizzas for dinner tonight if you're okay with Jacob having that."

I appreciated him asking me more than I could express without potentially sounding like a crazy person.

"Jacob will love that," I smiled because I knew just how much he would like it. "Maybe we could get some popcorn and watch a movie as well."

"Can we start a Toy Story marathon?" Tanner asked, popping up out of nowhere, more excited than any adult should be about watching a kids movie—okay I love them too, but I'll never admit it to them.

Grey and Tanner left after taking pizza orders from everyone and Aidan went with them, leaving just me and Blake in the house, and of course Jean. The whole place was just eerily quiet, and I didn't know what to do with myself. I didn't even need to go and get Jacob from school today because River was just going to bring him home. When I'd gratefully agreed to that this morning, I hadn't considered how lost I was going to feel when I had nothing to do all day.

My eyes fell to the door to the stairs leading up to the library. I suppose I could get a head start trying to figure out how to break the spell draining Jean and the baby. I was just feeling all magicked out at the minute, and while I had the barrier spell fresh in my mind, I didn't want to go confusing myself with something else.

I should have made my mother teach me more. I should have known I would need my magic to prepare me for adult life—a life where I potentially wouldn't have them beside me.

Blake disappeared into the guest room to spend some time with Jean, and I suddenly found myself alone. I couldn't blame him, with the mood I was in, I didn't want to hang out with me either.

I cleaned the kitchen—even though it wasn't dirty—as well as both of the bathrooms, then made a cup of tea. I wasn't in the mood for Netflix, which Tanner had helpfully connected to the TV last night for us, along with DisneyPlus which would make Jacob very happy.

There was still time before the others came home, so I went into my closet and grabbed the guitar I'd hidden when the others had come around. I didn't even know why I did it. It's not like it was a massive dildo or something.

I took the guitar and a fresh cup of tea to the outdoor sofa and closed the sliding door behind me so that I didn't disturb Blake. This was probably something we were going to need to discuss soon. This wasn't a small house, but it wasn't exactly massive either, and I imagined we were all going to be craving our privacy at some point. Sitting down, I wrapped a blanket around me to keep warm until the outdoor heater kicked in and looked down at the guitar with a sigh. My fingers plucked across the strings, and I let go of everything, all of the worries and grief that I was holding onto flowed out into the strings, and I finally let myself have time to work through my feelings for a change.

34

RIVER

Bringing Jacob home from school should have felt weird. It was like meeting Calli had given me a whole new element of a family I'd never experienced before. It didn't though. If anything, it felt completely natural. My wolf was adamant that Jacob was ours. In fact, he felt uneasy when he was out of our sight. School today had been difficult. Not only was I stuck trying to catch up with the work I had missed, but my wolf was riding me every second to go and check on Jacob. He needed to know that his pup was safe.

Driving home, we easily fell into a conversation about what movie he wanted to watch tonight. He had been so excited when I told him that Grey and Tanner would be bringing home pizza for dinner. He was such a cute kid. He was starting to come out of the shell of his grief, and even though I was under no illusion he would leave it entirely behind him, it was nice to see that it wasn't crippling him into silence as it had before.

We pulled up at the house, and as we climbed out of the truck, the soft sounds of an acoustic guitar and gentle singing drifted towards us. Jacob frowned softly and took an unconscious step closer to me. My wolf's attention was immediately grabbed as I realised it was Calli we could hear.

"Is that Calli?" I asked.

Jacob just nodded quietly before adding, "She only plays when she's sad now."

I looked down at him, and I saw just how worried he was for his sister. He was right, the song that drifted to us on the breeze spoke of loss and sadness, and you could hear every drop of Calli's grief echoing through her voice.

"It's okay to be worried about her," I told Jacob as I knelt down on the driveway beside him. "Calli is dealing with her sadness in a way that she knows how. She won't be sad forever," I promised him.

I could see the tears shimmering in his eyes as he took an unsure step closer to me. I knew what he wanted, and the fact that he'd ask for it from me filled my heart, even if he was a little unsure in the moment. I opened my arms wide, and Jacob all but threw himself into them, burrowing his face into my shirt.

"We've got you both, Jacob. We'll all get through this together," I told him.

Jacob lifted his head and asked, "Like a family?"

"Is that something you would be okay with?" I hoped to god that he said yes because I didn't know how I'd take being rejected by this little boy, and it had absolutely nothing to do with Calli. Of course, I'd be crushed if we had to take a step away from her until Jacob got older, but if he rejected us, I didn't know how my wolf would take such a crushing blow.

He looked at me, and I could see him process the information in his mind as he worked through the facts. Sometimes, it was hard to remember that he was still only five. After a moment, he gave me a small smile and nodded.

My wolf nearly exploded out of me in happiness, and I laughed at the glee that was radiating from him.

"You have no idea how happy that makes me, Jacob," I murmured, pulling him to me for another cuddle. "Now, how shall we cheer Calli up?"

Jacob rolled his eyes at me, and I laughed again. "She needs a cup of tea," he told me like it was the most obvious thing in the world.

"Let's go make her some tea then shall we?" I suggested, and Jacob happily bounced towards the front door, his previous sadness forgotten for the time being.

Walking after him into the house, it was easy to forget this wasn't home. Or maybe it was. Everything was confusing right now. It felt right to be here with Calli, but the house as it currently was wasn't going to be big enough for us.

Jacob was already rummaging in the cupboards in the kitchen when I caught up to him. He pulled out a tray, and a packet of cookies which I suspected was a secret stash of Calli's. He looked at me suspiciously as he pulled them out the cabinet and I held my hands up in surrender.

"I promise not to tell Tanner where you hide the cookies," I laughed, and he gave me one of his serious little nods before he added them to the tray.

Turning to me, Jacob's little hands came to his hips, "You have to do the hot water bit, I'm not allowed," he told me.

Realising he was right and reminding myself that I needed to remember Jacob was five and not the forty-year-old man he sometimes acted like, I started out getting the kettle boiling and getting a cup down from the higher cupboards that Jacob couldn't reach. In no time at all, we had the tray set up with a plate of cookies and Calli's tea on the side. I added a glass of milk for Jacob and decided to give the whole tea thing a go for myself.

Jacob stood at the sliding door, frowning at Calli. It was nearly impossible to hear her from inside, but he still watched her nonetheless, the concern radiated from him. He understood more than I think most kids his age did.

"She's been out there for over an hour," Blake said softly from beside me.

When I turned to him, I saw him standing next to me, his hair rumpled from sleep. He must have come out of the guest room when we weren't looking. We needed to keep an eye on him and make sure he didn't withdraw into himself, never leaving Jean's side. His wolf would be pining for her, and it was going to make things difficult for Blake if we didn't support him through this.

"I didn't want to disturb her," he told me, his eyes drifting to where Jacob stood silently at the door. "Maybe I should have."

I could feel his guilt at how Jacob was feeling. To be honest, we were all going to feel that for a long time to come. What Wallace had done was the responsibility of the pack. He was our pack brother, and his actions were our own. I was kicking myself that I hadn't watched over Calli when we brought her back to the house. But with Grey down and unconscious, my wolf was spiralling. He was my Alpha and my brother, and there was no way that my wolf or I would have agreed to leave his side. But what happened to Calli when we weren't there, I just didn't know how to deal with that.

"The others won't be back for a few hours," I started and then I drifted off because I didn't know what to suggest to Blake for him to do. What I didn't want was for him to go back into the guest room and just linger at Jean's side. She was already going to kick my ass when she woke up and found out how much time we let him sit there pining over her.

But it's not like he was going to stop, his wolf would be pushing him to keep watch over them both.

"I was thinking about heading to the cabin and picking up some more of my clothes," Blake said. "I just didn't want to leave Calli alone. I want to grab some work out stuff and try out the gym."

I sighed in relief and clapped my hand on his shoulder. He was going to be alright.

"You don't have to worry about me, you know," Blake said over his shoulder as he grabbed his truck keys and started to head towards the front door.

"I'm more worried about myself when Jean wakes up," I joked, and he laughed as he left the house, his laughter trailing behind him.

When I turned back to the door, Jacob was waiting patiently for me. I gathered up the tray, and he quietly opened the door, heading outside to Calli.

She was the most beautiful thing I had ever seen. She was curled up in the corner of the outdoor sofa with a blanket wrapped around her, and an acoustic guitar across her lap as she quietly strummed and sang to herself. The late afternoon sun bounced off her golden hair, making her look almost like she glowed. She sang of loss and grief in a song that I didn't recognise but which seemed to suit her mood perfectly. Her eyes were closed, but the sadness that radiated from her face showed me what she was truly feeling, what she was usually able to hide from us. Calli was hurting, deeply, in a way that would fundamentally change her if we didn't find a way to help.

"We made you tea," Jacob said quietly as he climbed onto the sofa beside her.

Calli startled, her eyes flying open as she looked between the two of us. She didn't seem too upset to see Jacob there, but her cheeks flushed in embarrassment when she took in the sight of me. I'm pretty sure it was only the fact that I had the tray with the tea that was making her let me stay. I smiled down at her, trying to go more for amazement than amusement but I wasn't sure it mattered, she was embarrassed either way.

"I didn't know you could play," I said, more just for something to say, as I placed the tray down on the table.

Jacob was there in a flash, grabbing his milk and two cookies before snuggling back into Calli. She looked down at him with a smile. I'm pretty sure he got away with most stuff because he was just so cute. I, however, got away with the intrusion because I passed Calli a cup of tea. I had quickly worked out that this was a get out of jail free pass with her and I would no doubt have to use it to my advantage on many occasions after today.

"River said that we could be a family," Jacob suddenly said.

Fucking hell, maybe I should have made an entire pot of tea.

"Did he now," Calli said, blowing on her tea and smirking at me over the top of it as she took in my sudden bout of nervousness.

"Yes, he said we could be like a family and help each other get through our problems if I wanted to," Jacob said nodding thoughtfully.

Was that bad? When he said it back like that, it sounded pretty bad. Had I just majorly fucked up by overstepping? Calli was just looking at me over the top of her tea, and I was shifting nervously in my seat. I reached out to the table and took my own drink just so that I could have something to do with my hands. Did it suddenly get hot in here? Wait, we were outside. Fucking hell, I was so fucked!

"Well, we were all talking about it this morning," Calli started to explain to Jacob. "You know that River, Grey and Tanner are my mates, right?" she asked him. Jacob nodded his little head, and she smiled down at him. "Do you know what that means?"

Jacob cocked his head to the side and then just as I took a sip of my drink, he said, "Are you going to make babies with each other?"

And I spat tea all over myself and the table in front of me.

Calli broke down into hysterical laughter, and Jacob just sat there looking confused.

"Mummy and Daddy were mates, and they had babies," Jacob reasoned.

"That's true," Call conceded as she coughed and brought her laughter under control. "What it means is that we all share a connection with each other and that fate decided we should be together, like Mummy and Daddy were," Calli explained to him.

"So you won't have babies then?" Jacob asked, and he actually looked disappointed by that. Weirdly, I realised that I was as well, and I was very much interested in what Calli was going to say next.

"Maybe one day, spud," she finally said, ruffling his hair. "But not any time soon."

My wolf huffed in disagreement, and that shocked me more than anything we had just spoken about.

"You will always be the most important person in my world, you know," she told him, pulling him closer to her. Jacob snuggled into her, and it was sweet to see them together like this. "River, Grey and Tanner, they want you to be that person for them as well if you are okay with that?"

"Calli," Jacob said sternly, sitting up, "You are their mate, you should be the most important."

He frowned at me like I had wronged his sister and I saw that forty-year-old man peeking through his eyes again.

"That's true," I agreed.

"I could maybe be second if you want," he said, suddenly sheepish.

"I'd really like that," I smiled down at him as he shuffled across the sofa and snuggled against my side instead.

I wasn't all that sure what to do at first; this was the first time that Jacob had made any move towards me like this. As I wrapped my arm around him, and he settled in against my side, I realised just how much had been missing in my life. My wolf pushed against the edges of my senses, reaching out, wanting to feel his pup. As he snuggled closer against me, I could have sworn that I felt his wolf pup reaching out back towards me.

"That might mean they come and live with us," Calli ventured cautiously.

Jacob just gave a sleepy grunt of agreement and then started to snooze against me. I looked up at Calli, and I knew tears were glistening in my eyes, even if I didn't want to admit it out loud. She smiled softly at me. This was happiness; just sitting here with my mate and our pup in the afternoon sun.

35

CALLI

Pizza night had been just what everyone needed. River seemed more relaxed into our situation after taking a nap with Jacob out on the outdoor sofa after school. I had seen how happy he'd been when Jacob snuggled into him and then they had both drifted off to sleep; it was possibly the most adorable thing I had seen in my life.

Jacob was tucked up tight in bed now, and it was the happiest I'd seen him since we'd lost our parents. I think this place was starting to feel more like home for him. Getting in touch with his wolf had no doubt helped as well. I needed to speak with Grey tonight about making sure we got Jacob to shift regularly. I didn't want to risk a spontaneous shift at school. Even though it had been drummed into him as soon as he could understand words, we needed to have the talk about shifting in front of people as well. At least we had River and Holly at school in case he needed someone to intervene for him. Oh hell, now I was nervous about something else entirely.

The ringing of my phone pulled me out of my thoughts, and I answered it without even thinking.

"Hello?"

"Calli?"

"Sera? Oh thank god, you have no idea how much I've stepped into it right now," I sighed.

I heard Sera chuckle down the phone. I may have only met her in person a few times, but she had been a significant presence in my childhood. She was never able to call my Mum as much as she wanted, but when she was in a place where she could, she always took the time to check in with us. Sera was the closest thing that my Mum had to a coven, and I think it was the same for her. She chose to mostly help the shifters that entered the underground, not trusting any witches into her inner circle, just in case.

"Sean has filled me in on some of your troubles and your … erm … discoveries shall we say," she said in her thick Irish brogue. I could still tell that she was making fun of me, though.

"Did he tell you about my talisman?" I asked her, almost frightened to hear her reaction. This was akin to admitting something to a parent and waiting for the bollocking that followed.

"It was a noble, if not foolish, thing that you did. But I am proud of you nonetheless," she sighed. "You understand what this means, though?"

"I was hoping we could find another solution," I told her. "A way to manipulate the spell into just enough of something else that it would still work for me."

"What do you mean?" she asked and I could tell I had piqued her interest.

"Maybe if it was targeted to just one side of my nature rather than a complete mask of everything?" I asked, hopefully.

"It would still be a mask, nonetheless. I fear it would not

work." My heart dropped in disappointment until she continued, "But you may be on to something. Changing the spell into something else …" she drifted off, and I could tell she was already working through the problem in her mind.

"Before I lose you to your theories, there is something else I needed to ask you," I told her.

"Hmmm, yes, sorry, ask away." I wanted to laugh at how far she had fallen into the problem already, but I still felt a small amount of guilt at creating it in the first place.

"I want to set up a warding around the pack property and mine, so we can know if anyone crosses it. We're going to be firmly on the witches' radar now, and I need to do everything I can to protect Jacob," I told her.

"That is a sensible idea," she confirmed. "I would tell you to send Jacob to me, but I think he needs to be with you if he has found a pack that he will be accepted into. That will do him more good than the underground ever could. Is he still showing no sign of magic?" she asked.

"Not that I can tell, but he had his first shift with the assistance of the pack Alpha here. I suppose that could be a sign for all we know."

"Hmmm, it is difficult because we have no one to gauge his progress against," she paused for a moment, and I could tell that she was running through the parameters of this problem and filing it away for later. "Now, tell me about this warding you want to do. It is a fairly simple spell, so I'm feeling like there is something you haven't told me yet."

I laughed because she couldn't be more right. What was it about me and making every situation I found myself in more complicated than it needed to be.

"Well, I don't want to just link it to me. I need it to link to specific pack members as well. At first, I thought about linking it to a talisman, but ideally, it needs to be more than just one of them. Then I got thinking about Jacob's tattoo. Would it be possible to do something similar here?" I asked her, rolling my eyes at myself.

Even as I said it, it sounded like a lame idea. Why had I not insisted that my mother teach me magic?

"It could work," Sera admitted, surprising me. "This type of magic is completely new, I haven't tested it out with any other kinds of spells, but in theory, I don't see why it wouldn't work." She went silent for a moment, and I could almost hear the gears turning in her head. "In fact, it's quite a brilliant idea. This could be something that would benefit many others if you could make it work."

I had already thought the same thing. If this worked, we could offer it out to other packs. It could go a long way to proving to them that not all witches were the same. But it could also be a turning point in the Wolf Hunts. It would prevent the witches from having the advantage of surprise on their side. The wolves could be protected within their own packlands if they had an early warning system in place.

We spent the next half an hour going through the spell work for the wardings, the process of casting it and linking it to the ink. As we started to get the final details finalised, I could tell that there was something she didn't want to tell.

"Spit it out," I sighed.

The line fell silent, and I was starting to worry that something might be happening at her end she didn't want to tell me about, that there was a problem with the underground where she was.

"There's something I never told your mother about the link," she admitted quietly.

"Why do I get the feeling that isn't going to be something good?"

She sighed, and I felt like I was going to throw up,

waiting for her to answer. There was only one thing that I could think about that she would have done and never dared to admit to my mother.

"I had to use blood."

All of the air just puffed out of me, and I fell silent. I didn't know what to say. We couldn't do it. The only thing my mother had ever warned me against was blood magic. She was completely against it. I had to believe that came from somewhere, from something I should be paying attention to.

"There was no other way to transfer the spell from me to the wearer, not permanently," she admitted.

"So there is the potential for a temporary transference then?" I asked her.

"A few days at best."

We both fell into silence again—me, from my attempts at trying to decide what I was going to do with this information. Unfortunately, I was still coming up blank. Sera, I assumed, from the shame of admitting she had kept this information from my mother.

"I don't know what to do," I finally admitted to her quietly.

I was glad I had moved up to the library when I realised it was her on the phone, and I wasn't sat with the guys all around me. I didn't need to be considering them as well right now. As selfish as it was, I didn't want their input. I needed to make a decision myself before I brought them in on this. The risk was mine to take. But not doing this, not placing the warding around us, that just pushed the risk onto the rest of them. Yes, I could still ward the house here for Jacob and I, but we would bring attention to the pack if anyone found out we were here, it would place the pack at greater risk just by being in close proximity to us.

"What effect has it had on you?" I asked her.

"None that I can tell. It was a strong spell, but I have only had to cast it twice."

"In other words, if I do this here, I may not be able to do it for anyone else?"

"Yes ... and if the Council finds out that you have the ability to do this, they may not give you any choice but to do it," she warned me.

She was right, of course. But right now we needed to be looking at our immediate problems, not the ones in the future. It may be shortsighted, but if our immediate problems could end up with all of us dead, what choice did we really have.

"Okay, tell me what else I would need to do," I finally asked. Just because I was getting the information didn't mean I had to use it. But at least this way I would be prepared.

Sera ran through the last few steps with me. It was so simple it was worrying. Sera assured me this was just another branch of natural magic. Yes, it involved sacrificing a piece of myself, but she didn't believe there would be any repercussions when that was done for the benefit of others. Even so, all I could hear were the echoes of my mother's warning bouncing around my head.

We said goodbye with a promise to speak again soon. Sera hoped to have a solution to my talisman free lifestyle the next time we spoke, but with all of the attention I was about to rain down on myself, I'm not sure she would be able to do anything in the time I would need her to. It already felt like it was too late. There was an ominous feeling that something big would happen, and I had a terrible feeling it wasn't going to be good.

Heading back down the stairs, I took a detour to the wine cellar and grabbed a bottle of red wine. I was in the kitchen, pouring myself the biggest glass I could find when Grey finally came up behind me, wrapping me in his arms.

"I get the feeling that your conversation didn't go as well as you had hoped it would," he murmured as he rubbed his cheek across the top of my head, scenting me.

It made me smile to see the wolf peeking out in the way he acted with me. I wasn't going to complain though; my wolf was practically giddy at the attention we were getting.

"We should be able to link the warding to the ink, but we need to use blood magic to do it," I told him, picking up the wine glass and gulping a fair portion of it down.

I felt Grey stiffen at my back. "You said blood magic was bad."

"That's what my mother always said, but Sera thinks it isn't. She used it for the masking spell for both Jacob and I, and she hasn't been able to feel any ill effects from it."

"Could your mother have been wrong?" Grey asked, but even as he said it, I could hear the doubt in his voice. It warmed my heart that he didn't believe she could be wrong just because she had been my mother. She would have liked him. She would have liked them all.

It was just that one small thought that blew the walls I held up around my grief wide open. It had been a long day, and it was getting harder and harder to hold it back, but I didn't expect it to overtake me so completely and so quickly.

I didn't need to say a word, Grey immediately scooped me up and carried me to my bedroom where he laid me down on the bed, pulling me against him. Lying here, with his arms wrapped tightly around me, I allowed myself to surrender to it, just for a moment. It stole my breath away as I felt like my chest physically cracked open. It was too much; all of the feelings I shut away from myself were flooding through me. It was overwhelming in a way that felt like I lost a sense of myself. I fell into a pit of everything I had shoved to one side, refusing to deal with it. I knew it was a stupid thing to do, I knew it would come back on me, but I had never anticipated it would be like this.

It was almost like I had fallen into a hole, a hole filled with sadness and loss, but then I fell further, past it all. There was nothing but darkness, an all-encompassing void, and once I was there, I wasn't sure if I wanted to leave. There were no problems here, no one who cared what I was or what I could do. No pressures and no threats. Would it be so terrible just to stop?

But images of my mates flickered through my mind, brief memories of the time we had spent together. Jacob and his smile, then his severe little frown, bubbled up in front of me. Then finally, my wolf, I could almost feel the warmth of her fur pressed reassuringly against me. She would always be with me. She would always be here to protect me. I didn't belong here. I belonged in the light with them.

I felt the pressure first, a solid band of pressure wrapped around my torso, holding me tight. It wasn't restrictive; it was more comforting, there was safety here, wrapped in these protective bonds.

"Calli," a deep voice whispered to me.

Blinking my eyes, the darkness started to fade, and the light began to filter through.

"Calli, come back to me."

As I kept blinking, awareness of my surroundings slowly filtered through to me. This was my bedroom. I was on my bed.

My vision cleared, and Grey was smiling down at me.

"There you are," he whispered, dipping his head down and laying a soft kiss on my lips.

"I'm sorry."

"Don't apologise, baby. We all know you're working through this the best you can. Just know that when you are, we're going to be right here beside you. You don't have to do this alone," he told me.

"The others ..." I started, not even sure where the question had been going.

"Are fine where they are," he smiled. "Let me be selfish and have some time alone comforting my beautiful mate."

I smiled, because how could I not when I was lying here and listening to Grey call me beautiful. When this gorgeous man was looking down at me with love in his eyes, how could I ever doubt myself? He was the image of perfection. His hair flopped down over his forehead in the most adorable way, and his brown eyes shone with affection. I gave in to the temptation and lifted my hand, brushing his hair back away from his face, how he usually wore it. The smile he rewarded me with would have been enough to shame a thousand stars.

"Are you ready to talk about it, or do you want more time?" he asked me, running his fingers through my hair.

It felt so good that I could feel my eyelashes almost starting to flutter closed before I made myself concentrate on the whole speaking thing that we apparently had going on.

"I don't feel ready yet, but I will, soon," I promised because I knew now that I had to. I couldn't afford to just zone out like that if Jacob was around. Apart from the fact that it wouldn't be safe, I knew it would frighten him as well. If I was going to take care of Jacob, then I needed to take care of myself as well. I made a mental note to get out the library books and actually read them. Once I'd done that, I'd sit down and speak with my mates.

"We'll always be here Calli, for whatever you may need," Grey told me, and I grinned.

Biting my bottom lip between my teeth, I had a thought about what I needed right now. It wasn't my fault, lying here on the bed, in his arms, of course, my mind only went to one specific place.

I felt the rumble of a growl vibrate through Grey's chest. It would seem his wolf was having the same thought that I was.

"Anything at all?" I asked, the question coming out more breathily than I had intended, but it had a distinct sex kitten vibe to it that I would swear to anyone who asked was definitely on purpose.

"Is there something you had in mind?" he smirked before moving his lips to my neck, peppering his way to my collar bone with kisses and soft bites.

The only sound I seemed to be able to make at that moment was a breathy moan which had Grey huffing out a laugh against my neck.

"I need to hear the words Calli. I need you to tell me how much you want so I know when you need me to stop."

Fucking hell, why did that sound so sexy. I didn't need to think. I knew exactly what I wanted. It was what I had wanted from the very first moment I saw him. Everything. I wanted everything.

Grey lifted his head, so he was looking me in the eye. Apparently, he was very serious about the fact that I needed to lay out any limits about what would happen. As frustrating as that was in the moment, I also really appreciated it. It was nice to know that his main concern was me and that I was comfortable. There were a lot of guys out there that wouldn't give me the same courtesy.

"I want you, Grey. I want every part of you. I don't want to stop," I told him, reaching one hand up to cradle his cheek as I spoke.

"That's all I needed to hear," he murmured before his lips met mine in a bruising kiss that made my toes curl.

Our hands became a blur as we tore at each other's clothes, I'm pretty sure I ripped my shirt, and I don't even remember taking my underwear off, but as Grey knelt between my legs gazing down at my naked body I could see his Alpha wolf shining through his eyes.

My wolf pushed at the edges of my mind, and I knew she was looking out at her mate.

Grey, with his clothes on, was gorgeous, but Grey, without his clothes, was breathtaking in an 'I'm worried about my sanity' kind of way. From his broad, toned shoulders, his six-pack and adonis belt, it was almost as if there was just too much for my eyes to be able to see. I couldn't just look at one part of him. I needed it all. God, if all three of them were like this, I didn't know how I would survive.

Somehow Grey had ended up kneeling between my legs in the mad rush to free ourselves of our clothes. It seemed like some kind of crafty planning on his part if I were completely honest. I was also 100% not complaining about it because I felt like out of the two of us I would definitely come out the winner.

Grey licked his lips before reaching down and taking one of my legs by the ankle and lifting it to his lips. I frowned in confusion until his lips brushed against my calf and his fingers slipped behind my knee. It was like he had found some kind of secret pathway that was connected directly to my clit, and my mouth dropped open as the ability to make sound completely left me.

Grey trailed his lips slowly up my calf and then started to move up my inner thigh. It was maddening in the very best kind of way, but he was turning me into a whimpering, writhing mess without hardly having touched me yet. I didn't know if this was some kind of mate magic or if Grey was just the god of everything related to sex, but I was very much on board.

When he reached the apex of my thighs, I knew that he would be able to see how wet I already was for him. I half expected him to continue with teasingly, light touches and kisses. So when he licked the full length of my pussy my back bowed off the bed from just that one touch.

His mouth sealed over my clit at the same time as he plunged two of his fingers inside me. With him licking and flicking at my clit and his fingers moving inside me, I became a panting, writhing mess on the bed as I felt the start of an orgasm already forming.

My hands somehow found their way into his hair, as my hips bucked off the bed, riding his very talented fingers. Grey didn't let up for one minute. He completely dominated me. His other hand slipping underneath me and closed around my ass, as he hauled me up closer to his face and feasted.

It only took him curling his fingers inside me once for him to detonate my orgasm and I came with a scream, not caring who in the house was able to hear me.

By the time my vision cleared, and I could focus on the grinning Grey between my legs, I couldn't help but grin back at him. The man was a God.

"You're beautiful when you come, baby," he whispered as he started to crawl up my body.

I licked my lips in anticipation. His cock was hard and long, and I was ready for more.

"I want to taste you," I told him, running my hands across his abs because there was no way I even wanted to try and stop myself.

"Not this time, baby. I want to be inside your sweet pussy when I come, and I'm afraid if I let you have a taste I'm going to embarrass myself before I have the chance."

"We have all night," I murmured, the sex kitten purr coming out to play again.

"If you don't pass out with exhaustion from coming harder than you ever have before, then I haven't done it right," he smirked, just as he lined his length up with me and slammed it home.

My eyes rolled back in my head as that move pushed me right to the edge of an orgasm again.

Holding himself over me, Grey waited until I focused back on him. He looked suddenly uncertain, and it wasn't a look you wanted to see on the face of a man who had just slammed his cock inside of you.

"What's wrong?" I asked, suddenly worried.

"My wolf," he started, looking confused for a moment, "he … I'm not sure."

"Do you need to stop?"

He closed his eyes and shook his head when he opened them again, his eyes glowed with the amber that was usually his wolf. I knew at that moment they were one, more than they had ever been while Grey was in this form.

"Tell me what you need," I said, running my hand down his cheek.

"To mate," he growled.

"We are mating," I told him, not sure which side of Grey I was talking to any more.

"To mark," he growled again.

"You want to mark me as your mate?" I said, seeing where this could be going.

Grey nodded, but he still looked worried. His wolf was obviously pushing for something that he wasn't sure about.

My own wolf pushed at the edges of my mind again, and I knew that my eyes would be lighting up with a similar glow as Grey had. She was more present than she had ever been, and she was making her intentions very clear. Grey was one of our mates, and it was time for him to make a claim as such.

"I would wear your mark with pride," I whispered, as I pulled him down into my arms and pressed my lips against his.

It was all that Grey needed to hear as he finally started to move inside me. He wasn't slow or gentle. He was an Alpha wolf, and at that moment, he showed me how he completely owned my body, and I couldn't have been more thrilled.

I pulled one of my legs up to wrap around his hip, and in his next thrust, he slipped just a fraction deeper.

"Fuck, Calli," he groaned as he hauled me impossibly closer to him, his hips pistoning away.

I felt his lips at my neck, and I knew his wolf was going to give me a mating bite, only because my wolf was pushing for me to do the same. I could feel my teeth shifting in my mouth, and before I even realised what I was doing, I was sinking them into the flesh of his shoulder. It couldn't have even been a second later when I felt Grey's answering bite, and as the taste of his blood hit my tongue, I came harder than I ever had in my life, just as Grey had promised me.

Grey managed to keep going and ride me through the waves of bliss that were surging across my body before he finally followed me over the edge, his breath huffing out of him as he finally found his own release.

Grey rolled to my side as he dropped to the bed, keeping me in his arms and pulling me close to him. His face was still buried in my neck as he peppered kisses around his mark. I sighed in happiness at the feel of him as I tickled my fingers across his abs again. I may have found my new favourite thing.

"Oh shit, Calli, I didn't use any protection," Grey said,

suddenly leaning back from me so that he could look in my eyes.

He was right. We had been too caught up in the moment to even think about it, which was stupid of us.

"It should be okay, I'm not at the right time in my cycle to get pregnant," I told him, which was the truth thankfully.

Grey nodded, still giving me a strange look.

"What?" I asked, feeling suspicious.

"Would you think I was weird if I said that I wouldn't be all that unhappy if that did happen?" he admitted.

"Yes," I said and then laughed at the shocked look on his face. "Okay, not weird. And you're right it's not a terrible thought, it's just really terrible timing to even think about something like that," I admitted.

Grey just nodded, and I could have sworn that there was a glimmer of disappointment in his eyes. It was strange. When it came down to it, we barely knew each other. But he was right; the thought of pups wasn't horrible to me. Maybe it was a mate thing. There wasn't anyone we could ask about it because my freaky magic made me unique.

While I was lost in my thoughts, Grey ran his finger over the mating mark he had left on my shoulder, and a shiver ran through my body at the sensation.

"We should probably talk about this," he murmured.

"Why?" I asked with a shrug. "It might not be what normally happens with shifters, but we're not really normal shifters, are we? It's probably a side effect of my wolf rather than a shifter mating with a turned woman," I reasoned.

"You're probably right," he nodded. "Fuck, it felt amazing as well."

I laughed because he wasn't wrong, but then a yawn suddenly forced its way out of me. Grey just smirked at me, and I remembered his earlier promise.

"Okay, so I might be a little bit sleepy," I shrugged.

He laid back down onto the bed, pulling me against his side. "Rest, we can talk about wardings and spells and all things to do with mating tomorrow."

I trailed my fingers across the scene tattooed on his chest. It suited him, he was all Alpha wolf and he should always be able to run free through the trees.

There was something about being in Grey's arms that made me feel like there was no safer place in the world for me. What we were building here, between the two of us, and with the others, was going to be something extraordinary, I could already feel it.

36

CALLI

I woke up the next morning, still curled up in Grey's arms. Tanner and River were nowhere to be seen, and I got the impression they must have left us alone for the night. I wasn't sure how I was supposed to feel about that. It didn't feel wrong that I'd spent the night alone with Grey, but I also felt a bit guilty that I hadn't been with them. Urgh, something else we were going to need to talk about. At least now I knew Jacob was okay with the idea of us all being together. Trust Jacob to just get down to the point of things. Maybe I could take a few lessons from him.

I slipped out of Grey's arms and sleepily padded into the kitchen. It was early enough that Grey didn't even stir as I left, and the house seemed pretty quiet. I found River asleep on the sofa, but Tanner was nowhere in sight.

I had a moment where I couldn't decide if it would be too disruptive to put the kettle on or not. The downfalls of open plan living spaces! But then I decided that my need for tea outweighed all other things, and also Jacob would probably be waking up soon anyway and there was no way he wouldn't be waking River up. The joys of living with a five year old, they don't really get the concept of having a lie in. So I flicked the switch on the kettle, without even the smallest bit of guilt, and grabbed mugs and the French press from the cupboard. If I was going to wake him up, I could at least make him coffee as well.

Once the drinks were ready, I headed over to the sofa where a now sleepy River was starting to sit up, and snuggled up against him. He seemed surprised at first, I suppose we didn't really do this much, but his arm soon came around me as he pulled me in tight against his side.

It wouldn't be long before we were disturbed, so for now, I was just going to enjoy snuggling with one of my mates.

"Did Tanner head back to the packhouse last night?" I asked as I sipped my tea.

"Yeah, he went to go over some stuff with Nash and then he was going to run a patrol."

"We need to talk about the warding and which property we're going to do first," I yawned, as Jacob stumbled out of his bedroom and into the bathroom.

I was a bit of a mess in the morning before I had a full cup of tea in me. Jacob was the same, except for juice, so when he just gave us sleepy grunts as he wandered back to his bedroom, I fetched him some juice from the kitchen and sat him up in bed with it for a bit.

When I wandered back into the living room to find my tea again, I was met with a wide-eyed stare from River.

"What?" I asked, suddenly self-conscious.

"You figured out the warding," he said slowly.

"Yeah, last night ..." I drifted off as I remembered the phone call, my meltdown and then everything with Grey, I hadn't actually told anyone. "I forgot to tell you all, didn't I?"

"Yeah, I wonder what could have distracted you so much," he said with a smirk.

I felt my cheeks flame as I blushed at what he was implying. Recalling how loud I had been, I knew he would have heard and Tanner as well if he'd still been here.

"Erm ... probably something else to talk about, maybe," I said, shuffling nervously on the spot.

River patted the sofa beside him, and I slunk over to him like a child waiting to get told off, which just made him laugh at me. As soon as I was close enough, he reached out, grabbing me by the waist and hauled me into his lap.

"Whatever happens between you and Grey, is between the two of you. Same as whatever happens with Tanner or me. We don't have to talk about it in the way that you're thinking about. You're not in trouble," he laughed.

"So, you're not upset that I spent the night with him?" I asked cautiously.

"He's your mate Calli. Of course, I'm not upset that you spent the night with him. Did it raise some strange feelings getting off on listening to you with my brother? Yes, but that's more for me to figure out," he said with a grin.

I could see his point there, and I couldn't help but laugh at his expense.

River nuzzled his face against my neck, and my toes curled in delight. "I can't wait to hear you making those noises for me," he said, his chest rumbling with the agreement of his wolf.

Just then, Jacob stumbled out his bedroom and back into the bathroom, without even casting a glance in our direction. He really wasn't a morning person. I had no idea what he was doing but he seemed like he was on a mission.

River pecked a quick kiss on my lips before lifting me up and setting me down on the sofa.

"I'll get breakfast started, what would you like?" he asked as he walked into the kitchen, taking his coffee with him.

"Pancakes!" Jacob's little voice shouted from the bathroom, making us both laugh.

"Pancakes it is," River said, shaking his head.

This must be weird for them, getting this insta-family but they didn't seem to be showing it if it was bothering them at all.

By the time Jacob had woken up properly, River had breakfast ready, and everyone else had gotten home and was in the kitchen helping out. Jacob ran straight to Tanner and got scooped up into his arms, which was a better greeting than he had given me this morning. They were both so cute together that it was hard to be annoyed though.

"So what did you want to tell us about the warding?" River asked once we were all sitting at the table and tucking into the breakfast feast they seemed to have put together.

"I went through everything with Sera last night, and I can get the warding put in place today. We're going to have to do one property at a time, so we need to decide which one we're doing first," I told them, shoving another piece of bacon into my mouth.

"You figured out how to link it to the ink then?" Blake asked, and I could tell that he was genuinely interested in the answer. He was really getting into learning as much as he could about magic and was proving to be a good study partner. I knew he wasn't going to let me live this down though, when he found out.

"Yeah, Sera told me how she did it last time," I said evasively.

It wasn't the answer that he wanted. He wanted specifics. But I didn't want to talk about blood magic in front of Jacob. I locked eyes with Grey and then cast my eyes to Jacob and back to him. He just nodded in understanding, and it seemed to ripple around the table.

"I think we should do here first," Tanner said, quickly changing the subject.

"I actually thought we should ward the pack first," I told them quietly.

Tanner cocked his head to one side in thought and looked genuinely confused. "Why?"

"Well, if you guys are going to be here most nights and Blake is here as well, I thought that the pack might need it more, you know, for Coby," I stuttered suddenly feeling like maybe I was overstepping.

Grey's face lit up in a blinding grin, and I had a feeling that I might have done something right. Unfortunately, I had no idea what it was.

"I'm only going to be able to set one before I'm going to need to rest. That also means that it's going to push back when I can start working with Jean even further," I looked to Blake to gauge his reaction, but he seemed okay with the news.

"We don't have a fix for the drain yet, so it doesn't make a difference right now," he shrugged. "I know you won't forget about her, Calli," he said with a soft smile.

I nodded in support at him. Even if it took me years, I was more determined than ever to get Jean and the baby back to him.

"So we're getting the first warding up today then?" River asked.

I nodded and then felt immediately guilty. It was the weekend art session at the library today and I'd wanted to take Jacob so I could spend some time with him.

"Well I was going to hang out at the house today," Blake told us leaning back in his chair and rubbing his stomach. "I've got a hankering for some cupcakes so I think I'm going to do some baking."

"Can I help?" Jacob immediately piped up.

"It's going to involve a lot of mixing and the super important job of adding the sprinkles. Do you think you're up for it?"

Jacob gave a determined nod and they immediately started to plan out what kind of cupcakes they wanted to make. I don't know what was more impressive, the fact that Blake had just jumped in without even having to be asked or that he knew how to make cupcakes from scratch.

I suppose this was the advantage of having a pack and people around you that saw you as family. There was always someone around to help out. And Blake was probably going to be around for a while if we didn't start looking for a solution for Jean, and even then, it could take years to find it. With the two of them and my three mates, Jacob and I were probably never going to be alone again. We really needed to figure out our living situation though. They couldn't be sleeping on the sofa forever. Maybe we could extend the house or something? Put in a couple of extra bedrooms and another bathroom.

"Calli," Grey's voice laughed, snapping me out of my thoughts.

"Sorry, what?" I asked, looking around the table and finding everyone was looking at me.

"Where did you just go?" Tanner laughed.

"Nowhere important, I should get ready then we can get started straight away," I said a bit flustered, standing from the table while everyone looked at me like the crazy woman I apparently was.

I rushed into the bedroom and pulled some clothes out of the closet, dropping them on the bed for when I was finished with the shower.

By the time I got out they were all waiting around my

room for me, I suppose it was to be expected. We didn't quite get to talk about it though because when I leant down to reach for my clothes, wearing nothing but my towel, Tanner suddenly exploded. "What the hell is that?" he growled and I whipped around to look behind me, confused what had suddenly made him so angry.

I felt Tanner's hands come to my shoulders as he turned me back to face him and then he tipped my head to one side and I suddenly knew exactly what it was that he'd seen. The mating bite.

"Someone needs to explain fast," Tanner growled. I could feel him vibrating in rage but his wolf was conspicuous by his absence. Did that part of him already know what it was, even if Tanner in his human form had no idea?

I tried to look at the mark again but I could only see the edge of it because of where it was placed on my shoulder. I'd seen it in the mirror before I got in the shower though. It was fully healed now but the silvery mark it had left on my shoulder couldn't be anything but a bite.

"So something happened last night," I started and Tanner turned around, his full fury zoning straight in on Grey, until he pulled the neck of his t-shirt to the side and showed him his identical mark.

River, who had been quiet up until now, stepped closer to his brother to examine the mark.

"You decided to place mating marks, like in the stories," River frowned.

"There was no deciding about it," Grey huffed. "Our wolves pretty much made the decision for us."

Tanner turned back to me and I could see the worry in his eyes. His fingers came up to trace the mark and a shiver ran through my whole body. It was like I could feel an echo of the pleasure I'd experienced when Grey had made it. A soft moan escaped my mouth and Tanner's worried eyes suddenly flooded with heat in response.

"Well, that's new," he murmured, before dipping down and placing a kiss over the mark.

My legs gave out from under me and Tanner caught me in his arms. It wasn't an unpleasant experience but it was a bit freaky. Was I going to turn into some kind of puddle anytime someone accidentally touched it?

Tanner chuckled and went to lay another kiss on the mark but I quickly darted out of his way, taking a step back, much to his amusement.

"So, you felt a compulsion to make the mark?" River questioned, drawing us back to the point we had started to discuss.

I ducked into the bathroom with my clothes and quickly dressed while I talked through a gap in the door to them.

"I don't know if it was a compulsion, I felt like I could have refused if I wanted to, but my wolf was adamant that Grey was her mate and she wanted him to wear her mark," I told them through the door before I stepped out fully dressed.

"It was the same for me. It was confusing at first because my wolf was more present in my mind than I'd ever felt him before, but it still felt like a choice," Grey nodded.

"Maybe we should look into the bond we have, it might be in the books upstairs," I said thoughtfully and caught Tanner's slump as he rolled his eyes.

"Why does everything involve homework now?" he groaned.

He was right, every situation we came up against seemed to start with us needing to turn to the library. I couldn't be more grateful to my parents for putting it there. How much of this did the Council know? And just how much were they actively keeping away from people? It felt like some of this stuff should be common knowledge, or at least something that was passed down through the Alphas. The packs would be so much better protected if some of this stuff was more widely known.

By the time I'd finished getting ready, I was thoroughly engrossed in my guilt trip of having to blow off the day with Jacob that I'd wanted to have. I reluctantly left my room and slunk into the kitchen to feed my tea habit and at least keep myself busy while I wallowed in the fact that I was failing at being Jacob's guardian. It felt like as soon as I had a grasp on one aspect of my life, everything else just flew out of control. I needed to start making a list, get a planner or something. Having a brilliant idea, I pulled out my phone and started to scroll through the internet. I found the perfect desk for the library on the Pottery Barn website. It was on sale, and wow it was expensive, but sooo pretty, so I bought it anyway. I added a chair to my basket and checked out. I'd check out Amazon tonight for some stationery goodies when I was feeling wiped out after setting the warding. Just thinking about it made me want to throw up—second spell of your lifetime and already dipping into blood magic, way to go Calli.

"How much of that stuff do you actually drink?" Grey laughed as he walked into the kitchen.

I took a step back and scowled at him because he'd just insulted my one true love, which only made him laugh even harder before he hauled me against him in a crushing hug. I couldn't even be angry about it because it felt too good—damn cuddly wolf, with his pettable abs.

"So what weren't you telling us earlier?" I heard Blake ask from the living room.

Turning I saw him and Tanner, lounging on the sofa, watching TV. I should have known that Blake would be the first to ask about the magic. Jacob was nowhere in sight and Tanner just pointed across to his closed bedroom door immediately knowing what I was looking for.

I sighed and steeled myself for the 'I told you so' I anticipated was about to come. "The last step to link the spell to the ink is blood."

The room went quiet, and I could see Blake working it through in his mind. He may only have a rudimental knowledge the same as me, but it seemed to come naturally to him. Tanner just looked confused and was staying quiet.

"I'm still not sure about this," Grey questioned, his arms tightening a fraction around me.

"Sera is convinced it will be fine," I shrugged. "I just don't know enough about it to be able to tell. I've been thinking about it, and I think the best thing to do is set up the warding for the pack and then here and then research it more thoroughly, so we know more about it."

"Shouldn't you be researching it before you do it?" Tanner asked, concerned.

I shrugged. "We could, but then it's going to delay the warding going up. Even if there is a risk, I'm still going to do it here. May as well include the pack in it if that's the case. I just want to be prepared for when the Council finds out what we've done."

Tanner frowned and looked on the verge of saying something stupid like 'I'm putting my foot down', so I raised a sassy eyebrow in question at him.

"We hadn't considered that before," Grey said carefully. "You're right that it's more 'when' the Council finds out rather than 'if'. When they find out your status as a wolf, I think they're going to be more interested in what you can do for shifters than thinking you're a threat. If they find out about the warding coupled with that, well we should be concerned about what the outcome is going to be."

"You're thinking we run now," Tanner asked him.

I was surprised they would be so willing to run, to leave everything behind. Their home was here, not to mention the business they had built at the garage and River's job at the school. I knew they said before that the pack would go with them, but I just couldn't wrap my head around that.

"It might be the better option," Grey sighed in defeat. I hated that it was me that had put that tone in his voice, even if it was through something I had no control over.

"Is Jean going to be able to travel?" Blake asked quietly, his eyes casting over to the closed door behind which his sleeping wife lay.

"I … I don't know," I sighed.

World's worst magic-user, right here.

"I don't want to leave here unless it's absolutely necessary though," I added. "I don't want to be forever moving Jacob around the world. He deserves to have somewhere he can call home, he's lost so much recently, I can't take this from him too."

I saw the sympathy in all of their eyes, even though a part of me hated it. I was also kind of grateful to see it there. They all cared about Jacob as well, and we were going to need as many people in our corner as we could get.

"Let's get this done then," Tanner said, with a nod of his head.

Everyone got up and started moving around the house, Blake and I had already gathered most of the supplies, and he and Tanner started to carefully pack them into a bag. We even had a map, marking out where each point would be and where to set up for the spell. After that, it was just a point of getting in the truck and driving over. I said goodbye to Jacob but he was so excited about making cupcakes with Blake that he didn't even seem that bothered to be left behind. He was a pretty easy going kid really.

When we pulled up outside the packhouse, Nash and Aidan were both waiting for us.

Walking over to the spot where we were going to set up, I had an overwhelming urge to shift. My wolf loved being here. These were the packlands of our mates, and she loved everything about them. I had to admit Mum and Dad had picked a very wolf friendly place for us to settle. I was starting to suspect that my Mum had known these guys were my mates, but I'd never know if she knew before or after they came here.

"Your packlands are beautiful," I said to no one in particular.

"I think you mean *our* packlands," Aidan laughed.

It was nice that he was so accepting of me being part of the pack. If I was honest, I had expected more of a response like I got with Wallace from the others as well. Wallace who was noticeably absent right now.

"I'm not part of your pack," I clarified—because I wasn't.

An awkward silence descended over us. I was getting really good at making these.

"How did we forget about that?" River suddenly asked.

I shrugged because the bitch voice that lived in my head decided it was because subconsciously they didn't want a mongrel like me in their pack, but I pushed that down into the same deep dark hole where I kept all my other repressed feelings—I was just a shining example of good mental health.

I was suddenly tugged to a stop because Grey, whose

hand I was holding, stopped dead without warning and that man was like an immovable object. He didn't even waver whilst I, on the other hand, nearly fell back on my ass.

"Calli," he said in his low growly voice that I loved so much.

I reluctantly met his eyes because I knew I was about to get told that, of course, I was going in the pack, and he knew what I was thinking; I just didn't want the others to know I was apparently some needy female.

Grey tugged my hand and dragged me into his arms—I just kept finding myself in them today, not that I was complaining. "Don't," was all he said before we started walking again.

Okay, that wasn't too embarrassing.

"Anyway, we need to talk about the pack connection and my weird magic before we do anything like that," I suddenly blurted out because apparently, the fact that the moment had passed without any weirdness wasn't enough for me.

"What do you mean?" River asked, cocking his head to the side. He had that tone of voice you get when you know something terrible was about to happen again, and you're not sure if you can take any more. Coupled with the kicked puppy look he had going on; it was pretty cute. For some weird reason though, it just made me laugh and then I felt terrible as the kicked puppy look got even worse.

"Sorry," I chuckled. "My father and I had a pack connection, obviously, and we could speak to each other in our wolf forms."

I just kept walking after having dropped that truth bomb like a boss. The others fell into a shocked silence which was a nice change to the uneasy ones we seemed to keep getting.

Nash suddenly started bouncing up and down in excitement. "I call dibs on researching this one," he said like it was the best present ever.

Well, at least my weirdness made someone happy.

"Like, how do you mean?" Tanner asked.

"We could hear each other talk in our heads," I shrugged. Okay, it was pretty cool, but I didn't want to make a big deal out of it for some reason.

"That's incredible," Nash squealed as his jumping up and down continued. "What range did it have? Could you turn it off? Did you have to be selective in what you thought or could you send specific thoughts? Could you communicate with anyone who wasn't in wolf form?"

"Nash! Dude, give it a rest," Tanner laughed.

"Yeah, let's just get through this part first before we start in on anything else," Grey said, giving him an almost fatherly smile. I wondered if that was what it felt like sometimes to be an Alpha, that you were in charge of a massive group of children—strong unruly children at that.

Looking around I realised we were already at the place we intended to use to cast the spell, once everything was laid out, I would need to walk the route for the warding and lay the stones. When I got back, I'd need to add my blood to the ink. River was already unpacking the bag of supplies we had brought, and now we were here, and it was all so real, I realised I was shitting myself. How did I even end up in these situations?

Huffing out a breath and letting my head drop back, I took a deep breath and closed my eyes. The wind rushed around me, and I could smell the woodlands, settling the wolf inside of me. The sun shone down on us, and the ground was firm beneath my feet, grounding my magic as well. I took a moment to find that sense of peace that I lacked, and then I dropped to my knees and started setting everything out.

"I don't like the idea of you walking this route alone," Grey suddenly said.

I looked up at him to find him squinting down at me, and I could see the tension vibrating through his body. Maybe I should teach him how to centre himself. Shaking the random thought from my head, I just told him, "We don't have any choice. Would you feel better if you followed along at a distance so you could keep an eye on me?"

He nodded firmly, and I thought about it for a moment.

"Okay, but it would be better if it were just one of you. And whoever it is, needs to make sure they don't cross over the route I'm walking for the boundary. You need to make sure that you stay inside otherwise once it's completed, it's likely I won't be able to include you within the link."

"I should do it," Aidan offered, surprising me. "That way if anything did go wrong it wouldn't be the end of the world if I can't accept the link. I'm not that important in the pack that you absolutely need me to link to the warding."

I could see that his words upset Grey, but unfortunately, they also made sense. Grey's pack was so small that they didn't have lower-ranking members. There just wasn't enough of them to warrant it. But if there had been one in place, Aidan, Blake and Wallace would be at the bottom.

Grey just sighed in reluctance and then nodded. I knew accepting this would be costing him, and as I stood to leave, I snuggled in against his side. He leant his face onto my shoulder, above his mark and inhaled my scent deeply. He was the type of man that would never want to accept that one of his pack was worth less than any other. And I loved him for it. Even if it was far too early to start throwing those words about, this would be doubly difficult for him because he also had to accept that someone outside of our bond was the best person to protect his mate right now. That was going to hurt him not just as my mate, but also as an Alpha.

River and Tanner stepped into our sides, and each wrapped their arms around us as well. It was the first time that all four of us had really been close at the same time like this. My wolf was practically drooling in joy in my mind. Grey accepted the support of the rest of our bond and then, what felt like far too soon, I stepped back.

The sooner we got this part over with, the better.

"I want you in wolf form and within sight of her at all times," Grey told Aidan, who just nodded and immediately shifted. "Be quick, Calli," Grey said with an edge of pleading in his voice.

"It should only take her about an hour to walk the route," Nash said, clearly trying to soothe him but failing entirely.

Grey locked him with a look that seemed to waver between 'shut the fuck up' and open despair.

"I've got this," I murmured to him.

He looked down at me, and I could see the concern shining in his eyes, weirdly, it made me feel better. He nodded and took a step back from me. The cold air rushed between us, and I instantly felt the loss of his presence. Knowing that showing him how much I hated him moving away from me wouldn't help him in this situation, I quickly turned and gathered up the small bags of stones from where we had left them.

I took a deep breath and set out walking the route to the first point that would form the corner of the square for our warding boundary. I couldn't look back. I didn't want to see their faces as I walked away.

It's strange how something as simple as walking alone could go from being a normal everyday activity to feeling as sinister as it did right now. Usually, when I was walking through nature like this, my wolf would be giddy with joy. She loved the feel of the earth between her toes and the fresh wind in her face. Now though, she was on high alert, regarding everything around us with suspicion. Her emotions felt like they were making mine spiral out of control, and it was hard to concentrate. Sometimes, it felt like two people lived in my head, and right now, it wasn't working for me.

Stopping on the path I was taking, I took a deep breath, I blocked out the worries and the emotions, and I brought to the forefront of my mind the purpose of this whole thing. Setting off on my route again, I thought about the pack and Coby and the need to keep them safe, about Jacob and how he needed a safe place where he could be with his pack. I thought about my parents and the trust they put in me by knowing I would look after Jacob when they were gone. Their smiling faces came to the forefront of my mind, and the love I always felt from them. I could do this. I could do this because I knew they were still with me. I was their daughter, and they had already given me all of the strength I needed.

The walk to the first point ended quickly, and I crouched down onto the ground, removing the small pouch of stones from my pocket. I started to dig down into the cold dirt with my bare hands, scraping away to make the hole for the warding pouch. I concentrated on my purpose with every movement, pushing my magic and my intention down into the ground. Placing the bag inside, I paused for a moment, my nerves flickering to life inside me again with the worry that this wasn't going to work, that I wasn't going to be good enough. I scooped the loose dirt back into the hole, pressing it down to seal the stones inside and the answering heat of magic I felt made me sigh out in relief. It was working.

Standing up, I brushed the dirt off my hands, turned

ninety degrees and set off walking in the direction of the next point.

The second and third points were about the same as the first, but when I approached the fourth, a feeling of uneasiness started to flow through me. The hairs on the back of my neck stood up, and my wolf was on full alert. It felt like someone was watching me from out in the woods. The snap of a tree branch had me whirling towards the sound, but all I saw was Aidan's wolf tracking me through the forest as he had been for the whole time. My wolf was convinced there was something else though, that there was danger nearby.

I continued walking because what choice did I have? I'd started this now, and I needed to see it through to the end. Pulling the bag of stones from my pocket, I gripped it in my hand, the weight helping to anchor me in the task I needed to complete.

I must have only taken a few more steps further when adrenalin suddenly surged through my system. My wolf forced through me triggering my shift, I'd only just shifted when something hit my side with enough force to throw me across the ground, skidding through the mud, my pain-filled yelp, the only sound that echoed around the forest.

Pain burst through my senses, my vision whiting out, and all of the breath rushed out of my lungs. Agony flared through me, but I shook my head and quickly got to my paws. The first thing I saw was the bag of stones laying on the ground where I had dropped, and relief swarmed my system when I realised that I hadn't lost them.

Next to them stood a snarling wolf, saliva dripping from his mouth as he growled at me—Wallace.

Pain shot through my left front leg as I put my paw down. I was definitely injured, but I wasn't going to show any sign of it to him. My top lip curled up as I growled back. This wolf was responsible for hurting Jacob, and for hurting me. I had shown him mercy before, but not this time. I knew I wouldn't be able to take him on alone; he had more than demonstrated that to me last time. But there was one thing that he hadn't taken into account. I hadn't come out here alone. I wasn't going to let him walk away from this in one piece this time.

I took a step closer to him, exaggerating a limp on my left front leg as I did. Lowering myself to the ground, I growled deeply, my ears flattening down on my head. My white fur bristled around me as my wolf relished in the anticipation of our attack.

As I had known he would, Wallace started to circle to my left. He was trying to come around my side and attack me where I was at my weakest. What he didn't expect, though, as soon as his back was turned, was Aidan barrelling into him from behind. I darted forward at the same time; my teeth found flesh and I locked my jaw as the force of Aidan's attack pushed Wallace past me. Something ripped, and Wallace's yelp was the one to fill the air this time.

The sound of his pain satisfied my wolf more than I was ready to analyse right now.

I whipped around, not willing to have my back to him for even a second. Wallace was quickly back on his feet, but this time Aidan stood firm between us, facing him down. This couldn't be easy for him, standing against someone he had considered his pack brother for years.

Wallace looked past Aidan to me, and I could see the hate burning in his eyes. At least he had an excuse for that hate now. The left side of his face was in ruins. His left cheek torn wide open to the extent that you could now see his white teeth shining through the ragged hole, most of his cheek now hung down off his jaw.

I should feel bad about this; I had essentially disfigured a man. But all I felt at that moment was satisfaction. Every time he looked in the mirror, he would be reminded of the consequences of coming after my family. That's if he lived long enough.

It must have only been a matter of seconds before Grey, Tanner and River rushed into the clearing in their wolf forms. I physically felt my muscles relax as soon as I saw them. I knew they would never let anything happen to me, and I finally felt the adrenaline begin to leave my system. Unfortunately, with that adrenaline crash came the reminder of the pain that I was currently in and it flashed up my front leg, nearly taking my breath away.

Wallace quickly cowered under the wrath of his Alpha as Grey came snarling at him. If he hadn't submitted at that moment, I knew without a doubt that Grey would have torn out his throat. The whole of the clearing was filled with wave after wave of his Alpha power and that power was pissed.

Tanner and River didn't stop until they were by my side. As soon as they appeared, Aidan shifted back into his human form and dropped to his knees in front of me.

"Calli, I failed you," he said, real sadness seemed to radiate from his voice.

I shook my head because, at this point, I had no other way to communicate with him in my wolf form. I needed to shift as well, but I knew it was going to be excruciating, and if I was honest, I was putting it off for as long as I could.

"I think she's hurt her front leg," Aidan quickly told River who was now kneeling beside me.

"Can you shift, Calli?" River asked, his hand coming up and running through the fur around my ears.

The answer was yes, I could shift, but now my wolf had no intention of doing so because she was enjoying her mate touching her too much. Reminding her that if we didn't get this sorted out, she would be lame in this leg for the rest of her life and also we wouldn't be able to finish the warding she reluctantly huffed out a breath and relented to me.

The pain that flared through my body as she receded, and the shift was triggered, was beyond anything I had ever experienced. The process of shifting what I was assuming was an already broken bone was not one I would recommend to anyone. For a moment, panic flared through me that I could be doing more damage to it by shifting now. I had never been in any situation where anyone had needed to do this. What if I was hurting my wolf? What if I wouldn't be able to heal this?

As the shift came to an end, in what was only a matter of a second or two, but felt like a lifetime, the pain slowly started to recede.

River cradled my arm as Tanner held me against his chest, I had absolutely no idea how I had ended up there. I was a sweaty panting mess though, and if I had the energy, I would definitely be moving because, ewww gross. He was just going to have to suffer through it right now, though.

"It's broken," River said, examining my arm carefully.

Grey snarled, and I heard his jaws snap as he advanced on Wallace again who had been sensible enough not to move from where he was cowering on the ground.

"Help me up?" I asked Tanner.

"Are you crazy, woman? Just take a moment," Tanner baulked.

"I haven't finished. I need to lay the last stones and complete the warding," I said, trying to struggle to my feet.

"Okay, I'll help you, just stop flailing about like that or you're going to hurt yourself even more," Tanner huffed.

Now, *that* I took offence to, but I wasn't going to say anything because I was getting my way and I didn't want him to change his mind. I did mentally flip him the bird, and he got the best stink eye I could muster in the circumstances.

Once I was on my feet, I retrieved the bag of stones, feeling the overwhelming relief of not losing them once more.

"It's important that you all stay where you are, we can't risk you crossing the boundary before the warding is fully set," I warned them as I shuffled over to the last point.

I could see them all watching me carefully. All of my mates had their fists clenched and muscles bunched, well the human ones at least. Grey's wolf was still pacing around Wallace like he was trying to decide if he was going to rip him to shreds or not. Well, there was no like about it; that was precisely what he was currently deciding. It wasn't looking good for Wallace right now, but I didn't have the energy in me to worry about it right now.

Dropping back down to my knees, I clenched my teeth when the drop jostled my arm and the pain flared through me again. I slowly dug out the hole in the ground with my good hand, placed the stones inside, and then sealed them in again. As soon as I pressed the dirt back into place, I felt the warmth of the magic answering me and then a rush of wind as it gusted around the warding leaving the now formed barrier in its wake.

"I felt that," River said, the astonishment shining in his voice.

"We need to do the last bit," I said, struggling up to my feet and staggering to Tanner who was now the closest to me.

As soon as I reached him, he swept me up into his arms, holding me close to his chest.

"Aidan, stay with Grey," Tanner said, looking at his pack brother who just nodded in agreement. "Let's get this finished and then get home so we can sort out that arm. We left Nash by the altar you set up to make sure that no one interfered with it," he told me.

I was grateful he said that. It wasn't something I would have considered, but they were right. If someone had disrupted this last step I wouldn't have been able to link the warding to the others and whilst it wouldn't be the end of the world because it would still have at least been in place, it was going to make life a whole hell of a lot easier for me.

When we made it back to the altar, Nash was pacing the ground and looking like he was about to lose his mind with worry. When he saw Tanner carrying me, I was surprised at how angry he looked.

"What happened?" he asked, rushing over to us.

He was hovering around us like he wanted to check me over, but he wasn't quite sure if he should. Given the way that Tanner had suddenly gone rigid at his approach, I would say he was doing the best thing at the moment by not touching me.

"Wallace," River growled from beside us.

"What?" Nash looked like someone had slapped him. His eyes cast over our shoulder in the direction we had come from. "Is he …" he trailed off, but we all knew what he was trying to ask. Was he dead?

"Not yet, we left him with Grey," River snarled.

I hadn't seen River this worked up since that day outside of the school when that drunk had accidentally hit me—which given the whole mate thing now, made so much more sense.

I couldn't get a read on Nash though. He seemed angry, but by the way, he kept looking over our shoulder, I could tell that he was worried as well. I couldn't blame him. How long had he known Wallace? Since they were kids probably. He probably grew up with him and was there when his son was born. Fucking hell Coby.

"You can go to him if you want. I won't be upset if you do," I told him quietly.

Tanner just tensed more but didn't say a word. This was an awkward situation, and I couldn't help but feel like I was fucking up their pack.

Nash looked nervously between us all before he gave a brisk nod and jogged away. A low growl rumbled through Tanner as he watched him leave.

"Hush now!" I scolded him, "He's allowed to be concerned about someone who is no doubt his friend and I don't even want to think about what is going to happen to him right now."

Tanner didn't calm down at all. If anything, he seemed more stressed out. But I just didn't have the energy for the drama right now, and if that made me a crap mate, then so be it, because right now my arm hurt like fuck and I just wanted to go home and maybe cry for a bit.

"Can we just get this done?" I asked more quietly. The energy was quickly draining out of me, and I just didn't have any more fight in me.

Tanner glanced down at me, and his eyes softened when he no doubt took in the state of me. He nuzzled his face against my neck, taking care not to jostle my arm, then gently placed me down on my feet next to the altar we had set up.

The next step was relatively simple. Magic didn't really seem all that complicated. It was more about knowing what you wanted it to do. It was a part of me, after all. It wasn't like I needed to summon it from anywhere with special words. I just needed to know how to tell it what I needed it to do.

Dropping down to my knees, I shuffled closer to the altar. It was just a simple cloth laid on the ground. On it, there was a bowl containing the same types of stones I had buried at each of the points. I picked up the ink bottle that Aidan had provided and emptied it over the stones in the bowl. Then, taking the knife that was laid next to it, I took a deep breath and sliced across the palm of my hand. I heard River hiss out a breath as he watched but apart from that neither of them made any move to interfere. I appreciated that more than I could express right now. Holding my hand over the bowl, my blood slowly dripped inside. I felt my magic swirl inside me with each drop and then fall into the bowl with it. It was a strange sensation. I'd pushed magic into other people before when I was healing them, but feeling it leaking out of my body now was completely different. It felt kind of unnatural if I was honest.

Once I was satisfied that there was enough magic in the bowl, I pulled my hand away and fell back onto my haunches with a puff of breath.

"Is that it?" River asked cautiously after a few seconds.

"Should be," I shrugged.

"That was … a bit anticlimactic if I'm honest," Tanner said, frowning down at me.

"Oh I'm sorry, I could lop off an arm instead if you prefer?" I snarked and then immediately felt bad about it. "I'm sorry that was uncalled for."

"Calli," Tanner said, dropping to his knees beside me. "You don't need to apologise. You of all people deserve to be pissed right now. Come on, let's get you back to the house so we can look at your arm properly."

Tanner scooped me up from the ground again and got to his feet with no effort at all. My wolf was practically purring in joy at the moment, and I couldn't help but roll my eyes at her. She didn't care though, and I had to admit it was nice to feel her happy and not grieving the loss of her pack.

It was a tense walk back to the house. River and Tanner were both on high alert, and the longer we walked, the tighter Tanner held me against him. Their wolves would undoubtedly be pushing for control right now knowing that there was a potential threat against their mate. The fact that they were holding back their shift right now was pretty impressive.

37
GREY

I was having a hard time keeping control of my wolf right now. He wanted to tear Wallace apart, fuck, I wanted to tear Wallace apart. But I needed answers first. I needed to know why he would do this. Why he would risk this when he was supposed to be protecting his son, because without him, Coby would be defenceless. Kelly wouldn't be able to protect him from the witches alone and surely he wasn't insane enough to think he would get away with this.

Wallace still cowered on the ground in front of me. My wolf thought he was pathetic. He hadn't even tried to stand against us when we came into the clearing. He had just attacked my mate like a coward. The betrayal stung more than the anger right now.

Emotions surged through me from my wolf. He wanted blood for blood. He wanted to hear Wallace's screams of pain, just as we had heard our mate's. His rage was nearly overwhelming, and the effort it took to fight it down was almost impossible.

If I stayed in this form, I wouldn't be able to keep fighting this. And I needed answers. I needed to know why? Why would Wallace betray me like this? Why would he betray his pack?

I pushed through the shift, my wolf fighting me every step of the way. As soon as I regained my human form, I pushed a wave of my Alpha power out and forced Wallace to shift as well.

Aidan stood quietly at my back, but I could feel his rage through our pack bond. He would be feeling the sting of this betrayal just as much as I was. Everyone would.

Nash jogged into the clearing, stopping at Aidan's side with an uncertain look on his face. He glanced down at Wallace, and a look of worry flashed across his face. I tried not to be pissed, but it felt like he was taking sides right now and it wasn't mine he stood on. That hurt more than I thought it would but I couldn't deal with it right now.

Turning back to Wallace, a growl echoed through my chest as my eyes landed on his form, crouched down on the ground. He looked a sorry sight. The left side of his face had been ripped open, and even though it had partially healed through his shift, he was still going to need stitches. His left cheek gaped open, and I could see the white of his clenched teeth through the ragged gap.

"Explain yourself," I gritted out, still fighting my wolf to keep control.

Wallace's eyes flicked to Nash and Aidan over my shoulder before they came back to me.

"Don't look to them; they can't save you right now. I gave you one chance, one chance Wallace. And still, you crept through the woods like some kind of coward and attacked my mate. This is the only chance I'm going to give you to explain yourself," I growled.

"She's a witch," he spat out. Pure hatred dripped from his

words. "She needs to die. She has you under some kind of spell. I did what I had to do to save the pack. They'll come back for us, for Coby. I did what I had to, to save you all."

"Calli was setting a warding spell to protect our lands from the witches, so we would know if they ever came back. She's not working with them," Nash said, stepping forward.

Nash looked at me uneasily, but I could tell he had something he wanted to say. I gave him a nod to encourage him to speak, not trusting myself to open my mouth. I barely contained my wolf right now. He was adamant that Wallace would always be a threat to our mate, and he wanted to put him down, to eliminate the threat. I was totally in agreement with him.

"It's a misunderstanding," Nash said, advocating from his pack brother. "He thought he was protecting the pack."

"I AM HIS ALPHA," I roared at Nash. I knew that I was taking this out on him, but I didn't give a fuck.

"Have you lost your fucking mind," Aidan gasped, stepping up beside me. "Why would you argue for him? You weren't here. You didn't see what he did. He waited for her to turn her back on him and then he went for her. He tried to kill her. Calli. Calli who has done nothing but try to help this pack. Calli, who helped us rescue his son. Calli, who is saving Jean and her baby at the expense of her own safety. Calli, who was only out here so she could try and make our pack, and his son, safer!"

Aidan turned away from Nash in disgust, pacing away from us. I could hear the frustrated growl from him. I'll admit I was surprised. I was surprised he felt so strongly about keeping Calli safe. Out of all of us, he had spent the least amount of time with her. My wolf was immediately suspicious, but I quashed that, I didn't have time to deal with more than one problem at a time .

Turning back to Nash, I could see the embarrassment on his face.

"I know," he whispered quietly. "I know what she's done and what we all owe her. All I'm saying is that Wallace is our pack brother and maybe we shouldn't lose sight of that as well."

"And what would you have me do?" I snarked. "Let him walk away so he can try to kill her again."

I looked down at the man in question still kneeling at my feet. He didn't say a word. He didn't even argue for his life.

"Why are you not begging for your life?" I asked him. I knew exactly how it sounded, but I wanted to know the answer nonetheless.

"What's the point? The witch has got her claws into you, you'll kill me because you have no other choice but to do so," he shrugged.

"Take him to the house, put him in the cage and stay with him," I said, turning to Aidan. "Under no circumstances are you to leave him until I get back with Tanner."

Aidan nodded and grabbed hold of Wallace, pulling him up to his feet.

Turning back to Nash, I snapped. "Go with him, but once Wallace is in the cage, I want you over at Calli's house, we need to talk."

I turned my back on them and started to walk away. My wolf was disgusted with Nash, suspicious of Aidan and furious with Wallace. My pack was falling apart, and all I could do was turn my back on them and walk away. I was a terrible Alpha. But if I stayed, I was definitely going to kill Wallace, and there was something about what Nash had said that was picking at my brain. We needed to find a way to prove to Wallace that Calli wasn't what he thought.

38

TANNER

By the time we got Calli back to the house, I was ready to shift and run. My wolf was so on edge that I felt like I was vibrating beneath my skin, trying to hold back the shift. I needed to run off some of this energy, but I knew if I gave in and shifted now, the only place I would be running to would be Wallace.

Jacob was thankfully in his room when we quietly slipped through the back doors. The distinct clicking sound of Lego filled the air. Blake, who had been stood in the kitchen with a cup of coffee when we slipped inside, froze when he saw Calli still in my arms.

"What the fuck happened?" he gasped when he saw us, rushing over to our side.

Calli had passed out when we were about halfway to the house and stirred briefly at the sound of Blake's voice. We quietly slipped into her bedroom, hoping not to worry Jacob that anything was wrong, and I carefully laid her down on her bed. Given the state of her arm, we decided it was best to let her sleep for a bit and walked back into the kitchen to try and not disturb her.

"Fucking, Wallace," River seethed, pacing up and down.

I knew he was fighting his wolf's agitation because I was feeling it too. We needed Grey back here to help because I was worried if River lost control of his wolf, it would be the final thing that made me snap as well.

"What do you mean, Wallace?" Blake asked, staring at Calli through her open door where she was asleep on the bed.

They had grown to be friends over the last few days, and I could see how concerned he was for her. Not to mention that she was the only chance Jean and the baby had. I could see why he was protective.

"Wallace fucking attacked her while she was laying the warding. He crept up on her through the woods when she was alone, and he fucking attacked her," River all but shouted.

I glared at him in place of trying to shush him quiet, and we all froze, listening to see if Jacob was going to come and investigate what had happened. If he saw Calli hurt again, I didn't know how he would deal with it.

"What! Why?" Blake whisper shouted once we had heard that the clicking of Lego was continuing on.

"We don't know, Grey is dealing with him," I told him, feeling the urge to start pacing as well. Instead, I started making Calli a cup of tea. I didn't know why because she was asleep, but I was hoping that the act of doing something for our mate would calm my wolf enough that I wouldn't feel like I was about to spiral out of control.

"Grey is dealing with him … how?" Blake asked cautiously.

We all knew what he was asking—was Wallace still alive? I shrugged because I had no idea. If he was then Grey had far more control than I did.

A few minutes later, Grey strode through the door, and even though I could see the anger flaring across his face, calming waves of Alpha power filled the room, and River quietly sighed in relief.

"How is she?" he asked, looking around for Calli.

"She fell asleep on the way here," River said, his teeth still gritted. "We're going to need to wake her so that we can look at her arm and assess the damage."

"How exactly are we going to do that?" Blake asked, looking unsure. "We don't have any medical training, and we can't exactly call in a doctor from one of the other packs to look at Calli."

We all fell silent, I hadn't thought about that, and I could tell from the faces of the men around me that they hadn't either.

"Fuck!" Grey shouted, his hands reaching up and pulling on his hair, as we all shushed him.

"Grey?" a sleepy Calli called out from the bedroom.

We all rushed inside to be by her side, me with the cup of tea still in my hand. Calli was struggling to sit up, and River sat on the bed beside her, his arm immediately coming around her back as he helped her get upright.

"How are you feeling sweetheart?" Grey asked, sitting on her other side with a look of such worry in his eyes. Her golden hair was rumpled around her head even though she had only been asleep for a few minutes, and she looked gorgeous.

"I don't feel too … ooo is that for me?" she asked, her eyes suddenly landing on the mug in my hand.

We all laughed because we just couldn't help it. Calli's obsession with tea was a borderline addiction. My wolf settled slightly, knowing we were helping her, and I passed her the mug with a smile. She sipped gratefully at it, and it took me a moment to realise which hand she was drinking with.

"Doesn't that hurt?" I asked, pointing to her arm.

She stopped drinking and looked at the arm in question. When she had been in her wolf form that was the leg which had obviously been broken, you could see the bulge in the leg where the bone didn't meet.

"I mean, it's a bit sore," she shrugged.

"Sore!" River said incredulously.

Calli passed her mug to the other hand and then started flapping her hand about trying it out.

"Will you stop that, woman!" Grey said, grabbing hold of her. "You're going to hurt yourself."

He cradled her arm in his hands like it was the most precious thing in the world, and even I could admit it was pretty sweet of him.

"It honestly doesn't feel that bad," she shrugged.

River scowled and then rolled the sleeve of Calli's sweater up. Gently running his fingers up her arm, he examined her face for even a hint of pain.

"I don't understand, you could see the break," River said, turning her arm over and pressing down on it more firmly this time. "You didn't heal this fast last time," he pointed out.

A growl rumbled through Grey at the mention this was the second time our mate had been hurt, and at the hands of one of our pack no less.

"Maybe it's got something to do with your magic," Blake murmured. "Because you've started to use it rather than repressing it."

Calli's head cocked to the side as she considered his words. "I suppose that could be it," she murmured, not looking convinced.

"I can't feel a break," River said, almost to himself. "But we would need an x-ray to be certain."

A knock at the front door had us all pausing and looking at each other in confusion.

"It's probably Nash," Grey murmured as Blake went to go and answer the door.

"Let's relocate this to the living room," Calli suggested. "I feel weird being in here with everyone else."

Grey nodded and helped her out of the bed, hovering around her as if waiting for her to collapse at any second. Calli was either ignoring him or just oblivious to it because she wandered out the room, sipping at her tea like nothing was wrong. I'm pretty sure that whenever she had one in her hand it was all she could think about.

When we all made it into the living room we found Nash looking reluctant to come inside at first, which confused me. As far as I was aware, he didn't have a problem with Calli. He'd been here before, and he didn't have a problem then. Something had changed. I glanced at Grey in question, and he just shook his head slightly. Grey was a good Alpha, but that pissed me off. I was beta in this pack, and it was my job to make sure that the pack held together. Something was off, and this was the last thing I needed on top of everything else.

"Alpha," Nash said, nodding his head at Grey, which just confirmed my suspicions further. Even River was looking confused now.

Grey got to his feet and stood between Nash and Calli, shielding her with his body. Hurt flashed through Nash's eyes, and I couldn't take the tension any more.

"What's going on?" I asked, looking between the two of them. Nash had tensed up almost like he was expecting Grey to attack him.

"Make your decision Nash, where do you stand?" Grey asked him, ignoring me entirely.

"With the pack, always with the pack," Nash said almost

pleadingly.

Grey's brow furrowed, and I could see that he was considering something. I was in the dark and it pissed me off. I was his fucking beta and Calli's mate. The fact that he wasn't cluing me in on this was disrespectful at the very least.

"I'd be within my rights to take his life. In fact, under the Council's rules, I'd be within my rights to take his son's as well."

I looked at Grey in shock, what the actual fuck was going on? We all knew Grey well enough to know that he would never harm a hair on Coby's head.

"You will touch that child over my dead body!" Calli shouted, jumping up from the sofa where she had been sat.

"Calli, I think you know me well enough by now to know that I would never do such a thing," Grey said, the shock radiating from his voice. I could see why he was hurt she would think such a thing, but he had been pretty convincing when he said that.

"I didn't, but you're fucking convincing when you're angry," Calli said sulkily, sitting back down on the sofa and then snuggling up against River.

"What I was trying to say, is that he knows the potential consequences and I don't understand why he would risk it," Grey growled, crossing his arms over his chest. He let out a sigh of frustration. "The only way I could see him taking this risk is if he truly does believe what he is saying."

Nash seemed to deflate in relief, and I instantly realised the issue. He had gone to bat for Wallace and was worried about what Grey would do about it.

"But, equally, I don't see how we are ever going to change his mind. He can't stay in the pack when he is a risk to Calli's safety."

The room fell silent as we all digested what Grey was

saying. I could see Nash weighing out the options and trying to find a different solution, but Grey was right, there was no other way.

"You could let him leave," Nash suggested quietly.

No one said anything at first because we all knew what he was suggesting. The problem was, would it be enough.

"I think I'm going to make some lunch and let you all discuss this alone," Calli said awkwardly as she tried to climb to her feet.

"You don't have to leave," River told her as she stood up.

Calli smiled softly at us before she started to move away. "This is a pack issue, and it's something you should decide together," she told us, and I could hear the hint of sadness in her voice.

It wasn't until that moment that I realised just how bad the loss of Calli's parents would have been for her. They were her pack as well, and she had lost them. Her overwhelming guilt made even more sense now and also the sadness I could hear in her voice. Here we were standing in front of her discussing the problems of a pack we hadn't invited her to join after she had just lost the entire pack she had grown up with. Jacob was too young to form a pack bond with. Like wolves, we were pack animals, and Calli was currently a wolf without a pack. It was no wonder that she was hurting so badly and I was the world's worst mate for not having realised sooner. We all were. How had we not seen this? Some wolves could survive as lone wolves. But to have had a pack and then lost it, it was a fate worse than death for most.

Calli moved over to the kitchen and started rummaging in the fridge, pulling out bread and sandwich makings. My eyes tracked her movements. Now that I'd figured out part of the problem, I was concerned. I didn't know how she was doing as well as she was and I couldn't help but wonder if that was because she wasn't. If she was hiding a far greater pain than any of us had realised.

"What's wrong," Grey asked me softly, only River and Blake could hear what he was asking.

"I just realised something," I murmured back. I looked between them all, even Nash, "We need to talk."

Grey just nodded and glanced over his shoulder at Calli. We couldn't do this in front of her, and moving out of earshot would probably hurt her, but it needed to be done. This needed to be dealt with as soon as possible.

We headed out through the sliding door to the outdoor sofa. At this time of year, it shouldn't be getting as much use as it was, but with the outdoor heater and it's relatively sheltered position, it was actually pretty nice sitting out here. River quietly closed the door behind us, but there was no way she would have missed us moving out here. I couldn't take my eyes off the door. Now that I had an idea of what could be possibly going on, my worry was spiralling out of control, and I could feel my wolf's sadness radiating against mine.

"Tanner, come on, you're freaking me out now," River said.

I turned away from the sliding door, and it felt like I was physically tearing myself away from Calli. My breath caught in my throat, and it felt like my chest was going to cave in from the pressure.

"Tanner!" Grey said, shooting up out of his seat in concern as he immediately came to my side. "Tanner, I can feel your panic, what's happening?"

Grey guided me over to the sofa, and I numbly sat down.

"Calli," I managed to gasp out.

Everyone looked confused at my sudden change of state. I could tell Grey and River were both starting to become concerned about our mate as well. I needed to get myself together. Then we could talk about this. It was just my beta-need to protect that was making me freak out right now. I didn't need to draw them into it as well.

Taking a few deep breaths, I reassured my wolf that we were going to fix this, and once I had him under control, I felt like I could reign my own emotions back as well.

"Have any of you noticed Calli having any kind of extreme grief reactions?" I asked the four of them. "Is she hiding how bad it is?"

I wasn't explaining myself well, but luckily they seemed to know what I was talking about.

"There was that time at the table when we were looking at the warding spells," Blake said thoughtfully, and I nodded as I remembered what he was referring to; when Calli had seemed to just slip away into her own mind.

"When I brought Jacob home from school the other day, and she was playing the guitar outside," River told us. "Jacob said she only plays it when she's sad now."

His face filled with pain as he recalled the moment we had all missed.

Grey frowned in concern. "Last night," was all he said.

"We've fucked up," I sighed. Because we had, there was no other way to see it. "Calli's parents were her pack. Why didn't we realise this before?"

They all looked equally shocked and ashamed, which was exactly how I was feeling as well.

"But Jacob …" Blake started.

"Is too young to have formed the bond and he only had his first shift the other day," Grey filled in.

"How is she surviving as a lone wolf?" Nash asked, turning to look back to the house "Her wolf's grief alone should have been enough to drive her half insane."

"Jacob," River said firmly. "She's holding it together for

Jacob."

We all nodded. He was right; there was nothing that Calli wouldn't do for her brother.

"Maybe it has something to do with her magic as well; maybe she doesn't feel it as much as a normal wolf," Nash theorised.

It was the wrong thing to say.

"She is a normal wolf!" Grey shouted. His chest heaved as he panted, and I knew exactly how he was feeling because it was pushing against me as well.

We needed to find a way to fix this.

"We have to bring her into the pack link officially," Blake said, surprising me with the amount of concern that he was showing. "She must be suffering ..." he trailed off.

It didn't need to be said, we had all heard the stories, and we all knew exactly how much she must be suffering.

"We need Aidan before we can make the bond," Grey said almost to himself, and I knew exactly what he was thinking.

We couldn't leave Wallace alone. We would have to deal with him first, no matter how much any of us wanted to fix this straight away. We had to deal with severing Wallace's bond before we could establish a new one with Calli. Grey could sever the bond without us, but the whole pack needed to be present to bring someone new into the bond.

"Go, now," I said, making a decision that I perhaps didn't have the right to make. "I'll stay with Calli and make sure she's okay."

Grey locked eyes with me, and I could see the emotions tumbling through his gaze. He didn't want to leave Calli, not now we knew this. The guilt that we had been missing this made it hard, but the fact that he was an Alpha and her mate, made it doubly difficult for him.

"Concentrate on your need to protect her to get you through this," I told him, and he nodded firmly.

"River, Nash, you're both with me. Blake, do you want to come or do you want to stay?" Grey asked him.

Blake looked uneasily at the door. We all knew that he was finding it hard to leave Jean, but we also knew that it could take a long time to find a solution to her problem. He couldn't sit by her side for the rest of his life. She was well cared for here, and we all knew just how much he loved her. We also knew how much she would kick our ass if we just let him wallow at her bedside.

"I want to come with you, if that's okay," Blake said, looking at me uneasily, and I knew what he was trying to ask me.

"I'll keep an eye on Jean; you don't have anything to worry about," I told him.

He smiled at me gratefully, and Grey clapped me supportively on the shoulder before he shifted into his wolf form. The others followed suit, and I watched as they disappeared into the trees. It would be interesting to see if when Calli joined our bond, she would bring with her the ability to communicate in wolf form.

Turning back to the house, I quietly went inside and found Calli standing in the kitchen. She stood at the counter with all of the food laid out in front of her. An empty plate was on the counter in front of her, and she seemed to be frozen in place, staring down at the knife in her hand. A blank look was across her face, similar to the one she had the other day when I found her sitting at the table. I could tell she was somewhere lost in her thoughts, but for a moment, a very brief split second, I worried why she was looking so intently at that knife.

"Calli," I said quietly, reaching out and laying my hand on her wrist. "Sweetheart?"

She turned towards me, her eyes focusing on my face and asked, "Do you want a sandwich?"

Taking the knife from her hand, I pulled her towards me and into my arms, she didn't even hesitate, and I loved that about her. She fit against me like she was made to be there.

"How about you go and sit down and relax? I'll make the sandwiches and come join you," I told her, shooing her out of the kitchen.

"Have the others gone back to the packhouse?" she asked as she wandered over to the sofa and sat down. I didn't miss the massive yawn she gave as she did so.

"Yeah, Grey wants to deal with Wallace first and get that out of the way so we can get on with everything else."

She looked uncertain as she sat there. I should have asked Grey when we would bring her into the pack bond, so I could at least tell her now and settle some of her fears.

I checked in on Jacob to see what he wanted to eat but found that he had fallen asleep on his bed. We needed to get him into a proper routine, it was playing havoc with the poor kids sleep having all of this disruption in his life.

I plated up the sandwiches I'd quickly made and took them over to the sofa where we ate in relative silence.

"So, how are you feeling after setting up the warding?" I said, desperate to fill the silence with anything.

"I'm a bit tired, but not too bad considering. I should be able to do the ward here tomorrow, it's much smaller anyway, and then we can start to think about the tattooing process for you guys."

I nodded. I wasn't nervous about the tattoo. It's not like it was my first ink. I may have been a tiny bit apprehensive about the whole magic thing, but Calli was doing it, and I trusted her.

"You don't want to rest or anything then?" I asked, then immediately kicked myself with how it sounded. I used to be so smooth when it came to women, when had I forgotten how to speak to them? Oh, that's right, apparently, once I realised this amazing woman was my mate.

"If I didn't know you any better, I'd think you were trying to get me into bed," Calli laughed, her voice dropping down into a seductive purr.

My wolf immediately sat up, panting at the sound of it. The idiot would be on his back begging for a tummy rub right now if I let him. I couldn't blame him though, I felt exactly the same way and had been ever since that night we'd had with Grey and us in her bed.

She was just so goddamned beautiful.

"Doesn't your arm hurt?" I asked her, shuffling closer to her on the seat even as I spoke.

"No, I can't feel a thing," she smiled, laying back on the sofa as I crawled my way over her.

I would swear to any god you asked me to that this had not been my intention, but now that she seemed to have waved the briefest of green flags at me, it was all that I could think about.

"You know, no one is going to be home for probably hours," she said, her hand coming up to run through my hair as her leg came up around my hip, drawing me down closer to her body. "And Jacob will be asleep for at least an hour."

My lips were so close to hers that I could feel her soft breath across them. When she licked her lips in anticipation, she lightly grazed my bottom lip with her tongue, and before I even realised I was moving, my lips were meeting hers in a bruising, desperate kiss.

Everything about Calli was perfect, from her soft lips to how she obsessed about her next cup of tea. She was everything for me. She was my reason to breathe, my first thought in the morning and every moment of every dream.

As I palmed her breast with one hand, she opened her mouth to me on a moan. Taking the opportunity, I slipped my tongue inside her mouth, and she met me with her own.

It had been years since I had just made out with a woman, but kissing Calli consumed me. My other hand came up into her soft golden hair as I stroked my thumb down her cheek.

I pulled my lips away from hers to try and get my brain to start firing again. She smiled up at me, her tongue poking out as she swiped across her bottom lip to lick them and my mind immediately went to what it would feel like to have those lips around my cock.

If all we had was an hour, I didn't want to waste a single second more. Standing up, I scooped her up off the sofa, and she wrapped her legs around my waist with a giggle. The sound made my heart flutter like a little girl but the way that her pussy was currently rubbing against my cock made me very happy to be a man right now.

Her lips crashed down on mine, as she ground against me, while I carried her into her room, kicking the door closed behind us.

We fell to the bed still wrapped in each other. I didn't want to let her go and it seemed like Calli was feeling exactly the same way as her legs tightened around my waist, drawing me closer to her.

"Is this weird because Jacob is asleep in the other room?" I asked, pulling back suddenly concerned.

"Jacob is asleep on the other side of the house and have you seen that kid sleep, nothing is going to wake him up for at least an hour," Calli told me. "But we can stop if you don't feel comfortable, we don't need to do this now."

"There is nothing that I want less than to stop right now," I murmured, peppering kisses down her neck. "I just didn't want you to think I was an ass," I confessed, grinning against her skin.

I felt her laughter and I couldn't help but chuckle with her too.

Pushing up on my hands, I gazed down at where she lay beneath me. The smile on her face lit her up with happiness. This is how it should always be. There should never be an ounce of sadness on her face, not if there was anything we could do about it.

"You're beautiful," I told her and then watched the way that the blush slowly moved across her cheeks.

"So are you," she whispered, threading her fingers through my hair and pulling me back down to her.

Our kisses became soft and gentle as I held her in my arms and worshipped her the way she should be for the rest of her life. I gently trailed my fingers across the skin of her stomach, feeling my way across the smooth expanse until I found the bottom of her ribs.

Calli sat up on her elbows and pulled her top over her head, then threw it off the side of the bed as I bit down on my lip, taking in the sight of her lace-clad breasts. Whoever had invented lace needed a medal. Her dusky pink nipples were pushing through the white lace in an almost sinful way.

I closed my lips around her nipple, drawing it and the lace into my mouth.

Calli's fingers threaded through my hair as she pulled me closer to her breast, her legs wrapped around my hips, pulling me back in against her body.

I'd been with women before, of course, I had, but none of

them were like her. She was the perfect picture of everything I'd dreamed about. If my wolf was right, and I knew to the very bottom of our souls that he was, she had been made for us, and she was perfect.

I cupped her other breast in my hand as I returned my lips to her mouth. I would never get tired of kissing her. I'd never get tired of feeling her tongue flick against my lips.

Moving down her body, I ripped her jeans and underwear from her in one tug. I was done waiting for this. I needed her more than I had ever needed anything in my life, my cock was so hard it was almost painful and the only sweet relief I would find was between her legs.

She looked down at me with a grin as she quickly whipped off her bra and threw it over the side of the bed where the rest of her clothes had ended up.

Suddenly, I was staring down at my naked mate, and my mouth went dry as I took in every delicious inch of her.

"You're far too overdressed for this party," she murmured out in a husky tone as she writhed beneath me on the bed.

It would seem that my mate was getting impatient. I could smell her sweet arousal tinting the air, and my wolf was howling joyfully in my mind.

It didn't take me long to strip the clothes from my body. Having Calli eye me greedily as I did, gave me all the motivation I needed.

I was suddenly met with a problem, though. "There are so many things that I want to do to you, but we just don't have the time," I complained as I made my way between her legs and ran my tongue along her pussy.

Calli's back arched straight off the bed from just that one touch, and the moan that left her mouth filled me with male satisfaction.

"It's not a race," she panted. "We have the rest of our

lives for you to take me in every single position you can think of," she purred, and I groaned at the mental image she was giving me.

Hiking one of Calli's legs over my shoulder, I ran my finger across the lips of her pussy. I could already see her arousal glistening and as much as I knew nothing was going to hold me back from them, I couldn't miss the opportunity to tease her just a little.

"Maybe this is something that we should save for another time then." I couldn't even get the words out without a grin on my face.

Calli's head snapped up from the bed, and she grinned down at me before she tried to carry it off with a shrug. Smartass, apparently two could play at that game.

I trailed a finger across her again before slowly circling her clit. Her pupils blew wide, and her mouth opened as she sighed with lust.

"Luckily for you, you're fucking irresistible," I mumbled before my mouth closed over her clit.

Calli stayed leant up on her elbow as she watched me devour her pussy and it was the hottest fucking thing I'd done in my life. I saw every ounce of pleasure flash across her face right up until she fell back against the bed crying out as her orgasm washed over her.

I could feel my wolf growling in satisfaction in my head. He couldn't be happier that we were here pleasing our mate but he was also pushing against the edges of my mind. His thoughts were starting to mix with mine and I shook my head, feeling confused at his rush of emotion. I'd never felt the connection with him like this before. He was always there at the back of my mind, but now it felt like he was seconds away from pushing for control without the shift being triggered.

My eyes refocused as I felt Calli's soft hands close around my face, and I saw her smiling in front of me. Her eyes glowed softly with the amber of her wolf, and the presence of my wolf surged stronger in my mind.

"Don't worry Tanner, he just wants to meet his mate," she told me, and I could hear the growl of her wolf echoing along her voice.

"Mate." I heard his voice strong and clear ring through my head, not certain if I'd said it out loud or not. "Mark."

My eyes widened in panic and confusion. This was what Grey had talked about after he had mated with Calli. His wolf pushed him to make his mark. At the time, I'd been pissed about what he had done. Even after they assured me it hadn't hurt her, I didn't believe them. I didn't think there was anything that would make me want to do it to her. But my mouth watered at the thought of biting into her now, and my cock quivered at the thought of seeing her wear my mark. I knew it was my wolf pushing me to do this, but a piece of me wanted to see something on Calli, marking her as my own.

"Are you sure about this?" I asked her once I was able to clear my mind.

In response, Calli rolled me onto my back, her knees bracketed my hips, and her hands rested on my chest. She looked glorious, sitting above me, staring down at me with love in her eyes.

I could feel the wet heat of her pussy against the head of my cock, and it was taking everything in me to hold back from pushing up and sinking myself into her. But I'd just given her the opportunity to stop, to slow down and I wasn't going to take that from her just because I was too impatient to wait for her answer.

"I've never been more sure of anything in my life, Tanner. I want you more than anything. I want the world to know that

I am yours, and you are mine," she told me as she slowly sank down on my length.

Her tight pussy gripped me as she slowly impaled herself, and it took everything in me to hold still, to let her take control of the moment. Once she had me fully sheathed, my hands came to her hips as I pulled her against me.

"How much is it killing you not to take control right now?" she asked, looking down at me with a mischievous grin.

"So much," I laughed.

She leant down, running her cheek along mine before she sucked the lobe of my ear into her mouth and teasingly bit down. I groaned in delight, but the need to move inside her was killing me right now.

"Take me, mate," she whispered into my ear and then she squealed with laughter as I flipped her onto her back.

This was how it should always be with Calli and me. I wanted to hear her laughter alongside her moans.

Snapping my hips back, I surged back into her, and her laughter soon turned into a throaty groan. I thrust hard and fast as her breath quickened and I could feel her starting to tremble beneath me. I knew she was close and so was I. I also knew what I wanted and needed to do and I was nervous. But the more I thrust between her legs and the closer I found myself to that precipice, the more the need took root in my mind. I could feel my wolf's presence with me and what had been his insistence before, became comforting encouragement. I knew that my eyes would be glowing amber with his presence because I could see the shine in Calli's own eyes as her wolf looked out at me.

I dipped my head down and ran my tongue from her collar bone to her ear. Her scent was intoxicating, as I nuzzled my face close against her.

I felt Calli mirroring my movements, and as her mouth opened and her teeth sank into my shoulder, it detonated the sensation of pure ecstasy as it flooded my body. I came hard as my teeth automatically found their way into her shoulder. As I bit down into her, the sweet taste of her flooded my mouth, and I heard her scream out her release.

My hips moved slowly as I rode out the wave of bliss, and then I released her from my bite, swiping my tongue across the wound for one final taste. Calli groaned and ground down against me again at the feeling, and I kissed my way up her neck to find her lips.

We laid on the bed, our limbs still wound around each other as we just basked in each other's presence. Calli's fingers trailed over the compass tattoo on my chest. I felt her finger trace the stylised G that had been put in the place of North.

"This is beautiful," she murmured.

"I always knew that Grey would be my Alpha. When Aidan started to get good with the tattoo gun I asked him to do this for me. Grey will always be my true North. I owe him my life," I told her, not ready to get into the full story right now.

Her head dipped and she laid a kiss in the middle of the compass before she snuggled back against me. She didn't ask me for more information and she didn't ask any questions. Calli knew what it was like to have to be ready to talk about something and I knew she wouldn't prod me for information like some women would. She was perfect for me, for all of us. I knew that Calli was my mate when I first saw her wolf, but I think I fell in love with her the second she stepped out of her truck that very first day. I'd never felt closer to her than I did right now. She truly was the missing piece of me, to all of us.

39

GREY

We arrived at the eerily quiet packhouse faster than I think we ever had. My wolf was still furious and had all but sprinted there. I was surprised the others had managed to keep up but judging by the winded look on Nash's face, I think it had been a struggle.

We had always been a small pack. We had dreams of expanding but knew it was something that would come with time. This place had never seemed so quiet and lacking in life before.

Wallace had to go, there was no other way for us to know that Calli would be safe. But there was an eerie feeling surrounding this place now, almost a foreboding warning that the pack was dying. I just had to hope that wasn't the case and it was just my nerves getting the best of me for what I was about to do.

As we approached the front doors, Kelly came rushing out the doors, running over to us. She dropped to her knees in front of me, tears streaming down her face.

"Please, Grey, please don't kill him. I'm begging you, please," she sobbed.

My brain stuttered at the fact that there was a crying woman in front of me. I had little experience dealing with women in an Alpha capacity, and I'm not ashamed to admit that crying women brought out an awkward side in me. It was more terrifying than facing down a black bear tripping on PCP.

"Kelly, get up," I started thinking that if I could just get her back to her feet, maybe she'd calm down a bit.

Unfortunately, it seemed to have the exact opposite effect, and she only started to wail louder. I looked at the others over my shoulder. I knew my eyes were wide with panic from the slight smirk on River's face. Nash and Blake both just took a step back shaking their heads, what good they were!

Taking one for the team, River stepped around me and gathered Kelly up from the ground, talking softly to her. She started to calm down, and he looked at me and did that eyebrow thing as if to say 'go on' except I had zero idea what it was that I was supposed to be saying to her.

"Kelly," I started, and she just began to wail again.

River rolled his eyes at me, and I was getting ready just to shake her until she listened to me—probably not the best of ideas.

"Sweetheart, no one is going to hurt Wallace," River murmured to her.

My wolf bristled at him calling her that, those sort of things should be reserved for our mate and I didn't like that he was using them for the woman who was essentially the mate of the man who wanted to kill Calli.

"Not that he wouldn't deserve it," I growled out.

I saw River flinch in anticipation at my words, but Kelly seemed to just weepily nod acceptingly at them rather than increase the waterworks like she had been doing.

"You know he came for our mate again? That he tried to

kill her?" I asked. I tried to keep my voice down because I knew that taking it out on her wasn't going to help, the problem was it just wasn't working.

"I know," she said, lifting her tear-filled eyes to me. "He started talking about how she was controlling your minds and that the only way to save you, to save the pack, was to kill her."

It took me a moment to roll her words around in my head and understand what it was that she was actually saying to me.

"So, you knew," Blake said, stepping around me and reaching the same conclusion I had. "You knew he was going to hurt her and you didn't call or do anything to warn us."

Kelly seemed to realise what she had admitted to, and suddenly the weepy woman in front of us was replaced by a snarling, pissed off beast.

"She needs to be removed from the pack," she spat. "She's a danger to us all, to my boy."

"Un-fucking-believable!" Blake sighed, throwing his arms up in the arm. He turned to walk away from her before whipping back around. "And the fact that she is the only chance that Jean and the baby have, that she is the only reason they are alive, means nothing to you?"

Kelly just rolled her eyes. "Jean and the baby are already dead, Blake. There's nothing that you can do to bring them back."

We all looked around each other in confusion, and I could see the worry rush through Blake's eyes as he tensed, ready to take off back to the house.

"Jean and the baby are still alive," River told her cautiously.

When had Kelly become this person? I had never seen her

act like this before; I'd never seen a look of such hate on her face.

She cast her eyes around us, suspicion flaring as she watched us like she was waiting for us to attack.

"She's dead; the witch killed her. Wallace told me."

"Jean and the baby are both very much alive," I told her firmly. "Calli was able to place Jean in a stasis, and she is restoring her health while we look for a way to break the spell on her and the baby. Calli is the only reason why she is still, and continues to be, alive."

Kelly's eyes widened. She didn't say anything, but I could see that her mind was spinning as she took in the information we gave her. What the fuck was Wallace playing at? Was this more than just his hatred for Calli and what she was? It was starting to feel like maybe Wallace was losing it.

"I don't believe you," she finally said, "Wallace wouldn't lie to me about something like this."

"Frankly I don't care if you believe me or not and I wouldn't trust you near Jean or my mate," I said, having enough of this conversation and just wanting to get this whole thing over with.

I stepped around her and started towards the house. It was time to deal with Wallace and then hopefully move on from this whole nightmare.

"Wait, you still haven't told me what you're going to do," she shouted after me.

Part of me thought that I should take pity on her and fill her in on what we had decided, but a larger part of me didn't give a shit. She had taken her side, and I didn't fault her for standing by her husband. That didn't mean I needed to give her any consideration, though.

I heard Nash tell her to come with us as I opened the door to the packhouse. She could come. I wasn't opposed to her being there. I suppose she did have a right to know; it was going to affect her after all.

I headed down to the basement and the room where we kept the cage. I found Aidan sitting against the wall outside of the room. I knew Wallace couldn't get out of the cage, but I was still a bit annoyed he hadn't followed the directions I'd given him about not leaving him alone.

"I know," he sighed as soon as he looked up and saw my face, "But I swear Wallace has fucking lost it or something, and I couldn't stand listening to him any longer."

I frowned but kept walking. What the fuck was going on here? I was starting to doubt whether it was a good idea just to send him on his way. I was already anxious that he was just going to come back and try again, or worse head straight to the Council, but what if there was actually something wrong with him.

Opening the door to the room, I stepped inside and came to a stop just outside of the cage. Wallace was back in the same position he had been only a few days before when he had somehow managed to convince us that he regretted his actions. Sat against the wall, with his elbows braced on his knees and his head hanging down, he looked a sorry sight.

I stood in silence, waiting for him to acknowledge my presence. I wanted to see how he reacted. Maybe I was foolish, but I was clinging to the hope there was something wrong with him, and he hadn't done this of his own freewill. It turns out hope was a bitch.

"Took you fucking long enough," he sneered when he finally lifted his head. "Too busy between the legs of your witch to come and kill me, had to keep me waiting as well, did you?"

"I'm not going to kill you," I told him, waiting to see what his reaction was going to be.

I'd known Wallace since we were kids. We grew up in the same pack together. I was nearly as close to him as I was the others. I thought that I saw a flicker of surprise flash across his eyes, but it was gone as quickly as it came and I wasn't sure if I hadn't imagined it.

"Then you're a fool."

"No, your pack brother begged for your life and reminded me that you were acting, however misguided and foolish, in an attempt to protect your pack."

Wallace just sneered at me again; it was almost like he wanted me to kill him.

"But that doesn't mean you can stay here."

His eyes snapped to me, and I knew he would understand what I was talking about. There was a way that these things had to be done. We were bonded, and I had to break that bond now.

"I won't have you in this pack when you represent a threat to my mate and my pack brothers. Wallace MacRath, you are no longer my brother; you are no longer *pack*. From this day on, my wolf is blind to you. You will no longer be bound to us, and you will no longer hunt beside us. I cast you out to a life as a lone wolf, may death find you quickly."

Silence fell across the room. Wallace's mouth fell open in shock. It was like he hadn't thought I would do it, maybe because death would have been the kinder thing to do.

River, Nash, Aidan and Blake all repeated the words behind me. It wasn't necessary, as Alpha, my word alone was sufficient to break the bond with the pack. It was more a final blow to reinforce their agreement with my decision.

Kelly was the first to break. "What does this mean? What are we supposed to do now?"

I could tell she was pissed, but they only had themselves to blame.

"You have until sundown to leave our lands and get as far from Arbington as you can. If I see you on our lands again, I will kill you without any hesitation. If you want you can leave Coby with the pack." It was more than I needed to offer. Coby was a minor, and there was no law that I had to give him safe refuge with the pack. In fact, pack tradition dictated that he should be cast out with his father. But at only seven years old, Coby shouldn't be held responsible for his parents' poor choices. Life as a lone wolf was hard. Wallace would likely lose his mind in a few years and then Coby would be alone in the world, the only future certain for him would be for him to come into his wolf at puberty and then take his own slow descent into madness. No pack would take him now.

Wallace locked eyes with me and nodded.

"No!" Kelly screeched. "I'm not leaving my son here with them."

"Aidan, Nash, escort them to the cabin to pack and help them on their way. Wallace, discuss this with your wife. If you decide to leave Coby with the pack, Aidan and Nash will bring him back to the packhouse after you've both said your goodbyes."

With that, I turned and left, River and Blake both followed me out. I headed up to the kitchen and pulled a beer out of the fridge for each of us. Passing them out before twisting off the top and taking a deep pull. How had this day got so out of control?

"You need to speak with Calli about Coby," River finally said.

I nodded but didn't say anything. My wolf was pissed. He wanted blood for what Wallace had done to Calli. Banishment wasn't enough for him. A part of me even felt guilty for it, but the moment I had rushed into that clearing flashed before my eyes, and I saw her standing there, her leg broken with Aidan trying to protect her from Wallace, and all that flashed through me was red hot rage.

I took another pull of my beer in an attempt to calm down and looked over at Blake leaning on the kitchen counter. He looked tired. I could see the tension lining his shoulders and the dark circles gathering under his eyes. As soon as this was dealt with and we had the wards in place, I needed to make sure I spent some time with him. I'd sit down with Calli and him, and we'd come up with a plan to get Jean back to us as soon as we could. The pack was crumbling around me, and I couldn't let another of our brothers fall by the wayside.

"I'm assuming we're staying until sundown?" River asked, and I nodded in agreement.

"Then let's use our time productively. I'm going to send Tanner a message about what's happened, so he knows what to watch out for, but then let's go over Nash's files on the vampire issue and make sure we're not dropping the ball while we deal with everything else."

Trust River to find us homework to do while we waited. Blake and I both sulkily followed him into the office Nash had set up. There wasn't much else I wanted to do less than this right now. Unfortunately, though River was right and we settled in for the most boring four hours of our lives as we sifted through document after document.

By the time the sun was starting to set, Aidan and Nash walked through the front door with a very confused looking Coby following behind them. The poor kid was white with shock, and I had no idea what he had been told about the situation.

I looked at Aidan first, and he nodded grimly at me. I'd get a proper report from him later, but right now Coby was more important.

"Coby," I said softly as he hovered nervously by the door. "Come sit with us for a minute."

I patted the sofa beside me, and he came over and sat down. He seemed more confused than scared, which was at least a good start. If he would be staying here without his parents, then the last thing we needed was for them to have made him terrified of us before they left.

"Do you understand what is happening?" I asked him.

River came over to the sofa and sat on his other side, and I was grateful for the backup.

"My parents have gone away, and I'm going to stay with the pack, with Uncle Aidan," he said quietly.

I glanced up at Aidan who gave me another nod and then turned back to Coby.

"Your Dad isn't part of our pack anymore because he did something that hurt someone and we couldn't let him stay here anymore," I explained.

I wasn't going to lie to the kid. He deserved the truth; finding out later would only make the whole thing more painful for him.

Coby nodded slowly in understanding.

"Am I in trouble?" he asked quietly.

"No buddy, you haven't done anything wrong." I gently wrapped an arm around his shoulder, and he snuggled into my side.

Coby was the only pup to be born into our pack so far, and we all had spoiled him rotten. He'd spent time with all of us, so we weren't unfamiliar to him. That would hopefully make this transition a little easier for him.

"Do you understand why wolves form packs?" River asked him.

Coby thought about it for a moment, but then he shook his head.

"Packs are like families, and our wolves need to be part of something like that. It helps them feel secure and that in turn helps us as shifters to live a normal life. When we don't have a pack, it can make our wolves unhappy, and that can throw a shifter out of balance," River explained to him. Coby nodded in understanding as he spoke. "Your parents wanted you to stay here with the pack so that you wouldn't have to feel that when you come into your wolf. They couldn't stay, but they wanted you to be somewhere you would be safe."

I'm not sure if that was maybe sugar coating it a bit, but as a general theme, he was right.

"Is my Dad going to get hurt without a pack?" Coby asked in concern.

And that was the kicker, yes he was, but how did you tell a worried seven-year-old that.

"He's going to need to find a new Pack," River told him, which was the truth, even if we all knew none of them would take him.

"Come on bud, let's go get you settled in upstairs," Aidan said, grabbing a duffle bag from beside the door I hadn't seen before.

Coby jumped up off the sofa and followed Aidan further into the packhouse. This was just so fucked up.

"Have I made a massive mistake?" I asked no one in particular, as I stared at the door Coby had left through.

"No, even if he hates us for this when he gets older, this is for the best. Wallace couldn't stay here; we all knew that. Letting Coby stay here at least gives him a life. He wouldn't have made it past puberty otherwise," Nash said as he came into the room and dropped down onto one of the armchairs.

"Did they cause you much trouble?" I asked him.

"Weirdly, no," Nash said with a frown. "Wallace packed up what they wanted from the house into his truck while

Kelly spent a bit of time with Coby and then they just drove away. She didn't even ask if she could stay with him; she just told him to be good and got in the truck. It was cold, man."

"That does seem weird," River said suspiciously.

"Hmmm." I thought about all of the potential problems this could bring us. "He's either going to come back and try again, or he's going to bring the Council down on us. We need to decide before that happens what we're going to do."

The others nodded thoughtfully, but really it wasn't our decision. It needed to be Calli's decision. She would be risking everything with the Council, and she needed to decide if she wanted to run.

Blake looked just as uneasy as I felt, and I could understand why. In his mind, Calli was the only way he was ever going to get Jean back, and he was right about that. If the Council took Calli, then he would lose her and the baby as well. I didn't think Wallace was going to give a shit about that though. He and Kelly were a problem, and they were a problem that was definitely going to come back and bite us on the ass.

40

CALLI

It had been fun spending the afternoon with Jacob and Tanner. We ate nearly all the cupcakes while we watched a movie and then we pulled out all the paints and art stuff we had in the house and started crafting to our heart's content. I'd thought Tanner would make an excuse to do something else, but if anything, the thought of glitter glue and googly eyes seemed to make him just as happy as Jacob was.

This was what Jacob needed; he needed some semblance of a normal life. The opportunity to just be a kid. It also helped that I was with Tanner, and Jacob was at the point where he absolutely idolised him.

Jacob had been non-stop all afternoon. They were organising a field trip at the school to go to Maine Wildlife Park and his whole class was excited to go. I was a little nervous at first, but Tanner told me that River usually went and Holly would probably help out as well. Some of the parents apparently went along as helpers, and while I could volunteer to go, we both agreed that it wasn't a sensible idea until I had some kind of solution on the talisman—which blew because I wanted to go to the Wildlife Park too.

The others didn't make it back to the house for dinner, and Jacob was fast asleep in bed before there was any sign of them. I was starting to worry that something had happened when Grey and River strolled back in through the sliding door.

I sighed in relief and settled back into the sofa, sipping at my glass of wine like I had been completely laid back the entire time. Tanner gave me a knowing smirk, and I just shrugged in response. They were my mates, and this was apparently our thing now.

"Did we miss dinner?" River asked, looking longingly into the now clean kitchen.

"It's 9:30, of course, you missed dinner," I laughed. You could tell they weren't used to running on the schedule of a five-year-old. As soon as they experienced a hungry rampaging Jacob, they'd get it, and I snickered at the image that filled my mind.

"Luckily for you, I made sure to put some leftovers in the fridge," I told River.

"I'll sort it, you …" Blake trailed off as he wandered into the kitchen and ushered River and Grey over to me.

Cocking my head to the side in confusion, I was immediately suspicious. Blake's behaviour, coupled with the fact that they were so much later than we'd thought, set me on edge. Blake managed to break the tension quite easily, though.

"How do I do this?" he asked suddenly, looking down at the glass dish in his hands that he had gotten out of the fridge.

I laughed at his confusion and then realised they were all looking at me. "How have you all survived this long on your own?" I asked in exasperation.

"Steak and pizza," Tanner said seriously.

For all that was holy! What the hell had I gotten myself into?

"Put the filling in a frying pan and keep moving it about until it's warmed through and put the tortillas in the oven to warm up. There's already grated cheese in the fridge," I told him. I was going to start labelling the leftovers from now on because there was no way that I was being turned into a cook for them all.

Blake happily went about the task of making fajitas for everyone, and Grey and River came over to sit with us. From the looks on their faces, they didn't exactly have happy news, and my anxiety immediately shot through the roof again.

"Please tell me he's not dead," I rushed out when I couldn't take it anymore.

"What? No, we severed the pack bond, and he left," Grey told me.

"Okay, then why do you look like that? I can tell that you have bad news," I said, shuffling anxiously on the seat and then took a huge gulp of my wine.

"We need to decide what to do next," Grey said seriously. "But also, Wallace and Kelly left, but they left Coby behind with the pack."

My brain stalled, and I stared at him blankly. They left him behind … and then I had nothing.

"What?" Was the only word I could get out.

"Wallace is a lone wolf now. Without a pack, he will most likely lose his mind. I wouldn't be surprised if the Council sent someone to have him put down. No other pack will touch him. That would have been Coby's fate if he had gone with them, so they decided to leave him with the pack," Grey explained.

"They left him with the pack," I repeated because my brain still wouldn't move past that point.

I knew all about the consequences of being cast out of a pack. The only reason that my father had survived was because he was mated to my mother, and he also had regular contact with shifters in the underground. They weren't a pack as such but with the way he took on the responsibility of protecting those that he could, it kind of formed a pack like instinct in his wolf.

I hadn't thought about the effects of losing my pack on myself, and clearly, Sean hadn't either. I had Jacob, though, and a strong need to protect him. My wolf saw him as her pup, and then there was the whole magic thing. Maybe that was what had sustained me.

"Calli," said River, snapping me out of my thoughts.

"They left him," I said again, not even knowing why. "I mean, where is he?" I shook my head, trying to get my thoughts back into some kind of order.

"He's back at the packhouse with Aidan," Grey explained.

My eyes started darting around the house, "But he's only a little boy, he needs a family," I suddenly said.

Grey's eyes softened, and he reached out and squeezed my knee with one hand.

"That's not what we need to talk about right now though," he said softly.

"Oh for fuck's sake, what else could possibly have happened?" I sighed. I was done with this now. I didn't know how much more I could take. Were we cursed or something?

Tanner laughed but was cut off with a glare from Grey, "What? It was funny," he sulked.

"We need to discuss what we're going to do next," River explained, but I could see the corner of his mouth tick up in amusement.

"He should probably come and stay here with us," I

mumbled looking around the house again like a bedroom was just going to spring up out of nowhere magically.

Suddenly, I was moving across the sofa, which was weird because I didn't do it myself. But when Grey's arms closed around me, and he crushed me against his chest, I realised that he'd just picked me up and put me on his lap. Not one to waste a perfectly good hug, I snuggled down against him with a sigh of bliss. How were men covered in such delicious muscles always so comfortable to snuggle? Like, it shouldn't be this good, I thought as my brain ran off with me again.

"I love that your first concern is for Coby," I heard Grey's voice rumble through his chest. "But we need to talk about Wallace."

"But Wallace is gone." I wasn't usually this dense. I didn't know what was wrong with me right now. I was going to blame Tanner. He must have damaged my brain cells through all of the orgasms.

Grey's chest rumbled in laughter beneath me, and I came to a mortifying conclusion. "I just said that out loud, didn't I?" I cringed.

"Would it make you feel better if I said no?"

"Yes, it definitely would," I nodded against his chest.

"Then, I don't know what you're talking about, you didn't say anything at all," Grey laughed. He was such a good mate.

When I looked up, I caught a glimpse of a satisfied Tanner smirking, and my cheeks flushed in embarrassment.

"So, Wallace …" I started trying to draw the attention back to where it apparently needed to be.

"He left too easily. We think he's either going to come back, or he's going to go straight to the Council," River said.

I nodded in agreement. It was the logical conclusion, after all. "We can finish getting the warding in place tomorrow morning," I told them. "That way if he does come back we'll know about it."

"Wallace coming back is the least of our problems," Tanner growled.

"The Council," I agreed.

And this was where all of our problems seemed to start and finish at the moment.

"Jacob deserves to have a normal life, to have a proper home, to be able to make friends and go to a proper school," I told them all. "You shouldn't have to uproot your lives and go on the run with us just because you're my mates."

"We know sweetheart, but do we really have a choice here? We know how bad the problem is, your parents built a whole underground to help people get away from it. I think we should get in touch with Sean and make arrangements to get out of town," Grey told me gently.

I looked around the house, and my heart was sad. This wasn't just a house; this was the house my parents had chosen for us. A place they had thought could be a home for us. This was all we had left of them. It wasn't fair that we had to leave that behind again.

"No," I firmly said.

This might be the worst decision of my life, but I seemed to be making them fairly frequently at the moment, and it felt like this was a path I was meant to take.

"It's not as simple as no, Calli. They will still come whether we want them to or not. We have no other choice."

"No, I mean it. I don't think we should leave. I think it's time to make a stand. To go before the Council and fight. We always have the underground if we need it, but I feel like I am supposed to do this. I feel like I'm supposed to make this stand, it's the only way that Jacob will ever get a chance to have a normal life," I argued.

"And if they come and take Jacob? If they hurt him because of what he is?" Grey argued, clearly not agreeing with me even in the smallest part.

"I have a contact that can get Jacob out if the Council takes him," I told them, and that was all I could say.

They didn't ask any questions, and I loved them all for that. They just accepted it.

"I don't like it," Grey finally said after thinking it through. "But you're right; it's either this or a life on the run."

"The Council isn't just going to change its views because we asked them to," River scoffed, apparently he wasn't on board with the idea either.

"No," I agreed. "But they've never had the potential of having real female wolves in packs before either. Or an opportunity to make fated mates a reality rather than a fairy-tale," I pointed out. "The Council is so corrupt because it's self-serving. I think they will see this as an opportunity before they see me as a threat."

"I don't think that's necessarily a good thing," River said anxiously.

"No, it's not, but it's a way inside, and we need a way inside," I told them.

"You want to make a move against the Council," Grey said cautiously.

"We don't have any other choice."

Grey sighed and sat back against the sofa. Tanner and River were both frowning in thought. I knew it was a lot to consider, but this was about more than just us. We could keep Jacob safe, and if we had to, I knew Sean could get him out. But if he had any chance of living a normal life, this was going to be the only way. If we couldn't make them change, then we needed to bring them down.

Blake brought a plate full of fajitas to the coffee table and passed plates out for everyone who hadn't eaten yet. I moved off Grey's lap to let him eat and found myself being pulled into Tanner's side. It was handy having multiple mates; there was always a snuggle buddy available when you needed one.

"Tomorrow," Grey said between mouthfuls. "We need to get the warding finalised, but I want to bring you into the pack bond as well."

A smile flickered across my face. I would love to be properly a part of the pack. Don't get me wrong. I felt like I was, but I was always going to be on the outside without the bond.

"If you want to that is," Grey added when I didn't answer him straight away.

"Of course I want to," I smiled. "You know this might change the nature of your bond though right?"

I just needed to check they were aware of the potential for the bond evolving into something else. If he turned around and said that he'd changed his mind now, I would be devastated, but I would understand as well—even if, personally, I thought the potential to talk wolf to wolf was badass.

"You mean the communication thing, right?" Blake pipped in, looking suddenly excited.

"Yeah," I laughed. "I don't think I bring any other weirdness with me. Or at least not that I'm aware of."

Fuck, was this a good idea? Maybe we should talk to Sera or someone about it first. The problem was I already knew what she was going to say. There was no way for her to know. There had never been anyone like me before, this would be the first time something like this had been done.

"It wouldn't matter even if you did," Grey said with a smile. "You are our mate, and you belong in our bond."

"Plus, how badass are we going to be when we can talk in wolf form," Tanner added giddily.

"If you can," I corrected him. "It might not happen."

He deflated a little as he thought about it and I felt bad for popping his bubble. Better now than him being disappointed once I joined the bond though, I'm not sure if I would be able to take that.

A loud yawn echoed through me, and Tanner laughed, squeezing me against his side.

"Did I tire you out, mate?" he growled softly in my ear.

"Yeah," I admitted, sleepily snuggling into his side.

"Come on, let's get you to bed."

I suddenly found myself being scooped off the sofa and into Tanner's arms as he walked us to the bedroom.

"Are you joining us?" I heard him ask over his shoulder.

I don't know who he asked, and I had no idea what they decided because I was asleep seconds later and I didn't even remember making it to the bed.

41

CALLI

I woke up the next morning sandwiched between two of my mates who were clearly made of fire. I could feel a bead of sweat running into my cleavage—so not sexy.

Wiggling out of the wolf sandwich I found myself in, I ducked into the bathroom and had a quick shower to cool down and, you know, make myself not smell like a sweaty mess.

When I came out of the bathroom, I was met with the sight of a shirtless Tanner laid on his back, his arms behind his head fast asleep. Next to him, River was laying on his side in just his boxers—very, very *tight* boxers. This was the first time I had seen River without his clothes on. In fact, this was the first time I had woken with him in my bed. I was kind of disappointed that I didn't remember any of it now.

Tanner opened one eye and sleepily said, "It's a bit creepy you know, just standing there perving on us."

"You love it," I laughed, as I climbed back into bed beside them, because why not? I was going to make the most of this while I could, we had a busy day ahead of us.

"What time is it?" River mumbled sleepily without even opening his eyes.

"Just after six."

"Good lord, woman! Why are you even awake?" Tanner groaned, dropping one arm over his eyes.

"Because two people were cooking me alive with their body heat," I huffed snuggling up against River because I wanted to pet his pretty, pretty abs.

He smiled sleepily, still not opening his eyes, and pulled me in closer against him. I ran my fingers down his chest and across his abs, exploring every dip.

He huffed out a laugh and squirmed on the spot. An evil part of me immediately wanted to dive on him and start tickling, but I felt slightly bad for waking him up, so I decided to be a good girl and just lay there staring at him like a creeper instead.

River's forehead wrinkled into a sleepy frown, and it was possibly the most adorable thing I'd seen for a long time. "You stopped," he complained.

"I thought it was tickling you."

"It was, but I still don't want you to stop," he sulked.

Instead of torturing him further, I lifted a hand and ran in through his hair where it had tumbled messily across his forehead in his sleep. Running my nails across his scalp, I played with the lengths of his hair while he lay sleepily next to me. It wouldn't be long until the sun started to come up and for now, a faint light glistened across his side, slipping down highlighting his chest.

He was a truly beautiful man; all three of them were. River was my only mate that I hadn't bonded with yet, but he was also the mate who seemed the most reluctant to get close to me. This was the first time he had even shared my bed, and we hadn't even kissed yet. Well not properly, there had been a few pecks here and there.

"What's wrong?" River asked. "You stopped."

I looked down and realised he had finally opened his eyes and was looking up at me, concern filled his beautiful brown eyes.

"I'm sorry, I just got lost in my thoughts for a moment."

"You're not nervous about today are you?"

"What part, potentially being attacked again while laying the warding, or joining the bond and possibly doing something weird to it?" I laughed.

"Both, either, you pick," he said with a sleepy smile.

Tanner shuffled across the bed and became the big spoon, moulding himself against my back. He gently kissed my neck, and I was about half a second away from turning into a puddle of lust when he ruined it.

"Wallace won't come back today. We only have the Council to worry about."

"Urgh, way to ruin the moment," I grumbled.

Tanner laughed, his lips still lingered on my skin before he gently bit down on my neck and a wanton moan slipped out of me.

When my eyes fluttered open, I saw River in front of me, his eyes full of curiosity and I tried to shut down the lust that was banking inside me. I didn't want to make him uncomfortable if he wasn't ready to take that step with me just yet.

"You did it again," River suddenly said. "Is it me, Calli? Have I done something to upset you?"

"No! No!," I quickly said, then realised that my quick answer just made it seem like I was hiding something even more.

This would be weirdly awkward with Tanner here, but I didn't want any misunderstanding between River and I.

"I just wasn't sure if you were in the same place I was. We haven't had much chance to spend time together, and I haven't even really …"

My rambling words were cut off as River's lips sealed over mine in a gentle kiss. Immediately, I melted against him and his arms wrapped around me, which given the fact that Tanner was still pressed against my back was probably quite awkward for him.

Tanner's lips kept peppering kisses down my neck and over my shoulder and my wolf, the wanton hussy, was practically panting in my head. I couldn't blame her, though.

River pulled back, his hand running across my cheek. "I want you more than anything else in the world, Calli. We just haven't had our time yet. And I don't really want it to be while Tanner is watching," he said, leaning up and looking over my shoulder at the man in question. I could just imagine the answering smirk he would have received. "Never doubt the way I feel about you. Soon, my beautiful mate. Soon."

I whimpered at his words, much to my shame, I didn't want soon, I wanted now. They'd both gotten me all hot and bothered, and now I had to wait. We were definitely cursed. I was calling it. Something needed to be done.

"I don't think our mate is going to be able to be patient," Tanner laughed behind me. "Maybe you should give her just a small taste of what's to come?"

River's face lit up in a grin that I was pretty sure meant things were about to go in my favour and I was about ready to drop to my knees and thank whichever god had smiled down on me.

"And what would you suggest?" River asked, his voice dropping low and husky as one of his hands trailed down to my waist.

I bit my bottom lip between my teeth, because I needed something, anything to stop me from panting in anticipation.

"Kiss her like you mean it," Tanner instructed.

River's hand brushed gently across my cheek before he brushed my hair back from my face. I expected a soft kiss, that seemed more like River's style. Instead, his lips met mine in burning passion as he rolled me onto my back. He used his hand to angle my head the way he wanted, and then he completely dominated me. His tongue slipped into my mouth and slid along mine as he hungrily devoured me. All I could do was hang on for the ride, and what a ride it was. Somehow, my leg ended up curled over his hip, and he wrapped his other hand around the top of my thigh as he held me tightly against him. I had no idea how he had ended up between my legs, but when his hard cock ground down against my pussy, I nearly exploded there and then.

"I think she likes that," Tanner said breathily next to us.

This was so different from anything I had ever done before, and I had never expected, with the close relationship these three had, that we would ever end up in a situation like this. Especially, not after I had been in almost this exact same position with Grey and Tanner. I wouldn't lie though, I was a very big fan of it.

As River leant back from me with a grin on his face, the bedroom door swung open and we all froze where we were as a sleepy Jacob shuffled into the room dragging his bunny behind him.

River stealthily rolled a fraction further away from me, so it just looked like he was lying next to me, and Jacob clumsily climbed up onto the bed before wiggling his way in between me and Tanner.

"You okay there, little guy?" Tanner asked him, and I could hear the amusement lacing his voice.

"Can I have some juice?" Jacob asked, snuggling in against me, as River flopped back onto the bed with a sigh.

Tanner burst out laughing and then scooped Jacob up off the bed as he climbed out himself. "I got your back, little man," he laughed, as he carried him out of the room with Jacob dangling over one shoulder.

As soon as the door closed, I couldn't help the laughter that burst out of my mouth.

"Talk about a bucket of cold water," River said, joining in with the laughter.

The mood was definitely gone, and I was a little mortified at how close we had just come to Jacob seeing something he definitely shouldn't.

"How about we get up, and you can make me breakfast instead?" I suggested.

River just grinned across me and shook his head. "I feel like I should be upset that I'm being tricked into something, but weirdly I'm not."

I grinned back at him because it was hard not to when this beautiful man looked so happy.

"I know it must be awkward getting used to having Jacob and me in your lives," I started out, intending to, I think, make some kind of apology for just how much we were changing their lives.

"Don't, Calli," River said, dipping his head down to give me a quick peck on the lips before he leant back to look at me seriously. "You and Jacob are the best thing that's ever happened to us. I wouldn't change anything for the world."

"Not even your own bathroom?" I asked slyly.

"Maybe my own bathroom," he conceded with a grin before rolling out of bed. "I'm going to grab a shower. I bet if you're lucky, someone will be making you a cup of tea," he teased.

There was no quicker way to get me out of bed, although as I was slipping through the door, I did wonder if I had stayed, maybe someone would have brought it to me. Then life really would be perfect, someone bringing me tea in bed. Swoon!

I found Tanner at the stove in the kitchen singing a song and dancing as he cooked up a pan full of bacon. Jacob was standing next to him on top of a dining chair, passing him things and singing along. It was possibly the most adorable thing I'd seen in my life.

Grey was at the dining table with Blake, and they had several folders laid out in front of them. Nash was with them hunched behind a laptop, frowning and mumbling to himself as he tapped away at the keys.

I walked over to Jacob and gave him a hug and a kiss while he excitedly explained what we had on the menu for breakfast. He was so excited about helping out that I realised I should probably include him more in stuff like this. My brain also felt a little broken because I could have sworn it was only like a minute ago we had been in bed, and I was starting to feel like maybe someone had sent Jacob through to disturb something they were missing out on and eyed Grey suspiciously. Grey looked up from his folders, looking the picture of innocence until he winked and answered something that Nash asked—well played Mr Thornton, well played.

Jacob quickly got bored with me and turned back to his new job of washing some fruit. Leaving him to it, I wandered over to the table to see what the others were so engrossed in. As I approached, Grey reached out and pulled me into his lap before his lips met mine and thoroughly kissed every thought out of my head.

"Good morning," he mumbled as he pulled away, "I missed you."

"Mmmm, I missed you too," I sighed, because I had. "What you up to?" I asked, looking at the paperwork that was spread out on the table.

"Just updating the books for the garage and the pack," Grey shrugged.

I frowned and looked at the papers on the table. I hadn't thought about the pack's financial running, but I suppose it made sense that they had to keep a set of accounts for that as well.

"Which reminds me," Grey mumbled quietly to me. "We wanted to establish the pack bond for both you and Jacob this morning, but I wanted to check with you before I said anything to him."

"I think that's a great idea," I said brightly. "A pack bond should really help Jacob, and now he's had his first shift it should help him feel closer to his wolf as well."

We needed to find time to work with Jacob on his shifting and making sure he was bonding with this other part of himself. It was strange to suddenly be able to feel another set of emotions in your mind, and it could be disorientating. We were fortunate that it happened to us at such an early age. I couldn't imagine how difficult it must be for someone to go through all that while trying to handle puberty as well. And that was the thought that brought Coby into my mind. I kind of felt responsible for him having lost his parents. If I hadn't come into their lives, he would still be at home with them now. What if me joining the pack wasn't a good thing?

"Hey, Calli, you went somewhere again," Grey said to me quietly, and I refocused my attention back on him.

"I was just thinking about Coby," I mumbled awkwardly. Maybe this wasn't something I should be involving myself with. Was I overstepping my bounds a bit?

"He's at the packhouse with Aidan," Grey told me.

"How old is he?" I asked suddenly.

"Seven."

My stomach dropped. I had ruined this poor child's life.

"Hey," Grey said, one finger coming under my chin as he tilted my head up so that I met his eyes. "Coby is going to be fine. He has his pack. This isn't your fault, you know."

"It is though. If it wasn't for me, if I never came here, he would still be at home with his Mum and Dad."

"No," Grey said firmly, his brown eyes flashing with emotion. "The actions of Wallace are not your fault. His prejudices and hate are the reason why all of this has happened. Coby doesn't have a Mom and Dad in his life because Wallace chose to put those things ahead of his son. The only fault here lies with them, not you."

I nodded because I knew he was right, even if a small voice in the back of my mind was still telling me it was all my fault. At the very least, I still felt like some of the blame laid with me, even if that was unreasonable.

"Shall we set a plan in place for this morning?" Nash said, breaking the mood and changing the subject.

I looked up and gave him a grateful smile, and he just smiled back at me. I really should try and spend some more time with the other members of the pack. I didn't know him that well, and I'd hardly spent any time with Aidan as well. I suppose now we didn't have the Wallace problem so close to home, that was probably going to get a bit easier. Plus, it would be nice for Coby and Jacob to get to know each other.

"First thing first, we need to get the warding set up around Calli's house," Grey said, taking charge. It was hot, and my hussy of a wolf loved his Alpha nature right now. He smirked knowingly down at me before he continued. "Then, I think we should bring Calli and Jacob into the pack bond."

Jacob excitedly came charging out of the kitchen with

Tanner hot on his heels, thankfully carrying huge platters of breakfast with him.

"I'm going to be in the pack?" Jacob asked, bouncing up and down on the spot in excitement.

"Only if you want to, little man," Grey told him. "This is an important decision. Do you think you want us to be pack?"

River slipped into the dining chair next to us, giving my knee a squeeze as we waited to see what Jacob was going to say.

It was an important decision, but I also knew there was no way that five-year-old Jacob was ever going to choose any differently. To him, this was his first chance at a pack bond and a step closer to growing that connection with his wolf. His five-year-old brain would never come to a different conclusion other than, hell yeah.

Jacob surprised me, though when he stopped bouncing and gave us his forty-year-old man look. Drawing himself up as tall as he could, he crossed his little arms over his chest and gave Grey his most serious face. I was proud of the little guy for standing up against this Alpha, even if Grey was trying to hide his smirk of amusement.

"That depends," Jacob said sternly. "What are your intentions towards my sister?"

I beamed at him because I couldn't be more proud of him than I was at this moment.

"That goes for all of you!" Jacob added seriously.

Everyone, to their credit, kept a serious look on their faces, even though I could tell that they all wanted to smile in amusement. I was having a hard job keeping my own grin of delight contained.

"She is my mate, and I will love her for the rest of my life," Grey told him seriously.

My heart swooned. We hadn't got to that stage yet, which

was probably a bit weird really given everything, but the fact that he would take the time to answer Jacob seriously meant the world to me.

Tanner knelt down beside Jacob so that he could look him in the eye.

"Calli is the most important person in the world for us, bud. And so are you. We would be honoured if you would consider becoming part of our pack."

Then it was River's turn, "We're going to be a family, remember."

I could see that Jacob's eyes were starting to get watery, and he was doing his best to keep his brave face on. He looked over at me, and I held out my arms to him. He immediately snuggled against me for a cuddle. I kind of felt bad for Grey now that he had both of us on top of him, but if it bothered him, he didn't show it. Instead, he just wrapped his arms around us both, and I felt the gentle caress of his reassuring Alpha power wash over us.

"I'll agree on one condition," Jacob mumbled against me. "River has to go on the field trip with me."

That immediately broke the mood, and everyone laughed at his, quite frankly, stellar negotiation skills.

"Already looking forward to it," River laughed.

"Then it's agreed," Grey said, giving us a quick squeeze. "Now, how about breakfast so we can get this day on the way?"

We descended on the food, joined by a delighted Jacob when he realised that not only was he going to be getting a pack bond, but that it was also going to be happening today.

We had just about cleared the platters of food when there was a knock at the door. It still amazed me the amount of food that these men ate their way through.

Tanner jumped up from the table and jogged over to the

front door to open it, Aidan strode in, and Tanner frowned at him in confusion.

"I thought you were bringing supplies for lunch?" he asked, clearly confused.

"Store's closed, we'll have to get takeout from the diner," Aidan said. "James has gone missing."

"What?" I asked, whipping around to look at him.

I heard Jacob whimper in distress beside me, and he shuffled closer to Grey, who pulled him into his side. Jacob had gotten quite close with James from their joined love of lego. Poor Mary! How was she taking all of this?

"Apparently, he went out last night just to put the trash in their cans, and no one has seen him since," Aidan said, looking to Grey in concern.

Grey pinched the bridge of his nose between two fingers. "We do not have time for this right now," he mumbled.

The room fell quiet as we all looked to Grey to see what he wanted to do.

"James is my friend," Jacob told him quietly.

"I know buddy, he's a friend to all of us," Grey said, before turning to Nash. "While we set the warding here, can you look into that issue we had before and see if there has been any movement."

Nash frowned but nodded in agreement. I knew he was disappointed. He wanted to be involved in the magic and the research because it appealed to his academic side, but so far every time something magic had come up, he'd been occupied with something else.

"We'll try to help find him," Grey said, turning back to Jacob who just nodded sadly.

I wouldn't let Jacob lose anyone else out of his life. He's lost enough already. We needed to get James back, no matter what it took.

A sudden realisation struck me, and I turned back to Aidan. "If you're here then where's Coby?" I asked in concern.

"Holly opened up the school office even though it's Sunday so we could get him enrolled this morning. She's showing him around and getting him all stocked up, so he's ready to start tomorrow. Now that Kelly isn't around, there isn't anyone to homeschool him. He was pretty excited to go in this morning. I get the feeling he's been wanting this for a while," Aidan said, coming over to the table and looking disappointedly at the now empty platters.

"I saved you some, it's on a plate in the oven," Tanner told him as he dropped back into his seat and a happy Aidan headed off to the kitchen.

"Coby should come and live here," Jacob said suddenly. "We can put bunk beds in my room."

Everyone had one of those awkward moments where they didn't know what to say. Personally, I didn't want to step on anyone's toes by saying he could stay with us, but also, I was only twenty and I had Jacob. I wasn't sure if I was ready to take on a second kid in my life.

"Coby is probably going to want to stay with the pack for a while, just until he gets used to things," River said being ever the diplomat.

"But you all sleep here now," Jacob said with a confused look on his face. He did have us there, I supposed. "He's like me, he lost his mummy and daddy, but he doesn't have a Calli to look after him."

Why is it that kids seemed to have that innocent logic that just got right down to the crux of the situation? He was so right.

"How about we look at getting some bunk beds and then when Coby feels ready, he can come to have some sleepovers if he wants to. Then we can see where he wants to go from there," I suggested. After all, I didn't know him, and he didn't know us. He probably wouldn't want to come and live with the woman who had made his parents leave him all on his own.

Jacob nodded, happy with the compromise, and I didn't miss the sigh of relief from more than one person at the table. It was quite funny how they got so nervous about keeping Jacob happy. Once he realised the power he held over them, they would be in for a hard time. Coby was a situation we all needed to sit down and talk about more. Because in his simplified way, Jacob was right. Coby needed the stability of a family, and he couldn't just be passed around from one pack member to another.

42

RIVER

We had been standing outside Calli's house for about half an hour in the cold guarding the altar while Calli walked the perimeter of where she wanted the warding to be set up. Jacob had gotten bored after about five minutes and gone inside to play with his lego. I couldn't blame him, and as he wandered back into the house, I could see the look of longing on Tanner's face. The depth of his newfound love of lego was pretty funny. Nash and Aidan had gone to the garage because we had a delivery of parts due that needed to be signed for and Nash needed some more paperwork for the books they had been trying to do earlier.

"They're right, we need a better solution for Coby," Grey suddenly said. "We need a better solution for all of us."

"Do you think now that Wallace is out of the picture, Calli might want to move over to the packhouse?" Tanner asked.

"I don't know. This is the house her parents set up for them. I don't think she's going to want to leave here," I told them.

Grey stared at the house in thought, and I could almost see the ideas and potential solutions running through his head.

"We could extend," he finally said.

It was the best option if Calli wanted to stay here, but this was her house. We were stepping a bit outside of our bounds with this. It was a weird situation, but it was one that we needed to discuss with her rather than trying to find any solutions and then just letting her know.

Before anyone could say anything else, I felt the snap of magic of the wards falling into place and the wind rushing past us as the warding boundary flared into existence. Calli came back into view, and a part of me I hadn't even realised was tensed, relaxed. She was safe and whole and not a single broken bone or bruise in sight.

Calli knelt before the altar. The bowl containing the ink already charged from our own wards sat on top. Picking up the knife, she slashed open her hand, holding it over the bowl as her blood dripped inside. I hated that bit the last time, and it wasn't any better this time either. When she was done, I was immediately at her side, wrapping a cloth around her hand to stop the bleeding. She smiled at me in gratitude, and I felt my wolf basking in her presence. This morning had been amazing, even if we did get interrupted before we even did anything. I needed to mate with Calli soon. I couldn't stand having this distance between us, and my wolf was pushing for me to make the bond. I hadn't meant to keep her at a distance. I'd just been concerned that everything was happening so quickly and I didn't want her to feel pressured into anything.

We all went back into the house to warm up, taking the ink with us, which meant putting the kettle on for Calli. Her tea obsession was starting to become pretty funny, but I supposed it wasn't much different to how some people obsessed over coffee.

Jacob was nowhere in sight, but I could hear the telltale click of lego coming from his room.

"So, lunch before or after?" Tanner said casually. I could tell by the tone of his voice that he was excited and I had to admit I was as well. I couldn't wait to see what having Calli in the pack bond was going to do. I was hoping for it to evolve into something like she had with her father, but I was trying not to get my hopes up too much. It was a shame that Coby wasn't old enough to form the bond yet. It would have done him good to have that to rely on while he was going through all this. I needed to make sure I picked him up from school when Holly had finished getting him ready for tomorrow because I wanted to have some time with him and make sure he was doing alright.

"After," Calli suddenly said, drawing me out of my thoughts.

"Are you as excited as I am, sweetheart?" Tanner purred at her, pulling her into his arms.

I rolled my eyes at his antics, any excuse to make a joke.

"Yes, but not for the same reason as you probably," she laughed. "This will be the first bond that Jacob has ever had, and I'm looking forward to going on a pack run with him."

My wolf was bounding in excitement at the idea as well. It had been so long since we'd had a pack run, months. As soon as we caught the scent of witch magic near our lands, we had put a stop to them, and instead stayed on constant guard. We needed this, all of us, a run together as a pack would help everyone bond as a pack and also just relax. We had so much going on that we needed to make time to do things like this more.

"Wait! Who's going to stay with Jean?" Calli asked, and we all froze. Shit! How had we forgotten about that!

We headed into the living room, all of us looking like someone had kicked our puppy. It was probably because we felt guilty we had forgotten about Jean and because I couldn't see a solution to how we were going to get around it.

"What if we wait until tonight and get Holly to come over?" Tanner suggested as he dropped down onto the sofa.

Blake was sitting in the armchair going through one of Calli's magic books and looked up when Tanner spoke. "What's happening tonight?" he asked, looking confused.

"The pack bonding," I said carefully.

"I thought we were doing that now."

"Well, it's just that we, erm, we thought we should wait until tonight so that Holly could come over and stay with Jean?"

"Why?" he asked, still looking confused.

"We didn't think she should be alone," Calli told him gently.

"Oh, right! I just assumed we would do the bond here," he told us surprised.

The obviousness of that solution to the problem slapped us all in the face, and it took a moment before anyone said anything. I could see the amusement on Blake's face when he realised we hadn't thought of that, but he was a better person than the rest of us because he didn't immediately laugh in our face.

"So, we do the bond here and then go on a run another day," Calli said with a nod of her head like it was now decided.

"You know you can go on a run without me, right?" Blake said in amusement again, looking around at us all.

"But then it wouldn't be a pack run," Calli said in a mixture of disappointment and confusion.

"I'm flattered that you want me there Calli and we will get to it at some point I promise you, but you need to do this. Of course, I want to go with you, but that shouldn't hold you back. It will do all of you good to let your wolves run together with Jacob for a little while. The last few days have been chaotic." Calli looked like she was about to break into tears of joy at the selflessness of Blake, but then he went and ruined it when he added on, "Besides, it'll give me more time to read and get ahead of Nash."

The two of them and this magic rivalry was going to cause problems, I could already see it. I kind of got Blake's obsession. He was looking for a cure for his wife. But Nash didn't have that excuse, and even with academic curiosity, I just didn't see why he was letting it get to him so much that Blake was doing it and he wasn't.

Nash and Aidan arrived back at the house a short while later. Calli had decanted the ink into a bottle to keep it safe, and she was now sitting at the dining table with Blake going through more books looking for the solution to Jean's problem.

"I should be able to start working on restoring Jean's energy tomorrow," Calli told Blake as she flicked through an old book I had seen her set aside on the first day she had shown us the library. It seemed to hold some significance to her, but she didn't seem ready to share that with us just yet.

"That's amazing news," Blake said, excited at getting one small step closer to having his wife and child returned to him.

Nash slowly walked over to the dining table to see what they were doing and as he approached, Calli gave him a friendly smile and pushed the chair out next to her. He didn't need to be asked twice, as he dropped down into the seat and Blake immediately started to talk to him about a text that had been referred to in another book but hadn't been able to find yet. He was confident it would be in the library upstairs, but realistically, it would take years if they had to read every book.

"Does anyone know the purpose of the drain?" Nash asked. "I know it allows a boost of power, but why do they need it? Is it just like an everyday thing, or are they collecting power for a reason?" Nash said as he flipped through one of the books on the table.

"Does it matter?" Blake asked, clearly confused. I was right there with him.

"Well, if it's just something they are using every day, then that's one thing, but if they're collecting it for a reason, is it possible they could have a way of storing it?"

"You're thinking that if it's stored, we could retrieve what has been taken," Calli said slowly.

Nash nodded without even looking up from his book. The rest of us just glanced around each other in surprise at even the suggestion.

"You realise that would be suicide, right?" Aidan said, coming over to join us at the table. "You're suggesting walking into some kind of witch strong hold and just taking it from them."

Nash shrugged. "I wasn't suggesting that, it was just a question. Perhaps if we knew the method of collection and storage, it would assist in breaking the spell."

Calli looked up from the book she had in front of her and frowned before she picked up her phone, typed out a message and then shoved it back into the pocket of her hoodie. I was about to ask her what she had just thought of, but Jacob suddenly came bounding out of his bedroom.

"Is everyone here? Is it time? Is it time?" he asked, jumping up and down in excitement.

We all looked to Grey because, at the end of the day, it was his decision. Some people might struggle having a sibling as an Alpha, but I genuinely didn't. I wouldn't want his job for the world. There wasn't a single part of me that wanted the responsibility of running the entire pack.

"Let's do this," he grinned.

Jacob was the first one out of the sliding door, and we all followed him at a normal pace. By the time we got outside, he was practically spinning in circles on the grass, not knowing where to put himself or how to contain his excitement. Calli just laughed and went over to join him as we all followed in her wake. I had a feeling that the dynamic of the pack would shift when she was officially part of us. There was something about this that just felt so natural. I didn't know if it was because she was my mate or something else, but it just felt right that Calli would be the centre of us.

"Okay," Grey said as he came to a stop on the grass a few feet in front of a practically vibrating Jacob. "This is how it's going to work; the pack will shift, and they will stand at my back in their wolf forms. There's nothing to be afraid of; no one here would hurt you," he gently told Jacob who just nodded.

"When it's time, I will speak the words to initiate the bond first with Calli and then with you. After that we'll shift, and I'll help you through your shift the same as last time. Is that okay?"

Jacob nodded excitedly and then turned to Calli with his eyes gleaming in happiness. I realised this was the first time I had seen him like this, radiating with the happiness that came from being a young child, and it saddened me to realise it. This was a positive step though, and hopefully, the pack bond would help him with his grief as much as we hoped it would help Calli.

"Okay," Grey said, turning to the rest of us. "It's time, unless any of you have any objections."

We all shook our heads, and one by one, the five of us shifted and stood at Grey's back. Tanner and I were on either side of Grey, stood just a few steps behind him, and Nash, Blake and Aidan formed a line behind us.

Grey turned to Calli first, and as he spoke, I could hear the love and emotion thick in his voice.

"Calli, I stand before you as your mate and as the Alpha of the Stoneridge Pack. You come to us today to become one of us, do you pledge yourself to stand by our side as our pack sister?" he asked, changing the usual words slightly so they would work for Calli.

"Yes," she replied in a strong voice. I was so proud of her, of the way she faced every problem head-on, selflessly. Even if she hadn't been my mate, I would have been proud to accept her into our pack.

"Do you agree to do all that you can to protect your pack brothers, to stand by our ideals and accept us into your family?"

"Yes." Her voice trembled slightly with emotion, but still, she stood firm.

Grey's Alpha power slowly seeped out, wrapping around each of us and wrapping around Calli and Jacob.

Grey repeated his words to Jacob, changing them slightly to meet his needs, and Jacob stood there tall and strong, making all of us proud to call him our pup. After Jacob gave his final agreement, Grey said the final words, "And now it is time to take on your true form and join with the pack as we raise our heads and call out for the moon."

Calli shifted into her beautiful white wolf, and it took

everything in me to stay where I was and not immediately go to her side. Grey's power increased in the clearing as he stepped closer to Jacob, helping him trigger the point of his change until he fell to his four fluffy paws on the ground. Grey quickly shifted and then as one pack, we tipped back our heads and howled as one.

As soon as the last note of sound was made, I was hit with blinding pain in my head. It felt like someone was trying to force my brain through a shredder, and my legs collapsed from under me as the pressure built inside my skull. As I started to come to, I could hear my pack brothers going through the same thing, and then I was flooded with panic for Calli and Jacob.

I could hear a quiet, high-pitched whimper that I immediately knew was Jacob and adrenaline surged through my system. Crawling on my belly, I dragged myself across to him. Calli had already somehow managed to curl herself around his body, and I laid my head across her back, giving Jacob a reassuring lick across his snout. He whimpered again and burrowed his head into the soft fur of Calli's stomach. The helplessness that flooded me was overwhelming. Our pup was hurting, and there was nothing that any of us could do to stop it. I had never heard of anything like this happening before in a bonding ceremony.

"*Fucking ow,*" was the first words I heard as the pain started to recede, and I felt like I could think clearly again.

I couldn't believe that Tanner had been able to shift back to his human form already. I didn't feel like I could move, let alone push through a shift. Fucking overachiever.

"*Hey! Rude!*" he laughed.

I lifted my head, immediately regretting the movement, as I realised that he had heard what I thought.

"*That's right, brother. I'm in your head!*"

"This seemed like a good idea in theory, but now I'm realising the error of our judgment," Grey laughed in my head.

"This is so trippy," Tanner laughed.

I looked around and I could see everyone looked as shocked as I was. Calli moved next to me, and I realised that she was still curled around Jacob on the ground nuzzling against him. He was laying so still that at first, I feared the worst.

"I don't like being in a pack," his little voice whimpered in my head, and my heart broke for him. That had been hard enough to go through as an adult; I couldn't imagine what it had been like for him.

"Sorry, little man. That was my fault. We didn't know that was going to happen though," Calli said quietly, and I could hear just how tired she was from her voice.

"Everyone sound off if you can hear each other," Grey instructed. *"We need to know how far the link stretches."*

Everyone spoke up and my brain just about fried from the amazement of this. We were all able to talk to each other in this form.

"I wonder if it will work in our human form as well," Nash said and I not only heard him, but I could feel his interest and eagerness to test it out as well.

Jacob burrowed further against Calli's side, and I could tell that he was done for the day. He wasn't going to be up for a run. We would need to spend the next few hours spoiling him rotten so that this didn't have any lingering effects for him.

Calli had come to the same conclusion when she suggested, *"How about I make you some hot chocolate bud, and someone can go and grab burgers from the diner?"*

"And chocolate cream pie?" he asked with childlike reluctance.

"Little dude, it wouldn't be right to have them without chocolate cream pie," Tanner told him, coming over to his side and giving him a lick on the face.

"Eewww," he grumbled, which just made Tanner laugh and do it again.

Jacob seemed to be cheering up a little and emerged from Calli's side, wobbling along on his little paws. He still hadn't gotten used to having four legs yet. It was cute because he was so small and I couldn't help but wonder how ridiculous we must have all looked when we were at that stage but full-grown wolves.

"We're shifters because we were born with two souls?" Jacob asked.

"That's right little man," Tanner confirmed bounding around him trying to get him to play.

"So why can't other wolves shift when they're little like me?"

"Because we don't have enough magic yet to be able to connect with our wolves. It takes time for that magic to build and the connection to grow enough for us to be able to feel them," Nash explained.

"Then why did the witches want Coby and the baby if they don't have any magic?"

We all stopped. Why hadn't we thought of that?

"I heard them saying that what they had gathered from Jean was the strongest they had ever got," Grey added with a frown.

"Do you ever get that feeling that you've been lied to your entire life?" Tanner added.

Calli shifted back into her human form and scooped Jacob up off the ground. "Okay, little man, seems as there isn't going to be a run today, how about we build a blanket fort to have that hot chocolate inside?"

Jacob gave a little yip of excitement, and they headed inside.

I waited until they had both disappeared before I spoke. It was only mind to mind so it wasn't like Calli could overhear, or at least I didn't think she could, but it still felt weird, almost like I was talking behind her back.

"That was intense," Aidan said before I had a chance to speak.

Everyone gave various noises of agreement, but there wasn't anything to add.

"Okay, everyone back inside. We can take care of lunch, get Jacob settled and then we need to discuss where we go from here. I want a plan in place for James and any potential leads on the vamp nest by the end of the night. We also need to start getting everyone tattooed with the runes to link them to the warding," Grey said firmly.

Everyone started to shift and move back into the house, but I noticed that Tanner was hanging back in his wolf form and looking at me strangely.

"What?" I asked when I finally couldn't take it anymore.

He gave a wolf huff of amusement before he shifted back into his human form. "Just checking how the link worked," he shrugged with a smirk.

"Jackass," I grumbled, shoving him on the shoulder before walking away.

I heard Tanner bark out a laugh as he followed behind me into the house. I had worried that this morning might have changed things between us, but he seemed to be business as usual.

43

CALLI

Burgers had been an awesome idea for lunch, and Tanner even got lemon meringue pie for me, as well as chocolate cream for Jacob. The only problem was, all that food at lunchtime had made everyone sleepy in the afternoon.

Aidan had disappeared to go and get Coby from the school and headed back to the packhouse with him. Grey and Nash went with them to use the office there and start going through some of the files they had, while Tanner was currently curled up on Jacob's bed with him watching a movie. Or rather they went in there intending to watch a movie, but when I stuck my head in there a minute ago, they were both fast asleep.

When I came back out of Jacob's room, River strode out of the kitchen with a cup of tea in his hand, and I swear my eyes bugged out of my head like they do in cartoons. He presented the cup to me with a flourish, and it was official, River was my favourite mate.

I sat down on the sofa with a grateful sigh, and Blake laughed at the look on my face.

"Dude, you have it so easy that you can make her that happy just by giving her a cup of tea."

River at least had the sense not to say anything in agreement and just smiled as he sat down beside me, carefully pulled my feet into his lap and started to dig his thumbs into my arches.

I was in heaven, I was about to slip into some higher plane of existence that was only accessible when you experienced the purest form of bliss.

Blake shuffled uncomfortably on the armchair where he was sat trying to watch TV, but his eyes kept shifting to where we were sat on the sofa.

"I think I'm going to go and have a lie down and hang out with Jean for a bit," he suddenly said, springing out of the chair and striding away from us without turning around.

"I think we made him uncomfortable," I said once he closed the door.

River just shrugged and didn't say anything but kept rubbing my feet.

"I feel bad though," I told him, pulling my foot out of his hand so that I could push him with it. "He lives here now, and he shouldn't have to run into the guest room because of what we're doing."

"You're right, we should head over to their cabin tomorrow and see about getting them moved back in there," he agreed.

"Wait, that's not what I said," I frowned, feeling confused. Was that what I had said? I could have sworn I didn't.

"Calli, Blake doesn't live here and don't you think he and Jean would be more comfortable in their own home, with their own things around them."

I nodded, but it still didn't seem right.

"What's wrong? Don't you want him to go?"

He should be feeling jealous that I wanted this other male in my house, but I didn't sense any of that from him, and it was refreshing. I had absolutely no interest in Blake or anyone else. These three felt like they were it for me.

"It's just that when he's here, he has access to the library without having to leave Jean and if I'm honest, I need the help with the research," I admitted.

"I'm sure Nash would be more than happy to help you research," River laughed. "In fact, I know that he would be. I think he's feeling a little left out."

"I know, and we may yet need him to help. But I think Blake needs this too. I think he needs to feel like he's doing something."

River nodded in understanding, his eyes fixed on the closed guest room door while he thought. "I'll talk to him tomorrow and see what he wants to do," he finally said.

"You're worried about him," I observed.

"Yeah, but I think we all are."

He was right. Blake seemed okay on the outside, but I got the impression that deep down, he was barely holding on by a thread. I was hoping that if I started to work with Jean tomorrow, it would help settle his mind a bit. If he could see that we were beginning to take steps toward a solution, he might not feel quite so helpless about the whole situation. Even if he was stuck with a half-witch, who knew basically no magic as his only way out of this awful situation.

"Come on," River said, patting my legs as he went to stand up. "Let's go lie down as well."

He didn't need to tell me twice, and I was up off the sofa like someone had set my ass on fire.

"Oooo, we should invite Holly over for dinner one night

this week," I suddenly said as the thought popped into my head.

"I don't know if I should be insulted or not that I'm taking you to bed and you're thinking of Holly," River said jokingly.

"Well, I mean if we're only going for a nap," I said with a casual shrug following him into the bedroom.

River spun around and grabbed me around the waist before hauling me up and throwing me over his shoulder. "Who says we're going for a nap?" he laughed, slapping me firmly on the ass as he strode into my bedroom and tossed me onto the bed.

This was a very different River to what I was used to. It was almost like after this morning, the last of his walls had come down, and a carefree boyish attitude was starting to come out. I could see now how this River had grown up around Tanner. I wondered if somewhere inside Grey, underneath all the pressures of being an Alpha, he had a similar side of his personality hiding inside.

River wasted no time, and as I gazed up from the bed, he slowly stripped the clothes from his body. I licked my lips as I took in the full display of him. He was already hard, and as he reached down and fisted his length, my mouth watered.

River raised an eyebrow in question at me and I wasted no time in stripping the clothes from my body. I should probably have slowed it down and made him wait, but that would have meant I'd be waiting too and I was so not okay with that.

Swivelling around onto my knees, I stalked towards him. My eyes set on what it was that I wanted. So far, every time I'd been with one of my mates, they hadn't let me take them into my mouth. I was fed up with being denied. I wanted him, and right now, he was entirely on board with the idea.

As soon as I reached the edge of the bed, I leaned forward and ran my tongue around the head of his cock, peering up at him through my eyelashes. The way that he gazed down at me with a look of complete awe on his face made me feel like the most powerful woman in the world. I loved giving head. It always turned me on to be in this position of power. I may have been the one on my knees, but as soon as you take a man into your mouth, he's putting the ultimate trust in you.

I shuffled closer, placing one hand around the base of his cock, I swallowed him straight to the back of my throat in one move.

"Fucking hell," River swore as I sucked down his length, gliding my tongue up his shaft as I slowly withdrew him from my mouth.

I felt his hands tangle into my hair as he took control, slowing down my movements.

"Touch yourself, Calli," he ordered, and my other hand immediately slipped between my legs.

I was already wet, just the thought of having him was enough to turn me on. Feeling the gentle movement of his hips now, as he fought back the urge to fuck my mouth was only making me hotter.

I circled my finger around my clit as I swallowed him deep again. I wanted to feel him surging into my throat, but River seemed adamant that he would hold himself back. I pushed two fingers inside myself as the heel of my hand worked my clit. Riding my fingers, I whimpered as my impending climax grew even closer.

"That's right baby, I want to hear you make yourself come. I want to hear you cry out around my cock," River told me.

Fucking hell, out of the three of them, River was not the one I would have bet on being the dirty talker.

His hips started to move faster as he glided along my tongue, the head of his cock, just pushing into my throat before he withdrew again. It was almost like he was teasing me, and I wanted more.

I whimpered as I peered up at him again, the amber gleam of River's wolf filled his eyes as he watched me. I was so close, but I needed more.

"Fuck, your mouth feels incredible, Calli. I can tell that you want more. Are you close, baby?"

I whimpered in agreement, and River bit down on his lip before his hips snapped forward again harder this time. He started to move faster, filling my mouth and my throat. Withdrawing my fingers from my pussy, I pinched down on my clit and came just as he pushed back into my mouth. I did exactly as he had asked and I cried out my climax, still taking him deep into my throat.

River pulled me up against his body and devoured my mouth. I could still feel the last of my orgasm slowly fading as he pulled back with a grin and then taking hold of my waist, picked me up and tossed me backwards, so I landed on my back on the bed.

My first instinct was to laugh, but the sight of River crawling up my body with his wolf gleaming through his eyes triggered a whole other emotion in me instead.

I felt my wolf pushing at the edge of my mind, and I knew that she would be looking out of my eyes now, watching her mate.

"You're incredible," River told me when he reached me, dipping his head down to seal his lips to mine.

He pushed inside me in one movement, and I felt the delicious stretch as he filled my pussy. Pulling one of my legs up over his hip, River slowly moved inside me.

It was a completely different pace to what we had been

doing before, but exactly what I needed. I held River close as he made love to me. He peppered my lips and jaw with kisses. Neither of us spoke. It was too early to say all of the things that filled my mind, but these three men were made for me. There would be no one else, even if we hadn't had the time to fully come to terms with all of the feelings that came along with that, they were still there. But there was a huge difference between feeling them and saying them out loud. Right now, though, we didn't need words. Every movement, every kiss was a declaration, and as we both reached our peak, our teeth closed down on the other, leaving our mark and our declaration to the world. River was mine, and I was his.

44

GREY

Waking up in my old bed was weirdly disorientating. This was the first night I'd spent away from Calli since I'd found out she was my mate. After a night working through the files with Nash, we were no closer to finding any answers. Whoever was making the property purchases and filing the renovation permits had so far managed to escape our discovery. Even worse, we couldn't see that anyone had even moved into the properties, they were all still empty as far as we could see. Which meant that if it was vamps that had taken James, they had somewhere else we weren't aware of and essentially we were back to square one.

We ended up calling it a night around two in the morning. At first, I'd wanted to head back to Calli's house, but then I got a weird vibe outside and decided to stay close by. I was probably just anxious because Coby was at the house now, and I was feeling the weight of what had happened to him pretty heavily. It was my fault; after all, I was the one that banished his father because I was unable to make him see the truth that was right in front of his face. I was a terrible Alpha.

My father wasn't going to let me hear the end of this. He already thought I was a failure for not growing the pack bigger.

I was in the kitchen pouring a cup of coffee when a pale-faced Nash came in.

"You look terrible, I thought you were going to bed at the same time as I did," I said, leaning back against the counter and sipping on my coffee.

"We've been summoned," he said in shock.

I nodded as I took a mouthful of my coffee. It was scalding hot, and it burnt my throat as I swallowed it down, but I needed it right now.

"We knew it was coming."

"I just didn't think it was going to come so quickly. That fucking dick!" Nash swore.

"Is it a general summons or have they named specific pack members?" I asked, my mind already spinning with how we were going to play this. I knew that Calli seemed to think we could argue our way out of this, but I wasn't so sure.

"They want you, Tanner, River and Blake. And you've been instructed to bring Coby with you as well."

I was surprised by that, but I suppose it made sense. If Wallace was going to the Council to report us, he would make some kind of play to get Coby back. Without the promise of a pack to take him in, though, that was a death sentence for Coby. So unless the Council had some way of forcing a pack to take them in, surely they wouldn't make Coby go with them. Young shifters were always protected in our society because we didn't breed easily. However, Calli was going to shake all of those beliefs up. If there was a way to get true female wolves, what would that mean for us as a species?

Coby was going to be so disappointed though, he'd been

excited about starting school today, and now he was being pulled away from it.

"Okay, we need to call the others. If they haven't specifically summoned Calli yet, that might work in our favour. We'll brief here before we head out. Are you okay staying with Jean and Calli while we're gone? I want Aidan to keep an eye on the packhouse. Something didn't seem right here this morning."

"Do you think the witches are back?" Nash asked, glancing nervously out the window.

"No, Calli would have told us if there had been a breach of the wards. I don't know, something just feels off," I shrugged.

Nash left me in the kitchen to go and call the others. I had finished my coffee and got started on cooking breakfast. Coby had taken a bowl of Cap'n Crunch up to his room to eat while he played on Aidan's Xbox. Calli would kill me if she found out, but it was all he had wanted, and I wasn't about to say no to him after I'd just broken the news that he wasn't going to school today.

Unsurprisingly, they all turned up just as I was plating the food up.

"Jacob is hanging out with Calli, and I've called off again. I'm not going to have a job soon if this keeps happening," River sighed as he dropped down into a seat at the kitchen table.

I felt terrible for him. We'd never had a time in the pack like this before where we had all been pulled out of our everyday lives to deal with urgent pack business. It was easier for us with the garage, but we wouldn't be able to keep it closed for much longer. We needed the income, and we couldn't afford to lose the business if people found somewhere else to go in the meantime.

"Once we're through this bit we should be able to get back to some form of normal, besides you've got a field trip to attend, remember."

River smiled and shook his head as he started to fill his plate. Jacob had us all wrapped around his little finger. I didn't think there was anywhere else we'd rather be though, he was an amazing kid.

"Yeah, if we're not all running for our lives," Tanner said casually as he shoved some bacon into his mouth.

We all just stared at him while he chewed. It took him a moment to realise that no one was saying anything before he looked up.

"What?" he asked.

"It's just shocking how you can say that without sounding like it bothers you," Blake said almost in amusement.

Tanner just shrugged. "I think part of me always expected I'd have to run from those bastards at some point in my life."

Nobody said anything, because what was there to say. Tanner had a complicated relationship when it came to his family and the Council. I couldn't worry about that right now though, because all I could concentrate on was whether we were even going to get a chance to run, or if it was already too late for us—too late for Calli.

"Nash is going to head over to Calli's when we leave to help keep an eye on things there," I told the others.

They nodded in agreement, and we all sat, and wordlessly ate, each of us lost in our own thoughts that were no doubt filled with the same golden-haired beauty. Or at least mine, River and Tanner's would be, the others had better not be thinking about Calli that way.

We all piled into the truck when we couldn't put off leaving for any longer. Nash was grabbing some stuff out of the office before heading over to Calli's and Aidan was working on an old Chevy in the garage. I think he was looking forward to having some time to himself away from the drama. Aidan had always been the quiet loner of the pack. I doubt he would have survived in a large pack like my fathers. He didn't gel well with too many people. Most shifters saw that as a weakness, too close to the nature of a lone wolf. It would have gotten to the point where he was either challenged one too many times, or he was eventually cast out of the pack. We all cared about him a great deal. We may have been a small pack, but we valued every single member, and Aidan was not an exception to that. His quiet nature meant that he saw things before many of us even realised what was happening. He was an asset in our pack. I trusted him wholly to watch our packlands while we were away and for an Alpha that was a big deal.

Tanner sat beside me in the front, and Blake and River had taken the back seat with Coby sitting nervously between them.

The truck ride to the Council compound was quiet; all of us were lost in our thoughts, and I could feel the nervous energy radiating from my pack members. I couldn't even try and help them either because I was a ball of nerves myself. If this didn't go our way, then we could lose Calli forever.

"Am I in trouble?" Coby finally asked, breaking the silence.

"No, of course not buddy. Why would you think that?" River asked him.

"Because the Council wants to talk to me."

This was so fucking hard because there was stuff that Coby wanted to know, but above everything else, I didn't want to bad mouth his parents to him, despite what they had done. But equally, he deserved more than to be lied to and walk into the shit show that was inevitably about to happen.

"They just want to make sure that you are happy staying with us," I told him. Because I suppose that was part of what this was all about. "They asked us all to come and see them because your Dad went to see them and told them some things about us."

Coby frowned in thought before stating, "Because he doesn't like Calli?"

The thing most people forgot about kids was that even though you weren't talking to them, if they were in the room, they were still listening to you.

"Yeah, buddy, he doesn't like Calli because her mom was a witch," Tanner told him honestly.

"But she helped you find me, and she's helping Jean and her baby get better."

"Yeah, she is."

"Then she's not bad," he frowned. I could see why he was confused. Things were very black and white in the world of kids, and us grown-ups just lived in shades of grey.

"So, he thinks she's bad just because her mom wasn't a wolf?" he asked.

"Yeah, he does." I winced as I said it because when you boiled it down to this simplest form, it was so idiotic and it was hard to admit to a kid that adults didn't always get it right.

"That's stupid," he said, pulling some earphones out of his pocket and putting them in his ears.

None of us could have said it any better. It was stupid. I just hoped that he made it out of today with some form of respect for his parents still intact. I might not have liked them now, but Coby deserved better than to grow up hating them.

Coby was staring blankly ahead out the car window listening to his music and once we were confident he was preoccupied, discussion soon turned to what we were going to do.

"How much are we going to tell them?" Blake suddenly asked, shifting nervously in his seat. "I feel like we should get our story straight before we go in there."

He was right, and we should have thought about this before we were only ten minutes away from the compound. I wasn't stupid enough to suggest we pull over. I'd clocked the two cars tailing us from our lands. They'd sent someone to make sure we didn't run, which surely wasn't a good sign.

"Wallace already knows that she can shift into a full wolf, but he doesn't know anything about the change in the bond. I think we should keep that part to ourselves," River said thoughtfully.

I nodded in agreement. He was right, if we did end up running for our lives, the changed bond would work to our advantage, and the longer we could keep that information from them, the better.

"He also knows that Calli is capable of practising magic," Blake pointed out.

Shit! He was right. I didn't know how the Council was going to deal with that. The fact that she could shift fully worked in our favour of arguing that she would be an asset to shifters and she was one of us. The magic, though, not so much.

"He only knows about the healing and the wards," River pointed out.

"He knows about Jacob as well," Blake added quietly.

"Maybe we should have had Nash get them out of town, just for a little bit," Tanner said.

It was easy to panic now when we didn't know what was going to happen, but the Council would probably have someone watching the house, and if they ran now they were only going to look guilty. Plus, it's not like Jean was in any kind of condition to run anyway. We didn't even know if we could move her.

"Call, Nash," I suddenly decided just as the gates were going into view. "Tell him to be ready to go if he doesn't hear back from us in an hour. Tell him to get Aidan to Calli's house now just in case."

What would be the point in having packlands if I didn't have Calli in my life? I wouldn't want to survive without her anyway.

River had his phone to his ear as we pulled into the compound. It was a long time since any of us had been here. It was almost like they picked the most intimidating building they could find and then painted it grey just to make sure that it sucked the life out of you whenever you came near.

The guards secured the gate behind us. It wasn't unusual, but it still didn't bode well for us. Just as they approached the truck, River turned to me, his face white and his eyes wide. "Nash isn't answering," was all he managed to get out before the guard pulled open the car door and glared at us.

"Alpha Thornton, the Council, is already assembled and waiting for you and your pack members," he told me. His eyes locking with mine in a sign of disrespect.

A growl rumbled out of me. There was no way I could have kept it in when River had just delivered news like that. My wolf was pissed, and I was worried. As I climbed out of the car, I could just feel it, this was going to go horribly wrong, and there was nothing we could do to stop it.

River and Blake rounded the back of the car and immediately took up position at my back. Tanner was already at my side like the good Beta that he was. We kept Coby protectively sheltered in the middle of us. We were in this together, all of us. We would show them a united force, even if it meant we were going down together. I knew my pack brothers would always have my back.

One side of the guard's mouth lifted in a sneer as he turned without a word and strode towards the Council building. He didn't need to say anything, we knew there was no other option for us but to follow him inside. As we marched through the double doors towards what felt like our doom, the cold shiver of oppression washed down my spine. How did anyone ever convince themselves that the Council was a force for good when they came to this place? They were supposed to stand for and support our people, but they hadn't been that for decades. It felt like every drop of life had been drained out of this place. There was nothing good here, no support, no caring leaders. It felt almost like we were being marched to our deaths, and I could only hope that wouldn't be the case.

Our escort pulled open a heavy oak door and waited beside it for us to enter the room without speaking. My wolf did not like this. He didn't like that we were not only going to walk into this unknown situation, but that we were leading our pack brothers inside, as well as one of our pack's pups.

I took point as we walked through the door into some kind of conference room. If this went as badly as I felt like it was going to, the least I could do would be to draw as much of it onto myself in an attempt to try and spare the others. That thought settled my wolf a little. He was happy to stand in front of Coby and our brothers like a shield. They were ours to protect.

I came to a stop in the middle of a room. A large conference table had been set up in front of us, almost like this was some kind of tribunal hall, that was when I realised that was precisely what this was.

Two men sat before us at the table, but the other three seats were vacant. Instead, three monitors had been brought in, and the other three Councillors' faces were displayed on them. I suppose it would have been strange for all of them to be able to get here so quickly. The Council had compounds like this spread out all over the country. The two Councillors in front of us were both wolf shifters. The majority of the shifters in this area were wolves. The other three Council members lived with their own kind in other parts of the country.

Looking at the five Councillors in front of us, I tried to gauge if anyone could potentially be swayed to our side.

Councillor Stone should have been the obvious choice. We knew him well, he was the Alpha of a pack close to my father's, and I had seen him frequently growing up. He should have a vested interest in the success of our pack, but I knew without a doubt that he was the least likely person we could rely on right now.

The only other wolf on the Council was Councillor Wells. I had absolutely no knowledge of him at all. His pack was further South, in Wyoming. He was new to the Council and the one Councillor who stuck out from the rest. While the others were all in suits, or at least a button-up shirt, he was lounging back in his chair wearing a grey t-shirt with a beat-up old brown leather jacket over the top. His hair was cut short, so it couldn't exactly get messy, but he had a few days worth of stubble. The smirk on his face wasn't unfriendly, but I didn't know him well enough to tell if the look he had going on was because he was going to cause trouble by standing on our side, or if he was just looking forward to the kill.

The other three Councillors were harder to read because of the screens. Councillor Gates was a bear shifter and Alpha to a sleuth in Montana. He had a thick white beard and close-cropped hair. He was dressed in a white button-down, but you could see where the arms bulged trying to contain the muscles underneath. This guy screamed bear in whatever form he was in. He wasn't someone I would want to see on the other side in a fight, and I could tell by the glare on his face that he definitely wouldn't be standing on our side.

That left the last two Councillors we could potentially see some support from them. They shifted into smaller predator animals, and if rumours were right, the rest of the Council members looked down on them for it. Hopefully, that meant they might side with us just to piss the others off, either that, or they would fuck us over just because they hated wolves in general.

Councillor Carson was hard to read. He was a fox shifter and controlled territories spanning from Texas right across the Country and into Nevada. It was rumoured that he had bought his way into the Council by clearing someone's debt to gain himself a nomination, but I had no idea which of the other four it could have been. He had white hair and thick bushy eyebrows and a moustache. He was frowning so hard it was almost like he was trying to get his eyebrows to meet in the middle.

The Coyote Alpha, Councillor Crane, was the only one out of the five that actually looked intrigued by us. He was the youngest on the Council, but he was fast coming up to his fifties. His long brown hair was swept back from his face, which was blank of any expression. Fuck, he was impossible to read.

It was true what they said; old white men really did rule the world, no matter what species you happened to be.

"Well, now that you've finally decided to grace us with your presence shall we get on with it?" Councillor Stone said, sighing like he had been kept waiting for hours by us.

Tanner shuffled uneasily at my side, and I was praying that he was going to get through this without losing his temper. Tanner was fairly laid back in general, but when he lost it, it was always epic, and even I had a hard time holding him back.

Councillor Stone waved a hand at one of the eight guards lined along the room's edge, and a side door was opened. In strode Wallace with a smirk on his face and hatred in his eyes. Or at least, I guessed he was going for a smirk; his face hadn't healed properly from where Calli had ripped his cheek open, and it was a mass of gnarled scar tissue which pulled one side of his mouth out at the side. I couldn't help the smile that pulled at my lips as I locked eyes with him. My wolf howled in glee at the damage our mate had left on him for all the world to see.

"Wallace MacRath has come forward and made some serious allegations about events occurring in his pack," Councillor Stone said, sitting back in his seat with a sneer.

"Wallace MacRath is no longer a member of my pack. He was banished when he attacked my mate and tried to kill her," I said confidently. "I told him that if I ever saw him again, his life would be forfeit and in accordance with this Council's rules, I am fully within my rights to take his life right now."

Wallace's face paled, and Councillor Wells barked out a laugh, much to the annoyance of the others.

"How about we hear the allegations first," Stone said quickly, looking slightly more flustered than his usual confident self.

Everyone looked at Wallace, who suddenly looked like he was starting to panic, he clearly hadn't anticipated having to stand in front of us and repeat what he had said.

"I've already told the Council what happened," he blurted out.

"Your Alpha, oh I'm sorry, your *old* Alpha, has a right to hear the allegations that you are making," Councillor Wells grinned, leaning forward in his chair and resting his elbows on the table in front of him. "Besides the other Council members, who have conferenced in with us, have yet to hear your statement."

Wallace started to shuffle on his feet, glancing warily across at us. His nervousness just added to the obviousness that what he was about to say was probably all lies. Coby stepped to my side, locking eyes with his father. I was proud of the kid, even if my heart was breaking for him.

"This is boring," Crane sighed. "Clearly he's lying, can we just wrap this up? I have far better things to be doing."

Councillor Stone glared at Wallace, and something passed between them. It would seem that Wallace was more scared of the Councillor than he was us because he soon started spitting out his lies.

"They are harbouring a known witch who tried to steal and kill my son. When I objected, they cast me out of the pack and wouldn't let me take my son with me. I … I was afraid that they might have done something to him."

"You fucking liar!" Blake swore, diving for Wallace only to be restrained by River.

I glanced at him over my shoulder, and at my look, he started to calm down, but I could see just how enraged he was.

"It would seem that this pack disputes the allegations that are being made," Wells grinned. "Perhaps they would like to tell their side of the story."

I hesitated for a moment. The three Councillors teleconferencing in were clearly bored and not paying attention, but the two wolves in front of us were far too eager to get on with things.

"A woman moved into a house in the town which borders our pack property. She arrived some months after witches were scented in the area. Wallace's child was taken from his cabin. While we were searching the surrounding area, I was injured, and she healed me. While I was incapacitated, Wallace tortured her for information and abducted her brother. She was not responsible for the kidnapping of his son and in fact assisted us in recovering Coby. She is also assisting us with healing Blake's wife, who was on the verge of death from a draining spell on her and their unborn child. When she shifted in front of us, my wolf immediately recognised her as his mate, as did Tanner and River's wolves."

Coby pressed himself firmly against my side, and I protectively curled an arm around him. He shouldn't be made to relive what had happened to him. He shouldn't be here at all.

Even as I said it, I knew it sounded bad. Councillor Gates seemed to be a bit behind the others though as the bear Alpha just waved his hand saying, "Who turned this woman? I am sure that her Alpha will be able to vouch for her."

The others though, were all paying far more attention than they had initially been. Wells looked like he was about to leap out of his seat in sheer excitement.

"She was not turned; she is a born wolf shifter. She has a dual soul and true shifter form," I told them, not an ounce of the fear that I felt radiated from my voice.

"Impossible," Gates dismissed.

"This is easily proved, bring her in," Councillor Stone said with a sly smirk on his face.

My stomach dropped. Calli was here. What? How? And then I remembered Nash's unanswered call.

Two guards marched through the same side door that Wallace had come through, dragging Calli between them. She didn't appear to be harmed, but she didn't exactly look herself either.

Tanner roared in rage and immediately shifted, springing from his spot to go to her side. I caught him by the scruff of his neck and hauled him to me. Whispering in his ear to calm the fuck down.

He snarled and growled at my side, but he stood tall, not moving from his spot.

"Enough," shouted Stone, standing from his seat and slamming his hands down on the table. "Control your packmate," he snarled at me.

"Like father, like son, hey Johnny boy," Wells laughed at Councillor Stone.

Calli's head whipped from Tanner to the table of Councillors in front of her.

"Oh, oh, this is just delicious! She doesn't know!" Wells cackled. "Have you been a naughty little pup and been keeping secrets from your beautiful mate?" he said sarcastically to Tanner, who had retained enough common sense not to turn his rage on the Council.

"Enough!" Stone shouted again, and I could see the rage simmering in his eyes.

"If you're all quite done," Gates sighed, "I want to see her shift."

The room fell quiet. I wasn't sure what to do, there was no way around this, but equally, I didn't want Calli to be put at any risk.

"Perhaps if you allowed her to come and be with her pack, she would find it easier to shift," River said confidently, and I was grateful for his quick thinking.

Wells just barked out another laugh, "You're funny, gotta give you points for trying though, right."

It was becoming glaringly apparent that he wasn't on our side.

Calli looked at me uneasily, but I could see the resignation in her eyes. There was no way around this. I gave her a nod, and a small smile graced her lips. I couldn't believe that she was taking the time to try and make me feel better at a time like this.

Gasps echoed around the room as she shifted and landed on the ground on four paws. She was a truly magnificent wolf with her pure white coat. She stood proud and confident in front of all of the shifters in the room who had, until seconds ago, wanted her dead. Now, they all looked at her like she was a piece of meat to fight over.

"Incredible," Carson said, leaning closer to the screen trying to get a better look. "She is a full shifter, not a half-beast like other females. How is this even possible?"

"She's a witch," Wallace screamed across the room.

"Will someone remove him, he's annoying me," Gates sighed.

Two guards grabbed Wallace and started to drag him from the room. "But she's a witch, she should be put down like the abomination she is!" he screamed as he was dragged through the door.

Coby whimpered and pressed himself harder against me and the hatred I felt for Wallace increased. He hadn't even acknowledged him. All he had done was shout his hate and lies.

As soon as the door slammed shut silence rang out through the room. Calli shifted nervously on her paws, not sure what to do. Even the guards on either side of her seemed a bit unsure. They probably hadn't expected her to actually shift into a proper wolf.

"Do you understand the potential that this has for us as a species?" Carson suddenly said.

"But what about this allegation that she is a witch?" Gates asked.

Calli took that as a sign to shift back into her human form, and as soon as she was back on her feet, one of the guards grabbed her arm again, but the other just stared at her in wonder.

"Tell us about this witch allegation, girl," Gates said abruptly.

Calli looked at me nervously, and I nodded to encourage her to speak. There was no point hiding it. It was out there now. Gates clearly had his own agenda, but if we could use that to get us out of here, I'd be willing to go with it for now. Unfortunately, the guard standing next to Calli was still staring at her, and it was starting to set my wolf on edge.

A low growl started to flow out of me, Calli was our mate, and I was at the point where I didn't want to take this shit anymore. That shifter needed to back the fuck off before I made him.

"I think you should take a step back Hunter, it would seem that the Alpha doesn't like the way you are currently staring at his mate," Wells laughed. I didn't give a shit though because this asshole, who was apparently called Hunter, took a step away from Calli.

Gates cleared his throat, growing impatient and Calli turned back to the Council.

"My mother was a witch, and my father was a wolf shifter," she said. If she was frightened right now, she wasn't showing it.

My mind quickly turned to Jacob, where was he? If they had gone to the house and taken Calli, had they taken him as well? Calli seemed way too calm right now to have been separated from Jacob, so I was praying that meant he was still safe at home with Nash.

"Did your mother have a coven?" Gates asked, but I couldn't see where he was going with this.

"When she was younger, but she left her coven when she met my father, and they ran away together."

"So, they mated?" Carson said in astonishment.

"Yes, they did. They were together for decades."

"And the witches, they're not aware of your existence," Carson queried.

"No, my mother's coven is not aware of me."

Clever girl. It was *technically* the truth.

"Tell us about this allegation of stealing the boy," Gates said, turning his attention back to me and trying to peer around me to see Coby.

"Wallace was warned that if he attacked Calli again, he would be banished. He didn't listen, so I had no choice. We gave him the option of taking Coby with him or saving him from the life of a lone wolf and leaving him with the pack. He decided that the best place for him would be with the pack."

Even as I said it, it didn't sound like the truth, even though I knew it was.

"Very gracious of you to allow the son of a traitor to remain in the pack," Crane said, watching me cautiously. "Can you give me your word that the child will not be mistreated?"

I was surprised that he actually gave a shit.

"Of course not," Calli gasped.

"So, you are fully prepared to give him a proper home then?" Crane asked Calli.

"Coby is a member of our pack, and he will always have a home with us," I answered before Calli could say anything. I didn't want her to feel like she was going to get backed into a corner.

"Boy, stand where we can see you," Crane said, addressing Coby who slipped to my side but didn't move away from me. "Has anyone hurt or threatened you?"

"No, Sir."

"Has this pack mistreated you in any way?"

"No, Sir."

"You understand that if you were to stay with them, you would likely never see your parents again?"

I could feel Coby shaking as he pressed himself against me. "Yes, Sir," he said, his voice finally breaking.

"If you wish to be sent to another pack, we can arrange that for you. Would you like us to do that?"

"No, Sir. I want to stay with my pack," Coby whispered, but we all heard him anyway.

Crane nodded, apparently satisfied. I was surprised he had shown so much concern for Coby. I might need to reassess my feelings about him.

It seemed to be going better than any of us had hoped for. Apart from Wallace crying out for Calli's head, no one else had mentioned execution. Maybe we were wrong about them.

"Crane is right, the implications of her existence to our species need to be considered. I vote that she be taken into custody by my pack, and we implement a long term breeding plan to see what type of wolves she can bear," Stone suddenly said, his eyes firmly fixed on Tanner as he spoke. The smirk that stretched across his face made me want to slit his throat. I had no idea how Tanner was feeling right now. All I could feel was rage, but it was coming from everyone, and it was hard to single out what was coming from who.

"You're suggesting removing your son's mate from him so that you can … what? Fuck her yourself," Gates managed to get out before he broke down into hysterical laugher.

No one joined in with the bear, but I caught the sneer of amusement that crossed Wells' face before he got it under control. Whatever plan he had, and he clearly had one, he was playing it close to his chest, for now.

"She needs to be studied. She can't be allowed just to roam free. If the witches were to get hold of her we could lose a vital opportunity for our species," Stone spat at Gates, who had managed to get the majority of his own laughter under control.

None of the rest of us spoke, it seemed like Gates was on our side at the moment, or rather not on Stone's side. Stone was firmly for taking Calli away from us, but I got the impression it was more about taking her away from Tanner than anything else. The other three had yet to weigh in an opinion. It was glaringly obvious that what happened next balanced on a fine line, and until it was apparent who was on whose side, I was going to have to let it play out. No matter how much that was killing me. These were men with massive egos, and agitating them would only ensure they sided against us. Hence why Tanner's father was so set against letting us keep Calli when he could see just how much his son cared for her.

"Well as long as you're only fucking her for her own safety," Gates waved him off, snorting with the laughter he was trying to hold back.

"The implications are wider than just for the wolves sat here," Crane interrupted. "We need to study her genetics. There could be a way for us to find the solution of how to breed true shifter females for more than just wolves."

"What, so you want her as well?" Gates snorted. "In that case, I'll throw my hat in the ring too. She's a pretty little thing, I'd let her warm my bed for a night or two."

The growl ripped out of me, and I was barely holding back my shift. This was my mate that they were so casually talking about using. As much as I wanted to see how this would play out, they were pushing it too far now. Calli looked terrified, and my wolf couldn't cope, seeing her there, standing between two unfamiliar shifters terrified of what was happening around her. I could feel my grip on my wolf starting to slip more. He was forcing his way to the surface, and I felt powerless to stop him. My Alpha power was building inside of me, and I felt like my skin was going to split open, trying to keep it restrained.

"That's some power that you're failing at holding back there," Wells said in interest.

He was right. This was more than I had ever felt before. I never used to be this strong. Something had changed, and I was kicking myself that I was letting it get out of control now, of all times. This must be due to the changed bond. Now was not the time to find out about this. If they thought that Calli could do this for them as well, we would never see her again. Losing control now would only put her at greater risk.

At the realisation that we were endangering our mate, my wolf pulled back, and I swallowed down the growing power inside of me. Only a fraction had slipped free, and that still seemed to have them intrigued. It was like acid sliding down my throat, burning away my insides, but I forced it down nonetheless.

"While Stone has a point about the breeding potential of our beautiful white wolf here, I think we can all agree that removing her from her pack would be detrimental to her health. And as he has already said, we couldn't possibly put her at risk," Wells started. His eyes locked with mine and I knew he was letting me know that he was standing with us, but it would cost us. "The best scenario that I can see, would be to allow her to return to her pack. But, to address Stone's concern for her safety, I would suggest that one of our guards accompany her. Besides, all you need to study her genetics is a blood sample Crane, correct?"

"Well, yes. We may need other tissue later down the line,

but for now, a blood draw would be sufficient," Crane agreed. He didn't even seem to be upset, his curiosity was peaked, and he was getting what he wanted.

"So, if we were to agree to allow you access to her blood now and further samples in the future, I'm sure you would be happy to agree that her return to her own pack, with protection, of course, is for the best."

"Well, if she agreed to attend the Council compound to allow for regular blood draws and collection of any other genetic material we needed, I can't see a problem with that," Crane quickly agreed.

The way he said it though set me on edge. What exactly did he mean by other genetic material? It didn't sound right, and he had agreed far too quickly.

"We don't want to interfere with her health, perhaps let's just see how things go," Gates intervened, surprising me.

Calli cast her eyes to him and then quickly looked away. Stone had caught the glance though, and from the look on his face, he was intrigued. He was going to be a problem. Especially, because he wasn't getting what he wanted, we would need to look out for him. He would be coming for us.

"It's agreed then," Wells quickly said, even though I'm pretty sure no one had agreed to anything. "The beautiful Calli will return home with her pack and Hunter here will accompany them as her guard."

Stone reared back like someone had slapped him, but Wells just pressed on, not giving him any chance to object.

"Hunter, take her through to the on-site doctor and have her blood drawn. Take one of her pack with you. We don't want the Alpha here to lose control of everything he's holding back."

And there it was. He knew, and now we were just going

to have to wait and see what he was going to do with that knowledge.

"Take the boy as well," Crane added. "He's seen enough."

Stone flew out of his seat, the chair flying back and smashing against the wall, before he stormed out of the room. Wells just cackled again and turned to the monitors showing the remaining Councillors.

"I will make arrangements to transport the samples for you, unless you would prefer to send someone to collect them."

They started to discuss things amongst themselves, effectively dismissing us without bothering to say anything. The guard, who had been looking at Calli in awe earlier, turned to us saying, "You're with me," and then strode out of the room. The other guard dragged Calli along with them.

I indicated for the others to follow, and Blake pulled Coby protectively against his side as I took position at the rear. I already knew what was coming, and I didn't want to slow down the others accompanying Calli to the clinic. I didn't trust Stone to try and just snatch her out from under us if the opportunity presented itself.

Wells closed off the feeds with the others just as I reached the door and finally called me back like I knew he would.

"If you have a moment Alpha, I'd love to have a quick word with you," he said, and I could hear the smile in his voice as he spoke.

River looked at me in question, and I nodded for him to follow the others before I turned back to the room and stepped back inside. Even the guards were gone now, and it was just Wells and I. How he had cleared the room so quickly, I had no idea.

He sat back in his chair, propping his feet in Stone's seat while he stretched his arms back behind his head. He watched me curiously as I walked slowly back over to him. I didn't get the impression that he was a strong Alpha, which meant he had gotten his position from his wits alone. That made him far more dangerous.

"I hope you realise just how much I've put myself out there today to make sure that you got to keep that beautiful mate of yours with you," he said slowly as he clasped his hands behind his neck. "I think it would be gracious of you to extend a hand of friendship in thanks, don't you?"

"How about we just get straight to what you want instead," I growled.

"Straight to the point, I like that," he grinned, dropping his feet from the seat and sitting forward again, bracing his elbows on the table in front of him. "You don't remember me do you?" he finally said, after taking a few moments to watch me.

I cocked my head to the side. I had absolutely no memory of him at all. I'd only been to the Council compound with my father once, and I had never been allowed anywhere near the Council chamber. I'd been left outside where a group of guards could keep an eye on me. I squinted at him then, trying to bring the memory further to the front of my mind.

"I'll admit I have changed a little over the years, but we all get older don't we. Look at you, a full-grown man and an Alpha in your own right."

I squinted at him as the memory hit me full force. "You were there," I said more for my own benefit than his.

"Yes, I was once your babysitter for a brief and wonderful day, and do you remember what we did?" he smirked.

My stomach dropped, and I felt like I was going to throw up. Fucking Fucking Fuck!

"You taught me how to manifest my Alpha power," I sighed.

Of course, that would have been him. The one fucking person outside of the pack that was intimately familiar with the power I held inside me. He had spent hours with me teaching me how to harness and how to push it out for the benefit of others. My father was too busy, and we had few other Alphas in our pack. No one that gave a shit about a teenage kid like me.

"It's her, isn't it?" he asked.

He didn't have to elaborate. He knew I was fully aware of what he was speaking about. He knew the power I had shown here today was far greater than anything I had before. Thankfully, I didn't think he was aware I had held most of it back.

"I don't know," I told him honestly. "It's kind of new."

He nodded thoughtfully, and my wolf pressed against the edges of my mind. He was seeing this man in front of us as a threat to our mate. He was right. Of course, he was also the only thing that was currently keeping Calli out of Councillor Stone's hands as well. Talk about a rock and a hard place—this was more like being stuck between a shit place and an even shittier place.

"Don't worry. I'm not going to try and take her from you. Logically, whatever effect she has on you, only works because you are her mate. I couldn't hope for the same outcome," he told me, then paused.

I waited, like the good little dog he thought I was, because I knew there was a giant ass-kicking 'but' about to be dropped.

"*But* of course, you belong to me now," he added coldly. "There will come a time in the future when I may need some additional power to back me up. When that time comes, you, your pack and your mate will stand by my side. Do you understand?"

I didn't answer him straight away. It's not like I was

playing hard to get or anything. I was just desperately trying to think of an alternative. Anything that could get us out of this building without having to agree to essentially become his bitch for life. But there wasn't anything. Centering my mind on the important issue at hand—actually getting out of here in the first place—I just nodded and strode out of the room, his laughter echoing behind me. Fucking fuck!

We just needed to get the fuck out of here, and then we could deal with all of this bullshit when we got home. It could line up behind the million other problems that we currently had going on. Fuck, I was starting to miss the times when we just thought we had a rogue vampire nest moving in, but then my thoughts immediately turned to James and I wasn't sure how much more of this I could actually take.

45
CALLI

My head swam again as I ducked down to get into the back seat of the truck. That butcher they called a doctor had taken way too much of my blood. There was no way I would be able to work with Jean tomorrow, which was stressing me out way more than the fact the Council was now aware of me, and apparently just wanted to chain me up and breed me. I mean what the actual fuck! I thought death was the worst thing that was on the cards for me. But from the way Tanner's father had looked at me, I was starting to realise that was just wishful thinking. And don't get me started on that Tanner's father was apparently on the fucking Council. I specifically asked them how close they were to the Council and he didn't tell me. In fact, he fucking lied to my face! I didn't have the necessary brainpower to even think about that at the moment, and by the way that Tanner couldn't even look me in the eye, he knew he had fucked up too.

Grey and Tanner both took the truck's front seats, and Blake moved onto the back bench with my new guard, Hunter. Still not sure how I felt about that, or how it was even going to work. He had pulled a massive duffle bag out of nowhere full of clothes, and the fact that he was prepared for this was weirding me out. Plus, the way that he kept looking at me wide-eyed like he was waiting for me to explode or something, was starting to get on my nerves.

Coby had the middle seat between River and me, and the poor kid looked like he was in shock. I couldn't believe that the Council would put him through that. Wallace didn't even try to talk to him once we left the chambers. He was nowhere to be seen, which I suppose could have been because of whatever happened after he left the room, but I had a feeling it wasn't.

I didn't know what to do. I wanted to reach out and comfort him, pull him into my arms and tell him that we were going to work it all out. That he was never going to be alone. But he didn't know me. All he knew was that I was the reason that his father left and got dragged out of that room, screaming like he'd finally lost his mind.

"I'm sorry about my Dad," he told me quietly, staring straight ahead.

I reached out and took his hand, and he held it so tightly it was like he was worried someone was going to turn around and tell him to leave.

"You don't have to apologise for him. He's not your responsibility. I'm sorry you had to go through that," I told him quietly.

Coby just nodded and continued to stare out the window, but he never let go of my hand.

As soon as we pulled out of the gate, there was a collective sigh of relief from my pack.

"Are you hurt?" River asked. I could see his eyes trailing over me as he started to check me over.

"No, it was all pretty civil, surprisingly," I said, still kind of in shock about how it had all gone down myself.

A scoff, from the back bench where Hunter was sat, had various eyes swivelling to glare at him.

"Of course, it was civil we're not fucking animals, you know?"

"I mean, we are, but let's put a pin in that debate for later," I sighed because I just couldn't right now. "They drove down the driveway. I felt them breach the wards, so I met them at the door," I shrugged.

"I'm sorry," Grey growled from the front seat. "That sounded suspiciously like you knew the Council was driving up to your house and you just walked out to say hi to them."

Ooooo, he was pissed.

"That's not exactly what happened. They drove up to the house, and I stepped outside so that Nash could protect Jean and Ja …" I trailed off, and a now-familiar sensation shot down my spine. "Someone just breached the wards at the house," I murmured, as all of the blood drained from my face.

The truck jolted forward as Tanner floored it, gunning the engine, but we were still about an hour out. There was no way we would get back to the house to help them. Jacob. Jacob was there with only Nash to protect him.

My wolf whimpered in my head as my thoughts started to spiral out of control. Coby gripped my hand tighter like he could feel my distress, and it was only the feeling of him clinging to me that kept me grounded at the moment.

"I need someone to fill me in on the situation," I heard Hunter demand from the back bench.

"We've had some recent problems with witches at the pack. Calli set up wards around the property so we would know if they came back," Blake started, but then his voice faded away, and I knew that his mind was in the exact same place as mine was, only he was spiralling out of control for someone else. "Jean," he muttered helplessly to himself.

"You have wards at your property?" Hunter said in awe.

"Now really isn't the time," River snapped at him. "Calli, look at me."

I felt his hands cup my face as he leant across Coby and turned me to face him, but even though his face was directly in front of me, I didn't really see him. All I could think about was Jacob. I couldn't lose him. I couldn't lose another person. He was so young. He didn't deserve this. He was just a little boy. He should be able to just be a kid without having to worry that someone was going to kill him at any given moment.

I felt myself moving as River unclicked my seatbelt and lifted me over Coby, straight into his lap.

"Stay with me, baby. We'll get to him as quickly as we can," he murmured, his thumbs moving across my cheeks, wiping the tears away that I hadn't even realised were falling.

I just nodded, but we all knew the reality of the situation we would be walking into. Nash was alone. He wouldn't be able to stand against them by himself. He didn't have a chance.

※

The journey to the house was possibly the longest hour of my life. Tanner hadn't even brought it to a full stop before I was opening the door and leaping from the truck. There wasn't one murmur of argument though because Grey and River were out of their doors as quickly as I was.

The front door of the house was hanging open, gently swinging in the breeze. There was nothing but silence, and that was more terrifying than if we had arrived to blood curdling screams. At least if you were screaming, you were still alive.

I wanted to throw up at that thought. At the thought of Jacob's little body lying broken and drained somewhere. But I couldn't stop, I couldn't slow down if there were even a chance. Maybe he had enough time to hide. His talisman could have shielded him from them. I almost felt guilty for thinking it, for knowing that Jacob could potentially have hidden while Jean and Nash were taken instead. But still, I hoped, even if that made me a terrible person.

When I walked in, the first thing I saw was the trail of blood that led from the front door into the living room. The whole living room was trashed. It looked like a tornado blew through here, but I could recognise the signs of a fight, and it looked like Nash put up one hell of one.

The blood trail ended at the body of a man I didn't know, and a sigh of relief whooshed out of me.

"Jacob," I shouted, rushing to his bedroom door, inexplicably expecting just to find him sitting on the floor playing with his lego. He wasn't there, of course, no one was there.

"Calli!" I heard Blake's voice shout, and I rushed out of the room in the direction of the guest room.

Inside I found River putting pressure on a chest wound that was still seeping blood from Nash's chest. His face was pale and judging from the amount of blood on the ground, he didn't have all that much left in him. Nash raised his weary eyes, and I immediately knew from the look of pain in them what he was going to say.

Blake was on the bed, Jean in his arms as he wept against her still sleeping form.

When I looked back down at Nash, I almost didn't hear

him as he whispered. "I tried Calli. I tried, but I couldn't save them both."

The realisation of what had happened slapped me in the face, and I looked at Nash in complete betrayal. He chose to save Jean over Jacob. He let them take Jacob.

"Calli, Calli, can you help him?" River shouted from the floor.

My first thought was no, why should I. But I knew that was the grief talking and not the real me. Dropping to my knees, I placed my hands over Nash's chest and started to push as much healing magic into him as I could. The only problem was, with the blood draw the butcher at the Council did, I didn't feel like I had all that much left in me. Leaving me only one choice. If I were going to save him, I would have to draw from my own life force. He was so close to the verge of death that it was the only way he had any chance to survive.

Just as I started to feel my stores depleting, Hunter burst into the room to tell us that the house was clear apart from one injured witch that they found in the basement.

"How injured is she?" I gasped out, remembering something that could just save Nash's life.

"Calli, you can't be considering healing her," River gasped, and I could hear the outrage in his voice.

"I don't have time to explain," I snapped at him. "The blood draw took too much, and I don't have enough magic to save Nash's life. If you want him to live without draining me dry, then I need you to bring that witch here," I told them firmly.

"What happens to you if he drains you?" Hunter asked like we suddenly had all the time in the world for a chat.

"I die," I answered him simply.

Cursing, he turned and ran out of the room, returning

moments later, carrying a terrified looking woman. He gently placed her to the ground next to me, and I could see that one of her legs was quite clearly broken. I couldn't believe they left her here just because of a broken leg. They could have easily taken her back with them. When Hunter said she was injured, I imagined she was on the verge of death, not just immobile.

Reaching out, I slapped my hand on her wrist nearest to me and clutched it in a death grip. "You will feed your power into me so that I can heal this man," I growled at her.

"Why would I help you do something like that?" she spat back, her unusual green eyes filled more with fear than anything else.

She was clearly in a lot of pain, I could see the sweat beading across her forehead, glistening against her ebony skin. Her long brown hair was hanging half out of the pony tail she'd scraped it back in. She looked like she'd been through hell, but I didn't have it in me to care right now. She came here with the intention of taking Jacob from me, whatever she'd been through, it hadn't been enough.

"Because if you don't, when I'm finished here, I will peel the skin from your bones and keep you alive long enough to feel every second of it," I seethed.

My wolf was pushing at my walls, demanding that I shift and tear this witch apart that was responsible for Jacob being taken. She didn't care that Nash would die, she saw him as being just as responsible.

Her eyes opened wide in fear, and I started to feel her power slowly leaching into me. I knew that she was drip-feeding it to me, no doubt in the hope that Nash would die before we could do anything about it. Almost like my magic had an opinion of its own, it reached out and clamped down on hers, dragging it from her. She gasped in surprise, her eyes opening wide in fear.

"How ..." she stammered, but I didn't have time to talk with her right now.

I could feel Nash still teetering on the edge. It wasn't enough, it wasn't fast enough. With a yank, I tore more of the magic out of her, and she screamed out in pain. I didn't have time to be gentle about it, and if I was completely honest, I had no fucking idea what I was doing anyway. The sudden flush of magic seemed to work though, and not only did Nash move away from the brink of death, but the wound on his chest healed over almost immediately, quicker than I had ever managed before.

I could hear Hunter's gasp of amazement—it was starting to get old if I was honest—but I was too busy wondering why the hell the others abandoned this woman here when she was so fucking powerful.

I could feel her magic coiling back through me. Almost like it was trying to tempt me to take it all for myself, but it felt wrong. No, that's not right. It felt different. Unlike my own and I didn't want it inside me. Once I could feel that Nash was healed enough for his shifter abilities to kick in, I broke my connection with him. The foreign magic was almost gleeful at not being funnelled out of me and started to build inside me. As hard as it was, I concentrated and forced it back into the unwilling witch, not willing to pollute myself with this foreign magic that I didn't understand.

Once I was done, I dropped her arm and then scooted myself back until I hit the wall. I stared down at the trail of blood that I'd left in my wake. Nash's blood. I didn't want to be in this room filled with all of these people. I needed to go after Jacob. I needed a plan. I wasn't going to leave him with them.

The witch was looking at me now, suspiciously. She didn't seem remotely bothered by the angry shifters in the room, no, all she seemed to want to know about, was me.

"Why did you do that?" she asked, confusion ringing in her voice. She must have seen from my face that I didn't know what she meant because she clarified, "Why did you give it back? You could have just drained me dry."

"I don't want it," I said with a shrug, as I clambered to my feet, feeling my head swim as I did. Fuck, I was still too drained to be much of any use.

Staring at the other's in the room, I realised what I was faced with for the first time, that I didn't want the comfort of my mates. I knew I was going to do something they wouldn't like, but I was so deep in my loss of my brother right now, that I couldn't bring myself to care. This was about more than us. It was about Jacob. Everything started and ended with him.

Nash was still unconscious, but at least he was alive. A flash of hate rolled through me when I looked at him, and I almost hated myself just for feeling it. River was still at his side, taking his pulse and checking that his wound had healed over.

Blake was still cradling Jean in his arms, and Grey was trying to console him. I couldn't blame him. I knew what he just went through. He just got a better outcome than I had.

Tanner wouldn't meet my eyes still, and was just glaring down at the witch instead, fixing his ire on her.

My decision made in my head, I turned and went to leave the room, but was met with Hunter blocking my path. He had that look on his face again, and I was just about done with it.

"Can you move? I want to get this blood off me."

"You just healed him," he said instead of moving as I asked.

I just couldn't right now, so I strode past him, and he automatically stepped out of my way. I didn't stop until I reached my room. Stepping inside my bathroom, I quickly stripped out of my blood-soaked clothes and dropped them into the sink. There was no point washing them; they were definitely destined for the trash.

The hot water did nothing to soothe me. There was only one thing that was going to make any of this better, which was setting out to find Jacob. Thankfully, with the assistance of the unwilling witch to heal Nash, I didn't fully drain myself. Don't get me wrong, I was wiped out, but still capable of movement. That's all I needed right now. Once I tracked Jacob down, I could assess the situation and go from there.

Stepping out of the shower, I towelled off quickly and pulled on a clean set of clothes. I immediately halted in my tracks as I left the bathroom, because sitting on the bed facing the bathroom door like he was waiting for me, was Tanner. Apparently, he thought we were going to get into this now.

Stopping in the doorway, I just stared at him. I didn't have words to deal with this right now. I felt betrayed because he lied to me, but also in the grand scheme of things, it didn't seem like that big of a deal. He obviously was estranged from his father, so it's not like he was in his life, but he should have told me. I deserved to know the risk that he posed, not just to me, but especially to Jacob.

"I know, I fucked up," he finally said, not looking up from the ground.

I couldn't see his face, but I could see the tears as they fell. Tanner was always my fun-loving, light-hearted mate. I'd never seen him like this before, and it broke my heart more than I realised it would.

My wolf whimpered in my mind. Her mate was hurting,

and even though she was angry with him, it still distressed her. It was the perfect way to explain my feelings. I was pissed, but those were my feelings and whilst we might need to work through this together, that didn't mean I wanted to see him in pain.

I sighed in defeat and moved closer towards him. He needed comfort, and I was his mate. Of course, I was going to give it to him. Reaching out, I ran my hands through his hair, and he pressed his forehead against my stomach. When I didn't pull away and just kept pushing my fingers through his shaggy blonde hair, his arms came up around my waist, and he pulled me closer to him. The sobs that racked through his body broke my heart. Tanner was hurting, deeper than any of us had ever realised, and he was finally letting it go. He clung to me like he feared I'd disappear if he let go and I held him back, clinging onto the bond that was growing between us because I couldn't lose that too.

When his sobs finally slowed, I heard his muffled voice talking against my stomach. "I fucking hate him so much."

I moved away enough to sit down on his lap and not make him let me go. He kept clinging to me, his head tucking under my chin as he soaked up the comfort I was giving him.

"When I was five, my mother died in childbirth. The next day he dumped me on the doorstep of Grey's father's pack. He was already on the Council by that point, and he said he didn't have time for me. He could have asked one of the other pack members to raise me, but he said he couldn't bear the sight of me. Nobody wanted me there. I ended up living in the basement of the packhouse because no one wanted to take me in. I was a lone wolf, and they didn't want me to taint their standing in the pack. I lived off the scraps that one of the women in the kitchens left out because she felt sorry for me. After a couple of weeks, Grey found me. He was only just six, but as soon as he saw me, he hugged me, and he's never let me go. He took me to his room, and he shared everything with me. His clothes, his toys, his food. We spent all our time together. I was there for nearly a year before his father even had any idea that he'd taken me in. He used to sneak these entire picnics out of the kitchen, and we would hide in the closet together eating them. By the time the Alpha found me, Grey and I were so close, he said I could stay. He gave me the room next to Grey's, and that was it. We've been together ever since."

"What about your father? Did you ever see him again?" I asked, shocked that anyone could treat a child that way. A child the same age as Jacob. Is that what would have happened to him if we had been in a pack when our parents died?

"I saw him a few times each year when he would come to the pack for Council business. He usually ignored me, or just outright told me that I would never be enough for him to recognise me as his son," he paused, but I could tell there was more he wasn't saying to me. I wouldn't push him on it today; he was hurting enough already. "I didn't mean to lie to you Calli. When you asked us if we had any connection to the Council, I should have told you he was my father. But I truly don't have anything to do with him. I still should have said something though. I should have realised that the fact he hates me so much would have put you and Jacob in danger."

His breath hitched as he said Jacob's name and I knew it was from pain. All of my mates had declared Jacob their pup. They would be feeling this just as much as I was right now.

"I need to speak with the witch," I told him.

Tanner just nodded and stood up, keeping his arm around my waist as I stood with him. "We've put her back in the basement," he said as he started to walk towards the door.

I loved that he would do this for me without question. I loved it even more that it wasn't out of guilt as well; this was just who Tanner was.

We walked out of my room and went straight down to the basement. We found the others stood quietly talking in the gym. The witch was nowhere in sight, so I assumed she was in the other room where the wine was stored.

Grey glanced up at the sound of our arrival and nodded when he saw us together.

"She isn't talking," he said, looking concerned.

"I'll speak with her," I said, moving to the door. Grey went to go with me, but I just told them, "Alone." Closing the door behind me before any of them could follow me through.

I found her curled up on the floor in the corner. There were a couple of boxes off to the side, which I chose to sit on, as I looked down at her. She glared up at me through her hair but made no move to approach me. From the look in her eye, I could tell she was scared, and she should be. I chose to say nothing, waiting for her to break the silence first. I wanted her scared; I wanted her terrified.

"What are you?" she finally spat. She was going for angry, but I could hear the fear in her voice.

"That doesn't matter now does it. What matters is how long you can hold out before you tell me what I need to know."

I stood up from the boxes, and she flinched back away from me. Holding out one hand in front of me, I slowly shifted my fingers into claws.

"They took my little brother, and I want him back," I said, staring down at her.

"The boy?"

"Of course the boy, how many other innocent children have you kidnapped today?" I spat.

If I wasn't mistaken, there was something that looked a hell of a lot like guilt in her eyes. I could work with that.

"Our parents died a few months ago. He's only five. What makes you think your selfish desires are worth more than his life!" I screamed at her.

She flinched again, but this time she mumbled, "It isn't."

I couldn't decide how to do this with her. I knew I could get what I wanted out of her if I hurt her. The thing was, that wasn't who I was. I could be that person if it were the only way to get Jacob back, I wouldn't even think twice about it. But I wasn't sure if it was entirely necessary. She was afraid, but I was starting to think that she might also be feeling guilty about the things she had done.

Figuratively crossing my fingers, I retracted my claws and crouched down in front of her. "All you have to do is tell me where they took him, and I'll do the rest."

She peered up at me through her hair. She had beads of sweat dotting her brow, and I could tell that she was in pain. It wasn't a surprise really; no one had done anything about her leg.

"I'll even heal you if you help me," I told her. "You know you could lose your foot if that fracture isn't sorted out, right?"

"I won't need my foot when I'm dead," she whispered. "That's what you're going to do right, kill me. That's what all shifters do to witches."

"Perhaps if you didn't break into our homes and steal our children, we wouldn't feel the need to," I spat before I could pull myself under control.

She gritted her teeth, and I saw the same look flash through her eyes. That was when I realised what her weakness was. It was the fact that Jacob was a child. She might not give a fuck about shifter adults, but everything was that much harder when you had to do it to a kid, especially one as young as Jacob.

I moved back to the wall on the other side of the room to sit down, facing her. It gave me plenty of distance if she tried anything, not that she would be moving that fast, I could see the bone sticking out of her leg from all the way over here.

"He started school this year. You should have seen him on his first day. We'd lost our parents already, and he slipped into a depression, he refused to speak nearly entirely. But that first day of school, he was so excited, it was like he was a little kid again. I tell you, that kid has an unhealthy obsession with Lego. He'd spend all day putting those bricks together. That was probably what he was doing when you forced your way in here. Just sitting there playing with his Lego, when you ripped him from his home and the only …"

"Just stop," she suddenly shouted. I could see her panting, her eyes wide and wild. "Do you think I want to do this? Do you think I like snatching children from their families and listening to them cry at night? See the things that they do …" she broke off on a sob.

It took absolutely everything I had right now to not just launch myself across the room at her and tear her apart. But I needed the information first.

"I don't have a choice," she hiccupped. "I can't survive without a coven with my type of magic."

I had no idea what she was talking about, and I didn't want to show my hand with just how ignorant I was on the issue of magic, just in case. I could offer her safe harbour with the underground, but I also didn't know if I could trust her. She was more than likely trying to manipulate me.

Her sobs were getting louder, and I wasn't sure how much more I could take. Don't get me wrong, I didn't give a shit that she was crying, I just needed the information before I lost control of my wolf and we killed her before we got it. I did feel a tiny bit sorry for her. I'm sure that she didn't grow up dreaming of doing these things, but also, have a backbone and some self-conviction, or, I don't know, some personal morals. The more I thought about it, the less sympathetic I was getting, which wasn't going to get me what I wanted, namely Jacob.

"Just tell me where they've taken him," I begged.

She looked up from the ground where she lay sobbing. There wasn't any fear or anger in her eyes anymore. She looked like she'd given up.

"There's no point. They aren't holding them at a second location since you stole the other child back. They've taken him to a coven facility. You won't even get close before they have you too."

I sagged back against the wall, my head slamming against the plaster. There had to be a way. I couldn't just give up.

"You're strong," she said slowly.

I peered down at her over the tip of my nose, she obviously had an idea, and it sounded like I was going to hate it. The problem was I was desperate and sometimes when you're desperate terrible ideas are all you have left.

"We could see if they would make a trade," she suggested slowly. "You, for the boy."

"Do you think I'm stupid?" I sneered.

"No, I think you want your brother safe, and you would be willing to sacrifice yourself to make it happen."

She fell quiet while I considered what she was saying. This was the worst fucking idea in the world. My mates were never going to go for it.

"What's your name?" I asked her.

She squinted at me suspiciously but eventually she told me, "Cassia."

"Okay, Cassia, I'm going to be frank with you because, well we just don't have the time to fuck around. I want to get my brother back and I want you to help me do it. I can tell that what you're doing isn't sitting right with you and I think you want to help Jacob too."

She didn't say anything to me, she just sat there looking at me, weighing up what I had just said.

"We need to learn to trust each other if we are going to get this done."

She nodded because it was true, we wouldn't be able to do this if we were going to be constantly looking over our shoulders waiting for the other one to betray us.

"What are you?" she asked me again.

Deciding to take a leap of faith and be the first to go with this whole trust thing, I started to talk. "My mother was a witch and my father was a wolf shifter. I guess I'm a bit of both." I shrugged like it was no big deal, but I saw the way that her eyes widened in astonishment.

"Why are you with them?" I asked her. I knew she would know who I was referring to without having to actually say it out loud. "They left you here when all you had was a broken leg. They could have easily taken you with them."

I scooted forward to look at her leg. Of course, I was going to heal it, regardless of what happened. My mother had taught me to heal and with it she had taught me compassion. Hopefully, that would go a way towards getting Cassia to trust me enough to agree to help me.

She at least didn't flinch as I moved closer to her and then carefully manoeuvred her leg out straight in front of her. I ripped the torn leg of her trousers further up so that I could see what I was working with. She flinched from the pain of the sudden movement.

"I'm sorry," I murmured to her as I continued to check her leg.

"I don't have a choice. My magic makes me an outcast and I need a coven to survive. When my magic reached dangerous levels, I had no other options. No one else would take me," she looked away in shame and I could see that she was just a person who had found herself in a shit situation while she was looking to survive. I knew how that felt. I'd just lucked out and found a pack and my mates, but it could have very easily gone in a very different direction.

"What if there was another way? A way you could survive without them?" I asked her.

She looked at me in suspicion and I knew that she needed more information than that. Unfortunately for her, I didn't trust her enough to give it to her just yet.

"I know you don't know me, and at this moment you have every right to distrust me because you're right, I am helping you because I need you to help me. But I can't tell you anything else right now, all that I can tell you is that if you can take that leap of faith and put your trust in me, I can give you another solution. But I can't help you until I know that I can trust you."

Cassia's eyes hardened and I knew she was doubting me. I felt like I'd lost her trust before I even had the chance to gain it. But in this situation, there just wasn't the time to make any grand gestures.

"I'm going to need you to feed me some of your magic so that I can use it to heal you, I don't have enough left to do it without you," I told her as I placed my hands over her leg.

She hesitated at first but then I felt the slow trickle of her magic as she started to push it towards me. There was something so different about it but I wasn't experienced enough to be able to tell if it was because it just wasn't mine, or it was because there was something entirely different about her magic altogether. That would be the sensible conclusion after what she had hinted at, though.

It didn't take long to heal her leg, and once I was fairly certain that the bone was set back in its proper place and fully healed, I picked up her leg and slowly rotated her ankle.

"How does that feel?" I asked her.

"Good," she said in astonishment. I suppose there was a part of her that just didn't believe I was actually going to help her. "Why would you do that? What's stopping me from just walking out of here now?"

"Well, a pack of very angry shifters, but I get your point. Like I said, I need your help and I need you to trust me to do that. This is a gesture of goodwill. Plus, you can't do what I need you to do with a broken leg." I shrugged. It felt like my go-to move at the moment.

Cassia fell quiet and I could see her weighing up her options. I stayed silent, letting her think it through. I prayed that my desperation wasn't showing on my face. This was my only way to get to Jacob. If Cassia got up and somehow walked out of here now, my chances of finding him went with her. This was a massive risk but also, it was our only option.

"I will go back to the coven and see if they will agree to the trade. I will help you through the trade. I will only help you escape if, between now and then, nothing happens that shows me I can't trust you," she finally told me. "You realise that once you are inside, you might not be able to break out. The cells are not heavily guarded but there will be an entire coven standing between you and the only door out."

It was more than I'd expected of her. Essentially, she was saying I will help you get in, but I might not help you get out. That was fine. At this stage, I'd settle with just getting Jacob out. I'd deal with my own situation once I was in it.

I nodded, trying not to show just how relieved I was.

"How long will it take you to get back to the coven?" I asked her.

"I can move through the shadows, I can be with them in seconds," she shrugged like it was no big deal, but I caught the glint of amusement in her eyes.

I nodded in relief. "I'll see you when you get back then."

She gave me one last look over before she literally just faded before my eyes. It occurred to me that she could have done that at any point, or perhaps the pain of her injury had been holding her back. Regardless, it didn't seem like she was quite as trapped here as we had first thought.

46

TANNER

Waiting for Calli to come out of the bathroom had been pure fucking torture. The fact that she was even able to touch me after that shit show had to be a good sign. I knew I should have told her. I fucked up. I'd really fucked up.

Now, we were all waiting in silence in the gym for her to come out from talking to the bitch that stole our pup. Grey didn't look like he was going to be able to hold out much longer. His pacing was getting more and more furious. The Alpha power that was leaking out of him was already thick in the air. He was so much stronger than I had ever felt him. Something had changed when we added Calli to our pack bond. I'd noticed it at the Council compound earlier, and I was hoping that no one else had.

Calli opened the door and wearily stepped through, gently shutting it behind her. From the look on her face, I could tell that whatever she was about to say, we were going to hate it.

"We've got a plan," she said slowly, dropping down on the weight bench with a haunted look in her eyes.

I dropped to my knees in front of her just as River sat next to her on the bench.

"We will get him back," I told her firmly.

She nodded, her eyes fixed firmly on mine, and I almost didn't want her to speak. I didn't want to hear the plan because I knew it was going to kill a part of me.

"We're going to make a trade," she said quietly, almost like she was just talking to me. "Me for Jacob."

I felt my heart stutter in my chest, and my lungs turned to stone as I lost the ability to breathe. I couldn't get my brain to even begin to try and interpret what she was suggesting.

"Absolutely not," roared Grey. "I'll go, make the trade with me."

Calli just shook her head. "It has to be me, and you know it. You promised me, Grey, you promised me you would do whatever it took to protect him."

Grey finally stopped pacing, and I could see him fighting his own nature as he tried to come to terms with what she was saying. "I also said that I would protect you as well, Calli," he whispered. "You cannot ask this of me."

He looked so broken, and I knew that my face was reflecting the exact same expression. River hadn't even spoken. He seemed frozen to the spot. I'm not sure if he was even hearing what we were saying now, still stuck on the part where Calli was suggesting giving herself over to the witches.

Aidan and Blake were staying quiet in the corner. They both looked furious, and I couldn't blame them. They would have the same pack need to protect Calli and Jacob even if it wasn't as strong as ours. I was surprised that Nash had been able to make the choice that he had, considering that Jean wasn't technically a part of our pack. His wolf should have pushed him to protect Jacob instead.

"It doesn't matter what any of you think," Hunter suddenly piped up from the doorway. "I am assigned as Calli's guard, and I can't allow her to do this."

"Tell me you at least have a plan to get out of there once you get inside. You can't be suggesting just turning yourself over and waiting to die," I asked her, completely ignoring Hunter. He wasn't one of us, and no matter what he thought his job was right now, he had no right to an opinion.

"Of course not," Calli said, sounding a little insulted. "My plan is to wait for the right moment and then make a move to escape."

"But escape how exactly?" River asked, keying back into the conversation.

"I'm not entirely sure yet. Cassia assured me that the cells are not heavily guarded. They know I'm a shifter, they won't suspect that I know how to use my magic, I should be able to use that to my advantage as soon as I'm alone."

"Calli, you don't know how to use your magic," Blake sighed, seeing the immediate flaw in her plan.

"I've learnt enough over the last few days to get out of a locked cell," she sniffed.

Grey came and dropped to his knees beside me, clasping Calli's hands in his own. "Promise me, promise me that you can get out of there," he begged her.

I saw her searching his eyes. I could almost see the thoughts running through her head as she decided whether she should lie to him to save his feelings. "I can't do that," she finally admitted. "But I think I can do this, Grey. Even if I can't, this is Jacob."

Grey's head fell to Calli's knees, and he held onto her hands even harder, almost like he was trying to keep her here, safe in this moment.

"I don't think any of you are understanding what I'm saying, I can't allow you to walk into a known witch stronghold," Hunter sighed again.

"Hunter, honey, it's cute that you think you have an opinion, but it's getting a little annoying now. Why don't you go upstairs and see if you can find something to eat while we talk," Calli said, dismissing him.

It was fucking hot. But now was so not the time to be getting turned on.

"This is a terrible idea," Blake muttered from the corner, while Hunter just stood in the doorway with his mouth hanging open.

He should probably get used to this. It wasn't like we were just going to let him walk in here and order us and our mate about.

"Unbelievable," he muttered, finally storming out of the room.

"We will need to make arrangements for how we are going to get the witch out of here to make the deal for us," Blake said carefully.

"She's already gone," Calli said sheepishly.

We all turned slowly back to her.

"How do you mean, already gone?" River asked carefully.

"She can do this freaky melting into the shadows thing," Calli shrugged.

"Do you trust her to come back?" I asked, needing to float it out there. "She could just go back to them, tell them our numbers and bring reinforcements back here to take us all."

Calli shrugged again and I could tell from the dark circles under her eyes, that not only was she physically exhausted, but she was mentally wiped as well.

"I think we can trust her. I think she wants out but doesn't know how to go about it. I told her that I can give her another option, but that I can't explain any more until I know I can trust her. I think she's going to take it. She's stuck where she is and I'm hoping that she's desperate enough to take a leap of faith."

"If we're even considering doing this, then we do it smart," Aidan suddenly piped up. "We fit Calli with a tracker, we make the trade, and we track her to whatever location they are taking everyone to. We gather as many allies as we can in the short amount of time that we have and we strike the facility and pull everyone out."

We all looked at the normally quiet Aidan like he had been body-snatched.

Grey's head snapped up, and I could tell that he was considering it. What fucking allies did we even have, though?

"Will the underground help us?" Grey asked Calli, possibly forgetting that Blake and Aidan weren't actually privy to this information. Thank god Hunter had already left the room.

Calli thought carefully for a moment. "Maybe, I don't know," she shrugged. "I don't even know if there are any in this country. I might know someone else though," she said, almost carefully.

"Babe, as much as I hate that I think you've got secrets from us, now isn't really the time to be coy," Grey sighed.

Calli looked uncomfortable as she glanced around at us. I wasn't sure how much more I could take of this either.

"The underground has allies," she finally said. "Who help us smuggle people out of the country if necessary."

"And you think you can get them here to help us in time?" River asked hopefully.

"It depends on ... well, which ones are moving their nest here," she said reluctantly.

Grey pinched the bridge of his nose between two fingers as his forehead wrinkled in anguish. Taking a deep breath, he just said, "How do we get in contact with them?"

"Sean."

"Do it," he sighed, and Calli got up, rushing out of the room, to no doubt, try to find her phone.

"We need a backup plan," Aidan said quietly once she had left.

"I already have one, if you plan to stay in Arbington, you need to go upstairs, make a scene in front of Hunter and storm out," Grey said coldly. "Those that want to stay with the pack get ready to leave."

"You can't be suggesting making Calli leave Jacob behind?" River gasped.

"No, of course not! But if we have to go to the backup plan, the Council will come down on us hard, and we need to put as much distance between them and us before that happens."

"What the fuck are you planning on doing?" River said cautiously.

"Once we have Calli's location, we pull the plans, we find a way in, and we call in the human cops as a diversion while we pull them both out."

The whole room fell quiet. What Grey was talking about would be enough to have us all sentenced to death.

"You're talking about exposing the supernatural world to the humans," Blake said quietly, almost like he just wanted to make sure that Grey fully understood what he was talking about.

Grey just nodded, sternly.

"I'll have Jean ready to move, I don't need anything else but her," he said, striding out of the room.

"You know I'm always with you," Aidan said, clapping a hand on Grey's shoulder before he followed Blake out.

Grey looked between River and me, almost like he was waiting for us to try to talk him down. It was fucking insanity. It would blow apart our entire world. But I didn't even need to think twice about it. I'd do anything for her.

47

CALLI

Hanging up the phone, I didn't know if I would throw up, cry, or just pass out. Hunter was at the dining table scowling at me over the top of a beer. I'd made sure to be out of earshot when I took the call and somehow ended up in Jacob's room.

His scent was thick in here, and it calmed my wolf, even if only by a fraction.

To say that Sean was furious was an understatement. He was taking the next flight over here, but even then he would be here far too late to be able to help. He said he would work his connections on the ride to the airport and promised to have something for me as soon as he could.

He confirmed what I already knew. The underground would not come out of hiding to help us with this. They couldn't risk so many to save just one. He did, however, think that the vampires could be a viable option, but he had already warned me that there would be a cost. I didn't care. I'd do anything if it meant getting Jacob back.

When I paced back into the kitchen to put on the kettle, Hunter finally spoke, "Calli, I understand your need to get your brother back, but I think you should let Grey do the exchange."

I looked at him, this stranger sitting in my house, drinking my beer, and thinking he even had a right to tell me what to do.

"What's my last name?" I asked him suddenly.

"I … what?" he stuttered, frowning in confusion.

"How old am I? When did I move here?" I said reeling off questions.

He at least had the decency to blush when he realised what I was doing. "Look, I get it, I don't know you, and you don't know me, but the Council …"

"I'm going to stop you right there before you start trying to get me to join your little cult. Why do you think you are here?"

He thought for a moment before he answered, and I could hear the conviction ringing in his voice, "I was sent here to protect you and keep you safe."

"Right, and why do you think that is." Now I was curious just how delusional this guy was.

"Because you're special, you could save our species," he said with such conviction in his voice, I was actually starting to worry about the amount of crazy that was finding its way into my life.

I couldn't help it, I started laughing, and that blush that had been from embarrassment earlier, looked like it changed to one of anger.

"I wasn't there, and even I think that sounds like bullshit," Cassia said, stepping out of the shadows in the corner of the kitchen and moving to sit at the table with Hunter.

He looked like he was about to piss himself with shock and he didn't even move an inch.

"He's not a very good guard, is he?" Cassia said, turning

to me as I walked over to the kitchen table carrying two cups of tea, and placing one in front of her.

"You'll have to excuse him, he's reassessing some life views," I said, taking a seat opposite Hunter, who was staring at Cassia like she had grown two heads.

"Why is he looking at me like that?" she asked, shifting uncomfortably in her seat.

"I'm not sure," I murmured as Hunter's eyes started to flick back and forth between Cassia and I. "Hunter, you stood in that room at the same time as I was when Councillor Stone was talking about removing me from my pack and repeatedly raping me until he could get me pregnant. How could you possibly think they have my best interests at heart?"

"That … that's not what he meant," he stuttered, rearing back like I'd slapped him.

"And what exactly do you think he meant when he talked about taking me to his pack and breeding me," I asked, genuinely curious.

"I … they just wanted …" and then he trailed off with a frown as he thought about it. You see this was the problem with most people, they were too ready just to accept what was told to them without actually thinking about it. "The Council is there to protect our people," he finally said, but there was far less conviction in his voice now.

"How many people have you seen brought before them?"

"I don't know, a few. I've only been stationed at the compound for three months."

"And of all of these people, how many of them were either killed or just disappeared? How many of them had done something, which now that you're thinking about it, was actually something that shouldn't be considered a crime?"

I knew I was pushing him too far too quickly, but as he stood up suddenly with an angry look on his face, I was still disappointed. "You don't know what you're talking about," he seethed, before storming out of the room.

I watched him leave with a sigh of disappointment.

"Change takes time," Cassia observed as she sipped at her tea. "He will see what is in front of him when he is ready."

"It could be too late by then," I murmured, my eyes fixed on the door he had just left through.

She hummed in agreement as she continued to drink her tea.

"I'm surprised you came back," I said, turning back to her.

There was something about Cassia that felt familiar in a way. It was hard to describe. I was trusting her to help me, even though I had no reason to do so. I didn't even know why, I was chalking it up to my desperation, but that didn't seem right when I actually thought about it.

"It's on," she said as I stared at her, trying to put my thoughts in line.

I nodded because this was the one job that she had and the one thing that I needed to happen in all of the world. This was the only way.

"How do we know they won't betray us and just keep them both?" Grey asked, sitting down in the seat that Hunter had left. I didn't even realise that he had come into the room.

"They will probably try," she shrugged.

Grey just nodded. I could see how much this was costing him. His overriding need to get Jacob back was warring with his need to keep me safe, but we couldn't do both.

I saw Tanner and River, hovering over at the other side of the room, unsure about what to do or how to act at a time like this. Cassia looked around at us, and with a sad smile, she stood up, "If you don't mind, I think I might use your shower," she said, looking down at herself.

She was in a bit of a state. One trouser leg was torn up to the knee and coated in blood from where she had broken her leg earlier. Her hair was in a mass of tatters around her head, and she even looked like she had a black eye coming in, but I wasn't sure where that had come from.

"You can use the main bathroom," I told her, pointing her over to the bathroom which Jacob used. There seemed something wrong about her using it, but I also didn't trust her enough to give her free access to my room. "I'll find you something to wear. We should be about the same size."

I stood up and moved towards my bedroom as Cassia disappeared into the bathroom. After rummaging through my closet and pulling out a few things for Cassia to choose from, I was relieved to find all three of my mates waiting in my room for me. Setting the clothes down on top of the dresser, I immediately walked into Grey's waiting arms, and he pulled me down onto his lap where he sat on the edge of my bed.

"I don't like this," he murmured as he dropped his head into my neck and nuzzled against my skin.

I held him tightly against me, even as I felt Tanner and River press against us, seeking comfort as well. I felt their arms wrap around me, and we ended up in one big huddle on the bed. My wolf sighed happily in my mind. She was beside herself with worry for Jacob and being close to her mates was the only thing that could even remotely soothe her right now.

"There's no other way," I told them all because I knew they were all thinking the exact same thing. "I won't survive losing him." My voice hitched as I spoke, and for the first time, I willingly let the tears threaten my eyes like they'd wanted to since I felt that first tingle of warning rush down my spine.

He's just a little boy. This shouldn't be happening to him.

The arms wrapped around me squeezed tighter, and the

first sob exploded out of me. I didn't even know why I was trying to hold them in. My mates were the only people in the world who understood how I was feeling right now. I knew that because they all had a bond with Jacob. He was just as much their pup as he was mine now.

"We're going to get him back," Grey murmured into my hair.

My phone started ringing on the bed beside us and River passed it across to me to answer it. When I saw Sean's name on the screen, my stomach suddenly flipped over as I fumbled to answer the call.

"Sean?" I said, my voice shaking as I answered.

"Calli," he sighed. "I have news. I've made some enquiries, and I've established the identity of the clan that's moving into your area. It's Davion."

My heart soared, was something going right for the first time since I'd got here? I was aware of Davion's links with the underground. He was one of the clan leaders that openly stood against the Shifter Council.

"Will he help us?" I asked, almost dreading to hear the answer. Because no matter how much this seemed like a fortuitous set of circumstances, fate had been a bit of a bitch recently.

"I've spoken with him, and he will help. But there is a problem Calli. He only has a fraction of his clan in the area and … well he says there is going to be a cost." Sean sounded uneasy about it, but I didn't care. We needed all the help we could get and to be quite frank, I'd pay any price if it got Jacob home safely.

"Anything, I don't care. How many can he send to help us?"

"Calli, I know your parents taught you better than to just

blanketly agree to anything, especially when it comes to a vampire," he scolded.

"No, Sean. My parents taught me to do absolutely everything within my power to keep my brother safe. I've failed them up until now because I've been reckless and selfish. I will give him whatever he wants," I snarked back at him. And I meant it.

I felt Grey stiffen beneath me. I knew he could hear the whole conversation, and I was impressed that he hadn't interrupted yet. Even if he did though, I truly meant what I was saying. Whatever it took.

"Look, I'm at the airport and about to board. I know I can't stop you from doing this, and truth be told, in your shoes I'd be doing exactly the same thing. Just be careful, Calli. Davion is bringing as many as he can to your house. He should be there within the next hour or so. I hope you've got some form of a plan, kid.

"We're working on it."

Sean sighed, and I could hear the noises in the background of him moving through the airport. I knew there was so much more he wanted to say, but he didn't. The fact that he was coming here despite the danger it would pose to him, showed just how much he cared about us.

"I'm proud of you kid," he said in a way that sounded far too much like a goodbye. "You get our boy back."

"I will," I promised him. "Thank you, for everything."

It was the closest we would come to saying goodbye, to acknowledging that there was a very real chance that I wasn't going to make it out of this. I was about to walk into the one situation that I had been avoiding my entire life. But I would do it willingly, for Jacob.

Sean ended his call, saying that he would see me soon, but I could hear the defeat in his voice. He was worried, and I suppose, he should be. This was a stupid idea, but it was the only one we had.

I stared down at the disconnected phone in my hand, not really sure what to do next.

"We should probably get those clothes to Cassia, so she's not stranded in the bathroom naked," Tanner said in an attempt to break the mood.

I smiled, or at least attempted to. We were going to be okay, Tanner and I. We still had things to discuss, but if we could get through this, what point was there in staying angry at each other. Time was too precious for people like us to waste it on grudges and bitterness. It could all be ripped away from us far too quickly.

"Right," Grey said firmly. "Let's clothe the witch, get everyone fed and ready. As soon as this Davion character gets here, we need to be firm in the plan and what everyone's role is going to be."

I got up from his lap, and Grey took my hand as he led me out into the living room. Nash was sitting at the dining table, his head was hanging down, and he looked like crap if I was honest. I was still too angry with him to care, though. I felt like he had betrayed me. With the pack bond being so new, and with how unsure I was if they wanted me in it to start with, the pain of losing Jacob was lined by me questioning if I could ever truly have a place with them.

Hunter surprisingly was in the kitchen with Aidan putting together food for everyone. I should probably take the time to talk to him properly, given that he was apparently going to be around now. I had no idea where he was going to sleep, and we were going to have to figure out how to keep him out of the attic library. Urgh, that could be tomorrow's problem!

I looked around but came up blank on where Blake was. I

don't know why I wondered though, there was only one place where he was going to be, and that was by Jean's side.

It was nice to see that someone had taken the time to take the dead body out of the living room, though. They'd even made an effort to try and clean up as much of the blood as they could, but it was going to take a thorough cleaning to get the rest of it off.

Grey sat me down on the sofa and then wandered over to the kitchen. I didn't like how he was handling me like a bomb about to explode, but I knew he needed to help soothe his Alpha nature and it didn't cost me anything to let him have it. Tanner and River sat down next to me, and I ended up curled up under River's arm, while Tanner pulled my feet into his lap and started to rub them.

It didn't take long for the guys to bring the food over and spread it out on the coffee table. Nash seemed to hesitate before he came over to join us. I kind of felt bad that he felt that disconnected with the pack. A little voice in the back of my mind told me that it was an impossible decision, he couldn't have won either way, but that little voice could fuck right off, because right now I was angry and I had a right to that anger, at least for now.

I'd almost forgotten about Cassia until she stepped out of the bathroom. She'd pulled on the jeans and t-shirt that I'd picked out for her. Annoyingly they looked better on her than me, but I would lie to myself and say it was the difference in our skin tones that just made the colours seem different.

I waved her over to us, and she slowly took a seat in the armchair, almost like she was waiting for someone to pounce on her.

"No one here is going to hurt you," I told her as she looked around warily.

"Yeah, we need you to get Jacob back," Blake said coldly

as he walked out of the guest room. I couldn't blame him for being pissed. She'd come here to try and take his wife and unborn child away, even if she had been forced into it.

"And we don't hurt women," Hunter muttered under his breath.

I'm not sure if I started laughing first or if it was Cassia, but as we clocked each other's laughter, it only made our own grow until I was pulling that weird, uncontrollable laughter face that never looked attractive. I was fanning my face with my hands to try and stop the tears from streaming out of my eyes as Hunter looked at me like I'd lost my mind.

"Fucking hell, you really are new, aren't you?" I managed to squeeze out before the laughter rolled away with me again.

Cassia had some kind of laugh wheeze going on that was just making me laugh harder, and most of the guys were grinning at the ridiculousness of the situation.

I coughed and managed to get myself under control. Opening my mouth a few times to speak, but quickly snapping it closed because I could feel the giggles starting to bubble up again. It took a while before I was able to talk. "I'm sorry, I think I might be a little hysterical," I told him, realising the truth in that statement.

"Calli," Nash mumbled, and my spine snapped straight. "I'm … fuck. I know that sorry isn't enough for what I've done, but I'm going to say it anyway. I am so, so sorry. This is all my fault."

I wanted to scream at him. I wanted to shift and tear out his throat. He swore the same oath that we did. He promised to protect Jacob as his pack brother, he accepted him as family, and then he just let them take him away. He protected an outsider over Jacob. I loved Jean. I didn't know her, and I would do everything that I could to protect her and bring her back to Blake, but she wasn't pack. What Nash had done felt like a betrayal, and I felt like a massive bitch for even thinking it.

"Calli, please," he begged.

"No," I finally said, my eyes fixed on the ground as I frowned because I couldn't bring myself to look at him. "You don't get to apologise to me, and you don't get to ask me for forgiveness. You know what you've done. You don't get to ask for those things until we have him back with us."

I knew it was unreasonable. That voice in my head knew that ultimately this wasn't Nash's fault, but right now I was barely holding it together and I just didn't have the strength to do that and care about everyone else at the same time.

"Nash, we need a tracker for Calli. Do you have one at the packhouse that we can use? Something as discreet as possible?" Grey asked him quietly.

Deep down, I knew that Grey was in an impossible position here, standing between Nash and me on this issue. But it stung that he wasn't taking my side.

Nash got to his feet and left. I didn't know if he did anything else because I still couldn't look at him. River's hand landed on my thigh, and I tensed. I didn't know why I did it. There were just too many emotions right now. But I knew that I'd hurt him when I unintentionally did it.

I was glad that Sean was on the way. I needed him now more than ever. He was the closest thing that Jacob and I had to family. When I got Jacob back, I needed to take a long hard look at our lives. We'd been exposed now, to not just the Council, but the witches as well. It was time to run. Wanting to stay here, to give Jacob this place to be a home, was nothing but naive. We needed to cut strings and run. Sean would help us. He would get us out, and then it was time to hide. A picture of Jean sleeping in the guest room flashed through my mind, and I was instantly hit with guilt. Leaving would mean not helping her. But I had to start making the right decisions. I couldn't keep fucking up. Jacob had to come first. And to do that we had to run.

"Let's go over the exchange," Grey finally said, breaking the silence in the room.

"The meeting place is set for the location you requested. They will try to double-cross you. Do not trust them in the slightest," Cassia told us. "I will take Calli to the pick-up location while the rest of you go to the drop off point to collect the child. He will be left in the clearing as requested, and when Calli has turned herself over, they will allow you all to leave. This is the most logical time for them to betray you."

"I'm confused, why are we even letting Calli go with them. If we know the location and both of them will be there, why don't we spring our ambush at the exchange and just walk away with both of them?" Hunter asked.

"Because a death charm will surround the child and if they are not able to leave the location with Calli in their custody, then he will immediately be killed," Cassia said glumly.

"What's to stop them from doing that anyway once they have Calli?" River asked nervously.

Cassia just shrugged. "Nothing."

This was so fucked up.

"So, Calli goes with them to the facility. We have a tracker placed on her so that we can track her final location, and then we spring an attack on the facility?" Hunter didn't sound at all convinced about the plan. "We should request assistance from the Council."

"Don't make me start laughing again, Hunter, we haven't got the time," I sighed slumping back in my seat.

"The lady is right, the Council doesn't do anything unless

they have something to gain from it and there is always a price," came a voice from the other side of the room as the sliding door snicked closed behind them.

"Davion, please, just walk straight into my home," I snarked without even looking up.

"Oh now, I know I'm always welcome in your home, precious," Davion laughed, and I could practically hear the sarcasm dripping from his voice as he busied himself in the kitchen making a cup of tea. He'd better make me one as well if he knew what was good for him. "It's been a long time precious, I was sorry to hear about your parents," he said as he finally walked over to the living room carrying two china cups.

I was somewhat impressed that everyone else in the room just sat silently taking this strange intrusion in rather than, I don't know, at least attacking him. There was something about him though that just made you want to look at him. I'd never been able to decide if it was because of some unknown vampire quality, or if it was just because he was that nice to look at. Davion had taken silver fox to a whole new level. I still wasn't sure if he dyed the grey in around the edge of his hairline or if it was natural. It just seemed too perfect to be real. His dark hair was always cropped short and styled perfectly, the grey highlights peppering the edges just seemed to somehow add to his sex appeal. He was the perfect package of smooth grace with the muscle tone to back it up. Sean had once told me that vampires were made to attract prey and Davion had that in spades. Everywhere he went, women would flock to him and sometimes men as well. But I'd seen the temper that rested behind that smooth façade, and it was deadly. He was not someone you wanted to cross.

"Thank you," I mumbled as I took the tea. I never knew what to say when someone said they were sorry for my loss.

A part of me wanted to ask them why? But I knew that societal norms frowned on that sort of thing.

Davion perched himself on the arm of Cassia's armchair, and she shrank back away from him, clearly terrified. He glanced down at her and grinned. "Don't worry dear, I've got enough of my own shadows without taking a sip of yours."

"You're the clan leader that's moving into our territory," Grey said with a growl, suddenly snapping out of whatever trance he seemed to have when the vampire first entered.

"Technically," Davion said, taking a sip of his tea, "we're territory adjacent, I checked."

Grey glared at him, and I felt the soft growl vibrating against his chest more than heard it. I put one hand on his knee and squeezed it in what I hoped he would take as a reassuring way.

"Will you help me?" I asked him, keeping my eyes firmly fixed on Davion. He had history with the underground and with my parents, but I still didn't know how much I could trust him. He was just a bit too smooth and polished for my liking. It screamed façade, and I knew without a doubt that I did not want to see what lay beneath.

Davion's face fell in a true expression of sorrow. "Yes, we will help you retrieve the little one, but we will need to be quick if you wish him to be returned to you in one piece."

I nodded gratefully. He wasn't asking for his price yet, which was probably for the best. I'm not sure the others would be so happy to agree when they realised the cost would be so high. And even though I had no idea what he wanted, I knew it was going to be a lot.

Grey started to explain what the plan was, if you could even call it that. It was Hunter that seemed to be the first to break through the weird normality of this meeting.

"What the actual hell are we doing?" he suddenly barked.

Davion lifted one eyebrow at his outburst and Tanner shrugged, fake whispering, "He's new."

"He's a vampire," Hunter said, pointing a finger at Davion like it was some kind of accusation. "He's an enemy to our kind. We can't sit here and drink tea with him. He's not going to help us. He'll only betray us to the witches."

"Why isn't he pointing his chubby little finger at you?" Davion asked Cassia, completely ignoring Hunter, who was now trying to subtly check his fingers.

Cassia just shrugged, but she did seem to relax a little more with having Davion next to her and looked a bit less like she was going to throw up.

"Why do you think he's an enemy to shifters?" I asked, merely out of curiosity than anything else.

Hunter opened his mouth to speak and then frowned and shut it again. At least he's starting to think for himself. "They work with the witches," he finally said.

"Actually, witches avoid vampires. They do not wish to mix with the shadow touched," Cassia sneered at the end, and I was starting to realise that life for Cassia wasn't as easy as we all just assumed it was, which was probably why she had so readily agreed to help us.

Davion looked down at Cassia but didn't say anything. It was strange how he seemed to recognise the brand of her magic, and if anything, he looked concerned for her rather than anything else.

"Then why does the Council not ally with them," Hunter said, looking somewhat smug about pointing this out.

Davion just looked exasperated when he glanced across at me. I shrugged and reiterated Tanner's earlier comment. "He's new."

48

CALLI

As I stood with Cassia in the shadows, at the edge of the clearing where we were meeting the coven, all I could think was just how much of a terrible idea this was.

"It's going to be okay," Cassia murmured to me so quietly, I wasn't even sure if she had spoken at first.

I had a death grip on my mobile in my hand, waiting for Grey to call to say that they had Jacob.

I knew Davion was hiding in the trees with a few of his clan members to make sure everything went smoothly, but I still felt like I was about to throw up. I was about to willingly walk off with a coven who wanted to drain my powers. We'd made sure to buy as much time as we could before we left and I'd pushed as much energy into Jean as possible without passing out. I wouldn't be able to do any magic to defend myself, but let's be real, I didn't know any anyway. What I was doing, was buying myself time before they started to drain me. Cassia was sure they would wait until my power had returned before they would start, otherwise, I'd die far too quickly, and they wouldn't be able to get what they wanted. That wasn't as comforting a thought as I had first thought it would be.

We saw a glow of lights illuminating the other side of the clearing just as my phone started to ring in my hand. Answering it quickly, I was greeted with the sweetest sound I'd ever heard.

"Calli?" Jacob whimpered.

"Hey, little man," I said, tears instantly springing to my eyes. "Did they hurt you?"

It was one of those questions that I both needed to know the answer to and didn't all at the same time.

"No, but they're going to hurt my friend," he said, sounding a lot more confident than before. "You have to help her."

Trust Jacob to have made friends while he was held in captivity.

"I'll see what I can do," I told him. "I have to go with them for a little bit. I want you to stay with Grey, Tanner and River, okay. Do what they tell you and make sure that you always have at least one of them with you until I get home. Can you do that for me?"

"I think so," he whimpered. "I don't want you to go though," he added quietly.

He was always so brave.

"I don't want to go either little guy, but I'm going to try to come home again real soon, okay?" My voice cracked even though I was trying to stop him from realising just how upset I was.

Cassia was standing off to the side, trying to give me the illusion of privacy, but I could see how much my conversation was upsetting her too. A part of me was glad. She should see first hand just what she had been doing to other families like ours. How many children had she ripped away from their families? I didn't know how anyone ever came back from something like that.

"It's time," Cassia said quietly.

"Jacob, can you pass the phone to Grey for me," I asked him in a hopefully cheery way.

I heard the shuffle of the phone as it was passed to Grey before his voice came over the phone. "I hate everything about this, baby."

"I know, me too."

Now that I could hear his voice, I didn't know if I could go through with it. But then Jacob's face flashed to the front of my mind, and I knew that I would do anything for him, even this.

Cassia held out her hand, and I quickly said goodbye to Grey before hanging up the phone and passing it to her. I felt like I was ripping out my heart and giving it to her to hold on to for a while, and in a way, I was. I needed to be strong now, and I couldn't afford to show them where my weak points were.

We slowly walked out into the clearing, and I could see the shapes of two people moving towards us, blacked out by the lights shining behind them.

"Sometimes, I'm still amazed at how stupid shifters can be?" a voice sneered before everything went black and reality just seemed to disappear.

༺༻

Waking up in a strange place will always be disorientating, but waking up shackled to the damp cold wall of a prison cell was not an experience I ever expected to have in my life. These people were constantly surprising me. I had always just assumed they would kill me. Go figure!

I made sure to stay as still as I could as awareness slowly started to creep in. I couldn't afford to give away that I was awake until I was fully prepared for whatever they were going to throw at me. The deja vu of my time waking up in the packhouse basement with Wallace was strong.

Searching inside myself, I found my magic still in a nearly depleted state, so I couldn't have been unconscious for that long. Surprisingly though, something seemed to be interfering with my connection with my wolf. It was almost like I was listening to her underwater. It was muffled and hard to feel, but at least the connection was still there.

I didn't feel any pain apart from a few aches from lying on this damp floor. What I could feel though was that the tracker that had been slipped into my shoe was gone. My stomach wanted to rebel at the thought that I'd lost my only way out of here, but I swallowed it down. I couldn't afford to give away too much right now.

Turning my mind back to the damp cell I was currently lying in, I tried to figure out something that could help me. Anything past the terror that was building inside me.

I didn't even want to think about what the liquid was that I was lying in right now. What I was hugely aware of was just how much this place stank. It was obviously where they had been holding people, and from the smell, I'd say they'd been there for a long time.

I steadied my breathing to try and get the pounding in my head to lessen so I could hear what was happening around me. Whilst my wolf was subdued somehow, she didn't seem overly concerned right now which made me think that I was at least not in any immediate danger, you know if you discount the whole shackled in a witch prison cell part.

Straining my ears, I sought out any sound at all to try and get a read for what was in the cell with me. I didn't know why, but I had the feeling that I wasn't alone. The faintest sound of a shoe scuffing across the ground registered to my left. It didn't sound too close by, but it was definitely in the same room as me.

I tried to keep my breathing level, but I felt like my heart was about to pound out of my chest, and my panic was making me breathe heavily, whether I wanted to or not.

The sound came again, and it was almost torture lying here with my eyes closed. My wolf was strangely relaxed, and I was starting to worry that they'd done something to her. She should be as panicked as I was that there was an unknown danger in this room with us.

I didn't know what to do. I could feel the cold metal around my wrists, so jumping up on the attack was out of the question. I had only the faintest threads of magic left in me and no idea how to use it defensively anyway. Whoever was in here wasn't going to wait forever for me to open my eyes, and I knew that lying here pretending to still be unconscious was only delaying the inevitable. My situation wasn't going to magically get any better in the next few minutes. But even though I knew that, I was still terrified and I didn't want to open my eyes. The next thought that hit me made me want to sob—I wanted my Mum and Dad. There's a genuine chance that I'm about to die here today and all I could think was that I wanted the comfort of my parents. I wanted to feel their arms around me and hear them tell me that everything was going to be okay. I missed them so much that it physically hurt, and now more than ever, I wanted them with me.

I could feel the tears leaking from my eyes, no matter how hard I squeezed them closed. Sometimes, it felt like it was the only way for the vast ocean of pain inside me to escape.

I didn't hear them move, but then I was so lost in my grief right now, I didn't think I'd hear if they started to talk to me. But I felt the small hand as it began to stroke my hair and the little voice that whispered, "Don't cry."

It was confusing at first because this small hand and little voice didn't belong in a place like this—a place where people were dragged to die.

The first thing I saw when I opened my eyes was so much red hair. It looked like an explosion of curls had started to attack the little girl they were attached to. She couldn't be more than four. She was definitely not older than Jacob. Judging by the matted mess of her hair and the thin layer of dirt that was coating her, she'd been here for a while. My brain just couldn't function with placing her here in this nightmare.

Her chubby little cheeks dimpled with the cheeky, impossible smile that she gave me when she saw me open my eyes and her brown eyes glittered with happiness—I think my brain just exploded from the sight of her.

"Sweetie, what are you doing here?" is for some reason the only thing that I could think to say.

Her face fell, and her bottom lip started to quiver.

"I've got you, angel," I whispered, pulling her into me as I sat up and then pulled her onto my lap.

She clung to me as she wrapped her little arms around me, and I rocked us where I sat.

"Are you Calli?" she eventually whispered against my chest where she had buried her face.

"You're Jacob's friend," I realised, and she nodded without pulling her head away from me. I cuddled her tighter to me. "He told me about you."

She finally looked up at me with her big brown eyes. "He looked after me, but they took him away."

"We're going to see him again really soon," I told her. "What's your name?"

"Abby," she whispered, snuggling in even closer to me.

Had she been sat in here alone all this time, shifters thrived with touch. It had something to do with our animals. To deprive her of that when she was only a child was beyond cruel and frankly, unnecessary. Wasn't it enough that they had her in this cell? Why did they feel the need to torture her even more?

We stayed like that, sitting on the cold, damp floor, and she eventually fell asleep against me. I didn't dare ask her how long she had been here or where her family was. I didn't know if I could bear the answers while we were still here in this place. When Jacob had first said he made a friend, I'd dismissed it straight away. It was going to be hard enough getting out of here. But there was no way I was going to leave her behind.

Now that my impossible task had become even harder, I took the opportunity to look around me and really take in my surroundings. The cell we were in was an enclosed room. The walls and floor seemed to be some kind of rough rock, almost like this place had been carved out of the ground. If it weren't for the door that kept us inside, I would have thought we were in some kind of cave. It didn't make sense, but then I suppose that wasn't really something I needed to worry about right now. The only thing that I needed to work out was how we would get out of here.

There wasn't a window; the only way in and out of here was through that one door. It looked like it was made of metal, in other words, I wasn't going to be breaking my way through it. I was going to be relying on someone opening it. Would it be too much to hope that it wasn't locked?

I rolled my eyes at my own naivety. Of course, none of this mattered if I couldn't get out of these shackles, which were attached to the wall. Judging by the chains' length, I didn't think I would even be able to make it to the door with them on.

I should have researched some kind of unlocking spell or done anything in preparation before just blindly walking into this situation with the belief that I would just escape. I didn't even know how to pick a lock, not that I had anything on me to use as a lock pick—what had I even been thinking!

I looked down at the angel sleeping in my lap and realised that my lack of forward planning could be responsible for getting her killed.

We sat like that for hours. No one came to check what we were doing, and no one brought any food or water. There wasn't even a bucket in here, which made me more confident that the liquid I'd woken up in probably hadn't been water. I pushed the thought out of my mind and looked down to find Abby starting to stir in my lap. When her eyes blinked open, and she saw me, she gave me a shy smile.

"When was the last time you ate?" I asked her, concerned.

She just shrugged her little shoulders at me.

"Do you think you can stand up sweetie?"

She nodded and clambered out of my lap before shakily walking to one of the back corners of our cell. She must have been here for a while because I suspected that she was starting to suffer from the effects of starvation.

I stood up, examining the shackles on my wrists. Each one was connected to its own chain attached to a metal ring embedded in the wall. I tried moving to the door, but the chains weren't long enough for me to be able to reach it. If I was going to try and get out of here, I needed to deal with the shackles first.

Examining the locks, all I could find was a standard keyhole. Honestly, I was surprised that they weren't made or locked by some kind of magic, but these just seemed like old fashioned shackles. God knows where they found them. This wasn't exactly something you could buy off eBay. Or at least, I didn't think you could. Ewww, I really hoped they weren't from some kind of weird sex shop.

I was just considering shifting one of my fingers into a claw to see if I could work some kind of miracle on the locks, when I heard the faint sound of footsteps echoing outside. Abby whimpered and crouched down into the corner, trying to make herself as small as possible.

I wanted to tell her that it was going to be alright. I wanted to say that I wouldn't let them hurt her. But I also didn't want to lie to her, and both of those things felt far too much like lies right about now.

The sound of keys jangling together preceded the noise of the lock clicking open. As it swung open, it revealed one very smug-looking male witch.

"Awake already I see," he sneered at me.

His eyes flicked to Abby in the corner, and I quickly spoke to draw his attention away from her.

"I came here willingly, there was no need to put me in shackles," I said, shaking my shackled arms at him to emphasize my point.

"You came here because you were desperate and no doubt intended to double-cross us as soon as you had a chance."

"Well, you can't blame a girl for not wanting to just walk to her death," I grinned.

"Oh, but we have such great plans for you," he grinned back at me and my blood ran cold. "If you're as powerful as Cassia promises, then we can drain you to the brink time and time again."

That didn't sound like something I was going to enjoy, and I needed to get out of here before they had the opportunity to start that nightmare. Thankfully, I still barely had any magic, and I knew from experience that it would take at least a full day before I began to feel anywhere near to normal levels.

"Come along then abomination, it's time to prove your worth," he laughed as he approached me with his set of keys. "Oh, and just so you know, if you try anything, my orders are to kill the kid *immediately*."

I'd wondered why they had put me in here with her, and now it became glaringly obvious. She was how they were going to make sure I did everything they told me, and if they could assure me that she would be spared during my time here, then I absolutely would, without hesitation.

The shackles unlocked easily, and I was shoved towards the door, the guard keeping to my back. It was almost like he didn't want to sully himself by touching me and just wanted me moving as quickly as possible. My wolf stirred in my mind, but I could barely feel her reaction to what I knew would typically enrage her. Something was very wrong, and I doubted I would be able to shift right now if I needed to. I'd never felt a loss of connection with my wolf like this before, and it was terrifying.

Even though my first instinct was to be as awkward as possible, I calmly walked towards the door. I didn't even flick my eyes over at Abby for fear of drawing too much attention to her.

It turned out that we were at the end of a dank corridor. There was only one way to go, and I slowly started to walk in that direction.

There wasn't much light here, and the smell was horrendous. The air was stale, and the aroma of fear and urine lingered. A lot of people had been through this place. There were six other doors on this corridor; three on either side. All of them were closed, and there was the same small barred window at the top that made me think they were cells as well. I strained my ears trying to tell if there was anyone inside them, but it was impossible to know without being able to tap into any of my wolf instincts, or even my magic, not that I knew how to use it that way. If there was anyone in there, they would probably be making as little noise as possible with one of the witches down here. No one would want to risk being taken upstairs. Being locked in one of those cells might have been every shifter's worst nightmare, but I didn't doubt that it was infinitely better than when they dragged you out of it.

The corridor ended with another heavy metal door and whilst it was open and unlocked now, once we walked through it, my guard quickly pulled it closed and locked it again. That meant, even if I could get out of the cell, I would have to get through this door as well. I needed that bunch of keys he was swinging about, but I couldn't see any way I would get hold of them.

A set of stairs stood in front of me, and I started my way up them. Admittedly, I took them as slowly as possible, but the shove to the middle of my lower back when I'd gotten to the top just seemed like overkill, especially because I stumbled forward and sprawled out on the floor much to his amusement—dick.

The room up here opened out into one massive cavernous room. It felt a bit like a warehouse. There was a set of stairs at the very far end, leading up to a walkway linking what looked like some offices up there. I could see the shadows of people moving around in the windows, but I had no idea just how many people were inside right now.

The room we had entered was mostly empty apart from the middle. There were some metal drums that had been set on fire around what looked like an enormous altar. I couldn't see much of it due to the small crowd of witches gathered around it. They were all wearing hooded cloaks like out of some teen movie and I couldn't stop myself from rolling my eyes at how ridiculous they all looked. They did match though, so you had to at least give them points for that. My brain ran away with me as I started to wonder if they had all gone to the same place to buy them, or if maybe they bulk bought and had boxes of them stashed somewhere. I suppose you'd probably need a spare for when you couldn't get the blood out of the one you usually wore.

Without realising it, I'd walked right up to them and was suddenly knocked down to my knees by the dickhead that was acting as my guard.

I felt my wolf surge again inside me, but it was like something was holding her back. She wasn't giving up, though, and she was fighting whatever it was that was holding her back so she could reach me.

The eight witches that had been gathered around the altar all turned as one to stare at me. It almost felt choreographed, and I had the ridiculous urge to laugh—unfortunately, I was one of those nervous gigglers, which seemed like an enormously bad idea right now.

One witch stepped forward out of the crowd and came to a stop a few steps away from me. Her hood was still pulled up and fell slightly over her face, but I could tell from the long red hair and her jawline that she was a woman. She quietly stared down at me until it started to get awkward, and I wasn't sure if she was waiting for me to say or do anything. I started to feel like I should say 'Hi' or something, but then I reminded myself that I wasn't here to make life easier for them and bitch slapped my British need to apologise into submission.

Instead, I just raised my eyebrow and continued to stare right back at her, or rather right back at her chin. Her flawless chin, she didn't even have the decency to have warts or anything. Rude!

"So you're the abomination we've been told about," she finally said, sneering down at me. "Not much to look at and I barely sense a scrap of magic in you."

She glanced around at the other witches, no doubt waiting for her groupies to reinforce just how big of a douche she was. A few tittered those annoying fake laughs, then one of them stepped closer.

"She was drained of her magic earlier when she healed another shifter and then me so that I could come and make the bargain with you, Aurelia," the cloaked witch, who I now recognised to be, Cassia spoke.

I knew she was a witch, of course I did, but there was a small part of me that still felt betrayed by her presence here. Which just didn't make sense at all. This was where she had come from, she'd already told me that she didn't have a choice but to be with them, even if I didn't understand what she had meant by that.

Aurelia continued to stare down at me, while Cassia shuffled nervously beside her.

"She is useless to us then for the next few days," she said, suddenly wheeling on Cassia. "We would have been better to keep the boy, even if he was a human, we could have used him to lure more to us."

Cassia shrank back away from Aurelia, and it became glaringly obvious just how terrified she was of this woman. I heard one of the others behind them quietly laugh at her unease, and my skin crawled with what these people were like.

"They will not be happy if they have to wait for what we promised them, the only reason why they passed us the information was because they needed this done quickly." Aurelia started to pace in front of the others, and I decided keeping quiet was going to be the best thing for me right now because I might be able to find out some information we could use at a later date, presuming I ever got out of this place.

"Why do you care about what they think?" a male voice scoffed in the crowd. "If she is as strong as Cassia promises, then we don't need them anymore. We can finally achieve our goal. Just because we agreed to work with them before, doesn't mean we have any need to honour that now that the end is in sight."

Aurelia just looked at him and nodded, and I couldn't keep the scoff from slipping out of my mouth. She spun around and lifted me up off the ground by my throat quicker than I could even flinch. She was faster than any witch should be, not to mention stronger, as my feet dangled at least a couple of inches off the ground.

"What could you possibly have to add to this conversation that you feel the need to interrupt us," she spat in my face before throwing me back to the ground.

"Not only are you cowards, but you're lying, cheating *cowards* at that," I wheezed.

It would have been sensible to just shut up and hope they sent me back to my cell, but I'd quickly realised there was no way that I was going to find an escape route from there.

"How dare you even think you are worthy enough to speak in front of our High Priestess," Cassia said, dropping to her knees and backslapping me across the face.

Slowly, I turned my face back to her, preparing to launch into all the reasons why she deserved these people, when she opened her mouth, and there sat on her tongue was the tracking chip Nash had slipped me.

My mouth snapped shut with an audible click of my teeth as I realised that Cassia was trying to help me—I also tried not to think about the fact that I'd had that chip in my stinking shoe only a few hours ago.

The giggler in the crowd started again, and even Aurelia joined in this time.

"Why would you think us cowards? Have we not proved to the supernatural world our superiority? We have found ourselves a new food source and you shifters cower in fear in front of us. That is not cowardice. That is the prey finally learning their place," Aurelia said, pulling herself tall as she started her 'big bad guy' monologue.

The sheen of madness flickered across her eyes as she continued to speak. "We were once 'the hunted'. The human scum searched the globe, ripping us from our homes and burning us alive for entertainment. But soon, soon we will show them. We already have the supernatural world cowering at our feet like the cowards *they* are. Next, we will put humanity on their knees as well."

I couldn't help it anymore, and the laughter just started to bubble out of me. Is that really where this was all heading? It was like every bad movie that had come before us.

"Global domination," I wheezed out before breaking

down into laughter again. "Oh my god, please tell me this is a joke. You want to take over the world!"

Now, I'll accept that maybe it wasn't as funny as I was finding it at this moment, but you have to admit, the cliché was alive and pissing itself laughing as well right now.

"Enough!" Aurelia roared, just as I felt her foot connect with my jaw.

I flew backwards and skidded across the floor a few feet. I'd forgotten that she was so fucking strong. Probably something to remember before I started to laugh at her again. Wiggling my jaw to make sure that it wasn't broken, I slowly sat up to find the crowd of witches sneering down at me. Cassia's fists were clenched at her sides and what looked like anger before now seemed like she was holding herself back from helping me.

Two of the hooded witches moved to Aurelia's side, trying to soothe her nerves like the sycophants they clearly were. But as they moved away from the altar, I finally got a clear view of it. The only problem, I wasn't sure *what* I was actually looking at.

It almost looked like one of the old stone tombs that you see in creepy ancient crypts, except the epitaph on the top was encased in crystal. There was something inside it, and whilst it was hard to make out, it looked suspiciously like a person. Around the altar were large chunks of crystal, too many to count, all evenly spaced out. It was ritualistic, but I had no idea what it was supposed to achieve. Were they trying to keep that person locked away? Could that be the answer to getting out of here? Was that someone that they were afraid of?

Aurelia had taken my moment of distraction to move closer to me and dropped to her knees in front of me. Gripping my chin in one hand, she squeezed it painfully, her fingers digging into the spot where her foot had only just connected. The pain flared through my skull and seemed to drill into my brain. Much to her enjoyment, I whimpered as white flashes of light momentarily stole my vision.

"She's radiant, isn't she?" she whispered, turning my face back to the altar. "They imprisoned her because they were afraid of her, afraid of all of us that would rally behind her. She wasn't just the strongest of us; she was the most beautiful creature that ever walked the Earth. She was made to be worshipped, and she will be. As soon as we free the Queen, the entire world will drop at her feet, and we will rise to stand by her side as she rules over them all."

Panic came to life inside me. This wasn't someone they were afraid of. This was someone they worshipped. If they were able to achieve this, it would be the end of shifters as a species. If she was as powerful as Aurelia believed, where would we hide? There would be no stopping them. All we had now was brute strength and luck. We wouldn't even be able to rely on that if the covens all united and organised under one leader. Aurelia was right. Together they would sweep across the country, and there wouldn't be a single shifter left alive in their wake.

"I'll see you in a few days, little abomination, if you're strong enough, maybe you will get the honour of being the first to die at the feet of our Queen."

She was laughing as she pulled her arm back, and her fist came flying at my face. Everything faded into blackness one more time, just as I realised how well and truly fucked we all were.

49

GREY

The fact that Calli wasn't with us right now was bad enough, but knowing where she was instead was driving me insane. My wolf was losing it in my head. He was ready to charge in there and retrieve our mate. I was having a hard time keeping his rage locked down, and I could see the others flinching every time he slipped through my barriers.

Davion was driving me crazy as well. He was standing with several of his clan members at the edge of the tree line. You would have thought they were here on a fun day out from how they were behaving. The next one to start laughing was going to feel my fist meet their face.

I kept trying to tell myself that they were here to help us, because they were—apparently.

Tanner growled under his breath and turned towards me with a look of exasperation on his face as two of the vamps started roughhousing.

"I know, but just suffer through it," I told him.

He gritted his teeth and paced away from me towards the others.

We had followed Calli's tracker for about forty miles until we pulled into a warehouse district not too far from the outskirts of Portland. It looked like it had been popular about fifty years ago, but now most of them seemed to have fallen into ruin. A couple of the warehouses were burnt out, and more than a few barely looked habitable. From a process of elimination, and the rough signal we were getting from the tracker, we were reasonably sure which warehouse Calli was in.

Two of Davion's clan had gone to scout the area. We were told to wait where we were since we would be too easily sensed by the witches. As Davion told us this, I knew he was right, especially because I could barely control myself right now, but it was still hard to accept. I needed Calli by my side. I needed to know that she was safe.

The five of us were waiting, either nervously pacing or stood, each of us as anxious as the other. I should be trying to soothe their nerves and reassure them that we would get her back, but it was hard enough trying to keep myself under control. I was going to be selfish, just this one time. If anything, I needed *them* now.

River and Tanner looked just as bad as I did, no doubt. This was pure torture. Aidan and Nash were doing their best to stand by them, but they looked almost the same as we did. I knew that Nash was struggling with his guilt over this whole situation. He blamed himself for Calli having to hand herself over, and there was a small part of me that agreed with him, no matter how much I hated it.

Deep down, I knew there was no one responsible apart from the witches that took Jacob. But it was hard to accept that when we didn't have her back yet.

Hunter was standing slightly separate from our group. His fists were clenched at his sides as he stared in the direction of where we assumed Calli was being held. I couldn't work him out. He genuinely seemed to want to help, but he'd come under Councillor Wells's instructions, and I didn't know just how much we could trust him, or if we ever could. Surely, everything he saw and heard was going to be reported straight back to the Council, and if not, at least to Wells himself. He was up to something, and we were now somehow getting dragged straight into the middle of it.

Almost like he could sense me staring at him, Hunter turned towards me, and I was surprised to see a genuine look of concern on his face.

"They've been gone too long," he said, striding over to me and then turning back to face the derelict warehouse district again.

"I know. But we don't have much choice but to wait for them now," I said. "We need Davion and the support of his clan. We can't run off half-cocked and without a plan of our own. It would put Calli at even greater risk."

Hunter just nodded, his eyes fixed on the warehouse. I couldn't work this guy out.

"I wish I knew if I could trust you," I told him as my eyes drifted to the same place, desperate for a glimpse of the clan members returning with news.

I heard Hunter's sigh, and caught a glimpse of him out of the corner of my eye as he turned towards me. He seemed to watch me, almost like he was measuring me up before he sighed again and turned back to watch the warehouses.

"This is a test," he finally said.

I didn't respond. There didn't seem much point to it. I knew he was going to explain either way. He'd already decided to make that leap of faith and trust me.

"Wells is testing to see how much he can trust me. He

knows that I may have been asking some questions before he sent me here."

I frowned in confusion as I replayed all of my interactions with Hunter in my mind up until this point. "But when you got here …" I trailed off trying to figure out what had happened in the last few hours and see them from a different point of view.

"I don't know if I can trust you either," Hunter shrugged.

"Quite the pickle," Davion crowed from behind us.

I spun around with a growl, ready to shout, scream, just do something really, other than standing here with my thumb up my ass. The grin that Davion gave me just boiled my blood even hotter.

"My men are here," he smiled, nodding over my shoulder.

Everything in me wanted to whip around and make sure that what he was saying was true, but my wolf was also fixated on Davion. He was the biggest predator here, and he was anxious about having him moving so freely around, essentially, our whole pack. The only ones missing were Blake who had stayed back at Calli's house with Jacob and Coby. Jean was obviously with them too.

The fact that I was staring so intently at Davion just made him grin wider—the fucker. It didn't take long for his two clan members to saunter up to his side.

"We had eyes on the witches, but the half breed girl wasn't there," one said casually.

The growl boomed out of me, and before I even realised I was moving, I had him by the throat. Picking him up off the ground, I shook him before growling, "You will speak with respect about my mate."

Davion just stood by and watched, intrigued. No one in his clan interrupted us. The clan member currently dangling from my hand by his neck didn't even seem that bothered about what was happening to him. In fact, I could have sworn he was smiling at me.

Growling in frustration, I tossed him at Davion's feet, and he just giggled as he climbed to his feet.

"Please excuse Nicholas, he is still young and has yet to learn the finesse needed for dealing with situations such as these," Davion said, reaching out and brushing some imaginary dirt from Nicholas' shoulder before he reached back and backhanded him across the face.

Nicholas' head snapped to the side from the force of the blow, but apart from that, he didn't move a fraction. He didn't retaliate or show any kind of anger, he just lowered his head and mumbled an apology to Davion, who had now just moved up to the top of my scary fuckers list.

The other vampire quickly picked up where Nicholas had left off.

"We were able to gain entry to the warehouse where the witches are located, and there seems to be a basement level we weren't able to reach. We're assuming that she is being held down there," he said. His eye flicked nervously between Nicholas and Davion as he spoke.

"Which coven are we dealing with?" Davion asked him.

"None, they're not members of any of the covens that we are aware of. I suspect that they may be the outliers we have heard about."

Davion rose one eyebrow in question but didn't speak. None of them did.

"What outliers?" I sighed, finally getting that they were waiting for me to ask like the assholes they were.

Davion turned towards me with a satisfied smirk. "We have been hearing rumours for some time that a group of witches have left the covens and gathered together against the Coven Council's rules. They are just whispers at the moment.

The Coven Council would obviously deny that anyone would make such an obvious move without their permission."

"Could they be making a move against the Council?" I asked.

"That would seem the most likely scenario," Davion shrugged. "It's not really our problem right now though, is it."

He turned back to his clan members effectively dismissing me, if I knew that I could do this without him, then it would be *his* neck my hand was around. Shaking my head, I tried to push the violent rage down. Something was going on with my wolf. He wasn't usually pushing so much emotion through to me. It was starting to affect me more than it normally would.

"How many are we dealing with?" Davion asked the second clan member. It would seem that Nicholas was well and truly on his bad side right now.

"Ten, that we could see."

"Then we need to assume at least twenty," Davion said, turning to gaze out at the building.

I had an idea for a plan, but I didn't want to presume to tell him what he and his clan members should do, especially since my plan would put them at greater risk.

"I will take my clan to breach the building from the roof. We will move down and take out as many as we can before the alarm is raised. Once it inevitably is, we will create enough of a diversion for you to take in your pack and retrieve your beautiful mate," Davion said, finally turning back to me.

I didn't argue because it was essentially what I was thinking as well.

"Fair warning to you though Alpha, you're on your own once you get inside. It is likely that a few of my members will get carried away once they get the taste of fresh blood. There will be no organised back up to assist you if you get into trouble. Once we get started, chaos will ensue. They haven't let their hair down for a while, sometimes I worry I keep them on too short a leash," he pouted, creepily stroking one hand down Nicholas' face who just leaned into it like a dog seeking the approval of his master.

Hunter, who had remained silent up till now, finally spoke up, "What end of the warehouse is the entrance for the basement level where you believe they are holding her?"

"North."

"How many were guarding the entrance?"

"None that we could see."

Hunter frowned, "Isn't it strange that they wouldn't keep her guarded?" he thought out loud.

The vampires just shrugged and then turned back to Davion who dismissed them with a nod of his head.

I was surprised that Hunter was so ready to run into this fight. I knew that the Council had told him to guard Calli, but I honestly hadn't expected him to care this much, much less risk himself to help us rescue her. I had the feeling that he was constantly going to be surprising me, but I couldn't decide if he was doing it because this was genuinely who he was or if this was some way to try and earn our trust for other reasons. Just his association with the Council immediately put him in the untrustworthy category for me, even though I knew that was wrong. After this was all over, I was going to have to make a point of getting to know him. I at least owed him that.

We wandered back over to the rest of my pack members who were waiting anxiously nearby. It didn't escape my notice that they didn't seem keen on mixing with the vampires. I couldn't blame them, Davion put me on edge as well, but they were only here because we had asked them to be.

I quickly ran over the very few steps of the plan with them—we needed to start planning ahead better. I could tell from the look on their faces that they didn't like it. We were relying too heavily on the vampires to draw all the attention to them. But, we were also relying on them to take the majority of the risk as well. If their plan worked as they thought, and I had my reservations that it would, they would be facing the witches alone, while we snuck in and out of the building. How were they going to feel afterwards if they lost clan members in this fight? More importantly, how was Davion going to react?

We couldn't worry about that right now, though. We just didn't have the luxury to. They were offering to help us, and we couldn't afford to turn them away. Besides, there was no way that we were getting inside without them. Well, no, that wasn't true. We would definitely be able to get inside. There would just be no getting out.

"It is time," Davion called out to us.

I glanced back over to where the clan was lingering, and I could see the blood lust already starting to form in their eyes. Davion really must keep them on a short leash if even the thought of going in there was starting to stir them up.

"Give us ten minutes until you enter, unless, of course, you start hearing the screams. Then it's probably a safe bet that they've already figured out we're there," Davion laughed and then they were all jogging towards the warehouse.

"What about the witch?" Hunter murmured as he watched them moving through the shadows towards the building in question. "The one that's on our side."

"She isn't on our side," Tanner sneered. "She had no choice but to help us."

I was surprised that Tanner, of all people, would feel that way. I would have thought that the fact that she had put herself at risk to get Jacob out, and Calli back out as well, would have at least softened him to her a little.

"If she has done as she had agreed, she should be with Calli by the time we are moving in. If she hasn't, then there is nothing we can do for her," I told him.

Hunter flinched, and I found myself even more confused by him, and even more certain that I was being played. Surely, there was no way he was sympathising with a full-blooded witch, not if he held any kind of allegiance with the Council.

Glancing back to the warehouse, I saw the last of the vampires slip over the side and onto the roof.

"It's time," I told my pack as I took off at a slow jog towards the warehouse. "Stay together, don't get separated, don't be tempted to chase after them and get isolated. We're going in quietly and hopefully slipping out the same way, but be ready for anything. We aren't leaving that building unless Calli is with us."

No one spoke, and no one disagreed. We had one goal in mind. We were a pack with one single purpose—now it was our turn to hunt.

50
CALLI

I woke up with a groan as pain shot through my body, and my stomach threatened to empty what little was left in it from whenever I had eaten last. Whatever that crazy bitch had done to me had made my head spin, and my link with my wolf seemed even further away now. I could barely feel her.

I realised that my head was laying on something soft, and when I looked up, I saw Abby's little smiling face above me.

"Hi," she said in her little voice.

"I'm sorry sweetheart. How long was I asleep for?" It seemed more sensible to call it sleep than forced unconsciousness.

"A little," she told me.

I mentally ran through a check of my body as the reality that anything could have happened to me while I was unconscious flashed through my mind. My clothes were still intact, and apart from the pain radiating out of my head, I didn't feel anything in my body that I was suspicious about. Just the thought made me desperately want to shower, though.

I pulled myself up to sitting, and Abby quickly snuggled

against me. The poor kid was starved of contact, and I couldn't blame her. She was bound to be beyond terrified being in this place anyway. Anger surged through me at the thought of what Jacob must have gone through being here. That crazy bitch, Aurelia, was mine. The fact that I couldn't feel my wolf's angry agreement at that thought though was worrying. What if this disruption to our bond was permanent?

I shook the thought from my head. I couldn't invite more problems. There was enough going on right now. What was important was concentrating on getting Abby and me out of this place as soon as possible. I wasn't going to let them hurt her, and I wasn't a massive fan of being sacrificed to whatever a witch queen was either.

Realising that I wasn't shackled this time round, I climbed to my feet and walked over to the door to see if I could find any kind of way of opening it.

"What are you doing?" came Cassia's voice as she stepped through the shadows in the corner of our cell.

"I was looking for a way out of this shit hole," I said, turning to where she was now stood.

Poor Abby had shrunk back into the corner with a whimper, absolutely terrified.

"It's okay, sweetheart. This is Cassia. She helped me get Jacob out of here, and now she's going to help us," I told her as I crouched down beside her and ran my fingers through her hair.

She settled a little, but her eyes were still wide in fear, and I could tell that she wasn't going to trust Cassia at any point in the future. I suppose I couldn't blame her for that, though.

Glancing over my shoulder at Cassia, I almost dared her to disagree with me. There was no way that I was going to leave Abby here. Cassia looked worried, in fact, she looked like she was shitting herself. I hoped that this wasn't the prelude to her changing her mind about helping us.

"The shadow touched are already here and entering the building from the roof," she told me.

"Why do you call them that?" I asked her, suddenly curious.

"Because that is what they are. They have faced death and walked away from it, but no one can do that without at least touching the shadows."

When she put it that way, it almost sounded poetic, romantic even.

"Why do witches not like shadow touched?"

"Because when the shadows touch you, when you bear their mark, they will inevitably come looking for you. And there are things that lurk in the shadows that not even the strongest witch wishes to face."

Okay, well kind of wished I hadn't asked that part.

"Your mates should be breaching the building soon," she said after we stood in awkward silence for a few minutes.

I knew it was supposed to make me feel better, but it didn't. This place was dangerous for them, and I would have preferred them to never come near this place at all. I just nodded in thought before turning to Abby.

"It's almost time to leave sweetheart," I told her, holding out my hand for her to take. At first, she just looked between it and Cassia, clearly not trusting me now that she had seen me with her. "Cassia helped me get Jacob out of here, and now it's our turn," I said again, hoping to soothe her fears.

Her reluctance stung, even though we had only met what felt like a few minutes ago. Eventually, she slowly got to her feet and came over to my side, where she snuggled against me again.

"We need to get everyone out," I said, turning back to

Cassia. "How many others are in the cells?"

Cassia's eyes widened in panic and flicked down to Abby before they returned to my own. She just shook her head, and the realisation felt like I'd been punched in the face. The others were already gone, which probably included Abby's parents. She held onto me tighter, and I could tell that she already knew.

What were we going to do? Where was she going to go after this? I looked down at her already feeling my chest tightening in panic before I shook it off and pulled my resolve around me. We didn't have time to worry about this. We had one goal for now, and that was getting out of here. Everything else could wait.

A noise down the corridor drew my attention towards the door. It sounded muted and far off, but that was likely because I couldn't rely on my wolf to help me.

Pushing Abby behind me, I backed us away from the door. I was surprised when Cassia moved in front of us, bracing herself for whatever was coming.

The sound of doors being flung open echoed down the corridor towards us, and that was when I knew it was them, and they were searching for me. Before I had the opportunity to shout out, I heard the lock being forced open on the other side of the door, and it was flung open. There, in the doorway, stood a panting Grey. His eyes were wild, and I could see the rage and fear warring in them before he strode into the room and pulled me against his chest, crushing me in his arms.

Tears welled in my eyes at the relief that I felt as he leant back and looked down at my face. His face creased in concern, and I wondered if he could sense the problem I was having connecting with my wolf. Could he tell that she was so out of my reach right now?

Abby peered around my side to look at Grey, and his eyes

widened in surprise when he saw her. I couldn't have been more proud of him though when he immediately knelt down to talk to her.

"Hey there, little one. You been keeping Calli company for us?" he asked, holding out a hand to her.

I could feel the soothing Alpha waves radiating from him, and I felt Abby's body relax even if she did hesitate before taking his hand. She still clung to my trousers with her other hand though.

"Let's go home, shall we?" Grey asked, not realising what he was saying.

Abby was immediately back at my side, pushing her face against me as her little shoulders shook. Grey looked up at me in question, but I could see from the tightness around his eyes that he already knew. There would be no going home for Abby. It simply wasn't there anymore.

I crouched down and scooped her up, holding her against me. She barely weighed anything, even for such a young child, it was evident that she was underweight. I felt a glimmer of a feeling from my wolf, but it was there and gone so quickly that I wasn't sure. It was just the echo of a feeling that couldn't quite make its way through the fog to me.

"Let's go and see Jacob, " I whispered to her, and she nodded against me.

I looked back to Grey, and he just nodded, glancing out of the cell door before he stepped outside. When I followed him, my eyes immediately fell on Tanner and River standing outside. Tanner's whole body wavered towards me, and it was like he physically had to hold himself back. I appreciated it so much that they were taking into account Abby right now, even if the only thing that I wanted was to feel their arms around me too.

I didn't know why it surprised me, but Nash and Aidan

were both standing out there as well, and the relief on their faces was touching. Standing at the base of the stairs to the main floor was Hunter, keeping guard and watching our backs. He locked eyes with me before giving me a firm nod and then turning back to the stairs. I had no idea what that was about, but it almost felt like acceptance.

"We move fast, and we stay close," Grey said, stepping forward and speaking to the others who started to move towards the door.

Tanner and River stepped to my side, and I felt Tanner run his hand down my back.

"Hey there," River whispered to Abby. "My name's River, what's yours?"

"Abby," she whispered, still pressed against my side where I had her sat on my hip.

"Hey, Abby. We're going to get out of here now, but it might be a bit loud and scary upstairs. Do you think you can close your eyes for me and snuggle in close to Calli?"

Abby just nodded and held onto me tightly. I pulled her around in front of me so that she could wrap her legs around my waist, and I could hold her tightly against me. She snuggled her face against my neck, and then she had me in a death grip, which was probably a good thing.

I gave River a smile in thanks, trust him to be the one to think about what it was going to be like for her up there. I'm not even sure I wanted to go up there, but I wanted to stay here even less.

Hunter spoke quietly with Grey at the bottom of the stairs, and they both grimly looked at the steps. I couldn't hear what they were saying, but it didn't look good. Nothing about this situation was good.

Cassia moved closer to me, again putting herself between me and the danger. Maybe it wasn't me she was protecting, maybe it was Abby. Tanner and River moved closer to my sides, and Nash and Aidan took up the rear.

We all stood nervously at the bottom of the stairs, waiting for Grey to tell us when it was time to go. I had no idea where I was going, but I was in the middle of the huddle, with my pack around me. They would guide me to where I needed to be, and I trusted them all implicitly.

The waiting was excruciating, and it seemed like everyone felt the same way as we all shuffled about nervously, the adrenaline rushing through us, pushing us into the need to take action.

Abby stayed gripped tightly to my front, and I had my arms wrapped around her, keeping her securely against my body.

"What's happening?" I whispered to Tanner when I couldn't take the waiting any longer.

He looked at me in question but then spoke, "Something is suppressing the sound between here and the next level. Grey and Hunter don't know what, if anything, is happening upstairs."

I strained my senses, trying to feel what they all no doubt heard, but there was nothing. The fog surrounding my wolf felt almost impenetrable, and my magic was still recovering, barely a flicker of existence inside me. I couldn't feel any spell when I was as drained as this.

I looked at Cassia at the same time that she turned to me.

"I don't know how to lift it," she said, sensing what I was going to ask. "They don't include me in things like this. It would take longer than the time we have for me to even be able to counteract the spell."

Grey had turned to listen to what she was saying and with a grim look on his face turned back to the stairs and slowly began to make his way up them. Hunter surprisingly stayed at his side, and it was strange to see him backing up the Alpha when that would ordinarily have been his beta's job, Tanner's job. Tanner was sticking closely to my side though, and he didn't seem upset about that. In fact, I'm pretty sure nothing would pull him from my side.

We all slowly followed, carefully placing our feet, trying not to make a sound. There was no way of knowing if the spell worked both ways, but more terrifying, there was no way to know what was waiting for us at the top.

Grey paused at the top of the stairs, his hand on the door handle as he looked intently at the closed door in front of him. I knew he would be trying to hear something on the other side. I also knew that if what Tanner and Cassia had said was correct, and I had no reason to believe that it wasn't, he wouldn't be able to hear a thing.

The anticipation was building as he slowly turned the handle and cracked the door open a fraction. Noises seemed to slowly seep around us, and the silence we had previously been surrounded by seemed more obvious and sinister. I felt a stirring deep inside me in response and recognised it as my wolf pushing through the fog trying to reach me.

After pausing for a moment, Grey pushed the door open and cautiously walked through. He was every bit the Alpha taking the lead with his pack at his back, but I wished he was safe and not having to go through this.

We followed through after him, the noise from before seemed to have moved further away, and there were sounds of fighting on the upper level. I assumed that was Davion and his people creating the diversion and my blood ran cold as I tried not to think about what that entailed.

We had barely made it out of the door before it slammed closed behind us and we were suddenly boxed in. There were only five of them, but Aurelia stood in front of us smirking at her own cleverness. Davion and his clan were nowhere in sight, but the sounds of fighting upstairs were still filtering down to us, so I assumed that she had sent some of her people up there to keep them busy.

The two witches behind us started to close in, and I felt River and Tanner spin, putting their backs to me. A quick glance over my shoulder showed that Nash and Aidan had done the same, and suddenly I found myself surrounded by my pack. It was comforting in a way, because I'd never had a pack like this before to feel like there was someone who had my back. But it was also terrifying. I didn't want them to put themselves at risk just to keep me safe. As Abby's death grip on me inexplicably seemed to tighten, I realised that it wasn't just me that they were protecting. She was so small, and there wasn't a single one of my pack that would put her at risk, even if she wasn't a member of our pack. They were good men, and they would fight to protect her, I already knew them well enough to realise that. Even Nash. He had been seriously injured back at the house, and he would have died if I didn't have the ability to heal him. He at least deserved the opportunity to tell us what happened before I judged him. I'd been too quick to judge, but at the time, with Jacob missing and not knowing if he was okay, I wasn't thinking rationally enough to be able to realise what was right in front of me. I owed him an apology. We just needed to make sure we made it out of here so I could give him one.

"If there is one thing you can always trust of a shifter, it's their extreme levels of stupidity and predictability," Aurelia cackled in front of us.

She smirked at me as she caught my eye. She really thought she had this in the bag. That we were going to go down easily. She had no idea what she was getting into.

"But you," she spat, whipping to Cassia. "Everyone told

me not to trust you. That the shadow touched witch could never truly be one of us. I should have known you would be the one to betray us, though. And after we took you in, us, the only coven that would let such an abomination exist amongst them."

Cassia's face twisted in the rush of emotions that surged through her. She almost seemed to be ashamed when Aurelia called her shadow touched. But by the point that she was done with her little speech, the only emotion left on Cassia's face was hate. She suddenly leapt at Aurelia with a shriek as a cloud of dark shadow seemed to wrap around her body before it whipped out to lash at Aurelia.

It was the breaking point that pushed everyone else into movement. The two witches at our back surged forward, and Nash and Aidan rushed to meet them. Tanner and River shifted into their wolves, circling to the sides to back them up. The two attacking witches, suddenly finding themselves surrounded, started to mutter a spell between them and the air grew thick with the rotten smell of corrupted magic.

The witches who had stood beside Aurelia advanced towards Grey and Hunter, pulling huge hunting knives from their robes as they grinned maniacally at them both. Grey shifted, but Hunter stayed in his human form as the two of them clashed with the witches coming for us.

I suddenly found myself alone in the middle of a battle-field, clutching a terrified four-year-old to me with nowhere to take cover and no way to fight if one of them came for us.

Aurelia and Cassia were lashing at each other with magic. I'd never seen magic used to fight before, and there was something quite beautiful about it. The way that the shadows seemed to flow around Cassia's form, gathering to take the impact of Aurelia's strikes and then whipping out to lash across its opponent. Aurelia's magic seemed to be adopting a similar tactic, but it looked very different. It was almost like it was supposed to be light, but it was dim and grey. It didn't seem to flow as seamlessly as Cassia's magic but instead surged in waves, almost like Aurelia had to force it into movement.

Sweat gathered on Aurelia's brow, and she seemed to be straining to get her magic to cooperate. Both of them were bleeding from various places where the other's magic had partially made contact. Cassia actually looked like she could win this fight until Aurelia pulled a knife out of her robes. Just as Cassia stepped closer for a strike, she plunged the knife into Cassia's stomach, with a cackle of insanity. Cassia's eyes opened wide, and her mouth dropped open in a silent scream. The shadows around her almost evaporated into nothing, but as Aurelia ripped the knife out of her, the last of them flowed to her stomach, seemingly trying to stop the flow of blood.

Aurelia dropped the knife to grab hold of Cassia's robes and dragged her closer. The sounds of fighting around me fell away, and I realised that I'd become so absorbed in the two witches fighting in front of me that I hadn't been paying attention to the others.

The two witches at my back lay on the ground. From the small movements they were making, they were both still alive, but the rapidly growing pools of blood around them seemed to indicate that it wouldn't be for much longer if no one helped them.

Tanner, River and the others backed away from them, returning to my side.

Grey had returned to his human form, and my eyes ran over him, relieved to find that he seemed to be injury-free. Hunter was in much the same condition, but unfortunately, so were the two witches they had been fighting.

At least their side was down to three, and most of us seemed injury-free. As the thought crossed my mind, Nash staggered next to me, Aidan's arm coming around him in support. I could see a deep gash running up one of his thighs. He shook Aidan off and returned to where he was standing at my side. When I caught his eye, he gave me a firm nod, trying to tell me that he was alright, but I could see the pinch of pain in his eyes.

Aidan just rolled his eyes, pulled the belt from his trousers and quickly started to wrap it around the top of Nash's leg, effectively slowing the blood that was quickly turning his blue jeans into a dark black colour.

"Let us leave, and you will still have time to save your two men," Grey's voice rang out, dragging my attention back to the scene in front of me.

Aurelia looked around us at the two witches laying on the floor and just sighed.

"Why would I save their worthless lives, they're clearly not worthy to stand in our ranks if you felled them," she said, before turning her attention back to Cassia, who was still hanging from her hands.

Like a creep, Aurelia inhaled deeply, dragging her face along Cassia's. "There was always something so intoxicating about your magic," she almost groaned. "Draining you has always been more of a pleasure than a chore," she said quietly.

Cassia's head fell backwards as she lost consciousness, and I realised that Aurelia had been slowly absorbing her magic right in front of us. The last of the shadows that had been trying to patch the injury to her stomach evaporated into nothing, as Cassia's blood started to slowly flow from her wound again.

A low growl sounded out of Hunter as Aurelia dropped

Cassia to the ground, discarding her like she meant nothing. But then that seemed to be her general attitude to everyone around her.

Grey and Hunter stepped back closer to the rest of us, and I heard Tanner murmur lowly to us, enough so that we could hear him but the witches most likely couldn't.

"Calli, pass Abby to Aidan. Aidan get the kid and Nash out of here as fast as you can. Hunter, grab the witch and follow them. River you're with Calli. Grey and I will cover your backs while you get out."

I knew exactly what that meant, and it was not a plan I was on board with. I wasn't going to let two of my mates sacrifice themselves to save the rest of us; there had to be another way.

"No," I whispered back. "I'm not going to leave you both here."

Aurelia stepped closer to us, her head cocking to the side in interest and I wondered if she was somehow able to hear what we were saying.

Movement on the other side of the warehouse floor caught my eye, and I realised that when the warehouse had fallen to silence, that had included the sounds from upstairs as well. A few clan members seemed to have made it down here and watched our exchange in interest. The red of the blood-lust shone through their eyes, but they made no move towards us.

"Return to the cells, and I will make sure that when the time comes, your deaths will be quick," Aurelia said, almost sympathetically.

Abby's grip on me loosened a fraction. At first, I thought she was getting ready to move across to Aidan, but then she leant back and her little hands came up to rest on my cheeks as she frowned in determination at me. Her little nose scrunched up in concentration, and that coupled with her mad, curly red hair, made her look like the cutest little thing.

I didn't feel it at first, but then that small glimmer of my own magic that I had felt earlier flared brighter inside me.

My eyes widened in shock as I looked at Abby again, realising what she was doing. She was like me. She was feeding my magic with her own. It wasn't much because she was so small, but it was enough for the connection with my wolf to clear a bit more and my magic to feel more solid inside me.

When she was done, she sagged against me in exhaustion, and I was so lost in the fog of confusion that I almost missed it when Tanner suddenly said, "Go!"

Everyone moved at once, Aidan took Abby from my arms and swung her around to his back where she held on as tightly as she could. Tanner and Grey shifted and flung themselves at Aurelia and the two remaining witches. Aurelia staggered back, caught off guard by the sudden movement and Hunter was there, swooping in to scoop Cassia up off the ground.

I felt River's hand close around my upper arm, and my eyes swung to meet his. I could already see his acceptance there. He knew I wasn't going to run from this. "Nash needs your help," I told him.

A look of desperation moved across his face, but then he nodded and stepped away from me, scooping one of Nash's arms over his shoulders and helping him move as quickly as they both could towards the exit.

Three witches were standing against us, including Aurelia, and as much as Tanner and Grey were trying, they couldn't distract them all, and the witches knew it. As the witches surged forward, two of them moved in on Grey and Tanner, and Aurelia slipped out of the crowd, strolling calmly towards me. The grin on her face made me want to slap her, and I almost wanted to laugh at the fact that I was about to. She was underestimating me. She still thought that I was drained and with no access to my wolf, but now, thanks to Abby, I had something to fight back with. I could feel my wolf closer to the surface, lending me as much of her strength as she could push through our fragile connection, but I wasn't strong enough that I could afford to give away the very small advantage I had.

I felt Aurelia's magic reach out and wrap around me as she walked a few steps closer, it almost felt familiar, but then the corrupted stench of it reached me, and I grimaced in disgust.

"Such a tasty little treat you were," she laughed. "I think I might keep you. Rather than draining you for our queen, I think I will take the lives of your pack instead. Then, I can keep you in a cage and drain you to the brink again and again and again for no reason but for my own amusement," she grinned, as she took another step towards me.

That was when I realised why her magic had a glimmer of familiarity to it, because it was mine. I could work with that.

Tired of her inane chatter and idle threats, I bared my teeth. My wolf was pissed, and so was I. This wasn't going to happen on her terms.

I dived for her, giving her no chance to reach for her magic. Grabbing her robes in both hands, I tackled her with all of my strength, throwing her to the ground. Tactically it was stupid, but there was something down here that I needed. Coming back to her senses, she lashed out with her magic, and I felt the burn as it slashed across my skin like acid being thrown over me. With a yelp, I shoved her away from me, and she fell onto her back, cackling in glee.

"You think too much like a wolf," she laughed, as she

slowly climbed to her feet and brushed down her robes. "Always going for brute strength because you don't have the necessary skill to learn how to wield what you hold inside."

She could think what she wanted. I'd closed my hand around what I needed, and as I climbed to my feet, I slipped it into the back of the waistband of my jeans.

I growled lowly, keeping my eyes fixed firmly on her. Out of the corner of my eye, I could see Grey and Tanner circling the two remaining witches, keeping them occupied enough that they couldn't interfere. The urge to start to circle Aurelia was strong, but I could see the red glow of the clan members' eyes slowly closing in on us, and I didn't want her to know that we were about to have company. It was the only way I could see we had any chance of getting out of here.

The smell of Aurelia's corrupted magic started to fill the air again, and it struck a chord of sadness with me to feel my own magic corrupted and twisted into something evil when this woman used it.

"It is quite ironic, don't you think? That I will take away your freedom using your own magic," she grinned as she said it, taking a step closer, so she was nearly in arms reach.

Aurelia's main problem though was the fact that she was just so fucking cocky. She'd drunk so much of the kool-aid that her brain was starting to be pickled by it. She was so convinced of her own superiority that she was blind to everything else happening around her.

I shrank back from her, making it look like I was cowering in fear, making it seem like I was buying into her bullshit.

The satisfaction and pride that shone in her eyes made me want to throw up. But it also made me want to laugh in her face as she took the bait and stepped closer.

She reached out to grab hold of my shirt just as I slipped

my hand behind my back and grabbed the handle of the knife. It was almost too easy to pull it free and plunge it into her stomach as she dragged me closer to her, pushing her own knife into her.

At first, she didn't react, but then she slowly lowered her eyes to the handle of the knife that I was holding in my hand, sticking straight into her gut all the way to the hilt. When her eyes met mine, it was my turn to grin.

"You have something that belongs to me," I told her as my free hand wrapped around her throat.

Squeezing tightly, I reached down with my senses, finding that small piece of magic she had managed to steal from me and ripped it free. I could feel Cassia's magic trying to follow mine, but I pushed it back down. There was something dark and twisted about that magic, and I didn't want it. I didn't want to risk the corruption that Aurelia and the others seemed so happy to submerge themselves in.

As I reclaimed that small part of me she had stolen, the connection with my wolf slammed back into existence in its full strength. It was comforting to be able to completely feel her presence again, but with the sudden surge of her presence came the sudden rush of rage.

Before I even realised what I was doing, I twisted the knife inside her, and she finally broke, screaming out in pain.

This was the person who had targeted my pack. She was responsible for taking Abby's parents away from her. She was the reason why Jean and Blake's baby was clinging to life. But the worst of her crimes was the fact that she had ripped Jacob out of his home and put him in that small, dank fucking cell where he would have been terrified.

My vision flashed white with rage, and I felt myself pull the knife out of her and plunge it back in again. It was almost like I wasn't in control of my body, even though I knew that wasn't really the case.

I heard a bellow of rage come from one of the witches facing off with Tanner and Grey, and I knew that my time was growing short before they tried to force their way through to me.

Aurelia locked eyes with me, almost like she couldn't quite believe what was happening. I pulled the knife from her body one last time, and with a grin, shoved her with all my strength into the waiting arms of the clan members who had gathered behind us.

The vampires immediately locked onto her, dragging Aurelia down to the ground as she screamed in rage, trying to fight them off. It was no use, though. The more she bled, the greater their blood lust.

I took a step back, shocked at what I had just done. My eyes locked onto the thrashing Aurelia on the ground as she tried to push the feasting vampires away from her. The two witches rushed past me, paying me no attention now, as they dived into the fray desperate to try and reach their insane leader. Hands grabbed my shoulders, but I didn't fight them. I could already tell it was Grey as he gently pulled me away from the horror in front of me. Just before I turned to leave, I caught sight of Davion standing in the shadows off to the side. The light was just enough to catch the soft smile on his face and the red glow of blood lust in his eyes.

As the smell of corrupted magic started to fill the air again, Grey pulled me away, and I turned and followed them out of the warehouse in a daze.

I would probably regret what I'd done in the morning, but right now, there was nothing but the glow of satisfaction from my wolf for having dispatched a threat to our pack, to Jacob.

51

GREY

Calli had been quiet for the entire ride home while she was sandwiched between River and Tanner on the back seat in the truck. She looked like she was in shock about what had happened. Calli wasn't the type to resort to violence, except in defence of Jacob. When she came out of the shock tomorrow, we needed to make sure that she realised she had done the right thing. Jacob would never be safe if she hadn't done it. Hell, Calli would never have been safe. Aurelia would never have stopped.

I pulled into Calli's driveway, and we parked behind Aidan's truck. At least we knew the others had made it back safely. River had been the only one waiting for us outside the warehouse, having sent the others ahead in Aidan's truck. He was just about to storm back inside when we had burst through the door in our escape.

As I turned off the engine, we all just sat there stunned. The past twenty-four hours had been the worst of my life. When I realised that Calli was still inside with us, and that Aurelia was targeting her, I nearly lost control of my wolf. It was only because I was determined not to let the others get past us, that I was able to hold my concentration.

I'd seen that bastard Davion hanging back in the shadows as well, watching to see how it all played out. I wouldn't be surprised if he'd been holding back his clan until the last minute. He'd implied there would be no stopping them once they got inside, but they seemed happy enough watching us with Aurelia without going into some kind of crazed feeding frenzy. Just that thought made me shudder though as images of them descending on Aurelia passed through my mind. Fucking hell, I hoped something like that hadn't happened to James. I like the guy, and he was good with Jacob. But even if I didn't, I wouldn't wish that on my worst enemy, no, that's a lie, I'd probably wish it on Tanner's Dad.

I didn't know how long we sat in that silent truck, but when the front door was flung open, and Jacob sprinted outside, we all moved at once.

Calli inexplicably reached him first, and I couldn't work out how she'd got out the car so quickly when she'd been sat in the middle. But she dropped to her knees in the driveway, and Jacob flung himself into her arms.

In between sobs and giggles, he finally managed to say, "You saved her."

At first, I thought he was talking to us about getting Calli out of there, but then he looked at Calli and added, "But she really needs a bath, and she won't go without you."

Calli laughed and scooped Jacob up into her arms as she stood up. He wrapped his arms and legs around her like a baby monkey and buried his face into her neck, inhaling her scent deeply.

The rest of us then moved as one, all wrapping our arms around the two of them, relishing the fact that we had our mate and our pup safe at home and in our arms. Mimicking

Jacob, I inhaled the scent of Calli mixing with Jacob, and for the first time in what had to be twenty-four hours, I finally felt my wolf settle.

Here at home, we were safe. Calli's wards still held firm and she would know if anyone breached them. None of us would be leaving any time soon, and no one would be left vulnerable for a very long time to come. We had learnt a lesson here today. The pack was vulnerable when we didn't stick together, and we needed to be more cautious. Even with the threat against Calli and Jacob, we had been too at ease here on our packlands, and we needed to be more on guard. We were a small pack, and we couldn't afford to keep taking the risks that we had.

The first thing we needed to do was get everyone keyed into the warding, and that was going to be the first job on the books for tomorrow. But for now, I just needed to get inside, feed my mate and then fall asleep with her in my arms with my brothers at my side.

"You're squishing me," grumbled Jacob from in the middle of us all.

Everyone laughed and stepped back to allow him some breathing room, and we all moved to go inside the house. What we saw when we got inside was nothing short of chaos.

Nash was sitting at the dining room table, while Aidan was looking at his leg. A very pale Cassia was laid on the couch with Hunter sitting beside her, holding her hand. He gave me a grim look when we walked through the door and then shook his head. My heart fell for the witch who had given so much to help us even when she didn't know us. Because it was obvious what he meant; she wasn't going to make it.

"Oh, for god's sake," grumbled Calli, putting Jacob down

on the ground and striding over to the sofa. "When are you going to learn?"

Calli moved Hunter out of the way and then sat on the edge of the sofa, placing her hands on Cassia's stomach. I watched as her face slowly relaxed and then the tension slowly drained out of her body. Calli was so beautiful when she was healing someone. It was like she went into a state of complete calm, and you could see every ounce of stress and tension drain out of her as she opened herself up to her magic. The faint smell of lilacs and twilight jasmine filled the air, and I breathed in deeply of the comforting scent that was my mate's magic. It was nothing like the rotting smell of the other witches we had faced.

Cassia's body relaxed under her touch, but she didn't wake when Calli pulled her hands back.

"Is she … is she gone?" Hunter asked. He looked beside himself with worry, and it just added to my confusion about him. I could not work this wolf out.

"Gone? Have some faith man, she's just asleep," Calli scoffed. "I don't have much magic left, but I had enough to pull her out of danger. She's not fully healed yet though, so I wouldn't recommend you move her. We'll have to make her comfortable here, and I'll try and do some more in the morning."

Hunter nodded and then rushed to Cassia's side, putting her head on another pillow and tucking the blanket from the back of the sofa around her.

Calli backed away, looking at him like he was crazy, before moving over to where Nash had sagged against the dining table.

"I'm sorry Nash, I don't have anything left in me," she said, kneeling down to examine his thigh.

The gash he'd received in the fight was deep, and it

looked nasty. Aidan was busy stitching him up, much to Nash's pained annoyance.

"Believe it or not Calli," Aidan chuckled as he looked up from his stitching. "We did get injured before you arrived and we dealt with it the old fashioned way," he laughed, slapping Nash on his thigh, which just made him start swearing and then hold his breath, ultimately turning red when he realised that Jacob was still with us.

Laughing, I pulled Calli up from where she was knelt and back into my arms. "Where's Blake and Coby?" I asked Aidan.

"They're playing Lego with Abby in my room," Jacob helpfully told me.

I grinned down at him, and I could tell that Tanner knew exactly where this was going.

"Well, it must be love if you're sharing your Lego with her already," I said, teasing him.

Jacob though, surprising us all, just scrunched his face up in concentration before giving us a serious nod and walking back to his room.

"I'm not sure what just happened, but it was definitely not how I thought that was going to go," I said confused.

Calli just laughed and followed her brother, and I trailed behind them trying to understand if my five-year-old pup had just admitted to being in love.

We found everyone working on what looked to be an enormous castle in the middle of Jacob's bedroom floor. It was the first time I had seen Coby actually look like he was having fun, but he immediately turned serious as soon as he saw me standing in the doorway. I couldn't work out if he were doing it because he wanted me to think that he was grown up and ready to be a member of the pack, or if he just hated me that much.

"I'm going to check in with Jean," Blake said, standing up quickly with a blush on his face. I didn't know what he was embarrassed about though, we were all developing a pretty hardcore Lego addiction by this point.

"Hey Coby, I'm sorry I haven't got to spend much time with you yet," Calli said, giving him a soft smile. "Have you guys eaten?"

Coby just nodded his head, and we all pretended we didn't see his watery eyes. It was easy to forget sometimes that he was just seven. I knew it had only been a few days, but we needed to come up with a permanent solution about Coby and where he was going to live. Calli had been right. He needed a family, not just a pack, and we needed to make sure that happened.

"We had pizza!" Jacob informed us.

"Pizza?" Tanner suddenly added from behind me scaring the shit out of me.

"There are leftovers in the oven," Blake informed us as he squeezed past and slapped Tanner on the shoulder.

Tanner immediately followed behind him, the thought of food being the only thing that could draw him more than a step away from Calli. I couldn't blame him. I was starving, as well. It had been a long night.

I noticed that Abby was quietly huddled in the corner, not quite joining in and looking unsure of herself. My heart broke for her. I didn't even know if she was aware that her parents were gone. Calli had managed to fill us in on at least that much on the ride back here. This little girl was all alone in the world, and she was just like Calli and Jacob. My wolf growled in disagreement in my head, and I couldn't agree with him more. She wasn't alone, she would be pack, and we would care for her like her parents would have wanted us to.

Calli crouched down in front of Abby, and the little girl

locked fierce eyes with her. It was almost like she was waiting for us to tell her that it was time to go.

"Shall we go play in the bath for a bit?" Calli asked, and she visibly relaxed before nodding. "We might need to borrow some pyjamas from Jacob, but we can get you some of your own stuff tomorrow, okay?"

Calli reached out her hand, and Abby immediately dived into her open arms. As Calli headed into the bathroom with Abby, Jacob shuffled about uneasily on the floor.

"You okay, little man?" I asked him.

He nodded, his eyes flicking to the door and then back to me.

"She's going to be right back," I told him, but I could tell that it wasn't causing him any comfort.

River stepped past me and crouched down beside Jacob. "Is your wolf telling you something, Jacob?" he asked him.

Jacob just nodded but didn't say anything. He looked confused, and I wasn't sure if he even realised what it was that his wolf was trying to tell him.

"Shall we find Abby some pyjamas for when she's finished with her bath?" River asked Jacob, and he nodded and started rummaging through his closet.

I looked down at Coby who was sitting awkwardly on the floor still, just staring down at his feet. We weren't doing a good enough job with him. We were failing him.

"Can Coby stay for a sleepover too?" Jacob asked, sticking his head out of the closet with an armful of pyjamas.

"Of course," I smiled, and Coby seemed to brighten a little.

"There are extra blankets and pillows in the storeroom down in the basement," Calli shouted out of the bathroom over the sound of running water.

"Fancy giving me a hand?" I asked Coby, who grinned and jumped up from where he sat.

It took us an hour to get all the kids sorted and tucked up in their beds. Calli and I stood in the doorway of Jacob's room watching him and Abby as they cuddled close to each other, sleeping in Jacob's bed. We had tried to set up a bed for one of them on the floor with Coby, but Jacob wouldn't hear of it. He wanted Abby with him and suggesting otherwise only seemed to upset both of them. In the end, it had just been easier to let them sleep in the same bed, but it wasn't exactly a long term solution. It was also something to worry about tomorrow because we were all starting to feel the exhaustion of the day set in.

"Let's head to bed," I whispered to Calli, pulling her against my side as she gazed up at me with a content smile on her face.

"It's sweet of you to offer, but I'm not one to go for crossing swords with someone I don't know yet," I heard Davion cackle from the dining table.

I sagged against Calli for a brief moment. We couldn't just have tonight. Rolling my eyes to the ceiling and wrapping my resolve around me, I joined him over at the table.

"Dude, it's called knocking, you need to learn about it," Tanner grumbled as he dropped down into a seat.

"Ah, as right as you are, your friend let me in this time. He was with the limpy one," Davion shrugged.

I looked around and realised that Nash and Aidan were both gone and must have headed back to the packhouse for the night. Blake wasn't in the living room, so he was probably still with Jean and Hunter was still hovering around Cassia. Something was definitely going on there.

"Did you lose any clan members?" Calli asked in concern as she took a seat between River and me.

"A few bumps and bruises, but nothing that won't heal while they're sleeping off the feast they just had," he grinned, and a cold shiver ran through my body.

This man was creepy, in an 'I'm unapologetically a vampire' kind of way.

I think he saw the uncomfortable horror on our faces and it just made him laugh louder. "It's not all good news though, a few of the coven did slip away, and they took the freaky crusty chick in the crystal."

Calli's face drained of blood, and even though I'd told myself that it would all wait until tomorrow, I really wanted to ask her what was happening. My wolf was prowling in my mind in agitation at the thought of a new potential threat to the pack.

"Even if you had recovered the body of the queen, you would not have been able to destroy it," Cassia's voice murmured from the sofa.

We all turned to look at her as she tried to sit up from the sofa, as Hunter tried to make her lie back down.

"Will you stop doing that," she huffed, slapping his hands away.

He looked like she'd just ripped out his heart and I was leaning more and more to the obvious, and frankly hilarious, conclusion of what was going on with him.

Cassia struggled to her feet and slowly made her way over to where we sat at the table. I didn't miss the way that her fingers reached out and brushed against Hunter's hand as she passed him. Or the way that he physically relaxed when she did.

She sighed in relief when she finally sat at the table, and I found myself feeling bad for her. I could tell that Calli wanted to help her, she was a natural healer and it must be hard for her to watch Cassia in pain and not be able to do anything about it.

"If they have the witch queen and the crystals they will be able to raise her soon," Cassia told us.

"They don't have the crystals," Davion said with a sly smile.

"You took them?" Calli gasped.

We knew what the crystals were, but I wasn't certain if Davion did. Each one represented a shifter—a shifter whose life had been ripped from them. At about the size of a football, there were more circled around the altar than I wanted to count. So many stolen lives.

Davion just shook his head. "There was a slight mishap, and they were destroyed."

I couldn't decide if that was worse or not. Obviously, if they were a power source for the witches, we couldn't risk them getting their hands on them again, but there was something so callous about just destroying the last part left of those people. Two of those crystals would have been Abby's parents. They deserved more respect than to just end up as the shattered parts of a broken crystal. Davion's usual joking face changed to a serious look that I was certain even he was unfamiliar with.

"You would not have been able to do it yourself."

He was right.

"So, what happens now?" Tanner asked.

"The coven was nearly wiped out. They will need to recruit a lot more members if they are going to perform the ritual to gather shifter essences into the crystals again,"

Cassia said with a grimace. "It will take time, but make no mistake; they will do it."

We all nodded thoughtfully. This wasn't over. This was never going to be over. This was the reality of our lives.

"We need to find a way to destroy the queen," Calli said seriously.

I looked at her in shock. She couldn't be serious. We were a tiny pack compared to the rest. Something like this should be undertaken by someone with more experience and more resources than us. But then I really looked at her. Calli was the greatest asset that anyone could have. And who else was going to do this? The Council weren't taking this threat seriously. Even the underground seemed more determined to hide than do anything about their problems. Who else was left to take a stand and stop children like Abby ending up all alone in the world?

We may be small. We may be inexperienced. But we had the courage to stand up and do more. My mind started working with a plan of where we needed to start. We needed allies, and we needed information. Looking around the table at the people who were sat with me I realised that we'd already made a good start, we just needed to make sure that we kept moving forward. My wolf growled in agreement. This threat to our pack, to our kind, had gone on for too long —it was time for the wolves to start the hunt.

NOTE FROM THE AUTHOR

I really hope you liked the book! It's equal parts terrifying and exciting setting off into a new series. Don't worry, this doesn't mean that the Destiny Series won't be getting finished off. There are two books left to go and both are going to be released over the course of this coming year.

I really wanted to write a book that spoke about grief. We live in a society that deals with grief in such terrible ways. Losing someone is heart-breaking and soul-destroying. Life can seem like it will never be the same again. I know from personal experience just how much grief can, and can continue, to affect your life. We, as people, always feel awkward around someone we know has suffered a loss. It's almost like because we don't know what to say, we choose to just ignore the issue completely. People expect you to work through grief and, after a suitable period of time, just be over it. Unfortunately, it doesn't happen that way. I wanted to shine a light on how normal it is to continue to live with grief in your life. How it can affect you suddenly and spontaneously in reaction to the smallest of things.

NOTE FROM THE AUTHOR

If you have suffered a loss and you are struggling to deal with grief, please reach out to someone for help. It doesn't have to be a professional, it can just be a friend or a relative. There are some amazing support groups and helplines being run by volunteers who are always available to talk with you. You are not alone. Thousands of us stand silently beside you. There is nothing wrong with needing to talk to someone, or in asking for help. We all need it from time to time.

This book wouldn't have happened if it wasn't for the input of so many people. Kris and Em, you know I love you. I can't express how much your continuing support means to me.

Izzie and Lin, thank you for beta reading all my weirdness. Izzie, I never did change all those 'sat' to 'sitting'. I'm sorry, but I'm a weird English person and I just couldn't bring myself to do it!

It really helps me if you write a review for the book, so that I can make sure that you all like what I'm writing. Constructive criticism is just that, constructive. It helps me to get better at what I do. Just try not to be too mean because I totally will cry if you are ☺ Also, on a purely selfish note, the more reviews you kindly write for me, the further the books can reach. It also helps motivate me in the middle of the night when I'm on my millionth edit and close to pulling out my own eyes.

BONUS MATERIAL
DESTINY AWAKENED

CHAPTER 1

How did typical twenty-year-olds spend their Sunday nights? One thing I knew for certain was they probably didn't spend it hanging outside a third-storey window of some douchebag's McMansion at 2:00 am. '*It may be time for me to reconsider some of my life choices,*' I thought as I pulled the dagger back out of the wall. My fingertips held onto a deep join between the stones, and I pulled myself up on the convenient handhold. Reaching up, I slammed the dagger back into the stone wall above me. It easily slipped into the soft cement between the stones, and I tugged down, testing it had anchored, before putting any weight on it. The window ledge was just one more reach above me, and I didn't want to ruin all the hard work of scoping out the house by falling now. Urgh! Why did they always install a safe on the top floor? Why not in the nice one-storey pool house at the back of the house? The one with the easy access points and no alarm. It was just selfish. Making a thief work this hard for a payday was just rude! With one last swing up, I finally had a handhold on the window ledge, and let out a sigh of relief.

It was easy to take a moment to contemplate the craziness that was my life while I just let myself hang from the window ledge. You could find total calm in the weirdest places. My name is Aria Graves. Just an ordinary college student with a side job to pay my way through college and set myself up for the future. Yes, my side job entailed crime, but could you really call it a crime when it was for the greater good? I mean, yes you could, but it helped me to sleep at night. Most of my jobs were like this. Break-in somewhere and steal something from someone who didn't deserve to have it. I tried not to get bogged down in the details. My morals tended to be quite fluid, but I had my rules, and I strictly lived by them. I wouldn't take a life, and I wouldn't hurt women and children. Let's face it, there were enough people out there doing that without me contributing to the problem.

My boss, Marnie, was the best middle woman a girl could have. She kept me honest. Marnie runs a private security business, and I technically worked for her, sort of on the books. I did the shady jobs. I'm a "consultant". It meant I could get a legitimate wage for doing less than honest work. I even paid taxes. Also, it made me feel fancy when I said it. Her side business was to help women escape domestic violence situations. My not-so-honest job was to break in and steal a skeezy husband's leverage or assets. I got the impression that it was personal for her, but I didn't pry. She was one of the few people I let close enough to me to consider her family, which was pretty sad when you thought about it. I tried not to. I grew up in the system moving from one shitty foster home to another. I'd seen some shit and been through even worse. I hated it. I hated the marks it had left on my body and the marks it had left on my soul. I was broken, and I hated that I'd let them break me.

Tearing myself away from my inner monologue, I rolled my eyes at my depressing-ass self. Letting go of the dagger, it held its shape for a heartbeat before I let go of the mental hold I had on it, and it faded from sight. It was handy being able to access weapons in this way. It wasn't like I made them with my magic, or at least I didn't think I did. They felt like they were always there, and I just had to reach out and take them. So, I did. It was kind of worrying that my life had devolved into something where that seemed necessary. Normally I didn't concentrate on them so much, but when it was the only thing holding you to the side of a building, it was hard not to give it your undivided attention. I hated calling it "magic". It was better thinking of it as a boost.

Nowadays, people around campus would brag about their magical heritage being one-fifth of this or a quarter of that. It'd been that way ever since the outing. Ever since the supernaturals had stepped into society and declared themselves more than just stories, the world had gone crazy. There was a section of society that just plain hated them, but then isn't there always. There was also a section that idolised them, and it seemed like most of my fellow students fell into that category. Me? I'd rather just keep quiet about it. I'd learnt the hard way that it wasn't smart to draw attention to yourself, and I was all about living a peaceful life. Under the radar had always been the best place to be. When I was in the home, I tried not to draw attention to myself. The quieter I was, the easier life was. Don't draw attention, good or otherwise, there was always someone who would hate you no matter what you'd done, and you did not, under any circumstances, want that person's attention on you. It was a lesson that had been taught to me through brutality, more than once. But it was a lesson I would never forget, and I had the scars to remind me every damn time I looked in the mirror. I was such a cliché.

Most of the world embraced the supernaturals, once they got used to them, but that had gone to shit recently—another reason not to advertise my magic. In the last five months, nine people had, well basically, gone postal. Always in public places and the casualties were always high. The common factor? All of them were apparently part human, part supernatural. I had no idea what I was; I had no idea who my parents were. But becoming like one of those nine people weighed heavily on my mind. No one was bragging about heritage at the moment. The government was even talking about some kind of registration.

I needed to get my mind back on the job. I couldn't hang outside this window all night. Disabling the alarm on the window was easy. I didn't even have to try. Electricals always fried when I fed my magic into them. I'd learnt the trick when I was a teenager. Hormones, uncontrollable magic, teenage drama and apparently cell phones, did not mix. It was rare that I ever managed to get a cell phone, and the destruction of one was a disaster to my younger self. However, it did give you a good solid foundation for a career as a cat burglar in later life. Ha, later life! I was only twenty. I couldn't help but laugh at my jaded-ass self as I quietly slid the window up and stepped inside. The library was laid out just as my client had told me. The fancy plush carpet quieted my footsteps as I crept across the room to the painting hanging next to the fireplace. Who hangs a painting next to a fireplace? It just screams concealed safe. Running my fingers along the edges of the frame, I found the switch to release the magnetic closure and swung the painting open on its hinges, revealing the safe beneath. The electronic safe. It was almost too easy. One little zap and it even swung open on its own. This bad boy was like some supervillain safe: stacks of money, folders of documents, there was even a gold bar in there. The job was just for the photos, even if my client had been told she could have anything she wanted. Flicking through the folders, I found the envelope with the photos. Handily, he had even left the SD card in there as well. This guy was organised for such a douche bag. Blackmailing your wife into staying with you was a dick move, beating her nearly every day of your marriage was the sort of stuff that should get that dick cut off. Fortunately for Mr. Douchebag, I only stole for a living; it was tempting to make an exception for this stain on society though.

I stuffed as much cash into the envelope with the photos as I could fit, before shoving it securely into my leather jacket. It wasn't easy starting a new life, and his wife needed all the help she could get. It wasn't technically part of the job, but why the hell not? It was easy to climb out of the window and silently closed it behind me before I jumped and landed in a crouch on the grass three storeys below. The only evidence I had been there was the now disabled alarm and the broken safe. Even if he did notice in the morning, his wife would be long gone, and there would be nothing that he could do to stop her. Hopefully, by starting over, she would finally get the life she wanted. Hell, she deserved it after everything he'd put her through.

I stepped onto the pavement and strolled down the road, hands in my pockets as casual as could be. I knew that no one had seen me go in or out, but one of my many rules, *never assume you've gotten away with it until you actually have*, always echoes through my mind whenever I'm walking away from a job. There was no point in running. People would remember the young woman in a leather jacket running down the road in the middle of the night. You couldn't even pull off being a jogger at this time. Best to just be someone walking home from a party. My auburn hair was pulled back into a ponytail, and the leather jacket and skinny jeans were just enough for me to not stand out in a crowd.

Not that you would be able to find a crowd anywhere at this time, but it also made me just normal enough to be forgettable. That was the key. Try to be normal. Try to be forgettable. In passing, I could carry it off; it was only if people got up close that they tended to notice me. I knew that men found me beautiful and I hated it. I hated the way they looked at me like I was something ready for the taking. It made my skin crawl. When I was in the home, it had always started with looks, leering looks. I shook my head, trying to clear the memories away. I hadn't had an easy start to life, but I had survived. I aged out of the system, and now I was just another young college girl making her way through life. Or at least that was what most people thought. Yes, I did have a night job as a cat burglar, but a girl has to eat … and buy the necessities like shoes and lingerie. Really it was the shoes and lingerie that were the most important parts. What can I say, even a badass bitch like myself liked to feel a little sexy at times. I'd discovered the lingerie helped me feel better about the scars and hey, if it works, why not?

I'd parked my motorcycle a few streets away, and once I slid on the saddle and put on my helmet, I let out a sigh of relief and, well, basically lust. I really loved this bike. It was the most expensive thing I owned and the first proper thing I had bought for myself. I tried to stash away as much of the money I earned as I could; college wouldn't last forever, and I needed to actually afford a life after. Thankfully, Marnie was making that more than possible. Turning the key, my bike purred to life, and I rode to the rendezvous point to drop the photos with the client. I loved riding the streets at this time. No one around, just me and the night air. I wished I could get away with riding without a helmet, but I didn't need to give any cops an excuse to pull me over right now.

Pulling into the bus station car park, it was easy to pick out my client. Huddled on the bench under the street light, she was clutching the sleeping toddler to her like she was expecting someone to rip her away at any moment. She probably was. The new ID Marnie had arranged for them would keep them safe, but this last step, waiting for the photos before getting onto the bus, must be killing her. I killed the bike engine before I got too close, trying not to wake the child. All of this must be hard enough on her as it was. If she could sleep through it, hopefully, it would make it easier for her mother. I pulled the bike into the parking spot a few spaces away and took off my helmet. Usually, I would just keep it on and pass across the package, but this woman looked spooked enough. I strolled up to her and sat on the other end of the bench. "Marnie sends her regards," I muttered, keeping my eyes on our surroundings. It always paid to stay alert.

The woman whipped her head around to me, her eyes big and fearful. "Did … did she ask you to bring me something?" she stuttered, pulling the toddler tighter to her. I gave her a soft smile and slowly unzipped my leather jacket. I had the distinct impression that this was a 'no sudden moves' kind of situation. The poor woman was terrified. God only knew what she had been through to get to this point. Reaching inside my jacket, I slowly pulled out the now fat envelope and sat it next to her on the bench. She cast her eyes to the ground, and I could see the dim light shining from the streetlight catch the shimmer of tears in her eyes. "You didn't look at them, did you?"

"Not really, just enough to make sure they were photographs. They were the only ones in the safe, so I figured they were the right ones. It's not my business what they are," I shrugged.

She picked up the envelope, frowning before straightening her shoulders and taking a steadying breath. It was like watching her physically pull herself back together and strap on her armour. It was at that very moment that I knew she was going to be alright. She had the strength to get herself through this. I could see from the determination that flickered across her face every time she looked at the sleeping toddler snuggled in her lap. She glanced into the envelope, her eyes going wide and her mouth falling open into a small 'o' of surprise.

"I figured you deserved some help in that new start you needed. It's not much, but hopefully, it should help get you settled"

Not much was probably about fifty grand. If the paper bands were to be believed, these were $10,000 bundles, and I had managed to shove five of them in there. Fifty grand wasn't that much to relocate and start a new life, and it probably wouldn't last her long, but at least it would give her a fighting chance.

"Thank you," she whispered. She pulled a wedge of notes off one of the bundles and pushed it towards me. There must have been about a grand there.

"I've already been paid, you don't need to tip me," I smiled across at her.

She finally met my eyes, and a stubbornness flashed across them. "You have to take it. I wouldn't be here if it weren't for you and Marnie. If this means that you can keep on doing this for other women, then I want you to take it."

Yeah, this chick was going to be okay.

"As I said, I've already been paid. You need every penny you can get, starting over isn't cheap and you've got that one to think about." I said, nodding my head towards the kid. I might have fluid morals, but taking money from this woman was not something I would feel good about.

"You don't understand," she whispered. "Living with him was the worst time of my life. I could have survived on my own. I got myself into that mess. I didn't think I had a way out. But once Hayley was born, I knew it was only a matter of time before he would turn on her, too. So from the day I knew I was pregnant, I started to hide money. He never really gave me much, but every chance I got, I hid as much as I could. It took me nearly three years to get enough to pay Marnie and a bit to start again. I found out about Marnie from one of my husband's employees. He slipped me a card when Reggie wasn't looking. I thought it was some kind of sick joke, but I cried for hours when I found out she was real. Then I pulled myself together, and I started to plan. I started to retake control of my life. No more cowering in the corner. From that moment on every time he hit me, I knew it didn't matter because I was getting closer to escaping. It was the only thing that got me through—knowing that I had control of what was going to happen. I needed Hayley to give me the courage to fight, but now that I've reached this point, I need to make it mine. I need to be the person that Hayley needs me to be. I won't ever be that weak cowering woman again. Please, I know this doesn't make any sense, but I need to do this."

I could understand the need to have control after someone had taken it away from you for so long. I picked up the bundle of cash and put it into my back pocket. She was determined, and she didn't seem like she was going to leave until I agreed.

"Come on. I'll carry your bags for you so you can carry the little one".

I stood up and picked up her duffle bag and the small

backpack which sat at her feet, while she gathered the kid up in her arms.

"You got your tickets already?" I asked, as we walked over to the only bus boarding. The bags were depressingly light, but at least she had the cash now to help get her set up.

"Yes, they're in the front pocket of the backpack, would you mind grabbing them for me?" she asked, hitching the kid up further, so her little head laid on her shoulder. She was a cute little thing with curly blonde hair that kept drifting across her face. She definitely didn't deserve to be raised by a monster. This was the best thing her mother could ever have done for her.

I pulled the tickets from the front pocket and passed them to the driver for her. He took a quick glance and nodded, casting a look over her. His eyebrows pinched when he saw the small bags. It was blatantly obvious she was a woman about to run and he no doubt saw this sort of thing all the time. I slipped one strap of the backpack over her free shoulder. "Are you going to be alright getting on carrying her, or do you want some help?" The last thing we needed was for her to fall down the stairs.

"I can manage," she whispered as the child nuzzled sleepily into her neck. "Can you just put the other bag in the hold for me?"

"Sure," I put a hand on her shoulder before she stepped onto the bus and she glanced in my direction. "You've got this," I smiled at her, and she nodded before stepping into the bus that was going to take her to freedom.

I watched her through the windows as she walked down the bus and fussed with getting the kid situated in a seat whilst trying not to wake her. Once I knew she was busy, I pulled the money back out of my pocket and slipped it inside the duffel before putting it into the hold. When I straightened, I saw the driver watching, he just gave me a half-smile and a nod before turning back to deal with another passenger coming over.

I headed back to my bike, casting an eye out for anything unusual. There was no one around. It was 3:00 am after all. The bus engine grumbled to life as I straddled my bike. I waited for it to pull out before starting the bike up and pulling away myself. It should only take about ten minutes to get back to my apartment. My bed was definitely calling me, and knowing that I had to get up at 6:30 am for my early lecture was threatening to ruin my good mood. Leading a double life really messed with your sleep.

CHAPTER 2

The alarm screamed at me to get up and, fighting the urge to smash the shit out of it, I turned it off before rolling out of bed. I'd managed to throw on some sleep shorts and a tank top before falling into bed a few hours ago. I should have just slept in my jeans to save those precious few minutes. I was going to be one grumpy-ass chick today. Luckily, I only had one lecture this morning. Then I needed to hit up the library to finish off a paper. I figured I could get back here by early afternoon and take a nap if I really tried.

Stumbling out of the bedroom, I crossed the corridor, into the bathroom. The bathroom was old but more than enough for my needs. There was a sink in a small vanity, a toilet and a shower over an old tub. It was clean, and it all worked. It suited me just fine. I turned on the shower to as hot as I could bear in an attempt to wake my sleepy ass up. As I was stripping out of my clothes, I caught a glance of myself in the mirror before turning away in horror. Why is it that movies always show women waking up in the morning looking like a goddess? My naturally wavy auburn hair was now a nest of tangles, evidence of the restless few hours sleep I'd had, and I had some lovely dark circles under my eyes. Hopefully, a shower would wake me up enough to fight off a bit of the scary look I had going on.

The water was blissfully hot when I stepped in. I loved to have scorching hot showers. When I was a kid, there was never enough hot water in whichever home I was in. I always ended up taking cold showers. At least with a hot shower, I didn't have to rush through to try and limit my potential for frostbite. Now that I was blessed with the gift of never-ending hot water, I spent as much time in the shower as possible. I'd actually found it to be a good thinking place. That and the fact that shower beer is actually pretty good. Nothing like drinking an ice-cold beer while the hot water works the kinks out your muscles. Bit early for beer now though. I'd kill for a coffee, though. It might actually wake me up quicker. I hated the nights where I had to get up early the next morning and pretend to be a normal person. I was the most uncoordinated sleepy person. All I could say was thank god for electrolysis. If it weren't for that modern-day miracle, I would probably have accidentally skinned myself one of these mornings. I did not have the necessary wits about me to be able to handle a razor when I was this tired. Best money I ever spent.

I quickly shampooed my hair and then slathered it in conditioner to try and fight the tangles. Leaving it to do its job, I lingered under the spray for as long as I could before rinsing and grabbing a clean towel. It wasn't practical in my line of work to have long hair as I did, but I liked it, and I didn't want to cut it when I could just tie it back. It fell to just below my shoulder blades, and once it was dry, it always had a soft wave to it. Thankfully, apart from giving it a quick blow dry I didn't really have to do anything with it. I wasn't really all that good at the girly stuff like styling hair and makeup. I supposed it was because I'd never really had anyone to show me. My style of skinny jeans, t-shirt and leather jacket didn't really go with a girly girl look anyway. I always made sure that my legs and back were completely covered. That was where all my scars were. I wasn't ashamed of them; I just didn't want to see the pity in everyone's eyes when they saw them. I'd grown to accept they were a part of me. They were evidence I had survived. I just didn't like sharing that part of me with others. I suppose that was why I didn't form relationships.

I quickly dried off and ran the hairdryer over my hair before looking in the mirror to see the damage my sleepless night had done. Now that my hair was not resembling a bird's nest, it wasn't too bad. I dotted a tiny bit of concealer under my eyes to cover the dark circles and coated my lips in cherry lip balm. There wasn't any need for other makeup, thankfully, because I didn't own any. My lashes were long and thick already and framed my hazel eyes nicely. I loved my eyes. I suspected the flecks of gold were due to whatever magical heritage I had but hell if I knew what that was.

I flicked on the news while I picked out my clothes. The newsreader was the same as every other morning, and she didn't catch my attention until she broke into the speech her fellow newscaster was giving.

"I'm sorry, Carl," she said, holding a finger to her ear and listening to whatever someone was reading to her. "We have a breaking news story coming through from a mall in downtown Los Angeles. Yesterday evening a young male, who appears to be in his early twenties, had entered the mall and gone on what can only be described as a killing spree. The pictures which we are about to bring to you may be distressing to some viewers." I briefly watched the news story unfold. The inside of the mall was the scene of a massacre

"... twenty-nine people were killed and many more injured ..." This was bad. This was the worst so far. "... congress went into an emergency session last night to discuss the registration act ..." I did not have time for this shit this morning.

Quickly dressing in jeans and a t-shirt, I grabbed my leather jacket and bag before running out the door. With my "job" I could have afforded an apartment if I'd wanted to, but Alfie's gym had been a home away from home when I was a kid. As soon as I was given the opportunity to get out of the system, I took it straight away, not caring where I would end up. Thankfully Alfie cared. There were a couple of back rooms at the gym he had converted into a small living area when he first bought it before he could afford to renovate the top floor for himself. The first room was set up as a living room and had a small kitchen in the corner. The sofa pulled out, and there were many a night that one of the kids in my self-defence class crashed with me when they didn't feel safe going home. Then there was a small hallway which had my bedroom on one side and a small bathroom opposite. Thankfully it also had a door which opened out into the alley at the side of the gym so I could come and go as I pleased. It was kind of essential in my line of work. It wasn't fancy, but it was everything I had always dreamed of, a space that was my own.

I couldn't thank Alfie enough for everything that he had done for me. The jobs I did for Marnie paid well, but Alfie wouldn't let me pay him anything for the rooms, so I helped out with the kids' self-defence class. I usually got about two grand a job from Marnie. I knew she didn't charge people like the woman last night that amount. She made up the cost with the profits from providing security systems for big corporations. I usually did four to five jobs a month, so I managed to put back a nice amount. I'd been with Marnie for just over two years now, and I had over two hundred grand set aside. From the outside, I lived like a regular student. My bike was the only extravagance I had bought, and I lived pretty simply otherwise.

Taking off at a run, I made it to the coffee shop on the corner with about ten minutes to spare. A latte and a breakfast sandwich should hold me over till lunchtime and hopefully keep me awake for the morning. Today was definitely a giant latte day, and obviously that needed to go with an extra shot and caramel syrup, but the best part was a sausage, bacon and cheese sandwich. Mmmmm cheese made everything better. I ate the sandwich on my way to college and had just started sipping on my latte as I strolled across campus to my lecture theatre.

There was a strange vibe on campus today. Usually, people scuttled to and from classes, but there were always groups hanging out chatting, guys throwing a ball around joking with each other and girls fluttering their eyelashes and giggling at them. Urgh, gag! Even at this ridiculous time in the morning, there was usually something going on. But none of that was happening today. I slowed my steps, casting my eyes around suspiciously.

Everyone had no doubt heard about the mall massacre. There were small groups of people huddled through the quad whispering to each other. Shrugging it off, I went into the lecture theatre and got settled in my seat. It was the same one I always sat in. Far rear corner, good views of the room, no windows or doors at my back and clear eye sights to all three exits of the room. Had I mentioned that I sometimes got paranoid? Call it a downside to the job. All the other students shuffled in and took their seats. It was weird that the room was so quiet with just some whispers here and there. It was never a busy lecture because it started at 7:45, but it was usually more animated than it was now, even if there were only fifteen or so people in here. Typically someone was going on about last night's party, or game, or whatever else it was that entertained them. The hushed silence lingered until the professor walked in, unusually accompanied by the Dean and another man I didn't recognise. He wore an ill-fitting suit and a scowl that screamed cop which immediately put me on edge.

"Students, if I could have your attention please?" the Dean said, addressing us as he strolled to the middle of the room. "I'm sure over the last few months you have seen the media reports of the number of attacks on humans increasing and the debate over the regulation and registration of super-naturals."

Murmurs ran through the crowd, and scowly crap suit heaved a case up on the desk at the front, opening it up and concentrating on the contents inside. Something not good was definitely about to go down. I cast my eyes to the exits checking they were still clear. The fire exit opening to the quad was my best option.

"Last night there was an attack on a mall. Twenty-nine people were killed, and we are still waiting on the numbers of injured." The murmurs immediately stopped, and everyone just stared in shocked silence. "An emergency session was called in congress last night, and the decision for registration was announced in the early hours of this morning. Every student on campus from the age of eighteen is now obliged to undertake mandatory testing. Anyone showing full or partial supernatural heritage will be taken for registration."

My blood ran cold. This did not sound good. I wasn't going to pass this test. I cast my eyes across the front of the room and back towards the exit. Scowly crap suit glared at me from the front, took out his phone and quietly spoke into it before slipping it back in his pocket with a smug look on his face. All of the doors opened, and three armed police officers stepped inside each of them. The Dean turned back to scowly crap suit and glared at him before continuing.

"This is a minimally invasive test. Just a finger prick and one drop of blood is required. If you can all make your way to the front, we can get this over with and back to your normal lectures. Come on, people, quick quick! I've got three more lectures to visit in the next forty minutes."

Everyone looked around confused. Could they even do this? Surely we had some form of rights here. This couldn't be happening. When did we start registering people? The problem came with them considering supernaturals were less than people. A few students got up, shrugging, and walked to the front. They were right; it was a quick process. Just a drop of blood in a tube filled with liquid that scowly crap suit looked at and then sent them back to their seats. No one else moved in the lecture theatre. The Dean had slipped out, no doubt going to deliver his speech to the next set of unsuspecting students on campus.

"If you do not step forward to take this test voluntarily, you will be compelled to do so," scowly crap suit growled at us.

The rest of the students slowly stood and filed to the front. I slipped to the back of the queue and cast my eyes over to the doors again. The room was locked down. There would be no escaping the test without a fight. My best option was to take it, fail and then look for an opportunity to slip away later. The twelve students in front of me filed through the test, all quickly passing and going back to their seats. I hadn't thought this through. Going last essentially meant I was now doing this with an audience. I steeled myself and approached scowly crap suit. He, surprisingly, scowled at me, and I fought the urge to roll my eyes at him.

"Not much need for you to take this, is there?" he growled at me. "You're a runner if ever I saw one, you already know that you've failed."

I smirked at him and silently gave him my hand. Fuck him if he thought he could intimidate me. He pricked my finger and turned it over to drip my blood into the tube he held. It immediately turned gold. Strangely, he looked confused about this, considering he had been so confident before. The guards around the room closed in on us, and I dropped into a defensive stance. Scowly crap suit pulled out what looked like a car key fob from his jacket pocket and clicked the button before a mother-fucking shimmery portal opened on the wall right next to me. I was so shocked by the sudden appearance of a portal which, let's face it, no one had seen in real life, that I failed to see the fist flying at my face and the guard rushing me from behind. Scowly crap suit punched me straight in the left temple and the bastard guard body checked me, sending me sprawling through the portal.

It was like being pushed through a cold, wet curtain, and I landed hard on the other side, smacking my head on the floor, sliding along the tiles and crashing into a wall. It hurt like a bitch and white light flashed across my vision as I tried to pull myself up, but collapsed back to the floor. I could feel blood running down the side of my face, and I thought I was going to throw up. Don't get me wrong, I can take more than a couple of punches to the head, but portal travel was just too weird for my stomach to take and it would serve them right if I threw up all over their shiny floor. I managed to pull myself together and look up just in time to see scowly crap suit step through the portal and close it behind him like he did this every day. Dick!

"Was that necessary?" a stern female voice said, before I felt hands lifting me from the floor and helping me onto a chair.

A waste paper bin was quickly shoved in to my hands, but the urge to vomit was fading, and I didn't think I was going to need it. I quickly took in my surroundings. I was in some kind of office. Most of the walls were lined with bookcases. There was a massive desk in one corner and a sofa set against the far wall. The woman who had helped me up off the floor had stationed herself between me and scowly crap suit, almost like she was protecting me. The only other person in the room was a man sitting behind a desk, glaring at scowly crap suit. At first glance, it seemed like these two were actually on my side.

"She's a runner. I needed to get her through before she even had a chance to think about it," he said, shrugging his shoulders, clearly not giving a shit.

I didn't bother wiping my blood from my face. Let it run and make a mess of the shiny floor. I wouldn't be the one cleaning it up. Scowly crap suit just glared at me more, like it was beneath him to be in the same room as me. He strolled across the room like he owned the place and placed my now-gold test tube on the desk before clicking the portal button again and stepping back to it.

"She's your problem now," he said, before stepping through and closing the portal behind him.

The man at the desk, who I hadn't paid much attention to at first while I was flying face-first into his floor, picked up the tube and gave it a confused look before raising it up to show the woman next to me. She couldn't keep the surprised look from her face and they just silently looked at it until I couldn't take it anymore.

"What the fuck is going on?" I screeched.

I'll admit it wasn't my finest badass moment. I pulled myself up off the chair, bracing myself on the desk and feeling pissier than I ever had in my life. I tried to do a stern badass stare, but I think my wobbly legs were throwing it off a bit.

The woman seemed to shake herself and turned back to me, clearly trying to paste a smile on her shocked face.

"Come," she pointed me towards a chair in front of the desk, "sit down before you fall down. Something needs to be done about this, Dominic, they can't treat them this way," she said, turning towards the man behind the desk.

I sat down in the chair, and she produced a handkerchief from, I don't know where, and gently pressed it against the side of my head. I was so taken aback by her kindness that I didn't even bat her away, which would have been my usual reaction. She was clearly distressed about my treatment, and it seemed like the smartest idea was not to make any enemies here before I knew what was going on. She fussed over me for a little while before she seemed satisfied, and sat down in the chair next to me.

"I'm so sorry that they have treated you this way, dear. We had no say in what was happening, and we only learnt they could potentially be sending someone here a few hours ago. Let's start at the beginning because I'm sure all of this is more than a little confusing for you. Firstly, let us introduce ourselves. This is Headmaster Farsight, and I am Professor Octavia. I don't know what they would have told you on the other side before they clearly brutalised you, but you have been brought to Packlands Academy to learn how to control your magic. The new laws the humans have made mean any half-blood supernaturals on Earth, such as yourself, have to be brought to one of our Academies. We are to classify your magic and teach you how to control it to prevent anyone losing control and further … incidents occurring." She grimaced at her explanation. "Granted, the means of getting you here was not supposed to be so violent."

"Incidents?"

I looked around the room again, and Headmaster Farsight drew my gaze. He was sitting back in his chair, still holding the test tube and looking intently at it. I didn't know what he thought it was going to do. He didn't look like any headmaster I'd ever seen or imagined. He looked, at best, in his late thirties. The suit he had on put scowly crap suit's to shame. This one probably cost a hundred times what his did. It highlighted his broad shoulders and skimmed what were no doubt huge biceps. He was attractive, but something seemed off about him that I just couldn't put my finger on. He looked up as if he realised that I was watching him, and he met my eyes with a kind smile on his face.

"I don't know how much your parents will have told you, but full-blooded supernaturals come into the majority of their magic when they reach the age of twenty. Some will have small amounts through childhood, but nothing major. Once they reach the age of twenty their magic flares and they come into their full powers. At that age, they are brought to the academies where they train to control and use that magic, whatever it may be. Most thought that half-blood children wouldn't have access to any form of magic, but it seems they were mistaken in that view. The humans believe some have undergone the same flare, but without anyone to teach them how to control it properly, innocent people have ended up hurt. The idea of regulation is not one which we support, but the humans are right that we should take responsibility for the half-blood children and bring them into the academies to help them learn how to control their magic."

Okay, what he was saying made sense in a way. But twenty? I had been able to use my own magic since I was twelve. Granted, over the last year or so, it did seem to be getting stronger. Maybe it was part of being a half-blood. Everywhere I went, I was a freak. These people seemed nice enough, but I'd been fooled by that before, and I wasn't falling for it again.

The headmaster got up from his desk and walked around to sit on the desk opposite me. "The way in which you were brought here was not how we had expected, and I can only apologise for the way in which you were treated. The humans are scared of us, and I can't say I blame them. Still, it is no excuse for hurting you as they did."

"I've had worse, this is nothing," I shrugged, wiping the blood from my face and holding the handkerchief to my cut to try and stop the bleeding.

I didn't miss the way their eyes widened as they considered me for a minute. Next would be the pity that I hated so much. A change of subject was definitely needed.

"So, what? You want me to go to school here now?"

"Yes, we can send someone to your dorm to pack your things and have them brought here. You start your classes tomorrow to determine what magic you have," the headmaster nodded.

"No," I replied. Might as well get straight to the point. They were not going digging through my stuff.

"No?" Professor Octavia repeated, cocking her head to the side.

"I'm afraid none of us has a choice in this ... erm, I'm sorry, what is your name?" the headmaster asked, raising an eyebrow.

"Aria Graves," I replied, lifting my chin. "I said, no. I don't want someone digging around in my things."

Professor Octavia knelt beside me and put her hand on my knee in an overly familiar gesture which I am sure she meant to comfort me, but had the complete opposite effect. Sensing my discomfort, she withdrew her hand, and there it was, the pity in her eyes.

"They won't let you go back Aria. You have to stay in this realm and learn your magic before they will even consider allowing you to return to the human realm and by then who knows if any of us will be allowed. There is talk of closing the gates, dear."

The headmaster was looking at the test tube again with suspicion.

"Why are you looking at it like that?" I asked, shifting in my seat. A dull ache had started in my head, and I needed to just lie down and probably throw up a bit.

"It's gold," he said, holding it out in front of him.

"Yeah, I can see that."

"The purpose of the test is not just to determine if you have magic, but what type it is. You are aware there are different types of supernaturals?" he asked, setting the test tube down on his desk but keeping it in sight. It was a little unsettling how much he seemed to be obsessing over it.

"I may have banged my head, but I'm not stupid," I snarked.

He lifted one brow again but continued, "Witch magic shows as green, red for vampire, blue for elemental, black for demon and white for angel. Shifters show up green as well because their magic is similar to witch-magic with it being rooted in nature," he explained.

"Right, so what's gold?" I asked.

"I don't know," he replied, looking at the little tube again.

"Well, is there like a manual or something? I feel like if

you're going to disrupt my entire life, you should at least have read the instructions."

"There isn't supposed to be a gold," he explained, and I swear I saw him roll his eyes. It made me like him just a little bit. A very small, tiny, little bit.

"Maybe I don't have magic. Maybe it's just a fault with the test. See, I knew this was a mistake, I should just go home," I said, standing up and looking around the room. "Just, you know, click me open a portal and I'll be on my way," I said, waving my hand in the area where the last one had been. Hey, it was worth a try, right?

"It doesn't quite work like that. You will have to remain for the first year, and if you come up as a null we will speak to the humans about returning you if the gates are still open at that time," the headmaster said, crossing his arms and calling me out on my bullshit.

"So, this is my prison for the next year then!" I snarked.

At least he had the dignity to flinch. "I hope you'll look at the Academy as your home, in time. I'm sorry we had to meet under such circumstances, but you will always be welcome here, Aria."

I considered what he had said. It seemed like for now, my only option was to play nice for a year. The problem was, did I keep my magic locked down like always and see if I could skate by as one of these nulls, or did I actually trust these people and maybe learn more about my magic? Who was I kidding? I couldn't hold on to a lie like that for a whole year with these people being constantly up in my space.

"Have you seen any signs of your magic, Aria?" Professor Octavia gently queried.

"Nope," I lied. No point in giving everything away until I at least gauged if I was in any danger here.

They both glanced at each other, suspiciously. Perhaps I'd answered that a little too quickly.

"Well, let's get you settled in your room," she replied. "One of the other teachers is in the human realm and will bring back your things. You've got today to explore, and then lessons will start tomorrow. We'll get this all straightened out in no time," she said, opening the door to the office.

The headmaster handed me a packet of papers and gave me one of those pity smiles that makes you want to punch someone in the face.

"This holds your timetable, a map of the academy and some other things you need to know. All of your books and materials will be brought to your room. You'll need to report to stores to pick up your uniform. I'll have Caleb drop off your things when he gets back."

I followed Professor Octavia out of the room and looked around as she led me to my room. "Where is everyone?" I asked.

"In class. Classes started a few weeks ago. We get a few extra students over the first month, those that come into their magic a bit later, but generally everyone starts at the same time."

"I meant the other half-bloods. Why hasn't anyone else been thrown through the wall yet?" I said, looking back at the office as if someone would fly out of it any minute.

"Oh, well, you're the only one so far, dear," Professor Octavia replied, walking down a corridor heading towards a large staircase. The academy seemed to be quite an old building. The corridor walls were stone, and the windows were set into it with thick glass panes. If we were in the "human realm", this would be hundreds of years old but who knew what buildings looked like wherever the hell this was.

"What do you mean? There must have been others,

everyone was bragging about having some form of magical heritage at my campus," I answered, looking around trying to take stock of where I was.

The windows didn't look like they opened, but being glass I should be able to smash one should I need to get out. I seemed to be on the ground floor. There was a large front door opposite the staircase which offered another exit if needed. I'd just need to find out if they kept it locked.

"Ah yes, I have heard of this. Half-bloods of your age are quite rare, dear. The gates only opened ten years ago, so any half-bloods your age would've come from someone strong enough to cross realms by themselves. I don't think any of those people would have had true claims. I'd be surprised if anyone else comes through a portal to us."

The professor started to climb up the stairs with me trailing behind her. If she was aware of me checking the potential exit routes, she made no sign of it. She just seemed quite content to show me to my room. They didn't seem like they were going to forcibly hold me here.

"So, I'm the only one then?"

This couldn't be good. I liked to live life under the radar, but now I was going to be the half-blood freak everyone knew about.

"So far, dear, but I would think it will take a couple of months before they get everyone tested so we may get another one. However, a few other academies are taking in students so they may not be sent here."

The corridor was lined with doors, and she stopped outside one and nodded her head towards it. "This is you, dear. I made sure you got a single room. I figured this whole process would be hard enough on you as it is."

"Thanks," I mumbled, grabbing the doorknob then screeching when I got zapped as if electricity ran up my arm.

I needed to calm the fuck down, I wasn't a screeching kind of girl, but this place had me on edge and acting like a big-boobed blonde chick in a horror movie.

"Oh, sorry, dear, I should have warned you about that—just the door configuring to you. Saves keys, you know. Only you will be able to open this now. Well, and certain members of staff if there's an emergency."

I nodded and opened the door. It was a typical dorm room. Bed in the corner, which was thankfully a double and already made up with blue cotton sheets. A desk on the opposite wall with some shelves, a bookcase and an armchair in the other far corner. There were two other doors. Sticking my head through each, I found a small closet and a bathroom. I gave a small prayer of thanks to the universe for the bathroom. I couldn't have gone back to sharing a bathroom.

"Well, I'll leave you to get settled in. Your welcome pack has the schedule for the day. Lunch will be in about an hour, and the cafeteria is marked on the map. Your things should be here by then, as well. If you have any questions, I'll see you tomorrow. We only have three academic classes on your timetable at the moment. No point adding things in when we don't know what your magic will be; you will have a lot of reading to do to catch up anyway."

She backed awkwardly out of the room before turning and striding away. The door slowly closed behind her, and I looked around at the empty room. I was exhausted, and I sank onto the edge of the bed, pulled off my boots and flopped back. My head was still hurting, I was exhausted from the night before, and everything I knew of the fragile life I'd managed to piece together for myself had come falling apart around me. I couldn't believe how much could change in what must have only been an hour.

I didn't have much in my apartment. They would no

doubt be able to pack everything into a few boxes. What if they never let me leave here? Maybe I should just tell them I already had magic and let them help me develop it into whatever it was going to be. My mind felt like it was spinning in circles, and it probably didn't help I was pretty confident I had a minor head injury to go with it. It was probably a good thing I was lying down. My mind raced with so many questions, but slowly my eyes slid closed, and exhaustion took over, pulling me into sleep.

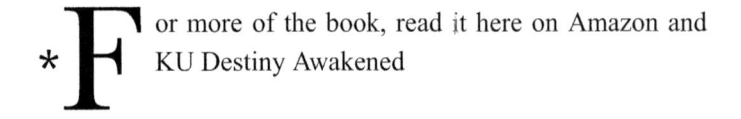

* For more of the book, read it here on Amazon and KU Destiny Awakened

ALSO BY CJ COOKE

DESTINY SERIES

Destiny Awakened

Destiny Rising

Destiny Realised

(Completed Chapter)

Revelations

Retaliation-Coming Soon

STONERIDGE PACK SERIES

Wolf Hunts

ABOUT THE AUTHOR

CJ Cooke lives in Nottinghamshire England, with her husband and son. She drinks more tea than could be possibly healthy for you and dances to her own internal song. She swears more than is probably socially acceptable, and yes, she's a bit of a weirdo, but as her husband always says, she's his beautiful weirdo.

If you would like to stay up to date with new releases and other news, you can sign up to my newsletter and check out my website

Other contact details:
Email: catherinejcooke.author@gmail.com

Printed in Great Britain
by Amazon